MW00605079

SMOKE, STEEL, & IVY

A FAIRYTALE RETELLING

AMY TRENT

Smoke, Steel, & Ivy

Copyright © 2022 by Amy Trent

All rights reserved.

No part of this book may be reproduced in any form or by any electronic or mechanical means, including information storage and retrieval systems, without written permission from the author, except for the use of brief quotations in a book review.

Smoke, Steel, & Ivy is a work of fiction. Any resemblance to reality is coincidental.

DEDICATION

In loving memory of my father-in-law, Mike

PART I

Once upon a time....

CHAPTER ONE

Ivy did not have time for bedtime stories or fairy tales, but she had even less time to argue with her youngest sister. "Once upon a time, our kingdom was so thick with magic, you could hardly breathe."

Mina pulled her feathered quilt up to her chin. "Was the magic thick like the ice outside on our cherry trees?"

Ivy opened her pocket watch to check the time. If she hurried, she might be able to make a cup of chocolate before the kitchen grew too cold.

"Or was it thick the way you call Papa sometimes?"

Ivy snapped her watch shut and cleared her throat. "They say—"

"Who's they?"

"People. People like our godmother—"

"Who has fey blood pumping in her veins."

Yet, Auntie Olivia had not made any such claim in years. Four years, to be exact.

"I wonder if I have fey blood," Mina prattled. "On my mother's side, I mean. It's very likely. My mother's family tree is much more exciting than Papa's."

Not this again. Ivy had no time for a recitation of their complicated family history, made all the more complicated by the web of monarchies that wove its way in and out of it. "They say you can still smell the magic. Even in our capital."

Mina sighed and nestled into her silk pillows. Mistress Kitty, the rotund, gray house cat, settled into a coil next to her head, purring loudly. "What does magic smell like?"

"Like moonlight. Newly cut grass." Ivy conjured memories of Amadanri's capital before the war, before the coal smoke soured the air and sooted the cobbled streets. "Fresh-baked bread. A summer rain right before dinner. Cherry blossoms on a windy day."

Mina yawned. "It can't smell like all of that."

"Well..." Ivy bent down to kiss her sister's head. "It's that note they all have in common."

"Do you believe in magic?"

Ivy tensed. If magic had ever existed, the last of it had fled their country years ago. Probably taking refuge in the Shale Mountains or hiding away in some distant little coastal country to be shipped across seas to safer lands. All that remained were traces in stories and customs, aside from the rumors that the fey still worked in magic. But Mina wasn't asking for history, and she was still doggedly pursuing the argument Ivy had tried to avoid all evening. Ivy pressed a hand to her forehead. Might as well get on with it. "I can assure you there is nothing magical about the opening night of a new opera."

Mina bolted upright. "I still want to go."

Ivy collected the scattered tomes of folklore around Mina's bed into a neat stack on her nightstand. "Mina, you are—"

"I know. Only twelve." Mina huffed, and the cat meowed distastefully before jumping with a thud off the bed. "You could have at least let me go to the play tonight."

"Must we do this again? You are too young. I already have my hands full enough as it is. Next year—"

"What if there isn't a next year?"

Ivy's heart hammered in her ears. "What did you say?"

"I saw Papa's report on your desk. If we are running out of

supplies for our soldiers, how long before we run out of supplies for ourselves?"

"Oh, Mina." Ivy smoothed her sister's hair. "You needn't worry over some silly pages. Papa needed my help poking holes in it, is all. He has a plan for peace, and I will tell you all about it. But tomorrow. I must get to work. I have Papa's appeals to sift through tonight, and you must get to bed."

Ivy rose and left the apartment she shared with her eleven sisters before Mina had the chance to uncover the truth: Papa had no plan. He had daughters. Twelve of them.

If only daughters could end wars as easily as fathers could start them.

Half a dozen vermilion dispatch boxes, stacked haphazardly on the marble-topped desk in the library, were waiting for Ivy. All the inner workings of Papa's government were in those boxes— briefings, reports, state correspondence—and awaited his nightly review and approval. But reviewing the boxes was too tedious for one man, so Papa had argued when he conscripted Ivy into service. She'd been more than happy to help, particularly when Papa told her that reviewing the appeals was to be among her nightly duties. Not everyone who committed a crime against the Crown was deserving of their kingdom's antiquated punishments, and everyone in the Kingdom of Amadanri was granted the opportunity to appeal to His Majesty's mercy. Magistrates combed the prisons daily to facilitate the honored tradition. It was all to the good, and Ivy was more than happy to apply Papa's initials to the appeals, setting aside the cases that clearly warranted further attention. But Ivy's interest in the matter had nothing to do with mercy or tradition and everything to do with ending the war.

She grasped the nearest red box and turned it over. The stack of documents landed with a thud that rattled the library's leaded windowpanes.

Trina startled, though she did not turn from her spinet. "Ivy!"

"Apologies," Ivy murmured, leafing through the stack. "I thought you might be at the play."

His story was hiding somewhere in Papa's box of appeals. Buried among the heart-numbing tragedies was a man with nothing to lose and a soul for sale. Ivy needed to find him soon, or else... Mina would be right. Ivy sighed. Summarizing the findings of the day's briefings and reports into a single, legible page came first. She wouldn't have the necessary focus otherwise.

Trina experimented with a chord progression. "You missed dinner."

The ice-covered branches of a bare cherry tree clacked against the library window as the wind howled low and long and mingled with the notes of Trina's spinet. A weak smile played across Ivy's lips. It was sweet of her sister to move the instrument down to the library.

Trina played a few measures. How she could infuse such feeling into a few notes was beyond Ivy's understanding. "Pen said to tell you your machine is ready. I told her to bring it by after the play."

"Excellent." Ivy scribbled a note in her dossier. She'd fight for increased winter rations in her summary. "Did Pen mention if she's tested it?"

"On every last one of us. Except you."

Ivy sighed. The flood of papers was never-ending. All of them important. All of them, Papa insisted, needed to be reviewed by another set of trusted eyes. All of them kept Ivy up at night and busy during the day. "I promise you'll see more of me when the war is over."

"If it ever ends."

Ivy cringed. That was the problem they were up against. The war, a disordered disaster, would grind to a bleak defeat when the snow melted, unless Ivy could succeed where their best generals had failed. "Did Sophia have a go with Pen's data?"

Trina laughed.

She'd take that as a no. "Would you ask Sophia to play with the numbers? Tell her variance and correlation."

"In exchange for?"

Ivy flipped through a new report detailing projected shortfalls of black powder. "My thanks and unyielding affection." She wished there'd been a report projecting when their weapons would become obsolete. Never mind, she knew the answer. "And if that doesn't work, my lavender brooch." Ivy moved the candles closer, though the smell of hot wax quickly made her second-guess the merits of her supper of cocoa and mints. The library needed more electric lamps. "Heaven knows I won't be needing it," Ivy mumbled.

Trina paused her playing. "The acoustics in here are better than I remembered." She scribbled a note on her sheet music.

Ivy never would have asked her sister to join her, but she was grateful she came. "Yes, the echoes keep me company." She grabbed another appeal. "The books too."

"And, of course, the statue of Adonis."

Ivy rolled her eyes and flipped to the end of the report. "Did you know the triplets asked to have him moved to our apartment?"

Trina's laugh was as musical as the rest of her.

Ivy's grip tightened on her fountain pen. Trina could still laugh. She could still enjoy her music, her days, even her evenings. The truth could swallow Ivy whole, as long as her sisters were happy. She would shoulder every inconvenience, every burden, to keep them as far from the war as possible. But she couldn't do it alone anymore. She needed help. Someone desperate enough to join her. Someone for hire...

She'd repeatedly scoured the ranks of their own soldiers for such a man, but had not found him. Earlier this winter, she'd persuaded Papa to send any colonel who could be spared in search of an officer who had the skill set she needed. All her most promising leads had literally come to dead ends, yet one or two of her persons of interest were presumed AWOL—a criminal offense against the Crown if they were ever found alive. Desperation had Ivy combing through the appeals, hoping against reason such a man would turn up in their prisons ready to make a bargain.

"Ivy darling." Ivy hadn't noticed when Trina had left her spinet, but her sister was now standing at her desk with a report in hand. "Why are these frostbite statistics from the front on your desk?"

Was every sister in the house suddenly interested in the war effort?

The reason for Ivy's involvement with the reports was simple enough—the news was terrible and tedious, and Papa did not deal well with either. It was Ivy's job to sift through all the bleak information contained in Papa's boxes, apply his initials, identify actions that must be taken, and make sense of it all in a succinct summary that Papa could peruse at his leisure the following morning. Preferably after his breakfast.

Ivy took the report from her sister and set it aside. "When soldiers lack proper boots"—and functional weapons, ammunitions, rations, and fuel—"the cold can be dangerous." She tucked an arm around Trina's shoulders and gently steered her back to the spinet. "This is why I want Papa to agree to my new strategy."

"Enough, Ivy. We are practically the same age—"

"Still ten months your senior." Ivy bussed the empty teacup from Trina's spinet to the sideboard.

"—so you will tell me the unvarnished truth." Trina's playing tumbled to a thin pianissimo. "How bad is it?"

Ivy poured her sister a fresh cup of peppermint tea. "It's not good."

Trina's music stopped. Fear pooled in the shadows of her face.

Oh no. "But it's nothing for you to worry about." She swirled in a spoonful of honey.

"What are we going to do?"

"Well..." She set the cup and saucer gently on top of the spinet. "Our boys have fought hard. Now they're safe behind snowdrifts and iced roads." To say nothing of the enemy's frozen rails. "It gives us just enough time to rally."

"Can we?"

Ivy picked out a simple C major on the spinet. "Resourceful

minds always rally. It's a matter of getting the right people and the right tools together." Ivy had lost her touch for this. Reading too many reports in which lives lost were distilled to numbers and statistics would do that to a young woman. It's why she was so eager to propose a different approach. But Papa had refused to hear her. Again.

Trina took a sip of her tea. "Is that why you insisted Pen make your funny little machine?"

Not exactly. Ivy returned to her desk and scribbled Papa's initials at the bottom of another briefing, this one detailing the dwindling grain stores. Hardly a surprise. The draft had taken nearly every farmer from their fields. "The heart is a metronome." Ivy removed her spectacles and rubbed her eyes. "If its beats are cataloged on paper, I can eliminate uncertainty."

"What sort of uncertainty?"

Ivy replaced her glasses and reached for the next briefing. A lengthy report on sustained mental trauma, accompanied by stress, among the wounded and honorably discharged veterans. Gracious. What would happen when all the soldiers returned to civilian life? "Human error."

Trina shook her head. A cacophony of sounds flowed from her fingertips.

Ivy initialed the report and grabbed the next. "If I had a map of a man's beating heart, I could tell you when he was lying. If I could log the numbers against his respiration, I could know he was hiding something without him saying a word."

"If you get to know a man, you can tell when he's lying without a score of his heartbeats."

A blond pixie of a young woman kicked the library door open wide. "Unless he's like Pops, and lying is his native tongue."

Ivy's younger sister, Pen, marched into the library carrying a smart-looking steel box with an assortment of tubes and wires piled on top of it. "I don't know how you do it, Ives."

"You learn to discount everything he says when he opens his

mouth." Ivy scrawled Papa's initials in the corner of the report, then rushed over to her sisters at Trina's spinet.

"I meant I don't know how you do *that*," Pen said, dragging a chair closer.

"The boxes?" Ivy asked.

"The pages of cramped squiggles. I'd sooner go blind than spend all my waking hours looking at them." Pen set the machine on top of the spinet and began connecting the tubes.

"How was the play?" Trina asked.

"Rubbish. I only went to see Sophia and the triplets charge the actors afterward. That was spectacular."

Ivy pinched the bridge of her nose. "I'll have to have a word with them." Chasing after young actors was a recipe for scandal.

"Don't bother," Trina said. "They're determined to carry on Papa's tradition."

"Agreed. Now..." Pen patted the chair. "Have a seat, Ives."

Ivy complied.

"Two tubes around the chest. They measure breathing." Pen strapped the tubes around Ivy. "Wires connect to these bits of metal that rest against the temples." She placed the leather strap with connecting wires around Ivy's head. "A cuff to measure the pulse on the right or left arm. And more wires to wrap around the forefingers."

"The point of the wires being?" Ivy asked.

"Tracking eye movement and perspiration."

"Ingenious!" Ivy winced. "And uncomfortable."

"You have to stay still," Pen said, attaching the last of the wires to Ivy's fingers. "Now then, Trina, ask away." Pen clasped Trina's shoulder affectionately. "Remember, yes or no answers only. Better make them easy for her." Pen's trademark smirk surfaced.

Trina took a sip of her tea. "Is your first name Ivy?"

"Yes."

The machine began to whirr, and modest squiggles appeared on a rolling feed of paper.

"She speaks the truth!" Pen beamed.

"Is there a young gentleman who inspired this machine?"

"Trina!" Ivy said.

"Yes or no answers, if you please," Pen said, pressing her lips together, her eyes twinkling.

"No," Ivy said.

The sisters peered at the machine's tracings. The squiggles had grown. Considerably.

Pen's eyebrows wiggled. "You looking to audition an assistant?"

Trina giggled. "Perhaps a tall, dashing one?"

Ivy's heart beat faster. The squiggles grew frantic on the machine's tracings below. "All right, you've had your fun. I need to get back to work. And the two of you should get to bed."

"So bossy," Trina said.

"Typical eldest child," Pen agreed, turning off the machine.

Trina closed her spinet. "Remember you have a bed too, darling."

Ivy twisted the wires off her fingers. "I can't sleep. Not until I've reviewed all of Papa's boxes. I've got his appeals to consider too." Maybe tonight there'd be someone promising among the typical horse thieves and drunk-and-disorderlies.

"If Papa doesn't review his boxes, why should you?" Pen asked while she disconnected the remaining tubes and wires from Ivy.

"Papa does review the boxes. He just needs a second pair of trusted eyes, is all."

Pen tore off the tracings and handed it to her sister. "Papa riffles through the boxes looking for fan mail."

"Or invitations from favorite courtiers," Trina said with a yawn.

Ivy tossed the tracings on the desk and grabbed the box of appeals. Anything not to look her sisters in the eye. "Papa is a busy man." Although, Ivy must admit, it was not the monarchy or the war that occupied his days. "Someone needs to champion mercy. Half a dozen innocent men have been granted clemency this winter alone." Ivy brushed her dark curls away from her face. The truth gnawed at her, but if she told Trina and Pen, they'd be plunged into needless worry. She wouldn't do that to her sisters. Not now. Not ever.

Ivy thanked her sisters, insisted she must get back to it, and wished them a good night. Alone once more in the library, she sifted through Papa's boxes until only the box of appeals remained.

The grandfather clock echoed the late hour. She checked the time against her pocket watch. Three minutes slow. Ivy poked the fire. It crackled a reproach of sorts but wrestled out of its cozy embers. She tossed in a log and rubbed her palm against her pinstripe skirts.

Ivy read through the appeals, disheartened by the guilty and innocent alike. She scrawled Papa's initials on the majority of the appeals, indicating he agreed with the sentencing, but made a modest stack for the secretaries of the men she believed deserved more careful consideration.

One last crumpled note lay on her desk, a receipt of sale of some kind. The magistrates were a sloppy lot, but if Ivy was anything, she was thorough. She downed the last sip of her now-cold cocoa and smoothed the note flat.

A barrel of spiced wine and three shearlings transferred...

Gracious, the note was from last summer. Ivy flipped it over and saw three paragraphs of writing in a tight, neat hand.

Ivy read aloud. "'I petition His Majesty for mercy as the circumstances of my arrest were not considered during my sentencing.'" Ivy's finger fell to the recording stamp bearing yesterday's date at the bottom. So it was an appeal, but not an appeal drafted with the assistance of the usual court magistrate.

His Majesty must be made aware that until my arrest I served with distinction.

Ivy's heart began to race.

Captain in the north regiment.

Her tired eyes dashed and jumped across the page, pulling out bits of crucial information.

Extensive knowledge of explosives.

That was good. That was very good, but not enough, given the risks. Ivy's finger raced across the lines. Until at last she found it.

Sentenced to life in prison.

Ivy fisted the appeal into her dossier, which she tucked under her arm. She grabbed Pen's machine and raced out of the library.

This man—imprisoned, coldly articulate, and furious—could be the key to saving the kingdom and winning the war, if Ivy could persuade him to try.

CHAPTER TWO

Collin strained against the leather belts and cuffs that fixed him to the metal chair. He did not like sitting with his back to a door. Never mind the nerves—all that twisting to try to catch a glimpse of who was walking in and out was brutal on the neck. Then again, his discomfort might have more to do with yesterday's torture.

"Please, don't struggle."

Who strapped down not only a man's arms, but also his ankles and head, and then said the word *please*?

Electric lights hummed from the vaulted ceiling of the crypt. Wires wrapped around Collin's temples and threaded back to the box of gears at his side. The steam that hissed from the boiler... That was a far more pressing concern. The noise muffled entire catalogs of sound. The condensing steam on his skin distracted him, made his mind wander to concerns—chiefly, the electrical conductivity of water.

The boiler presented too many distractions for collecting reliable information.

And collecting information was all that mattered now.

Collin cleared his throat. "Is all this really necessary?"

The sharp sound of well-heeled boots clacked against the slick grave markers on the crypt floor. "Yes, they are necessary."

They'd sent a woman. Marvelously good of them to find one with such wonderful perfume. Orange blossoms and jasmine, with a hint of chocolate. "I meant converting the abbey's crypt into a noisy boiler room. Haven't the dead earned their peace?"

"Progress is no respecter of persons, dead or living." A pen scratched, and papers shuffled. "More importantly, the war has limited our resources." The click of a pocket watch opening and closing. "In more ways than you know."

"Hence the makeshift interrogation chamber and homemade tinker toys?"

A rustle of skirts and a huffy sigh. "This machine monitors your beating heart, the strain of your blood through your veins, even your respiration, and transmits the information pictorially."

"To what end, madame? Or is it mademoiselle?"

The woman bent to examine the scribbles, but Collin caught no details. Maybe ink-black curls. The yellow glow of the lightbulbs made it hard to tell. "To put it simply, this machine tells me if you are lying."

Collin snorted. "You need a machine to tell you if a man is lying?"

"No. I need an excuse to tie you up." Collin's interrogator stood before him now. She was a young woman. Her hair was dark and piled on top of her head until it tumbled down her back. She had dark, lovely eyes—sharp and intelligent, though maybe a little small. Her mouth, though, more than made up for that. Defined. Expressive. Full. And those gorgeous lips twitched into an amused pout. "One learns caution when she has a disadvantage of three stone." The young woman ran her fingers slowly, carefully across the box of gears. "And it is fun, isn't it? Advancements. New toys. Technology civilizes us." She returned to scratching notes in her dossier. "It's proof of our refinement."

"And here I thought it was mercy and brotherly kindness."

The young woman's lips flattened into a firm line. "You will answer each of the following questions with a yes or no answer. Do not speak otherwise. Now, then, is your surname Dobhareach?"

Collin sighed. "Yes."

"And is your name Collin of Thuaidh Fuar?"

"Yes."

"Is your name Meleager?"

Why not? "Yes."

The young woman bent over the tracings and scoffed. "They can't all be your name."

"Well, they were at one time. I wear names out rather quickly. Much faster than the average man."

"Yes or no answers, Mr. Dobhareach, or would you prefer Mel?"

"No, that was at least two names ago."

She flipped through the files in her dossier. "No wonder I didn't find you sooner. Half your aliases are presumed dead."

Collin's chest tightened. She'd been looking for *him*?

His interrogator continued. "Are you a citizen of His Majesty King Rupert the Just's Kingdom of Amadanri?"

"Yes."

"And were you a captain in His Majesty's royal army?"

"Yes."

The young woman paused and bent over the machine's tracings. She brought the spectacles that hung from the chain around her neck to her eyes. "Either you are comatose or more practiced at telling the truth than any man alive." She straightened. Her clever fingers checked the wires connected to Collin's temples.

Collin watched in silence as she paced in front of him. She was tall, but her frame was slight. The black, pinstriped skirts that were bustled dramatically, as well as the impeccable tie around her throat and carefully tailored cut of her blouse and vest, gave only the illusion of age and experience.

"Something wrong with your machine, mademoiselle?"

"Unlikely." She scribbled a note in her file. "Then again, it is possible that an external source of stress is necessary for calibration in this instance." Her lips twisted into a deathly smile.

"What is your age, Mr. Dobhareach?" Before Collin could answer, the woman took a perch on his right knee. She was sitting in his lap and staring at him with her onyx eyes.

Collin swallowed. He felt moisture slide down his back, but he doubted he could blame it on the steam in the room. "One and thirty."

"You are thirty-one years old?" She briskly smoothed her skirts.

"Yes."

"I have here in your military record that you were twenty when you enlisted four years ago." She shifted her files to rest a hand on Collin's shoulder. "Are you sure you are thirty-one?"

Her clothes made a lovely crinkling sound when she moved. And her hands, small though they were, had a weight to them that was distracting. "I suppose I wear my years out faster than the average man too."

She laughed. And Mars, she was a prism when she laughed. Just like the ones Gran used to hang in the windows when he was a boy. She absorbed Collin's carefully collected theories and reflected them back as a pretty puzzle of uncategorized thoughts and emotions. Distracting thoughts about wanting to hear her laugh again and learning her favorite dance.

"Are you twenty-four?" she asked.

Commitment was important. So was keeping this woman as close as possible for as long as possible. "No."

She leaned over to examine the graph that now had some admirable squiggles across it. "At last!" Her voice fell into the comfortable register of satisfaction. "It would appear that the intro-duced stress to our little interview has more accurately calibrated your responses."

"Meaning?"

"I've caught you lying. You are twenty-four." She flipped through some of the records in her dossier—but stayed on his knee. "Although

I must admit I am surprised. No one would believe you're only two years my senior."

"Charming."

"Now, then, let's talk about desertion."

Collin swallowed. The back of his neck prickled. "If you insist."

The woman studied Collin's face. She gently pulled free his hair trapped underneath the leather strap. He'd been wrong about her eyes being too small. She was lovely. "I understand that you disobeyed the orders of your commanding officer, abandoned your post, and deserted your men. Is that not so?"

"Yes."

"I can't abide a coward."

"I suggest you reverse that opinion. We need more cowards in this kingdom."

The mademoiselle was once again fidgeting with the wires at his temples. Her fingers felt electrifying against Collin's skin. "Is that so?"

"Yes." Collin spoke with conviction. Her fingers paused. "My order was to execute a couple of farm boys turned Olcceart fighters. I refused."

"Why?"

"I have too much respect for human life to do anything so stupid." Collin closed his eyes, trying to shut out the fear-drenched memories. He needed to concentrate. Not easy to do when an attractive young lady was sitting on one's knee. "One day, this war will be over. The enemy will be our neighbor."

"Unless he is our dictator."

"We will need those two farmers for the bread they grow."

The woman arched an eyebrow. "Farmers do not grow bread."

"You understand my point." Collin winced against the high-pitched whine that started in his ears. "The senseless slaughtering on both sides must end immediately. Our people need to buy and sell goods somewhere. Our kingdoms are too small to exist independently. We need each other."

"And what do you need, Mr. Dobhareach?"

"I need you to untie me. I'm far more persuasive with my hands free."

The woman rose. "Are you a hero, Mr. Dobhareach?"

Collin swallowed against the swell of panic. He felt it rattling inside, close to taking over. "I could be, if you like."

She wasn't the sort to blush, but she was the sort to smile wickedly into her folder of notes. "You were decorated in the Battle of Amaideach. Not a single man of your company was wounded, and such a decisive victory. Your strategy was brilliant, yet unconventional."

"Human life is the most important commodity on earth. Far more precious than weapons or gold."

"Explain to me how you managed to disarm an insurgent group that outnumbered you three to one?"

"While the parties called a cease-fire to resupply at the river, I infiltrated their ranks, targeted their armory, and destroyed it."

"Not very sporting of you."

"It's a bloody war. Both sides are trying to kill each other. It doesn't have to be sporting. I found a solution without shedding a drop of blood."

She was pacing once more. "Burning an armory is risky during a cease-fire."

"It didn't happen during the cease-fire." The squiggles on the machine's tracings were growing larger.

"How did you—"

"I planted a timed detonator." Collin twisted his wrists against his restraints until the leather bands dug into him.

"Controlled explosives?" She nearly dropped her dossier. "I've been trying for years to persuade—"

"Who are you?" Collin asked.

The mademoiselle startled and blinked. "I'll ask the questions, Mr. Dobhareach. Where did you study explosives?"

"Gran fancied me a surgeon." Collin winced. The wires at his temples pinched. "But the apprenticeship required connections and resources we didn't have. So Gran farmed me out to every chemist in our town, not to mention hatters, tanners, cobblers, soapers... She hoped it would be enough to get me into the army's medical corps."

"Was it?"

"Yes." Collin shut his eyes tight against the memories. He wished he could shut his nose, his ears. "My talents and experience lent themselves better to the inorganic."

"Elaborate."

He could hardly breathe. There were too many memories too close to the surface. "Chemical combustion."

The young woman flipped to a different page in her dossier. "Yes, your regimen's armory had a considerable store of grenades, shells, and other incendiaries." She snapped the dossier shut. "Yet, our stores of black powder have been depleted for months."

Collin shrugged. "Charcoal, sulfur, and saltpeter are not the only chemicals that combust." Truthfully, they were not even among Collin's favorites. "I improvised."

She laughed, but this time it was a single beat of dismayed wonder. "I take it those lumps of putty in the armory were something dangerous?"

"Not on their own, but with some persuasion."

"A detonator?"

She was a quick study. "Yes. What are you going to do?"

"With the putty?"

"With me? I've been questioned before. And yes, I enjoy your brand of interrogation much more than the old dandy who insisted on slapping me, but to what end?"

She took a deep breath and twisted her spectacles chain between her fingers. "You've been charged with insubordination, desertion, and treason." She fumbled, and the chain slipped out of her fingers. "Ordinarily, life in prison would be the consequence of such actions, but your experience and skills cannot be ignored. It is as you say—we need more cowards in this war. We are running out of manpower.

We need a clear strategy and a decisive victory to force a peace, and then we need everyone back in the fields so we can at least harvest some potatoes come autumn. We need our men back so that there will be babies again next spring. The birth rate has fallen at an alarming rate—"

Collin groaned. It was always the simple, albeit disappointing, answer.

The young woman tore off the tracings and went about adjusting the toggles of the machine. "You seem to be our only dog left in this fight. Believe me. I've been looking for ages."

She was standing in front of him, so he could see it now. Stupid, really, not to notice it earlier. "You have a sweetheart fighting out there, don't you?" Probably a celebrated but completely incompetent baron turned petty officer. "You hope to have a baby of your own come next spring. Who are you doing this for?"

She flinched before she tossed a loose curl out of her face and straightened. "I should ask you the same question. Your record has no family listed. Your wages were sent to a poorhouse in Durbronach before they were garnered."

The whining in his ears had distilled to the sound of his own pounding pulse. Collin arched his back and dug his nails into the cold, wet metal of the chair arms as he strained against his scientific fetters. "Look," he said in a voice louder than he'd intended, "I'm going to break your clever machine if you don't untie me. My patience is worn out."

"Calm down. I'm nearly finished." The woman peered at the squiggles of the machine's tracings and opened the case of her pocket watch. "Excellent. I won't have to sit on your knee again."

"We wouldn't want to upset your man in uniform," Collin mumbled.

"Brilliant, Mr. Dobhareach." She scribbled in her dossier. "Distilling an armed conflict that has lasted these four years, not to mention the pain and suffering of countless souls, into a woman pining for a presumed sweetheart." She gripped her pen until her knuckles turned white. "Brilliant," she repeated through clenched teeth.

Collin's simple construct shattered. Exactly like Gran's favorite prism had when the explosions started. All that colorful light disappearing instantly into countless shards. Collin's mind raced to fit the shattered pieces into a working theory.

"I want peace, Mr. Dobhareach. Peace for us all." Mars, she'd become almost wistful.

"Why me?" Collin asked.

She raised an eyebrow. "I need someone I can trust."

He scoffed. "You'd trust a deserter?"

"No. I trust tight leashes." The young woman snapped her files shut. "Your appeal is impossible. No one likes a coward—desertion, et cetera. Clemency in this case would be a scandal. I'm afraid you will live out the rest of your life in prison." She brought forth the tarnished pocket watch, rubbed her thumb against the surface. "Unless you agree to help me. Then you'd be a hero. A gallant and dedicated officer with a strong moral compass who has always obeyed a higher law and turned the tide of the war."

"There were witnesses to my insubordination. You can't just rewrite—"

"I'm very persuasive with a pen." She replaced her watch in her vest pocket. "If you help me, join my task force, the charges against you will be dropped. You'll be a free man after the war. Do we have an agreement?"

Collin rattled his fetters. "And in the interim?"

Her eyes narrowed.

"My wages have been garnered during my stay in your capital prison. I'd like them back. With interest."

"And, no doubt, a raise?"

"Fifty percent. It's a small price to own a man."

The woman bristled. "I don't like your phrasing."

"Eighty, then. To drive home the ugly truth of our bargain."

She paled. Her lashes fluttered, and her boot skidded slightly against a gravestone as she took a step backward. "You're in no position to make demands."

"And you're more desperate than I realized. Three hundred percent and a farm on the outskirts of the capital when all this is over."

Her chin trembled. "You're not the only man to appeal to His Majesty."

But she had let slip that she'd been looking for someone like him, probably for some time. The steam hissed from the boiler and settled on the uneven stone floor. "You forget I served for the past four years in the army. I'm well aware of the talent pool you have to draw from. I am one of the last explosives experts left with both his hands and all his fingers."

"And a beating heart." She opened her dossier and scribbled a note. "Fine."

She bought it? The straps bit into his skin as he struggled to sit upright. "You really think I can help you win the war?"

She froze. "You have to!" She spread her shaking hands wide and gestured around her. "This all crumbles away if you don't. We end. All of us! There's nothing I can do about it alone. And believe me"—she clutched her dossier and raked a trembling hand across her cheeks—"I've tried everything else." She shut her eyes tight before smoothing the front of her vest. "Others may be content to pretend there is no immediate danger. I know otherwise. Now." She tried to catch her breath and piece together her courage, her armor of composure. "Will you swear your allegiance to King Rupert?"

"That's impossible. The man is a selfish, incompetent disaster. Not to mention an ugly, beady-eyed toad—"

The door scraped open, and the guard appeared. "I heard shouting, Your Highness."

Oh.

Collin winced. He was an idiot.

"Thank you, Constable. I'm almost finished."

The door slowly creaked shut once more.

"I can't grant your appeal unless I can vouch for your allegiance."

"Then let me swear it to you." Collin swallowed and looked up into her face. "Princess."

Princess Ivy, eldest of King Rupert's twelve daughters, tore the final tracings from the machine and exited the crypt.

CHAPTER THREE

The door to the crypt needed replacing, oiling at the very least. The hinges shrieked with every swivel. It was almost enough to keep Ivy behind them.

She pushed through the door. "Constable." Ivy willed her voice not to shake. "Mr. Dobhareach is to be taken from the crypt and detained in the abbey cloisters until I return."

"Very good, Your Highness."

Ivy tried to smile. Papa was always getting after her about her frown. "Constable Jefferies, is it?"

The man nodded.

"Mr. Dobhareach is not to be harmed." Ivy's stomach twisted at the thought of the young man's purple and yellow bruises.

The constable bowed.

"Thank you, Constable." Ivy added the final tracings to her dossier before she buckled it shut. She only had to march one foot in front of the other, and then it would be over. Sunshine was at the other end of those dark, narrow stairs. Once she felt the warmth on her skin, she'd be able to breathe again.

It didn't sit right with her. She'd needed the demoted captain to sit still for her machine to work, but she hadn't needed him shackled to the chair like some animal. The fact that she'd felt so much safer because of it was appalling.

Her hands still shook as she crossed the lawn between the abbey and the palace. It was too cold and too early for anyone to be on the commons. The wind blew hard with all the strength of winter's bitterness. It carried the endless, inescapable coal smoke of the capital to her face, triggering tears. Good. The wind could be blamed for her tears today. She'd put them away as soon as she stepped inside the palace.

Bluffing was all she had. And she'd failed. No one respected a little girl who cried in a corner and begged for help. She needed to be strong. She needed to demonstrate experience and confidence, and she'd done a passable job. Until the end.

He'd asked for reassurance of her faith, as if it were commonplace to put her trust in a deserter. As if there were nothing concerning at all about risking everything on a man who knew his way around a timed detonator and had refused to swear allegiance to the king.

But he had instead sworn it to her. Ivy's skin prickled with the memory.

Ivy knew what she was risking. She knew that the coal smoke could, in a matter of weeks, turn into the smoke of burning buildings. And souls.

He'd looked for faith. Instead, he'd found her raw desperation.

Ivy patted her cheeks dry and pushed open the kitchen door. The kitchen whirred with activity. The servants moved with the familiar purpose of a busy house.

Frankfurt, the butler, bowed as low as his old back would permit. "Good morning, Your Highness. Any signs of spring sunshine this morning?"

"None that I could see through the coal smoke." Thank heavens for that. Ivy needed all the time winter could buy. "It's as cold as any winter day I've known. I wouldn't be surprised by more snow."

"Maybe so, but I am an eternal optimist. Early springs do happen. Cup of chocolate, ma'am?"

If only there were time. "No, thank you. But, Frankfurt, I feel a distinct draft."

"The chimney, ma'am. It was damaged in our last storm, and on windy mornings like these, we feel and hear the damages. Mrs. Stoddard has spoken with Her Majesty."

But of course to no end. Ivy opened her dossier and scribbled a note in the margin of Mr. Dobhareach's final tracings, right under the terms of his aid. She'd have to review the household budget again. Hopefully, willful neglect, and not a lack of funds, was the reason for the delayed repairs.

"Is my father taking breakfast—"

"In his apartment, ma'am."

Ivy nodded her thanks and quickly made her way out of the frigid kitchen.

King Rupert sat hunched in his special chair. Not the throne. That was too old and dirty, not to mention uncomfortable, for day-to-day. King Rupert liked his luxuries—gilded wood carvings on all the paneling, silver mirrors with gold leaf frames, heavy wool rugs from the Easterlies, and fine silk cushions stuffed with goose down.

"I don't understand why I can't have a footstool to match," King Rupert said with a mouthful of eggs and lox.

"Papa, it speaks so plainly of the boudoir," Ivy said.

"If I want a footstool, I should have a footstool."

"And if you wanted to conduct matters of state in your dressing room? Or in your bedchamber?"

"Then I should do it." King Rupert's jowls hung like those of a mastiff. And something about the dim glow in his eyes was faintly reminiscent of one too.

"Papa, it wouldn't be appropriate for courtiers or dignitaries to follow you into your personal areas."

"Oh, they don't care if I don't care." King Rupert frowned and added generous spoonfuls of salt to his eggs.

"Papa, I wondered if you, or perhaps Adelaide, have approved the repairs for the kitchen chimney."

"You've interrupted my breakfast for a smoking chimney? I am the king, Ivy." He gestured with his hands. Always with the hands when he was frustrated or blundering through political duties. "I don't have time for petty problems. Don't I have my hands full enough with the succession crisis?" He shoveled another bite of eggs and lox into his mouth. "And the war?"

Ivy gripped her dossier tightly. She didn't need another lecture on the war. "Of course you do, Papa."

The king licked his fingers before mopping his mouth with the vermilion linen. "What do I say? What do I always say?"

"'Bring me solutions, not problems.'" At last, Ivy had a solution. A great big important solution that could save not just lives, but the entire country. "Papa, there is a man I want you to meet."

The king spread inordinate amounts of marmalade on his toast. "Have I told you about my opera?"

Ivy swallowed. She'd learned long ago that her father would not consent to tedious political discussions unless every one of his current pet projects had received the appropriate care and attention.

"Opera?" Ivy poured herself some cocoa from the sterling chocolate pot at the sideboard. King Rupert was enormously fond of his sweets. Particularly on dreary winter days such as these.

King Rupert smiled up at his daughter. A more satisfied smile didn't exist in all the Shale Mountain realms. "I wrote an opera."

"Papa, that is wonderful." Ivy stirred her cocoa but remained standing at her father's side. He'd not invited her to sit. "Tell me all about it."

King Rupert nodded. "I wrote the lyrics. You know I'm a sensitive, introspective man." He picked up the knife on the table and began cleaning his nails. "I wrote the lyrics, and Minister Rosecrans begged to see them."

"I have no doubt." There could not be a more sycophantic courtier than Rosecrans.

"I wrote it for Adelaide, you know. She is so fond of the opera."

Adelaide was also fond of her solitude. "Yes, but—"

"Minister Rosecrans was so enamored with my lyrics that he immediately commissioned a score and instructed the royal theater company to perform it."

Oh dear. Ivy sipped her hot chocolate and flinched. It was far too sweet. Perhaps there would be enough time to salvage the situation. Ivy would have a word with the head of the opera house and persuade him to perform a different opera. Berlios was talented—his wife, Gilda, even more so. The pair of them could rewrite an aria, translate it into a different language if necessary. One pretty little song would be enough to satisfy Papa. He was, after all, merely looking for a creative outlet, an opportunity to impress Adelaide.

"That is wonderful news. I can't wait to hear it." And that was entirely true. The sooner Ivy understood the details of the situation, the sooner she could manage it and protect all parties involved.

"I can't either. The first performance is tonight."

Ivy choked on her chocolate, spilling quite a bit of it on her tie. "Tonight's opera? The new opera? It's your opera?"

"Of course it's my opera!" King Rupert narrowed his eyes. "Is that so shocking?"

"It's just...so soon?"

"Well, it's been in the works for some time. To tell you the truth, I'd forgotten about it."

Ivy's heart beat fast. "Well, that can't be helped. You're a busy man, Papa."

"Made all the busier for smoking kitchen chimneys."

"Might I inquire what inspired the opera?" She set the cup and saucer on the sideboard and blotted her tie with a spare linen napkin.

King Rupert's brow furrowed. His elaborate, curled wig slid

dangerously forward. He no longer wore the powdered ones. These days, he favored the blonds. "Horses."

Ivy's heart sank. "Horses? Well, they are beautiful, noble creatures."

"No. I was thinking about the big, fat ones."

The mantel clock ticked bravely, and King Rupert chewed his crunchy marmalade toast. "You wrote an opera about big, fat horses?" Ivy asked.

King Rupert nodded. "And the star is a horse who thinks he's not big or fat enough, but the prettiest horse falls in love with him, and then it turns out that he was always the biggest, fattest horse of them all. Do you think Adelaide will like it?"

"I'm sure it will leave her speechless. Have there been many rehearsals? Surely you must have attended one or two?"

"Oh no. Of course I was kept apprised of the progress, until the reports proved too tedious to keep up with. I approved the budget. They were all so worried about creating all the horse costumes, but I said, 'This is for your queen. I want you to spare no expense and make this the finest opera this country has ever seen.'"

An ache crept down Ivy's neck into her spine. Why hadn't she reviewed the budget this season? She'd asked, but Papa had insisted it was taken care of. She should have insisted. What had possessed her to neglect the financials, not to mention the opera house? If only she had stopped by, she might have learned something telling. Her sisters went to the opera all the time. Of course, they would not have known what to look for. Trina would have been too mesmerized by the music to notice anything amiss. Beatrice, too, if there were any passable flutists, and there always were. Jade would have spent all her time poking holes in the plot. Pen would be beside herself, observing all the "social irony," as she called it. The triplets and Sophia would have had eyes only for the young gentlemen. Poor dears didn't have much to look at these days. The younger set would have fallen asleep. Little Mina was still too young to even attend.

Not one would have thought to approach the director afterward to excavate what that telling note of panic meant in his voice. Not a one would have sought out Gilda to learn what was keeping her up at night. Because they didn't have to. That was Ivy's job. They could go to the opera and enjoy themselves. Ivy would go, and her mind would only wander in the dark as she worried about whether the opera's budget allocation might be better spent in rural schools or in research for the war effort. Confound the war!

"Now, Ivy, you said you had someone you wanted me to meet?"

"Yes, Papa." At last, she could show King Rupert the contents of her dossier and win approval for her plan.

"Good. Bring him to the opera tonight."

"No, Papa. That is not a good idea. Now, if we could look at my proposal—"

The king waved the proposal away with his fork. "Well, of course it is a good idea. It is my idea. Bring him to the opera. It's good to mix a little business with pleasure."

Ivy was sure it was not.

CHAPTER FOUR

"Gran, are you magic?" Little Collin asked.

How Gran fumed. If Collin's face wasn't already bruised, Gran would have boxed his ears. As it were, she banged the pots on the stove until she could speak. "It's not magic. It's information." She slapped a ball of dough on the table in front of Collin.

Collin floured his hands and began to punch and roll the dough until it lost its tackiness.

"Information is all that matters." Gran dropped the rolling pin in front of Collin. "Repeat it back to me."

Collin grabbed the pin and struggled to tame the dough into a flat circle. "Information is all that matters."

"That's right," Gran said. Her temper once again returned to a controlled simmer. "You tell people what they want to hear, you make them happy, and they pay you."

"How do you know what they want to hear?"

"You listen. You watch. Context, Collin. Say it!"

"Context."

Gran took the big knife and began to cut the flat circle of dough into an odd jumble of shapes—all of them four-sided, none of them squares. "How something is said, what isn't said, how the body is carried. It matters! You gather the pieces of information together..." Gran's callused hands had a natural tremor to them, like the fiddlers who came through town in autumn. Except Gran didn't play the fiddle.

Collin grabbed a piece of dough and stretched it gently. "Until you have a theory."

"That's right." Gran snatched the piece of dough from Collin and tossed it into the pot on the stove. It sizzled and crackled in the hot oil until it turned a golden brown. "You tell them the story they want to hear." Gran fished out the fried bread with a slotted spoon.

"But that's not honest."

"It's the most honest profession in this world. You only affirm what they already know." Gran slit open the fried bread and added a pat of butter to the inside.

"But you trick them." Collin handed Gran another stretched piece of dough.

"I stay alive." Gran tossed it in the pot. The oil sizzled and hissed. "How many north winters could a fortune-teller survive if she didn't play to win?"

Gran placed the two fried breads on Collin's tin plate and held it out to him. A signal that he could start, so long as he continued to do his part.

"Sometimes people can only believe in themselves after someone else believes in them," Gran said, sitting down to the table after all the dough had been fried. "After they hear their story told."

"How do you know if the story you told is the right one?"

"They tell you." She tore off a piece of her fry bread and popped it in her mouth.

"How?"

Gran gave Collin a pained look while she finished chewing. "Repeat it back to me."

"Context. Information is all that matters."

"It's as precious as gold. And people give it away, every day, every moment."

The snow blew hard against the window, but the prism glittered in the cold winter sun. Little rainbows decorated the kitchen table. They were all that decorated the table.

"I don't want gold. I want more fried bread and butter."

"Then you can't afford to be so foolish. Only old grans make fried bread for little boys with faces covered in bruises. You need to be more careful next time. You know what trouble is now. Hurt, fear, pins pricking the back of your neck. You must learn what it looks like. How it smells. What it sounds like. Do you understand?"

Collin nodded.

"Good. Now tell me. What do you hear?"

He heard men, mostly the young privates, some a half-dozen years younger than his twenty, screaming in pain. Explosions ricocheted so close that Collin would have torn his own ears off from the ringing if he'd had a spare moment. The medic made sure he did not. And in the days (and years) that followed, it was not the sight of blood that haunted him, but the metallic smell of it. Fresh but insolently stale too. Dried on his forearms, still wet on his fingers.

"Am I going to die, mate?" the private with the patchy mustache asked. Collin tried to read him in an instant and formulate a theory for what the wide-eyed youth, with blood soaking the front of his uniform, wanted to hear. Collin didn't know, but his comrade had asked for words, and, Mars, he deserved them if this was his miserable end.

"Only for a moment. And then you'll live forever in the Great Beyond. Where there is only light—"

"And no turnips." He coughed out blood, and drops of it landed on Collin's face.

"No. None." Oh hellfire, Collin didn't know what to say. "And no mud or freezing rains."

"And butter and fig pudding at every meal."

"That's right. And you pick who you share it with. Every time."

"Every time," the lieutenant colonel repeated.

Collin was standing in the road outside his camp. He'd done everything he could to ensure that he'd never get his boots caked in mud again, but here he was, four years after getting out of the medical corps, standing on a country road so destroyed by the wind and sleet that no sane person would venture onto it for another six weeks. Maybe seven.

The lieutenant colonel's humor was certainly not improved for the ordeal. The old raisin seemed determined to make a point of it. "The enemy steals from us. They dishonor and disgrace us, and every time, they must be punished." He circled the two boys lying face-down in the mud before unholstering his pistol and offering it to Collin. "You are the captain of this regime. The honor falls to you."

It had been four years since Collin had held a pistol. The last one hadn't been nearly so clean.

"Dispatch them. We can't have the enemy stealing our supplies."

Collin held the cold weight in his hand. Why did the lieutenant colonel have to come? Collin had done a good enough job keeping everyone out of trouble until now. They'd held their line, fought bravely, even waged a few successful campaigns under Collin's command, but not enough to garner this kind of attention. Collin had made sure. His shoulders sagged as his boots sank deeper into the mud. "They can have my rations. Their crime is absolved as I freely give them—"

"The rations are not yours to give. They are the property of His Majesty—"

"I will not murder these children." Collin's fingers clenched tight around the pistol.

"If the enemy deems them fit enough to wear their uniform, then they will be treated as soldiers and deserve a soldier's death. A bullet in the head for each of them, Captain. That's an order."

Screams chased away by weak whimpers echoed in Collin's ears, even though the road was silent. The smell of blood already lingered and kept him company through the coldest nights. And the ringing. The damn ringing. "Turn them over," Collin said.

The lieutenant colonel nodded to his men.

Collin would not look at the boys. He didn't need a larger cast for his nightmares. "Your names and ages?"

The ringing drowned out their words. But he saw the lieutenant colonel blanch.

Collin nodded, still staring at the brightly polished author of so much fear and destruction in his hands. "Lieutenant Colonel, ask your men to step away. Every soldier should be allowed to face death on his feet."

The raisin nodded, chest puffed up in pride. "Exactly so." He motioned for his men to fall back.

"Behind me, gentleman."

The lieutenant colonel chuckled. "A medic's penchant for safety."

"In wartime, it comes in handier than you'd think."

Their boots *slurched* and gurgled in the mud. The wind blew a low moan, and Collin felt his heart keep time to an inevitability he wished he'd realized sooner.

It was time to leave the army.

The farm boys turned to Collin with eyes full of white.

"Run," he told them as he raised the pistol to the sky and fired into the open air.

∾

The princess' footsteps announced her arrival long before the guard, the gaunt one who repeatedly misplaced the keys in his back pocket. "It appears you have a visitor."

Collin rose. Six days had passed since he refused to execute those boys. The four spent in this prison had taught him a new kind of wariness. His eyes found the drops of chocolate on her tie. She was breathing quicker. Flushed cheeks. Something had changed.

"Thank you." Ivy nodded her dismissal. The guard quickly ambled back to his pocket novel. "I apologize for the accommodations. I've arranged something more comfortable. If you'd be so good as to follow me."

Collin would. The princess was better company than his memories. "I take it your morning went well?"

"Abysmal." Ivy led Collin through the cloister and heaved open the sanctuary door.

"I'm not really dressed for church." Collin buttoned the top button of his soiled and tattered shirt all the same.

Ivy strode quickly down the choir aisle. "And I've no patience for it this morning, but it's the fastest route."

A painfully thin friar spotted Ivy and waved her down. "Princess Ivy!"

"Father Michael."

"If I might have a word. I've had the most distressing communication."

Collin drew up casually to Ivy's side, leaning his back against a column darkened with decades of candle smoke. He watched walls fall down in Ivy's eyes, only to be shorn up immediately by her smile. It was an exceptionally winning smile.

"We've learned that His Majesty is displeased with the Archbishop of Ryland."

"Oh?" Ivy shifted her dossier to her other arm.

"Apparently, the archbishop prays too much for His Majesty's liking."

Collin's scoff bounced off of the centuries-old sculptures and stained glass, inspiring grave disapproval from the few praying friars.

Ivy's smile disappeared into a look of sympathetic concern. "Surely not."

"Would you be willing to speak to your father on our behalf? We are only too happy to pray less if it would—"

"Father Michael, I'm sure this is just a misunderstanding. Let me talk to my father, and I will sort this out."

"Bless you, my child. Will you be attending the opera tonight?"

Opera in wartime? It was nice to know the capital had its priorities straight.

"Oh yes, and I think it best you invite as many parishioners as you can. My father does adore a crowd."

"I'm sure several dozen members of my congregation would love to attend. However, there is the question of admission."

"The balcony will be free to the public."

"Excellent. However, a tangible incentive would be more enticing."

Ivy's shoulders tensed. "I'm sure there will be a public reception after the opera with several barrels of spiced wine and the usual fare."

"Excellent, Your Highness. Excellent as always."

"Good day to you, Father Michael."

"And to you, my child. And to..." Father Michael took in Collin for the first time, no doubt noting Collin's torn and soiled shirt. He raised his hands in a prayer above Collin's head. "And to you, my son."

Ivy pushed through the abbey doors and headed out into the west courtyard. "You are very quiet, Mr. Dobhareach."

"I was listening. A lot was being said just now."

"A lot is always being said. It would be nice not to be the one who had to say it for a change." Ivy examined her pocket watch. It was a marvelously intricate, albeit tarnished, piece. An emerald inlay, if Collin had to guess. "It would also be nice if one didn't have to answer for any of it."

"Your Highness?"

"I'll need an hour before the opera to coordinate the public reception. Thank heavens the shipment of ale arrived from the coastlands." Ivy stopped outside what Collin imagined was the college garden. A beautiful magnolia tree had bravely bloomed early, emboldened by its tactical brilliance of growing in a wind-protected corner. Poor tree. Its blooms would shrivel in the next snowstorm.

Ivy opened her dossier and began to scribble. "My father has requested that you attend the opera with us tonight."

"Has he?" Collin sauntered closer, curious to see what sort of notes Ivy took.

"I'd imagine you have no formal wear." She looked up at Collin with a sly smile. She snapped her dossier shut and marched across the courtyard toward the common.

Collin followed. "Sadly, my dinner jacket was confiscated with my other personal effects when I was thrown in your prison."

A group of fellows passed by in their green and vermilion scholarly robes. Ivy smiled and nodded. But her eyes were hollow and the shadows under them deep. They crossed the common, the dried and yellow grass accented with only the scantest tufts of foolhardy green clover. "It is not my prison, Mr. Dobhareach—"

"Dobha-reach," Collin corrected. "You're adding syllables that aren't there."

Ivy stumbled but quickly regained her footing. "It's impossible to pronounce."

Collin shrugged. "If you have a lazy tongue."

"I'd take care not to insult the woman who haggled for your freedom."

"Are you in the habit of taking in stray men from makeshift prisons and inviting them to the opera?"

"Mr. Dobhareach—"

"If I'm to be your date this evening, then you should know I go by my first name, as no one can ever pronounce Dobhareach. And captain is perhaps a more appropriate title than mister."

Ivy twitched a black curl out of her eyes. "Let me impress on you, Captain..." She opened her dossier and riffled through the papers.

"Collin."

"Yes, thank you. Let me impress on you, Captain Collin, how delicate a situation this is."

Collin's gaze settled on Ivy's neck and wandered to her tweed jacket. What was she doing out in the elements in only a jacket? Gran wouldn't have stood for such nonsense.

Ivy's fingers on Collin's jaw quickly redirected his attention. "My father takes great stock in first impressions."

"I don't think there is anything I could do to persuade your father that I am essential to winning the war."

"Not with a torn shirt and that attitude. Try to keep up, Major." She turned off of the main avenue, down a small alley.

"It's captain."

"I've promoted you. I can't have a lowly captain leading my task force. Now, tell me how you kept all your fingers while still managing to blow up so much of Olcceart's artillery?"

Collin's heart beat faster. He raked his fingers through his hair. Mars, this would be funny if it were happening to another man. "Working with explosives... It pays to be risk-averse."

"Explain."

A particularly bitter, far-reaching wind found them in the shadowed alley. Why didn't she have a coat? Collin would have offered her his own, had he one to offer. "Explosives can be highly unstable. A single blunder can be deadly. A few spilled drops could take off your hand. In the quiet confines of a workshop, there is risk. How much more so in the theater of war? I didn't want to lose any of my extremities. I didn't want to be responsible for the lost limbs or lives of my..." Of the other boys who'd stood with him shoulder to shoulder. The ones who'd by now perished, with the rest waiting out the winter to do the same. "I found a way of making nitrated glycerin more stable."

"The putty?"

Collin nodded. "Adding it to kieselguhr made it practically inert."

"By raising the activation energy?"

"Just so." What would Gran make of her?

"An inert explosive isn't very useful."

Collin shrugged. "A detonator changes the equation. Every time."

"It must be nice to work in absolutes." Ivy directed Collin down a busy street. Cabs and hacks jostled one another. Horses shook their bells and flicked their tales against the staccato of their hooves. She had to shout to make herself heard over the din. "Your detonators and knowledge of explosives will be a real advantage, not that we have many. I won't sugarcoat the situation." They turned down a quieter street. "We face an industrial nation, mobilized to outfit a conquering army with the latest technological advantages."

"Yes, their machine weaponry is impressive."

"And effective." She tucked the dossier under her arm and gripped her wrists behind her. "The Republic of Olcceart was ready to win the war with the first invasion. They have prolonged the fight because it is a boon to their economy and national pride."

Convenient to leave out that it was her father and his ridiculous trade war—and idiotic posturing—that had led to that first invasion.

"Although, I do wonder if there is not something devious going on. A clandestine goal to decrease their population. Some of our neighbors appear preoccupied with purifying their kingdoms." Ivy's voice faltered. She retrieved a pair of leather gloves from her dossier and tugged them on. "The rumors I've heard of forced marches and exile... It is a dangerous time for our fey friends."

Collin wanted to know the rumors she'd heard. He wanted to know how much she understood. He wanted to know if she couldn't sleep at night because of it. If she couldn't sit with a quiet cup of tea alone now. If she had woken up bone-tired but too scared to fall back asleep because she had dreamed the very worst. And knew it was real.

A part of him, the part deeply bruised from all he'd seen and survived, wanted to reassure her that her fears were unfounded. But

Collin couldn't outright lie. He could, however, admire how soft her lips looked.

She was off again, and Collin had to jog a few paces to catch up. They turned down High Street, past blocks of smart townhomes, the prettiest outfitted with window boxes filled with white and purple flowers.

"Aren't the violas charming?" Ivy asked. "You think I'm like them, don't you? Pretty little things sheltered away and oblivious to the struggle." She fussed over the button of her glove. "The horrors we are facing."

"Have you been to the front, ma'am?"

She continued to struggle with the button. "No."

So she read reports and imagined she knew enough to play with the fates of so many men, pretending they were little more than toy soldiers in a ridiculous skirmish over ice fields!

"Four years ago, at the start of the war," Ivy said, "I toured the hospital tents." She squinted into the sunshine. "For all of twenty-four minutes, before I was escorted back to safer ground." She shivered in the wind. "Papa was furious, but I had to do something." She once again turned her attention to the loose button on her glove. "One does not forget shed blood."

Collin watched her continue to struggle. She'd seen it, heard it, smelled it. It haunted her too.

"I begged to return as a nurse, a mechanic, a secretary, anything. But the safety of a princess is weighed differently than that of our boys," she said grimly. "Even if there are twelve of us."

Collin approached and offered his assistance with the stubborn button.

Ivy accepted. "Papa deigned to let me help with the paperwork he ignores. But helping with his dispatch boxes is not enough, not when young men are dying, and they spend their last moments covered in their own blood, talking of turnips."

Collin's hands slipped from the button. He fumbled and held Ivy's gloved hand in his own. He dared not look into her eyes.

"Every time I bring this, or any bit of bad news, to Papa's attention, he changes the subject, or he tells me that I needn't worry, but when I press, he bellows, 'Then bring me a solution.' You are my solution, Major."

Collin had to say something to change the subject. "The violas are a favorite of Her Highness?"

A frown accompanied her impatient huff. "Why must every woman have a favorite flower?"

She was going to make him work for this bit of intel. "Then you prefer roses? Tulips? Gardenias?"

She walked on. "The sweet pea, if you must know."

Collin grabbed his elbows and hugged his arms to his stomach. His lungs became poor servants. "My Gran grew sweet peas."

The sweet pea was a curious flower known for its scent and not its form. And the memory of the smell ferried Collin back to the bare-foot kingdom of a little boy. Gran would soak the seeds the night of the first autumn frost, and they'd plant the swollen black pearls the next morning. He had to say something, or he'd start to cry. "Early spring days like these, ones that could easily be mislabeled as late winter—"

"Where you want nothing more than to hold a cup of something hot in your hands."

Exactly! "Where the balance of your life hinges on dry, wool socks."

"Where you imagine the sun has lost its strength."

Mars, but she was forlorn. Her smile rivaled the ones he'd seen at the front. "These were the days that Gran and I would look for the cotyledons among the crocuses." They'd check the sweet peas' progress daily. Gran had taught Collin when to tie the sweet peas to the fence post. When they were young. Before they made up their mind to be troublesome.

Ivy turned up a new row of dazzlingly white townhouses.

"How do they keep the coal smoke off the stone?" Collin asked.

"They don't. The facades are washed regularly. I read the details of your desertion."

Collin winced. Was there really nothing better to talk about from his file?

"You impressed me, Major. If we win this war, and win we must, and the dust settles, and we go home and discover that we are no longer capable of gentlemanly sensibilities"—Ivy shrugged—"then we've lost something even more precious. You agree?"

"Emphatically."

Ivy nodded. She turned down an alley.

Collin followed. She almost had him convinced he was a hero. That wouldn't do. "War is too easy an excuse to use a fellow as something less than human. And war makes the necessary functions of intelligence—spying, assessments, interrogation..."

Ivy turned pale.

That was better. "It makes it too easy to use these for one's personal gain."

Ivy jabbed Collin's chest with a gloved finger. "You were not sufficiently stressed to make my polygraph helpful. I did what I could."

"You did what you wanted." They had that in common at least.

"I don't believe in violence, Major Collin, but you have me reassessing my stance. Slapping you now seems like a good idea." Ivy marched up the stairs to a slim residence shouldered between far larger real estates.

"A gentleman knocks," Ivy mumbled.

Collin reached around Ivy on the little stoop and lifted the brass knocker up and down.

A woman in a turban opened the door. "Ivy!" she screamed, embracing the young woman. "It's been ages. How are you, my dear?"

"Fine, Auntie. Fine."

"Lies, my dear. I see the dark circles under your eyes. But come

in. Come"—the turbaned woman turned to Collin, and her eyes
danced—"in," she commanded, ushering Collin into her home.

Incense filled the salon. And art. Paintings and silver-plated glass
photographica filled the walls. Exotic orchids and vines spilled off of
the slender tables. Books lay in stacks. "I'd offer to take your coats, but
goodness, you are without them."

"Which is why we've come. Auntie Olivia, this is Major Collin.
He is Papa's guest at the opera tonight, but alas he has no dinner
jacket."

Olivia turned an appraising eye to Collin. Given his sorry state—
torn and soiled shirt, threadbare and filthy trousers, matted hair filled
with coal smoke, and dirt, sweat, and yellowing bruises covering most
of his skin—it was absurd to be discussing dinner jackets. Gran would
have told Collin to wait outside and doused him with a bucket of
water before she greeted him.

"Major?" Olivia extended her hand graciously.

Collin pressed it warmly. He liked this maternal woman. He
liked even more that she belonged to Ivy somehow. Collin bowed
over her hand. An extraordinary ring of andalusite and sapphires
adorned her index finger.

"Major, this is Madame Olivia. She was—"

"Is, my dear. Is," Olivia extolled. "Death does not erase
friendships."

"—a dear friend of my mother's. And has been a godmother to me
in her absence."

Collin's brow furrowed. He should have remembered the
princess' family history. He should have known when and how that
mother had become absent. Olivia would know. She'd know all the
gossip about Ivy and her family. And judging by her open, friendly
manner, she'd be more than willing to share with Collin. It was too
easy. Ivy would have to be warned about revealing so much information in the future. "A pleasure, Madame Olivia."

A wide smile spread across Olivia's face. "A joy, Major. Now, then, tea, coffee, cocoa imported from the far-off forests of the Easterlies?"

Collin knew better than to refuse friendly hospitality. "Tea, thank you."

"None for me, Auntie. I must be going. I've a promise of spiced wine I must keep. Would you please help the major prepare for the opera?"

"I'd love to."

"Thank you. Is Ottis in? I'd love to say hello before I disappear."

Olivia busied herself at the tea service. "Ottis is out inspecting the tulips' progress at the abbey, though I told him there is none to be found yet."

"Will you give him my love when he returns?"

"I'll treat him to his favorite biscuit in your honor."

"And would you join us in our box tonight?"

"Alas, my dear, I have important preparations to make for an upcoming expedition."

"And here I am demanding last-minute favors." But not apologizing for them, Collin noted. "Safe travels, Auntie." Ivy bussed Olivia's cheek.

"Take one of my coats, Ivy. It is too cold, and you are too small to be playing this sort of game with the wind. You don't know the wind the way I do. He has no compunction when it comes to young ladies. The major would agree with me, but as he is coatless himself, he's hardly an authority on the subject. We will soon remedy that, aye, Major?"

Collin agreed.

Olivia rolled her eyes and gestured an order for him to assist the princess. He readily complied, joining the princess at the armoire near the door. She'd already made a selection from among the jewel-colored offerings.

"May I?" Collin asked, taking the coat and holding it open for the princess. Ivy hesitated before she shrugged into the indigo wool.

Collin adjusted the collar, smoothed the shoulders. His hands tarried, and he was seized with the impulse to hold this young woman close.

Olivia clasped her hands together. "Just lovely."

Ivy met Collin's eyes and had the audacity to smirk. "Yes, it's breathtaking."

Collin flushed. His arms retreated to his sides.

"Auntie, where did you find this wool?"

"Oh, you know me." Olivia turned her attention to Collin. "I'm always interested in sponsoring the young and talented."

Ivy nodded. "Now out of my way, Major. I've more pressing business than spiced wine to see to before tonight. Budgets. Broken chimneys. And an avalanche of correspondence from our easternmost charities."

"Charities?" Olivia brought the major a steaming cup of tea.

"Hospitals mostly. A few libraries. Even a poorhouse."

He felt himself pale. Pins prickled the back of his neck. What did she know? More important, what did she suspect?

When Ivy had left, Olivia rounded on Collin. "Don't worry, Major. When I'm done, you won't even recognize yourself. Now, then, let's start with your mustache."

CHAPTER FIVE

It was a simple yet elegant plan. The rifle was not concealed but hiding in plain sight. One in a lineup of many props for the opera that evening. However, this rifle was loaded. And fitted with a clever telescope that would make the task of aiming a bullet at King Rupert's skull all the easier.

CHAPTER SIX

"Where have you been?" Trina asked.

Ivy struggled with the buttons of her vest. "Oh, Trina, you look lovely!"

Wearing her best violet silk, Trina was serene, poised, lovely.

"Did you have a go at the abbey's organ?" Ivy asked.

"Mm-hm." Trina helped her sister with the row of buttons down her back. "I did. Right after I removed a robin's nest from the C-major pipe. I don't know what those monks have been doing for the past six months."

"Hiding so they don't get drafted." Ivy fumbled with the buckles on her boots. "Did you save a dress for me?"

"I did, except Daphne stole it." Trina handed Ivy an impressively ruffled petticoat.

"Trina!" Ivy wiggled into the petticoat. "What in heaven's name am I going to wear?"

Trina heaved a green gown out of the armoire.

"No!"

"Ivy darling, this is what happens when you wait until the last moment to change."

With eleven sisters, it was what happened. Wardrobes were pillaged. The most fashionable styles conquered. The most flattering colors captured. The posturing of victorious strategy decisive. "You know I can't stand green," Ivy said, tossing back the dress.

"Green suits you, Ivy."

"It doesn't matter. If your name was a plant as well as a color, you'd understand why I am weary of the association."

"I thought only Papa still teased you when you wore green."

Ivy huffed, stepping out of her pinstripes. "Papa still thinks I'm twelve years old."

Trina had the gown up and over Ivy's head before Ivy could say another word. "Has Papa approved of your strategy?" Trina concentrated on lacing Ivy into her gown.

"No. I didn't even have a chance to explain. Papa was all, 'I wrote an opera. Are you coming to the opera tonight, Ivy? I wrote it!'" Ivy gripped the back of her desk chair.

"Breathe in," Trina instructed.

"Why do we do this to ourselves?" Ivy said, holding her breath.

Trina tugged hard on the laces of Ivy's bodice. "Because it's fun."

"Did you know that Papa wrote this opera?"

Trina paused before tugging the laces with renewed vigor. "No. But I do know that Berlios wrote the score, and he is wonderful." Trina tied the laces extremely tight.

"If Berlios is so wonderful, why don't you marry him?" Ivy teased. The same way she had teased Trina back when they'd worn their hair in braids with matching ribbons.

Trina tossed Ivy a jeweled necklace. "Well, for one, he is conveniently taken and has been for at least twenty-five years. And two, he's not an organ enthusiast. I keep trying to persuade him to write more for our organs, but he never does. Now hold still."

Before Ivy could object, Trina had threaded a circlet of silver leaves into her coiffeur. "Oh no, Trina. The injustice of this is too much."

"But you look so pretty! Besides, Papa is too nervous this night to say anything."

Ivy struggled with the clasp of her necklace. "That doesn't sound much like Papa."

Trina shrugged and turned her sister toward the electric lamp. She opened a pot of red cream.

Ivy shook her head. "Absolutely not."

"I swear I will not overpaint the way Gwen does."

"No."

"But, Ivy, the lights will be so dim, and if you aren't done up like the rest of us, you'll stand out like an old—" She cut herself off.

Ivy flinched. "Go on, say it. An old maid."

"Oh, forgive me, Ivy. I didn't mean that. It's just you are running yourself ragged. You are in court meetings all day. You pore over ledgers and reports from the front all night. You hardly sit down long enough for a meal. You can't even spare more than ten minutes to get ready for Papa's opera. Harriet says you've aged at least five years since January."

"Harriet would say that. She's obsessed with her beauty rest."

"'Holistic health' is her favored term."

"Did you know she wants me to institute meditation at the war front? How in heaven am I supposed to do that?"

"Could be on to something."

"If both sides were interested in meditation, then don't you think we would have been able to negotiate a peace by now?"

Trina shook her head, but she was practical and persistent. "Do you think I look too done up? I promise I won't take any liberties. And you will be so glad for the extra five minutes spent on your pretty face."

"Would it make you happy?" Ivy asked.

Trina was already patting cream onto Ivy's lips. "Very much."

When Trina was finished, Ivy was happy she'd indulged her sister. "You winged my eyes."

"I did." Trina smoothed her white silk gloves past her elbows.

"You said you wouldn't take any liberties." Ivy stepped into her vermilion slippers. If she couldn't be a fellow, at least she could wear their colors.

"I lied," Trina said. She handed Ivy a fan. "Shall we?"

"Trina, have you thought of studying music at the college?" Ivy asked, inspired by the colors of her gown and shoes.

"I'm not sure that's done, Ivy."

"Never mind that. Are you interested?"

"They do have a lovely organ over there."

"But what would you think about all those books?"

"Egads, Ivy, do they bite?"

Ivy rolled her eyes.

Trina crossed hers and then pushed her sister out of the room.

Ivy bounced her closed fan in her palm as she wove her way through the halls. "I'll have to have a word with Professor August. It's absolutely absurd for those scholars to get up and have only a handful of pupils to teach when there are hundreds of bright minds eager to learn."

"Ivy, please pace yourself."

"Why? So I can sit on my hands and just wait for this stupid war to end and for my country to reevaluate its antiquated ideals?"

"No, so I do not break a heel or a limb." Trina pointed to her silver shoes.

Ivy slowed, appropriately chastened.

Trina considered her sister. "Will you tell me what is going on? The last time you acted like this was on the eve of your hospital tour."

"Nothing is going on." Ivy smiled in spite of herself. Trina folded her arms. "Papa told me to invite Major Collin Dobhareach to the opera tonight."

"You have a date to the opera?"

"Not like that, but yes."

Trina stopped to fasten an emerald bracelet around Ivy's gloved wrist. "He must be handsome."

"He's absolutely top-notch. At least I think he is. His face is a little too purple at present to tell. But that's not the point."

"What is?"

"His mind. He could win the war for us."

"Emphasis on 'could'?"

"I have to persuade him."

"I'm sure you already have."

"No, I must persuade Papa. He has to agree to my plan."

"The plan. Of course." Trina continued down the stairs. "I suppose relaxing and enjoying the opera is not part of tonight's agenda for anyone unlucky enough to be in Papa's box."

Ivy's brow wrinkled. "Are you not in the royal box tonight?"

"Heavens no. I want to listen to and enjoy the opera. I'll be in the family box above. Far away from all the whispered politics that will keep everyone, I'm sure, from enjoying Berlios' brilliance."

"Do you know what the opera is about?"

"Haven't a clue."

Ivy considered that discussing business tonight might be more constructive than her sister supposed.

CHAPTER SEVEN

Olivia proved most helpful. Most. In a single afternoon, she had transformed Collin from a tattered, filthy inmate to the picture of a gentleman. Collin tried to thank her, but she swatted away his sentiments with a free hand. "Never underestimate the power of a hot bath."

Collin smoothed his freshly cut brown hair back at the sides. The woman was a genius with a straight razor. "To say nothing of a shave and new haircut."

Olivia mumbled something about the dearth of well-groomed young men before tying off a few threads on the lining of Collin's new jacket. Not only had the woman procured and fitted Collin with a full ensemble, but she'd also supplied a cascade of invaluable facts regarding Ivy. She'd even explained how a set of triplets could have such vastly different hues and statures.

"They have different mothers, of course. Princesses Daphne, Angelica, and Gwen were born within hours of each other, so in the beginning, they really did look like triplets. Rupert says he didn't plan any of it. He claimed these things just happen." Olivia snorted.

"Rupert is many things, but he's never been one to quibble over race or skin color. Pretty faces, that's a different story."

Olivia handed off the jacket, which Collin immediately shrugged into.

Olivia nodded and opened a drawer of her credenza. She rummaged around before finding a white tie. "Constance would have loved this."

"Constance?" Collin bent down.

"Constance, Ivy's mother, was a dear friend." Olivia sighed, adjusted Collin's collar, and looped and twisted the tie until it was a sharp bow. "She died in labor with her last. The baby was breech." Olivia blinked rapidly. "It's not fair. To this very day, it's not fair."

Collin nodded. "How old was Ivy?"

"Not old enough. Four."

Collin sipped his cocoa. It was a thicker, sweeter drink than Gran had ever made. Olivia had said it was Ivy's favorite. "Has Ivy ever explained why cocoa is her favorite drink?"

Olivia chortled. "A little preoccupied with our lovely Ivy, are we?"

Collin shrugged. "I must understand if I am to help. I need all the information I can gather to do so."

Olivia opened a box under the settee and pulled out a white silk scarf. "Information is all you require?"

Collin replaced his cup in his saucer. "If you have enough information, you can solve any problem."

"Is that so?" Olivia found two pearl cufflinks in her abalone shell and handed them to Collin.

There was insufficient information to know if Olivia was teasing or merely disinterested. Gran would have known instantly. Collin slipped his fingers over the smooth stones. "Ivy has no true sisters, then?"

Olivia snapped the hatbox shut and reached for a second. "Katrina, the second eldest, is Ivy's full sister, although the girls don't make much of this. They all seem to get along with each other. They get on surprisingly well."

"There have been four wives."

"Adelaide makes five."

That's right. The king was newly remarried. "And how many mothers?"

"Nine. No, ten. I keep forgetting that the youngest's mother was the lady's maid and not the lady herself." Olivia handed Collin a new salve.

He patted it onto his yellowing bruises. "I need an illustrated family tree."

"So does Rupert."

Olivia stopped to inspect the shine of Collin's shoes. "King Rupert calls himself generous and has recognized all the children as his, despite his reluctance to formalize the unions with many of these women. Although, as most of these unions took place simultaneously with other marriages, I can't quite fault him on the legality. The rumor was always if a match produced an heir, then the king would have divorced and remarried immediately."

Collin handed back the jar of ointment. "Ivy is not the heir?"

Olivia pulled a black top hat from her wardrobe. "The monarchy must pass to the king's son."

Collin accepted the hat. "And if the king were to die before a son is produced?"

Olivia slammed the wardrobe shut. "It would be a disaster. For years, friends at court have tried to persuade His Majesty to settle the question of succession. But the king's solution has always been to divorce another wife, find a new mistress, remarry—"

"There must be someone. A cousin, an uncle, a nephew."

Olivia shook her head. "The family tree bears no clear answers. The question of succession would be far more pressing, but of course, there is a war... And you know more of the war than all of us." She handed Collin a cane, which he politely declined.

Collin held the smooth, silk hat in his hands. "And what would happen to the princesses if their father left the question of succes-sion...unresolved? Untimely end and all that?"

"Oh goodness, I don't know."

Collin didn't either.

The little dog whimpered at Olivia's feet. She scooped him up in her arms. "But... God save the king until we do."

CHAPTER EIGHT

Ivy considered that the people who recommended mixing business with pleasure were the sort who never actually did any business, and the people who suffered through the mingling of leisure and work never had any time for pleasure to begin with. But what could be done? Privilege came with power. Unfortunately, the overwhelming responsibility to do right and make good was tied to neither. The work always fell to the less privileged and less powerful. Children, in this instance. And, more specifically, since Rupert had no sons, eldest daughters.

The opera house's facade of windows and framing looked like fine lace against the dark topaz sky. The exterior stairs were filled with clusters of excited patrons.

"There's nothing quite like opening night, is there?" Trina asked, her face flushed with excitement as she alighted from the carriage. "You can taste the energy."

"What does it taste like?" Ivy asked. Hopefully not spiced wine. Tracking it down had been easy enough, but then Rosecrans had insisted on serving from crystal punch bowls rather than the kegs. The bowls had been lost, only to be found in the armory of all places.

Why did crystal even matter? Ivy was sure that she and every other patron would be so tired by the end of the opera, and so desperate for a drink, that they would happily supply their own shoes as cups if need be.

"It tastes like the first cool autumn morning after a long hot summer. It tastes like the first peppermints of winter or the smile that comes from finding the first crocus in spring."

"Or sweet pea cotyledon."

Trina smoothed her skirts. "What's a cotyledon?"

"Do you remember when we used to grow sweet peas in the garden?" Ivy asked. "I can't remember the last time I had a chance to putter about in the dirt." She missed it.

The girls had reached the atrium of the opera house. It was packed with people. "Nice that no one stops and salutes for princesses these days," Trina said.

Ivy shrugged out of her cloak and piled it on top of the rest. The poor cloak-check attendants had their hands full tonight. "There's too many of us to keep track of."

Ivy and Trina summited the stairs to the second floor of the opera house. "So many stairs," Ivy grumbled, tightly clutching the banister. "I wonder how much time I waste climbing them. If I could just squeeze them out of my schedule—"

"Ivy darling, I'd listen to you if I thought you might say something sensible about extra sleep or a relaxing pastime, but I know you."

Ivy paused to acknowledge an officer of the royal guard. "Good evening, Captain Hector. Congratulations on the new promotion."

Hector bowed to the princesses. "Thank you, Your Highness."

"Trina, Hector has just been promoted to captain of the royal guard." Ivy found a genuine smile while addressing him. "I was so pleased to hear some good news. How is your family? Has Elenore regained her appetite?"

"That she has, ma'am."

"Wonderful news, Hector. Please tell her to keep up the good work."

Hector's stoic face broke into a cracked smile. "That I will. Thank you, ma'am."

Ivy turned to Trina. "Hector's dear Elenore is expecting their second baby. It's terribly important work she is doing. Without women like Elenore, our kingdom would dry up." Ivy nodded to Hector and walked with Trina to the private staircase leading to the family boxes. "Half our secondary schools are empty as it is, but I read a report last week that said that enrollment in our kinder enrichment will fall by forty percent in the next two years."

"That's awful, Ivy."

Ivy looked down at the throng of people in the atrium below. It was far too hot, and it was spinning. No matter how hard she gripped the railing, everything still spun. Splendid. Ivy shut her eyes tightly. "We will be paying for this war for the rest of our lives, which won't be for much longer if we can't think of a way to end it."

Trina took her sister in hand and led her to the double doors, decorated with banners in the emerald and vermilion colors of Amadanri. "Lucky for all of us, we have you thinking one step ahead, but, Ivy..." Notes of warning in Trina's voice gave Ivy pause. "No more tonight. Try to enjoy yourself. Please? Mr. Top-Notch—"

"Major Top-Notch."

"Major Top-Notch needs an introduction to Papa, and that's all. Escape the politics and business for one night and try to enjoy the opera."

"It's about horses," Ivy said, exchanging an embrace with her sister. "Big, fat ones."

"It's about sitting in the dark next to that handsome gentleman," Trina whispered.

"Is he here?" Ivy asked, too tired to turn around.

"I'm going to leave you to flirt before you have to stumble over my introduction."

Collin stood at the top of the stairs. He adjusted his white bow tie with the same disdain of a puppy kicking at a new collar.

Ivy had been right to take him to Olivia. No one knew how to smarten the way she did.

Ivy wished very much that the missing punch bowls had been located sooner. If they had, then she would not have been standing with her neck and shoulders bare in the dreaded green monster of taffeta and tulle.

Ivy took a deep breath. She had to assume her role. Puppies needed a firm hand after all. She sashayed to Collin, her jaw tilted at an unnatural, stiff angle. "Good evening, Major. You clean up nicely. Olivia must be thanked. I'd no idea you were this handsome."

"Yes, I've been told I'm top-notch after a good scrub."

Ivy's eyes narrowed, but she kept her smile soft. "Were you eavesdropping, Major?"

"Eavesdropping is appallingly rude." The major held open the door of the box.

"But instructive?" Ivy supplied.

"You'd have to be a fool to ignore perfectly good information."

"Even if taken out of context?"

Collin considered. His gaze traveled the length of the green monster.

She'd let him stand there awkwardly holding the door open a moment longer for that. There wasn't much she could do in a green fairy-princess dress. She adjusted a pin in her coiffure, and a calculated black ringlet tumbled to her shoulder. "Are you fond of the opera, Major?"

"I think I will be after tonight."

Ivy gathered her abundant skirts and brushed past the major into the royal box. "My father has written the lyrics of our evening's entertainment."

The major followed, and together they surveyed the theater below. It was a red and gold affair. Red curtains. Red rugs. Red chairs. Red tapestries and gold columns.

"Have you been to our opera house before?" Ivy asked.

"I've not."

"Then you should take your time admiring the ceiling. It is considered one of our national treasures. The coronation of Grandpapa, Cornelius the Circumspect. You see that cherub there?" She leaned closer to Collin and pointed upward. "The one stealing the grapes? It's said to be Papa."

Collin was not looking at the ceiling. He was looking at Ivy.

"No interest in fine art?"

"I find more beauty in the natural world."

Ivy brushed her tresses over her shoulder. "Then let me direct your attention to the architecture. A frieze of our lake country and mountains was incorporated into the balcony faces."

"The gilded ones?"

"Yes, Papa is fond of gold." But she had to admit the gilded columns and friezes glinted beautifully in the luster of the electric lights.

Ivy smiled with satisfaction. She'd seen to it that all public spaces were the first to be retrofitted with electricity.

"Don't you love electric lights?" she asked. "They can be dimmed and extinguished with a mere toggle. Genius."

"You are a true neophile."

Ivy arched an eyebrow. "They are safer than any gas lamp or candle. And the application here, with all of these people packed into this venue, is perfect. You know my sister Trina—"

"The one who accompanied you to the box?"

"Yes. She has convinced her musically inclined friends to experiment with the lighting to enhance their production. I know this is what theater has done for ages, but the electricity makes it more exciting, don't you think?"

"It's intriguing."

Ivy found her seat next to the empty throne. "It's more than that. The right machine can enhance our lives. It could save our country from the poison we've been served. The war has brought everything to a head, but even if peace were declared tomorrow, our crisis would continue."

"Crisis?"

The orchestra tuned. Patrons below were finding their seats. The red and gold palette became unbalanced with the addition of so many colorful gowns.

"We are running out of space. We are running out of pasture. We are running out of food. Our population is concentrated in our capital, but there isn't space for everyone, let alone for trade. We need innovation. We need it to outwit our enemy, and we need it to pull us out of this mess."

The din of the chatter and tuning instruments made the theater vibrate like crickets' wings.

"Is this what you think about all day?" Collin asked.

"No, Major. I think about how your cheek and jaw are top-notch."

Collin took a seat next to Ivy. "Curious features to fixate on."

"But yours are so pronounced," Ivy teased, running a gloved finger quickly across his jaw.

"Still. Shouldn't my eyes, my smile, even my character matter more?"

"Not when they are still bruised and cut." Except the purple had faded considerably, and the cut was healing nicely. They were hardly noticeable. Ivy turned her attention to smoothing her bodice. It wouldn't do to linger on any of the major's features. "Not when there's a war or a crisis of population density and a lack of basic resources."

"But when the war is over, and we've solved the density and resource problem, what matters then?"

Ivy turned and met Collin's gaze. She felt a curious gear shift inside her. She felt that someone at last had stopped to wonder if her heart was that of an automaton or a woman. And she felt her heart wind tight at the word *we*. "Sweet pea cotyledons."

The theater went silent. A curious groan, the kind that came from every person in the theater rising to their feet simultaneously, reverberated in the silence. King Rupert and Queen Adelaide entered the box, followed by Minister Rosecrans and his daughter and son-in-law. A very smart lieutenant of the royal guard in his dress armor stood at the doors. The glint of the electric lamp off his silver breastplate was particularly distracting. Two additional officers followed. They wore the guard helmets with the elaborate red ostrich plumage.

King Rupert, wearing his ever-fashionable scowl, did not even nod to the crowd. He crossed in front of the box and slouched into his chair. Beautiful Adelaide nodded to the assembly and her attendants. She caught the eye of the handsome lieutenant and smiled before she took her seat next to her husband, her senior by more than thirty years.

Adelaide was the exact opposite of Papa. Papa was hunched forward, scowling. His curly wig again slid too far forward on his wrinkled brow. Adelaide was perfectly erect, rigid, a placid smile frozen on her smooth, pretty face. Her hair was swept back in a formal coiffeur and adorned with a gold tiara. Mama's tiara.

Ivy's heart twisted. The guards stood at attention. That was the cue. The audience once more erupted in a groan as everyone found their seats.

"Good evening, Papa. Are you excited for your opera?" Ivy asked.

The king did not bother with a greeting. "Someone I'm supposed to meet?" Papa tapped his thumbs together, a tic that surfaced only when he was nervous. Perhaps Ivy had been wrong to pursue this meeting on opening night.

"Ivy?" the king barked as the concertmaster began tuning the musicians.

The smile fixed to Ivy's face soured. "Papa, may I present to you Major Collin. The major is going to help us win the war. With your approval."

The king looked past Ivy to Collin. His eyes narrowed until they were small and black, like burnt peanuts. "Who are your parents?"

Collin's shoulders tensed. His neck and spine formed a line as rigid as his tone. "My mother was a snake charmer."

The king's beetle eyebrows bristled. "And your father?"

Collin's lip curled, but the bitterness in his eyes kept it from becoming a smile. "He was a snake."

The king grunted. Collin clenched his jaw. A promising start all around.

Berlios came out and bowed to the audience. The overture started. Trina was right. The music was beautiful, and tonight might have been fun if Ivy had not been sandwiched between two fuming brutes.

The overture ended. The curtain rose, and the opera singers stood onstage. Their dresses were beautiful, opulent. Each was fitted with an impressive wire horse sculpture. The electric lights reflected off the bent and twisted steel. The audience gasped, astounded by the visual splendor. King Rupert grunted again, this time approvingly.

The star tenor moved to center stage. His horse sculpture was a bucking stallion, front legs pawing the air. The orchestra paused. The tenor sang with an eyebrow arched high in supplication to whatever higher power would listen. "I'm a big, fat horse. I'm a big, fat horse."

The chorus of wire-horse-clad singers responded, "He's a big, fat horse. He's a big, fat horse."

The tenor, using all of his technique and many years of experience, tried in vain to elevate the words as he sang. "I'm the biggest, fattest horse of them all."

The chorus continued with unbridled enthusiasm. "He's the biggest, fattest horse of them all."

Ivy swallowed. The ornate costumes. The individual (and no doubt expensive) wire sculptures. The inventive score. All tried, but failed, to distract the audience from the laughable lyrics.

The patrons sat in stunned silence. The soprano had a beautiful aria about being the prettiest, but loneliest, horse. Still, the lyrics were so grotesque in their inanity that it was painful in the extreme to witness it. Who had encouraged Papa to do this? It could not have been Rosecrans alone. Ivy turned to her father. Tears streaked his jowls. Her jaw dropped.

In his usurper horse solo, the baritone insinuated that the tenor horse wasn't nearly big and fat enough for the prettiest horse. That was when Ivy began to twitch—and when she noticed Collin's mischievous eyes were focused on her.

The baritone sang out, "I'm a bigger, fatter horse than you!"

The chorus followed with, "He's a bigger, fatter horse than you."

And then the reprise.

It was madness. There was nothing to be done. There were no musical devices, no clever costuming, nothing to detract from the fact that this was inane, stupid, and made a complete fool of her father. Ivy felt her cheeks flush.

"Are you all right?" Collin whispered.

Of course she was not all right. They were two songs and one aria into the opera, and she already saw patrons squirming with repressed laughter. The work that Ivy would have to do to massage her father's bruised ego would be insurmountable. The gymnastics she'd be expected to execute to explain why substantial resources had been allocated to an opera that ran for only one night, while men at the front were cold and underfed, would be impossible. This was a disaster. And it was only getting worse. Two of the wire horse sculptures onstage had tangled with each other. The performers were locked together. Ivy heard Pen snicker in the family box above before being hushed by Trina.

Ivy smiled broadly, tightly. "Isn't it impressive?" she whispered to Collin.

"That's one word for it."

The curtain fell. The electric lights glowed bright. Applause thundered in the theater. The king rose, arms outstretched. Papa did love a crowd. He waved to his public, and when he grew tired of the din, he finally fell back into his ornate chair.

"What did you think?" he asked Ivy.

Ivy swallowed. "It's astonishing."

"And you, Lieutenant?"

"Major," Ivy corrected, not that Papa heard her.

"I wish my Gran could have seen it."

Surprising, since Major Collin didn't seem to be the sycophantic type.

The king smiled and was preparing to push on, but Collin continued. "She would have laughed herself silly."

Oh no. Ivy winced.

The king puffed out his chest. "It takes a certain amount of intelligence to appreciate fine art. I shouldn't have expected the son of gypsies to understand."

"And I didn't expect an entire city to go to such lengths to protect the fragile ego of their monarch. Not to mention the resources. If such efforts were spent on the war, it would have ended ages ago."

The king rose, face purple with anger. "I don't want to ever see him again."

"Yes, Papa."

The king left hastily, followed by Adelaide, the attendants, and the guards. Ivy and Collin remained.

The applause ended. The din in the theater grew to a deafening roar. Ivy was too angry to speak, and although she was fuming with frustration, she was also relieved. Collin was honest. He didn't nettle the truth for the sake of convenience.

"Forgive me." Collin bowed over Ivy's hand. "I must take my leave, ma'am."

"I thought you had a stronger stomach, Major."

"I've no stomach at all for seeing you in pain, Ivy."

Wasn't that forward? "And so you'd run away while I must endure?" And mop up this mess. Something could be salvaged from the situation. Necessity demanded it.

"Come with me," the major said simply.

Ivy would force him to play his bluff. He deserved it for being so blunt. "Where would we go?"

"Back to Olivia's for the night. Across the mountains to the Easterlies in the morning."

"You'd turn me into a deserter as well?"

"I'd have you back when opera season ended."

Ivy felt for her watch but remembered she'd no pocket on her bodice. "Just in time to win the war."

"Exactly so. Although, if we put our heads together, I'm sure we'd be able to do something about it sooner."

"Put our heads together?"

Collin took a step forward. "It's a place to start."

He was top-notch. Ivy would have to be careful.

The theater had deflated somewhat after intermission, evidenced by clusters of vacant seats and quieter jabber.

Adelaide still looked serene and young and beautiful, but the strain of the evening was starting to show on Papa. He was perspiring and looked small and hunched in his chair.

The entr'acte commenced, and when the orchestra had finished, the tenor once again stood in center stage. The chorus of wire sculpture horses were outfitted in mock uniforms and carried rifles. Ivy wished she had joined her sisters in the family box above. What with Collin gone, she was...lonely. She would have happily asked any of them why the horses were now in uniform. She must remember to collect their theories back at home.

The tenor began a reprise of the same big, fat horse nonsense. "I'm a big, fat horse. I'm a big, fat—"

Crack, crack, crack.

Three small explosions came in rapid succession, then Papa was on the floor, gripping his wig in one hand and his chest with the other.

Time and space seemed to fold in on itself. Adelaide sobbing.

Everyone shouting. Guards shoving into the box. "Get back! Move back!" boomed the guards.

The electric houselights glowed to full strength. Opera patrons were fleeing toward the exits, screaming. Others were huddled on the floor, crying. The performers ran off the stage. Some dived into the pit. The upright bass was completely destroyed by one of the charging horses.

Confusion. Hysteria. Panic. Ivy pushed all of them down. "Papa, are you hurt? Papa, can you hear me?"

The king's face was pearl-like, white and shiny with sweat. "Ivy?"

"Are you hurt, Papa?"

Adelaide, clutching her husband to her chest and sobbing, demanded, "Who's done this?"

CHAPTER NINE

The midmorning sun streamed into the breakfast room. Ivy stirred her cocoa and placed the spoon carefully on the saucer. Even so, the gentle clattering made her wince. "I'll need your report as soon as possible."

Hector hesitated. "Wouldn't it be more prudent for His Majesty to review—"

Ivy set her jaw and pushed up from the table. "His Majesty has adjourned to the Summer Palace. He didn't fancy staying in the capital and getting shot at again. Please send your reports to me. A royal currier will ferry them to the king after I've reviewed them."

Hector bowed and left.

Frankfurt quietly spoke at Ivy's side. "Major Collin, Your Highness."

"Please show him in. Oh, and, Frankfurt, the chimney repairs—they've been approved. Additional funds allocated. I sent word yesterday but wasn't sure—"

"Already underway, ma'am. We're all of us grateful."

"As am I." At least something was moving in the right direction.

Collin entered, dressed in the traditional sage-green coat and trousers of the army uniform. His medals hung handsomely from his shoulders. His helmet with the ostrich plume was tucked carefully under his arm.

Collin looked as if he was ready to fold Ivy into his strong arms. "Ivy!"

"Good morning, Major." She should have scolded him for the informal address, but she liked it too much to say anything.

Collin stooped over Ivy's outstretched hand. "Tell me you haven't lost sleep over this."

"I witnessed an assassination attempt on my father. I've not suddenly taken to spooks and fits of things that go bump in the night." Ivy had slept for exactly two forty-minute spurts last night. Her waking hours had been spent consoling her younger sisters and then consoling members of the court, who'd been far more hysterical.

"But how are you?"

The major asked questions that no one else ever posed to Ivy. More impressive, he listened to the answers. "I am faced with an even taller mountain of work to conquer. Not only do I need to expedite a successful conclusion to our little war, but now I must walk a delicate line of inquiry about last night." Ivy rubbed her brow. "It'd be lovely to fall apart or, as my father has decided, leave for the Summer Palace, but someone must see that things get done."

"And things like a decent night's sleep, a proper meal, and revelry—"

"We've had quite enough revelry, haven't we, Major?" Ivy remembered the major's star in her pocket. She sauntered over to him and adjusted a medal at her eye level before pinning his promotion to his collar. It was a poor excuse for familiarity and an even poorer flirtation, but the major had to be kept close. "Papa approved your orders before he left."

"And they are?"

"You are to assemble a task force of experts to assist you in building a doomsday machine, a final solution to end this ghastly war with minimum loss to human, particularly civilian, life. You will report to me and only me from here on out. I will oversee your progress, your financials, and your strategy. Due to the sensitivity of your mission and the inquiry that must take place here at home, you will relocate your operation to the lake holdings in the mountains."

Collin placed a hand across his abdomen, and for a fleeting moment, Ivy thought he might be sick. He fingered the brim of his helmet. "Close to the north border, then?"

"A safe distance, of course, but yes. We have a manor house well suited to our task."

"Will you join me?"

Ivy was too tired to play this game well. And the major had those premature flecks of gray in his hair that made him appear so...upright. "As often as duty permits."

"You place so much trust in me."

"I've run out of options." Ivy passed her thin hand across her brow. Why did fatigue have to result in pounding headaches? The other symptoms were tolerable, but the pounding was tedious.

"Are you feeling all right, Princess?"

"The library." Mornings were always deliciously dim in the library. The bright sunshine in the breakfast room glinted off the gold filigree of the china and stabbed Ivy's brain through her eyes. "I've collected leads for you in the library. This way, Major."

Ivy's tweed skirts rustled as she swept out of the room.

"And what leads have you from last night's gun show?"

"Not enough."

"Have you questioned your sisters?"

Ivy stopped in the hall. "Sir, your insinuation is both dangerous and absurd."

"Of any creature I know, sisters are the sharpest observers."

Ivy rubbed her eyes. "Also the second-most-prone to hysterics." Courtiers being the first.

"You must have had your hands full consoling all of them."

"I'd thank you to keep your distance from whatever my hands are full of, but the threat to stay away from my sisters might not be understood."

"Ivy, you must trust me. Collaboration is nine-tenths of all success."

Ivy pushed open the doors to the library. "Is that so?" She crossed the lavish Easterlie rug to the black-marble-topped desk.

Major Collin followed. "I've no idea, but I hope so."

The darkness helped with the pounding tremendously. A nap on the sofa would help even more. "What about the last tenth?"

"Desire and dogged determination."

Amusement coiled warmly inside her. Collin knew how to play. "The girls have been here. And they have moved my files."

"Ah, yes. I will help you look, but I confess I suspect this an elaborate ruse to spend a morning alone with me in a dark library."

"You should be so lucky. Look for a stack of papers in my writing."

"And your longhand looks...elegant and sophisticated with looping—"

"That's Jade's poetry."

"And whose are these?" The major held up exacting sketches of the basilica's rotunda.

"That's Pen's."

"Pen?"

"My sister Princessa Penelope Augusta."

"Pen's. Of course. And these sketches?" The major held up a pen-and-ink that Pen had designed to replace a rose window in the college's library.

"All Pen's. She is our illustrator."

"And what is this one?" Collin asked.

Ivy leaned over the desk, deliberately brushing against the major's shoulder.

"That is some sort of gadget for Trina's organ. She is tired of the pigeons making nests in the pipes."

"I think this is my favorite." The major held up a sketch Pen had sworn not to make. It was a study in line work, one of those fluid ones where Pen refused to pick up the pencil, of Ivy writing at the desk in her nightie, her hair down and her glasses on. "Do you always bite your nails when you write?"

"I wasn't biting my nails."

"What were you doing?"

"I run my fingers across my lips when I'm thinking. Like this." Ivy demonstrated.

"No, you don't. You're a reformed nail-biter who has learned the art of subtlety."

Ivy tidied a stack of papers. "Everyone has a tic."

"We don't get to choose our tics to complement our best feature, Princess."

"As attractive and enticing as my lips may be, they are not my best feature."

The major swallowed. "Forgive me—"

"My best feature is my pragmatism, followed closely by my resolve. Agree with me, Major."

"My sincere apologies for not speaking to those qualities first."

"An apology is not the same as agreement."

"I will not agree to a statement I do not know is true."

Oh, he didn't! "Then you are a pig who maintains that a woman's finest attribute is only skin-deep—"

"No. I spoke to features in a flirtatious conversation. A certain extent of insincerity is warranted in a flirtation, no? You twisted the conversation to attributes. And while there is much to admire about you, Ivy, I cannot yet speak to what are your finest attributes, and therefore, I will not agree that they are your pragmatism and resolve."

"You refuse to be backed into a corner."

"I refuse to distill a woman who takes care of her family first and self second as being merely pragmatic and resolute, particularly when she is clever and quick and has the most beautiful lips I've ever seen."

And wasn't his sincerity sweet? Perhaps the game was too much for him. But Ivy could not run the risk of the major falling apart and needing to be smacked and sent off to a remote corner of the kingdom. "Pretty words. They do not end wars."

"Who did these sums?" The major riffled through a stack of papers.

"I did."

"You were evaluating the war effort with calculus?"

"Someone has to make sense of the numbers."

"I see. Someone verified your work, of course."

"Sophia obliged me. She has quite the head for numbers, when she can be persuaded to take her eyes off the young men."

"Sophia is a mathematician?"

"My protégé. Trina is our musician. Jade, our poet—well, when she isn't lost in a game of chess. Pen, our artist." Ivy paused. Better not to overwhelm the major with a recitation of every sister's talents.

"I think I found what you're looking for." The major had wandered to the statue of Adonis. At his feet was a modest stack of papers. Ivy suppressed her groan. Her sisters were forever hiding Ivy's regalia near the tacky copy of the naked hero.

"Keep it. They are all for you. Leads on who might prove helpful in your assignment. It's not much, but it is a place to start."

Major Collin flipped through the dossier of class rankings from the college's School of Chemistry, honors students from the School of Mathematics, promising officers who distinguished themselves at the front without getting their boots dirty.

"Where do you think you'll start?" she asked.

The major snapped the dossier shut. "With your sisters."

CHAPTER TEN

Ivy was a fury come down from heaven, and Collin was sure lightning bolts would flash from her eyes at any moment. "Was I not clear when I warned you to stay away from my sisters?"

He was right. There were sparks.

Collin tossed down the stack of leads. He didn't need to waste any time perusing them to know there was precious little ability or promise among the usual suspects. Ivy would have found them and recruited them herself if there were. She needed to consider a different talent pool.

"Pen has the mind of a mechanical engineer, and her draftsmanship is extraordinary. Sophia is a fine mathematician under the right circumstances. Trina is a natural problem solver, and I suspect your other sisters are equally talented."

"Absolutely out of the question."

"Have you changed your mind about coming with me?" Collin lowered his voice. "I might be able to get by with just your very attractive calculus."

At that moment, a young woman with a crop of blond hair slid down the banister of the library's spiral stairs. "Well, don't do that when the rest of her is so lovely. Am I right, Ives?" She smacked Ivy on the backside with her portfolio.

Ivy went pale. "Pen, what are you doing?"

"I forgot my favorite namesake. Shame to just smudge about with charcoals when it's such a remarkable day outside." Pen swung the curtains open. Ivy winced in the bright sunshine. "The door was open."

Ivy rubbed her temples. "It most certainly was not."

Pen drummed her fingers on her portfolio. "You must be Major Top-Notch." Pen splayed a hand across her heart and batted her eyes unnaturally. "I've heard so much about you."

Collin shifted closer to Ivy, raking his fingers through his hair, and did his best not to laugh.

Ivy rolled her eyes. "Pen, this is Major Collin."

Pen wiggled her eyebrows and thrust her hand forward. "Pleased to meet you."

"Major, this is my sister Princessa Penelope Augusta."

"Half sister, really. I'm one of the bastards."

Ivy clenched her fingers tight. "Pen!"

"But Pops is a nice guy. So here I am. Raised with the rest of them. Call me Pen. Everyone does."

The major bowed over Pen's hand but was surprised when she grasped his fingers and shook firmly. "Delighted to meet you, Pen. May I see your portfolio?"

"No," Ivy said.

"Yes," Pen said, handing it over and wiggling her eyebrows at her sister.

Collin leafed through more sketches of sisters, and as tempting as it was to muse over the depictions of Ivy, he was looking for something very specific. "This one." He stopped on an image of gears. "Tell me about this one."

"Ah. Ivy asked me to add an alarm to our mantel clock. But I thought, why not just build a new clock from the ground up? Of course, I wanted to design my own gears, which required a study of the existing model."

"You tinker?" Collin asked.

"No." Ivy spoke before her sister could. "No."

Pen crossed her arms. "Now, hang on. Who built your lie detector?"

Ivy grabbed the portfolio from Collin and handed it back to her sister. "I told you, it is a polygraph. I am the lie detector."

"You built that clever machine?" Collin asked Pen.

"Trina lent a hand. Organs are apparently more machine than feeling instrument. Which is, interestingly, what many of us have heard said of Ives." Pen patted her sister on the back.

"Hysterical," Ivy deadpanned.

Collin cleared his throat. "Wonderful, would you bring your sister Trina here? I'd like to ask her some questions."

Pen's smirk turned into a wide grin. "Sure."

Ivy held up her hand in protest, but it was too late.

Pen whistled. "Coast is clear!"

Some of Ivy's sisters pushed open the double doors. More appeared on the spiral staircase.

Ivy's shoulders sagged. "You were listening at the door?"

"And upstairs," a short, sober-looking sister with green eyes said.

"Oh, don't look cross, Ives," another sister said with a giggle.

A sister in blue tickled Ivy's chin with the feather from Collin's helmet. "We had to."

"Mr. Top-Notch is here."

"*Major*," Pen clarified. "Major Top-Notch."

"Although why he stayed is beyond me. You are an abysmal flirt, Ivy." That had to be Sophia. She had ink stains on her thumb.

"Thanks for that," Ivy said, rubbing her brow.

"It's true, though," Pen said.

"The poor major should get an extra-special medal for putting up with you," a sister in red said.

"I tried to shoo them away, Ivy." Trina looked dismayed. "I promise I did."

"You should have tried harder," Ivy said.

One of the princesses had taken Collin's helmet and added it to Adonis' head. Ivy looked like she was about to faint. She looked more distressed than Collin was comfortable witnessing. Other men would look away, but then they'd miss all the exquisite information. Collin put his hands in his pockets and leaned against a bookshelf.

"*You* should have tried harder, Ivy," one of the triplets, if he had to guess, whispered. "Major Top-Notch is a fox."

Collin cleared his throat. Loudly.

Ivy's lips twitched, and for a moment, Collin's heart beat faster as he wondered if she agreed.

Ivy breathed in, and before she exhaled, her shoulders were squared and her chin raised. She sauntered closer to the major. "And he is practiced enough not to turn pink with embarrassment." Ivy entwined her arm around the crook of Collin's elbow. "Major Collin, let me introduce my sisters. You've met Pen. And Trina you almost met last night."

Collin placed his free arm across his chest and bowed his head, enjoying the weight of Ivy's arm on his. "Your Royal Highnesses."

Ivy introduced Jade, the sober one with green eyes; Sophia, who did indeed have ink on her thumb; the triplets, Gwen, Angelica, and Daphne; Beatrice in red; and Harriet.

"But where are Rachel and Mina?" Ivy asked.

"Rachel is with Mistress Floof," Harriet said, yawning.

"Our cat is about to have kittens, Major Collin," Angelica supplied.

"And Mina?" Ivy asked.

Angelica shrugged.

"She must have gone to help her," Trina said.

Ivy's brow furrowed. Her hand briefly tightened around Collin's arm. "Major, it is time for you to leave. Girls, please say goodbye."

Collin was enveloped by sisters.

"I'll show him out," Sophia offered.

"Nice try, Sophia, but I need you to review the sums I worked out over breakfast."

Sophia stomped her foot and huffed. "You know I hate it when you get crumbs and cocoa stains all over the parchment!"

"And you know I'd sooner handcuff myself to Major Collin than leave you alone with him." Ivy grabbed Adonis by the waist and hopped up onto his pedestal to fetch the plumed helmet. Collin offered her his hand as she scampered down. "Your hat, Major." Ivy again placed her hand on his arm. "Shall we?"

There was no snow yet in the dormant gardens, just mud and dried leaves. "Your sisters are lucky to have you," Collin said.

"We are lucky to have each other, Major." Ivy smoothed away the crease her arm had left in Collin's sleeve.

"Come with me." It was the second time he'd said the words. The first time had been to give voice to an absurd fantasy that needed to be mocked lest it turn into something more dangerous—a dream. Now, it was the obvious next step. "I'm serious."

"Why?" And the reasons radiated off of her like swirling points of light. Some of them were ridiculous trivialities, others concrete and specific, like how his stomach bottomed out when she smiled at him, how his heart beat faster when she touched him.

Ivy's cheeks were pale and hollow. She folded her arms and shivered in the sunlight. "Don't tell me that you, too, are worried the capital isn't safe anymore."

"I need you." Never mind that keeping her close was the surest guarantee he'd survive the war outside of prison. It was ironic that finally landing in one had at last cleared a path forward. "We all do. Yes, I can round up some men to help build your machine and do your dirty work. But I can't lead the way you can." Collin removed his military jacket and slid it around her shoulders. "You're a leader, Ivy. You find the right gears, put them in place, and solve the problem without any thought of personal gain. That's a rare talent."

"It would be safer," Ivy said, pulling Collin's jacket close against the threatening snow. "The army of correspondence we will need to send—especially in the beginning. The lake holdings are remote and far away from the heart of the conflict." Ivy ran a finger across her lips. "Still, we wouldn't want to run the risk of exposing our last hand."

Collin stepped closer. "No, we wouldn't. Surely you must know how to quietly disappear for a few weeks."

"Careful now, Major. You don't know what I know."

Collin was too cautious to assume her words were flirtation alone. War did not eliminate a man's past, it just kept people from looking for a bit. Hopefully long enough for Collin to prove himself. Still, if the princess was having some fun, then he could too.

Collin leaned in, his arm braced against the vine-covered wall beside Ivy, his voice rumbling and low. "I mean to find out."

Ivy traced Collin's features with a single finger. His skin prickled in the cold winter air, certainly not from her warm touch. "You make a sound argument, one that has nothing to do with your handsome eyes or how trim your shoulders look in uniform."

There was the glint of mischief in her smile and now an irksome flutter in Collin's stomach when she touched him. Ivy brushed the snow off the major's shoulders. A flurry had started as they stood in the garden. "There may be some late-season skating at our lake operation. My sisters are fond of skating."

"Better hurry up there. No telling how long the ice will last."

"Exactly so."

"And do you skate, Princess?"

Ivy examined her watch. "When time permits."

"I see. You're afraid of having fun."

"I'm too busy for fun." Ivy shrugged out of Collin's jacket and handed it back to him. "Now, off you go."

"Ma'am." Collin saluted and left, noting with a smile that his jacket now smelled faintly of chocolate.

CHAPTER ELEVEN

Ivy shivered once more in the snow. "He's gone. You can come out now."

Trina pushed aside the vines, most of which were still covered in brown leaves, and joined Ivy, wrapping her into the shawl she wore. "What did he want?"

Trina took Ivy in arm and strolled her through the vines toward the kitchen garden, where she'd been hiding.

Ivy fiddled with the case of her pocket watch. Open and shut. Open and shut. "Ice skating."

Trina placed a quieting hand on top of Ivy's watch. "Ice skating?"

"The major accused me of being afraid of fun."

"Did he?" Trina considered. "And that of course is..."

"Not true."

"Of course. Yes. Not true." Trina pulled Ivy down next to her on a garden bench. "What did Major Collin really want?"

"He wants me to go with him. In fact, he wants us all to go with him. He is quite impressed with Sophia's numbers, Pen's drafting, your ingenuity."

"I like him more every minute." Trina blew into her hands. "Will you go?"

Ivy pinched the bridge of her nose.

"Ivy darling?"

"What am I to do, Trina? I know better than anyone that my sisters are the most talented mathematicians, strategists, and engineers in the capital. I can't not provide the major with the best resources, but I can't willfully put my sisters in danger—"

"Does it follow that we would be in any less danger here?"

Ivy huffed and kicked at a pile of brown leaves that had found shelter near the bench.

"Sorry, please continue," said Trina.

"I can't turn my back on the capital and uproot us all or jeopardize the mission with a silly brouhaha in the papers."

"Silly brouhaha?"

"'Princesses run off with handsome officer and new recruits.'"

Trina brushed the snowflakes out of Ivy's curls. "But it does rile that the major said you are afraid of fun?"

"Everything about the major riles." In a rather splendid way. "He's an excellent flirt."

"Is that why you were tripping over yourself so abominably?"

"I'm out of practice." Ivy flipped her watch closed. Out of time too. The inquiry demanded immediate attention, of course, and she had a looming meeting with the housekeeper about the sugar crisis. At least it was not a cocoa crisis, although she knew that was coming. She shivered and hoped the kitchen would now be warmer with the chimney repairs underway.

Trina pulled the shawl tighter around them. "You know what I'm going to say."

"Practice makes perfect?"

Trina bumped her shoulder against Ivy's. "You are perfectly capable of making this decision by yourself. You know your mind better than anyone. You see the whole machine and all its moving parts better than I ever will. You can make this decision."

"I have. It's just... I'm not sure you will like it."

"You want me to stay behind with Harriet, Rachel, and Mina?"

"And Bea and the triplets. We can't all go. It would look suspicious."

"Like we've abandoned them," Trina said softly.

Ivy pulled her sister up to a stand beside her. "I can't keep track of the triplets, not when it comes to young men. Bea is always cross with me. I'll have my hands full enough as it is with Pen, Sophia, and—"

"And the major."

Ivy smiled. That part would be fun. "I was going to say Jade."

Their slippers made muffled sounds on the snow-dusted walk.

"You certainly could use the practice." Trina stamped the snow off her slippers. "I'll do it, if you tell me exactly what Major Collin said before we rushed the library. Without Mina's ears, we couldn't make out the fun parts."

Ivy winced and pressed her cold, bare fingers to her brow. Poor Mina. She'd finally cried herself to sleep this morning in Ivy's arms. Where was Mina? Ivy quickened her pace. Little Mina had not taken the news of Papa's departure well. Poor dear was probably huddled up, fretting about him, alone and terrified. Ivy had tried to persuade Papa to take her with him.

"She'll feel safer here with her sisters," Papa said.

"She's only twelve. She needs you." Never mind that they all did.

"The Summer Palace is no place for young people."

"Papa, she's scared. She wants to come with you."

Papa smoothed his puckering waistcoat and preened in the mirror. *"Nonsense."*

Ivy tried to explain about the fear and the trauma.

"So fix it," Papa snapped. *"They can't come along. All their worried faces would put Adelaide out of sorts. And you know we can't have that."*

Not with Papa desperately trying to conceive an heir with Adelaide.

"Find another solution," he barked.

Now, in the bare garden, Ivy's shoulders carried the burdens of the kingdom's problems and solutions as well.

Trina tsked. "Major Collin must be just as poor a flirt as you to merit that kind of frown."

Bless Trina. She always knew when to pull Ivy back to the present. "He was charmingly insincere and remarkably handsome." Tall and dark, with a distinguished nose and intelligent eyes that not only told stories, but begged to be trusted with hers. "He thinks my calculus attractive."

Trina winced. "Weeks in the mountains and time to practice will do you both good. How did the other meeting go this morning?"

The light snow danced through the neat rows of peas and cabbages. What the gardeners did to keep the greens from freezing every night was beyond her. She'd like to know. Of course, that would require time. And there was never enough of it.

"Which meeting?" Ivy asked, turning back to the kitchen. "The Committee of Public Safety wanted reassurances that the court would not allow the assassination attempt to go unpunished. They demanded a public inquiry."

"What did Papa say to that?"

"Papa had already left. But he promises to do the utmost to ensure the safety of the monarchy and its future, et cetera." Ivy yawned.

"You need a nap, darling."

"It will have to wait." She bussed Trina's cheek in parting. "I should find Mina."

Ivy swept through the kitchen and stormed past the butler's pantry but retraced her steps when she heard soft voices.

"Kitty did marvelously well. Didn't she, Frankfurt?"

Ivy toed open the door and found both Mina and Frankfurt on their knees, admiring the gray cat and her new litter of kittens.

"She did indeed."

"And she deserves only the finest of cream for her efforts. And maybe a nice, fresh trout."

"It's a fine job," the butler said.

Ivy felt less tired as she watched her youngest sister fussing over the mama cat and kittens. Mina belonged more to the nursery than anyplace else. But something about growing four inches since the winter solstice had her looking the part of the young lady. Even if she wasn't ready for it.

Frankfurt stood to attention, but Mina continued to stroke Kitty's rumpled gray fur.

"Thank you, Frankfurt," Ivy said. "Would you tell Mrs. Stoddard I'll just be a minute?"

The butler nodded and left.

Kitty purred loudly. Mina continued to stroke her head.

"Mina darling, have you been hiding in here alone all morning?"

"Of course not. Frankfurt was here. And Rachel was around but left exactly when we could have used an extra pair of hands."

Mina did not look at Ivy. She bit her quivering lip and stroked Kitty's head with an intensity that would have had the poor mama cat running for safer cover if she were in any sort of condition to run.

"Mina." Ivy caught her sister's hand and pressed it between her own. "I know you were upset when Papa left, but there is no need to worry. Papa is perfectly safe at the villa. And I will make sure we are perfectly safe here."

"That's not why I was upset." Tears threatened to spill out of Mina's eyes.

Ivy bent down and scooped up a blind and deaf kitten that had wandered too far from its mama. "Tell me what's wrong." She placed the warm lump next to the others in the basket.

Mina blinked her eyes rapidly, but even so, a tear slid down her nose. "It's about the opera."

Damn the opera. Ivy handed Mina her handkerchief. "Sweetheart, it all sounds much worse than it really was. It was all just a lot of shouting in the end."

"I know. I was there." Mina buried her face in her hands. "I was backstage."

Ivy's heart froze. "You were backstage. After we both agreed that you staying in was for the best."

"I am not too young for Papa's opera." Mina huffed and stamped her foot. "And you are not my mother!"

This was true. Mina's mother was not on friendly terms with the palace. Not since Adelaide. Ivy swallowed and retrieved her watch, flipping it open. She could spare a few minutes on the rug with her sister. Ivy slid to her knees and nudged the silver water tureen closer to the mama cat. "Darling, you are only twelve. Why did you not listen to me?"

Fresh tears streaked Mina's cheeks. "Ivy, I saw him."

Ivy caught a distorted reflection of her own pale, frightened face in the silver tureen.

"I saw Papa's assassin." Mina shook with fresh sobs.

Ivy's mind stumbled over shock before it raced with questions. "Why didn't you say something earlier?"

"I tried!" Mina wailed, and now Ivy understood why she had been so desperate to be with Papa this morning and why she'd been so inconsolable last night, understood the words Mina had no doubt tried to say through all the sobbing.

"You did. You certainly did. Will you forgive me for not listening sooner?" Ivy squeezed Mina's shaking hands in her own and willed herself to stay calm. "I'm listening now. Whenever you are ready, tell me what you saw." Ivy knew that Mina had important information, but she also knew that the trauma and fear of last night would make sharing them a challenge. She'd have to be patient.

Mina closed her eyes and hugged her knees to her chest. Ivy rubbed small circles across her back. "I wore your black silk dress. I traded my lilac gown for it..." Mina trailed off.

"Traded with whom?" Ivy asked, hoping an easy question might help build momentum for this difficult conversation.

"Sophia."

Always Sophia. "Go on. I'm listening." Ivy smoothed the hair out of Mina's eyes.

"I rode in the second carriage. You were so late and in such a rush, I didn't even have to hide under Rachel's cloak."

Another reason to hate the stupid crystal punch bowls. "But you hid at the opera?"

"Trina would have tattled on me. Besides, Berlios is always inviting Trina to sit backstage. But really, he's trying to get her into the orchestra pit. He says no one has an ear like Trina. He wants her to conduct. Protégé, he's always calling her. What is a protégé?"

"It's a pupil, one with extraordinary talent."

Mina sat on her knees again and ran a finger across the nursing kittens. "I sat backstage. The chairs were just behind the curtains. No one even knew I was there, which was a good thing, because I could not keep my face straight with all that big, fat horse nonsense. I forgot my binoculars, not that they would have done any good—the lights were so bright, I couldn't see anyone in the audience."

"Did you stay behind the curtain through intermission?"

"No. I tried on one of the horse sculptures. They are so heavy. I almost fell over. But no one saw me. I got back to my chair just as the lights flickered, and I watched all the singers and stagehands look scared during the entr'acte. Then the curtains opened, and the horses were in uniform and had those muskets." Mina shut her eyes and grimaced, her lips trembling. "And then there was gunfire, really loud, right by me. I jumped far back into the corner of the stage, and I hid against the pull ropes."

"Poor Mina." Ivy knelt next to her sister and stroked her brown hair. Mina threw her arms around Ivy, hugging her fiercely.

Ivy was desperate to press Mina for details, but her sister shook in her arms.

"There was so much screaming and shouting. And then I saw him."

Ivy did not speak. She had to listen and not influence. Mina was supplying few details, and any that Ivy could prod from her would not be as reliable as what she offered freely.

"He was holding the rifle, and it was still smoking." Mina swallowed and shook her head. "And he opened up the barrel and looked inside before tossing the gun onto the pile of props and leaving."

Ivy's heart hammered. "Do you remember anything else?"

"He wasn't in any hurry. And he wore a fancy suit and waistcoat." She bit her lip. "He was very handsome."

"Handsome like Papa?"

Mina grimaced. "Papa is not handsome. The ladies just let him think so."

"Would you recognize this handsome man if you saw him again?"

"Yes, I would. He was standing very close."

"Close enough to see his freckles?"

"He had no freckles."

"Close enough to see the color of his eyes?"

Mina thought a moment. "No. The lighting backstage was funny."

Ivy nodded. "Was he one of the actors?"

"I saw all the actors onstage before intermission. I saw all the stagehands scurrying backstage during the singing. None of them was in a fancy suit."

Ivy cradled her little sister close. "You saw something very important. Thank you for telling me. Will you promise to tell me if you ever see the dashing assassin again?"

"You're making fun."

"Only because I don't want you to worry and because Kitty needs a gentle hand now."

Kitty's eyes bulged with every stroke of Mina's hand. Mina eased up and scratched the cat gently behind the ears. The purring started to rumble loudly once more.

"Do you think we'll catch him?"

Ivy willed a confidence into her voice that she did not feel. "Of course we will."

With the description of a dashing, handsome assassin in a fancy suit, how could they not?

Sutherbee's was an old, dirty brick building with painted gold letters on the front window. It was the sort of place that no one ventured into in broad daylight. The cobbles in front of the establishment were blacker than any other part of town. The coal smoke was thick and fierce in the narrow street, making Collin's eyes itch as he exited the cab. He hopped over the closed gate, ran down a short set of stairs, and shouldered open the door.

Inside, chairs were stacked on tables. The counter was bare but polished clean. And though the stone floor was stained and worn, it was mopped.

A young man sat at an organ. He played a few notes, and the pub reverberated with the sound. A lock of hair purposefully fell across his brow as he scribbled with a pencil, played a few more chords, nodded, and scribbled more. "Yeah, we're closed, mate. Come back at sundown."

"You play the organ here?"

"It's the only paying gig in town that will let me compose."

"I'm looking for an organist."

"Look, I'm really sorry for your loss and all that. But I cannot play any more funerals for the present." The young man adjusted some toggles on the pipes and played chords that rumbled inside Collin's chest.

"It's not a funeral, but for the record, how do you feel about weddings?"

The organist raised an eyebrow and looked at Collin. "I'm flattered, mate, but I'm not interested."

Collin chuckled and ran his hand along the polished wood of the bar. "That's not what I meant."

"Then why don't you play it straight, and tell me what you want?"

"I want your ears in the palace."

The organ notes stopped abruptly. "Excuse me?"

"Princess Trina is an organ enthusiast. I need someone I can trust keeping tabs on her and her sisters." He needed a conduit of steady, reliable information.

"And who told you I was the man for the job?"

Collin set his helmet on top of the organ. "You did. A young man alone in a pub, and you are drinking"—Collin sniffed the glass at the side table—"seltzer water with a splash of cranberry juice. You're obviously in good standing with Sutherbee."

"Or I made a copy of the key when he was drunk."

"Either way, you are resourceful and disciplined. It's what I need."

"Why?"

"Because, despite best efforts, things rarely go like clockwork."

"Whose best efforts?"

Collin squinted. Carefully tied cravat. Short, even fingernails. Fastidiously groomed right down to the obnoxious curl that hung across his forehead. Perfectly clean spectacles. Neat pencil marks. Clean sleeves. And not a scent of liquor about him, despite his surroundings. If he was willing to stake everything on the information this chap supplied, then he might as well go all in. "Princess Ivy's."

The organist toggled a couple of switches above his keyboards. "Look, I'm a patriot. I don't go in for plots against the royal family, even though I've certainly heard my share of them."

"Yes, I'm sure you've heard everything working here. It's why I need you." Musicians had the best ears after all.

The organist studied Collin as he rolled his pencil between his fingers. "You worried there's going to be another assassination attempt?"

"I need more information." Collin shifted his weight. Gran would have scolded him for squirming. Only liars squirmed. "Will you help me?"

The organist scoffed. "Sure, I'll just plant myself as a music teacher for all those young ladies."

"That wasn't exactly what I was thinking." Collin brushed his thumb across the new insignia Ivy had pinned to his collar that morning. "But what an excellent idea."

CHAPTER TWELVE

At least it had stopped snowing. Snow had made Collin's journey to the lake house nearly impossible, and in the six days since his arrival (and since he'd last seen Ivy—not that he was counting), snow had fallen nearly every day. From the east-facing window of his bedroom, he could see the sunshine sparkle off the undisturbed drifts. The day was warming. Too bad the roads would be muddy by the time they met the princesses.

"Remember, you can't speak," Collin said to Tim. "You're a mute. This all ends the moment you open your mouth. Understood?"

Tim clenched his jaw and ground his teeth.

"It's the best I can do, given the circumstances." To say nothing of the risks. "This way, at least, we're both away from the front. Agreed?"

Tim opened his mouth, but Collin raised a finger. "Ah-ah! No talking. If you need to say something, write it down. You do know how to write—"

Tim picked up a pencil and proceeded to write a string of curse words and Collin's name.

"Yes, Gran would have been the first to agree with you about my father. Now then, is there something you can do about my wet boots? They'll be destroyed by the time I return."

The lake country was wet and cold. All the unmelted piles of snow were dirty with mud, but the air was crisp and fresh. The mountains stood at attention, ready to assist the princesses. Mountains tired easily of war. They would have been happy to assist anyone in ending it.

The coach stopped at the crossroads, where the major was to meet them.

"And why couldn't we have taken a carriage and a team from home?" Sophia complained as she shook out her skirts.

"Because we are trying to keep a low profile," Jade explained.

"And a fine job we're doing of that too." Pen spoke as the coachmen tossed their fifth trunk from the coach. "No one would ever suspect us. Clearly, we are up to nothing more than a little snowshoeing and ice skating."

Ivy stepped down from the coach, tugging on a glove. The mountain air made her head spin. Terribly inconvenient.

"Ives!" Pen called, hopping from one trunk to the next. "Was all of this really necessary?"

"That depends entirely on whether or not we find cocoa in the lake house pantry," Ivy said. Truthfully, she did not want to risk being ill-equipped in any way. It had been ages since they'd been to the lake house. Ivy had insisted on packing it all—abacuses, compasses, rulers, reams of paper, and yes, cocoa.

Sophia scowled and plunged her fists into her muff. "Because we all know what Ivy turns into without her precious chocolate."

Jade munched a biscuit. "You know half these trunks are filled with your clothes, Sophia."

Sophia rounded on her sister. "Why did you even come, Jade?

You could have just as easily stayed home and played chess with yourself."

The fight would have escalated had Major Collin—on horseback, no less—not trotted into view, ponying an additional smelly, four-legged beast beside him.

"Ladies." Major Collin alighted from his horse and tied off the pair of beasts to the obliging fence post. "Our steward is just getting some supplies in the village. He should be here any minute with the cart for your...five trunks."

Ivy buttoned her coat and smiled in spite of her headache. Seeing Major Collin again made the long night spent in the coach almost worthwhile. "I should have brought five more, make it an even ten for you."

"And I should have brought more horses. I don't know if all of you and your trunks will fit in the cart."

Ivy looked past the major and saw a man in a pea coat driving a cart and team of horses toward them. "No carriage?" Ivy tried desperately to sound disinterested.

"None with wheels." Collin stroked the neck of the bay mare he'd ridden. "One or two of you will fit in the cart, but someone should ride with me."

"I'll ride with you, Major," Sophia quickly offered.

"No need, Sophia. I'll walk back," Ivy said.

"You will not," Pen said, mounting the other horse. She always made it look so simple. "You can barely stand."

Collin rubbed the bay's long nose. "She's a very gentle, sturdy old girl."

A stout young man with a strawberry beard and a scowl stopped the cart and horses beside the princesses. "Damn waste of time. Might as well buy sawdust and mill it myself." He jumped down and touched his knitted cap and gave a slight nod to Ivy and her sisters before groaning at the sight of the five trunks. "Five? And women to ferry besides."

"I believe you know Matthew." Collin assisted Matthew in lifting the trunks onto the cart.

"No." Ivy started to panic. "How do you do? More importantly, who are you?"

"I'm the steward of Your Highnesses' lake house." His face was red now from the strain of heaving the trunks. Ivy would have liked to have seen Collin's turn a similar shade, but he seemed unfazed by the exertion.

Jade sauntered forward. "If memory serves, you were once upon a time a kitchen boy?"

"That's right. I became the chef's assistant, and then I took his place."

Ivy's toes were freezing, but she'd happily stand in the road all afternoon if it meant she didn't have to mount a horse. "How did you become steward?"

Matthew grunted. "By default. Everyone else left."

"Delightful." Ivy jumped when a cart horse chuffed at its reins.

"My sentiments exactly." Matthew unbuckled the top trunk and riffled through the contents until he found Sophia's fur-lined cloak. He kicked the trunk closed, climbed up to the driver's bench, and spread the cloak over himself like a blanket. "Now, if you don't mind, I'd like to get back home before I freeze."

Jade and a grouchy Sophia climbed up beside him.

"Shall we?" Collin asked. He assisted Ivy as she clambered onto the stupid creature.

"Are you going to tell me why you didn't bring enough horses, Major?" Ivy asked.

"I wanted an excuse to hold you." Collin climbed up behind her and clicked his tongue. The horse lumbered forward.

"And we needed a smelly, half-ton chaperone?"

Collin spoke quietly in her ear. "I needed a chance to tell you privately there's a problem."

Ivy tilted her head back until it rested against the major's shoulder. There was always a problem. But the major's shoulder felt solid, almost reassuring. "You invented a problem just to get me close?"

"Of course, Princess. I flooded the lower level of the foundry so I could wrap my arms around you for this ride back."

His arms did feel comfortable around her waist. "Is that all you did?"

"Then I froze the water solid and shut off all the electric power."

"How novel. What does your engineer make of this?" His missive had stated that he had found both an engineer and a mechanic.

"This, too, is problematic. I could not pry an engineer away from the college. All the army engineers, of course, are otherwise occupied. I improvised."

"So cryptic, Major. Should I be worried?"

The major shifted the reins, freeing a hand to rest more casually around Ivy's waist. "Always."

The horse stumbled for a moment in the mud, and Ivy clutched the major's arm.

"Steady," he said quietly and slowly.

"I hate horses. I'd be happy never to ride another for the rest of my life."

"Easy. Betsy here will take that personally."

Ivy sat up straighter. She examined her watch. At this pace, they were another ten minutes from the lake house.

Ivy felt Collin's arm tense around her waist. "Your father's watch?"

"Something like that." Ivy snapped it shut and placed it in her pocket. "You had best make better use of your time, Major. Tell me the specifics."

"Four inches of ice in the foundry."

"And the turbine?"

"Frozen solid."

The uneven stride of the horse did not make the ground feel steadier, and this news was distressing. The pine trees that lined the road started to spin, but what could Ivy do about it now?

"What else?"

"My engineer, Monty, is not presently motivated."

"Specifics, Major."

"He hasn't been sober for days."

"A flooded foundry, a frozen turbine, and a drunk engineer." Ivy inhaled slowly—it sometimes calmed the spinning sensation. "You're skirting around the real issue, Major."

"We retrieved a prototype of what the enemy has been manufacturing all winter."

"Ah." Now they were getting to the heart of it.

"It's a mechanized rifle."

Ivy shut her eyes tightly and willed her mind to stop spinning. "Machine rifles and a network of rails to transport all the ammunition and spare parts to wherever they wish. Now I wish you had just wanted an excuse to hold me."

The major's voice rumbled low and soft behind her. "As do I."

"You retrieved one of their rifles?"

"It wasn't easy." The major said each word distinctly.

"Who else knows about this?"

"My man in the capital."

"You have a man in the capital?"

"He'd be the first to tell you not to be jealous. It's not like that."

"We need to tell the others. Just as soon as we right the foundry."

"Has your father approved—"

"My father has abdicated all his wartime responsibilities to me." Ivy dug her fingers into her palms. "He is preoccupied with producing an heir." The horse trotted up to the lake house, an old manor on the edge of the frozen lake. Old, but with exactly the type of country elegance that was missing in the capital. Ivy slid down from the horse and marched toward the foundry.

Collin saw quickly to the horse but wasn't far behind.

Ivy pressed her fingers to her right temple. Stairs. That's right. The foundry was nearly at water level, out of necessity for the turbine.

"Ivy?" Collin called.

"You said four inches." Ivy turned. "The ice is up to the second riser. That's at least six."

"Damnation and hellfire," Collin said evenly.

"You've a mechanic."

"The best alive."

"Excellent. Bring him round. I've questions that need answers." Ivy's knees buckled. She grabbed on to the railing and hoped the major didn't notice her knuckles turn white. "But first... I'm feeling peckish."

Ivy found Pen in the kitchen, along with Jade. "Where is Sophia?" she asked.

"She claims to be in need of peace and quiet." Jade leafed through a notebook on the table.

"Probably ran off in search of the major's young men." Pen winked at the major.

"How would you sober up a young man?" Ivy asked her sisters while examining the contents of the larder. If the organized shelves were any indication, Matthew was fastidious.

Pen kicked her feet up onto the table. "I'd let him talk to Jade and then Sophia. One of them is bound to do the trick."

"Hysterical," Jade said without looking up from the book.

"You know it's true." Pen rose and stretched. "Black coffee, fresh air, a swim in that ice-cold lake, if all else fails."

"None of those will lower his blood-alcohol level. Discarding his booze, however, will," Jade said.

"Do it." Ivy pulled out a tin of marzipan.

"Come again?" Pen helped herself to a piece of the almond candy.

"The major's engineer is off his trolley. I need him working within the hour. The entire foundry is covered in ice, and we don't have time to spare."

Pen's eyebrows rose and fell as she no doubt considered the possibilities. "Come, Jade. Let's go make a new friend."

Ivy almost felt sorry for the young man, who appeared in the kitchen a half hour later, swaying on his limbs. What he must have endured from her sisters to be on his feet.

Young. Nose red. Cheeks pink. "Monty, is it?" Ivy did not wait for his reply. "We have a moisture problem in the foundry. Would you agree?"

"Yes, ma'am."

"Are you up to the challenge?"

Monty blew out a foul-smelling breath.

Pen, standing behind him, clapped him on the back. Monty startled. "Of course he is."

"You've met my sister Pen," Ivy said.

Monty squinted. "I met...a sister."

"Don't feel too bad, Monty. There's always too many of us to keep track of," Ivy said dryly.

Pen elbowed him in the ribs, and poor Monty looked as if he might be sick.

"Where's your mechanic?" Ivy asked, turning to Collin, who was leaning against the wall, his arms folded comfortably across his middle.

Collin straightened. "Tim is...ah...I don't know."

Ivy drummed her fingers on the table. "Pen, have you any ideas?"

"We need a pump."

Monty shook his head but grimaced in pain with the motion. "You can't pump ice."

"You could flood it, let the ice melt, and then pump out the water," Pen said. "Not all of the lake is frozen."

"A steam-powered pump would be ideal." Monty ran his fingers through his hair. "So would a drink."

Ivy snapped her watch shut. "Careful, or I'll ask Jade and Sophia to take you for a swim." Although, she could use a cup of chocolate herself. Her hands were still freezing. "We cannot flood the foundry. I need the generator working as quickly as possible." She pressed her fingers across the table. "Could we salt it?"

"Salt?" Pen took a seat, stretching her long legs across the table.

"Would it harm the turbine?" Collin asked.

Monty shrugged and just about fell over from the movement. Pen pushed the tin of marzipan toward him.

"Let's experiment," Ivy said.

CHAPTER THIRTEEN

Collin watched Ivy from the stairs. No need to get his fresh pair of boots wet. The risk that the moisture would seep into his socks was unnecessary. "Matthew is not going to be happy about this." An entire barrel of Easterlie sea salt lay scattered over the foundry floor.

Ivy sprinkled the last of the pink salt into the turbine. "Can you move the blades?"

"I don't know," Monty said. "Would you stop shouting?"

Pen covered Monty's ears with her hands.

"Get it spinning, then come inside. I can't have my draftsman and engineer freezing off their fingers." Ivy stomped the salty slush off her boots. "Where have you been, Major?" She bundled past him on the stairs. She moved with such haste, a breeze trailed her, one scented with orange blossoms, jasmine, and chocolate. "Never mind. I need to meet your mechanic. What's his name?"

"He goes by Tim." Better to leave out the details at this point.

"How did you find Tim? Pen says Monty was expelled from the college for drunk and disorderly conduct. Am I to understand that Tim distinguished himself in a similar fashion?"

"No, ma'am. Tim and I fought together."

"He was enlisted?" She outpaced him.

Collin jogged a step to catch up. There was much more information to be had from her eyes, although her neck was pretty. "Conscripted."

Ivy burst through the kitchen doors.

"What the bloody hell?" Matthew barked. He turned back to Jade. "How am I supposed to cook anything without salt?"

"You have more than one barrel," Jade said.

"Astonishing observation." Matthew pulled a bowl of eggs from the larder. "Different salts have different flavors." He cracked an egg cleanly and bounced the yolks from shell to shell until the egg white fell into a glass bowl. "Different dishes require different flavors." He reached for another egg. "I had one barrel of Easterlie sea salt." He cracked the egg with one hand. "What am I supposed to use in its place? Coastlands sea salt? Highland rock salt?"

"If that's the pink one, I've used it up." Ivy pried the lid off the marzipan tin and retrieved a square.

Matthew groaned and threw the eggshells in the sink. "I leave my kitchen for a half hour and return to find it overrun by *women*."

Jade grabbed a whisk and attacked the bowl of egg whites. "Don't talk to me like I'm some sort of cow who got out of her pasture."

Matthew slammed his hand on the kitchen table. "God's finest gift to man was the cow. Look me in the eye and tell me you could live in a world without butter."

"Stop slamming things. You'll deflate my egg whites."

"*Your* egg whites?" Matthew roared.

Collin flinched and steered Ivy farther down the hall. "Tim's this way."

Ivy took the stairs two at a time. Her black and gray suit was completely at odds with the periwinkle and gold interior of the great hall.

"The lake house was designed by His Majesty?" Collin asked.

"Redecorated. Papa is fond of pastels. And gold." Ivy stomped through a mirror-lined hallway on the second floor. "And his own reflection. This house was my mother's wedding present from her family."

"A nice present."

"Papa was never fond of it. He said it was too dreary. I haven't been here since I was...Mina's age, I suppose. He was determined to redecorate it to his own tastes. But he tired of the project. Many of the rooms are untouched."

Ivy threw open the doors to the east wing.

"There's one thing you should know about Tim." Collin knocked on the door, and when Tim didn't answer, he banged on it.

"Let me guess. He's imaginary?" She crossed her arms and leaned against the wall.

"Tim, open up," Collin said.

Silence.

"Tim!" Collin roared.

The door unlocked but did not open. Nice.

Collin held the door open for Ivy, and he felt a prickle of sweat at his collar. Talent... No, not just talent, but genius manifested itself in peculiar but patterned ways. Regimentation. Obsession. Peculiarities. They were all telling symptoms of an underlying cause—genius. Ivy needed a genius. Tim was a genius. He was also ready to strangle Collin for the mess they were in.

The young man was sprawled on an unmade bed. The blue and gold silk brocade coverlet had been kicked off and lay on the floor in a lifeless pile.

"Tim, I have someone I'd like you to meet."

Tim, with shirt untucked and suspenders loose at his hips, remained motionless on the bed.

Collin felt the heat in his cheeks and pulled at his collar. "Tim, Princess Ivy—"

Tim held up a hand and glared at Collin. He folded his hands behind his head and closed his eyes.

"Are you thinking or napping?" Collin asked.

"Major?" Ivy asked.

"Excuse us, Tim." Collin ushered Ivy out of the room and closed the door but kept his hand on the knob. Always easier to act without a critic. "Tim is mute."

Ivy's mouth opened. Her brow furrowed. "Mute? As in, he can't speak?"

"The war does strange things to a young man." True enough. "We all deal with it in different ways."

"Does he understand?"

"Oh yes." More than she knew.

She smiled. Collin was learning fast to be wary of such smiles. "Open the door, Major."

She went first to the armoire, pulled it open, and started throwing things out. Old and dirty clothes tumbled to the floor.

Tim sat up and stared at Collin with fury and death in his eyes.

She went next to the nightstand. "Have you really nothing of any interest in here?" She pulled out the drawer and rummaged around, mumbled something about being worse than the triplets, and then dumped its contents on the floor.

"What are you doing?" Collin asked.

"I'm looking for a reason not to throw you both out of my lake house." To Tim, she said, "Collin tells me you are the best mechanic he has ever seen. I'm looking for proof. I haven't found any yet."

Tim clutched the white sheet as if afraid Ivy would take it from him. His features looked all scrunched and wound up, like a gear ratcheting down a pulley. Kinetic energy and all that.

"You must have something. A clock. An invention. A portfolio. A toy..." Ivy dropped to her knees and checked under the bed.

Tim raised an eyebrow and then clenched his wiry fingers into fists that he then shook in Collin's direction.

"Ivy." Darling. "Have you gone mad?"

"What do you mean 'gone'? This is her natural state." Pen sailed into the room. "Name's Pen." She thrust her fingers in front of Tim's nose. He gingerly shook them. "Matt said there was a party in the east wing."

Ivy stood up, holding a small sculpture of a rabbit fashioned out of scrapped clock parts. Exposed gears, wires. Brass oscillating weights. Old, rusted hour hands for whiskers. Ivy handed the rabbit to Pen. "What do you make of this?"

Pen smiled. Tim looked like he'd just been shot—surprise, fear, shock, a bit of pain. All mixed up and plastered on his face at once. Poor Tim. He was a goner.

Pen checked the front, turned over the back, swung a whisker down. "I think..." She pulled out the right whisker, placed it in the back of the bunny, and wound some instrument inside.

Tim rose quietly, reverentially.

Pen looked up. And again beamed. "Aren't you tall and lanky?"

Ivy drummed her fingers on the bedside table. "Tim is mute."

"Ah, and here I thought he was just stunned by his good fortune to find not one but two pretty girls in his room. To say nothing about a handsome army officer. Can't leave the major out, can we?" Pen looked at Tim. "There's a second winding point, isn't there?"

Tim nodded. He fitted the key back into the whiskers and gently wound them. He then motioned for Pen to set the clockwork rabbit on the floor.

The mechanical beast hopped across the room while its whiskers twitched.

Pen cracked a smile and tossed her short crop of hair out of her eyes. "Brilliant."

Ivy arched an eyebrow.

It was all the cue Pen needed. "Inventive. Resourceful. Elegant workmanship. Balanced too. Which is impressive in a piece with this much movement." Pen placed the rabbit in Ivy's hand. "Altogether very clever."

Ivy examined the little automaton before placing it on the bedside table. "You made this, Tim?"

It was as if Pen had asked the question. His eyes didn't move from her. He nodded.

Pen smacked him hard on the back. "Aces!"

Poor Tim looked mortified but also pink. Very pink. Especially in the ears.

Pen pushed all the rubbish off his table, grabbed a charcoal, flipped a piece of paper over, and began to sketch.

Tim moved his suspenders back over his shoulders and watched over Pen's shoulder. His eyes moved from her very short hair to her hand and grew wider and wider at her sketch.

Ivy returned to Collin's side. "What was it you asked Tim to make for you?"

Collin pressed his lips together, causing his untrimmed whiskers to bristle out. "A heater of sorts."

Ivy folder her arms primly across her chest. "A heater?"

She was cute when she was condescending. Collin grabbed Ivy by the elbow and steered her to a small room at the end of the hallway.

A small contraption was propped against the wall with a bellows quietly expanding and compressing. Gears moved, and a row of boots moved back and forth on a belt.

"It's drying your boots?"

"Warming them too. I hate having cold feet."

Ivy pressed her lips together. "An obsessive steward. A drunk engineer. And a mute who makes toy rabbits and boot warmers."

Now, hang on. "Tim's uncle was the finest tinker west of the Snake River." To say nothing of east. "Tim never left his shop. Until the war."

Ivy sat down, unbuttoned her own boots, and made room for them on the belt.

Collin continued. "Matthew is obsessed with his cows and will talk your ear off about cheese recipes, but he can rattle off four dozen formulas for chemical explosives. *And* he has the right nose to help me mix them. Plus, he's an excellent cook."

Ivy's glasses caught the light as she checked the temperature of her boots. "Are you telling me I should have been interrogating cooks instead of army captains all this time?"

Collin leaned closer and spoke in a soft, teasing growl. "Maybe. Have you considered that some of us will need to eat while we plot to end the war?"

"I brought enough cocoa to share." Ivy placed her gloves on the belt too.

He wanted to draw circles with his thumbs across her bare hands. "Food, Ivy. Butter and bread are not a bad start."

"Tell that to your engineer."

Collin took up a pleasantly warm and dry glove from the machine and handed it to Ivy. "He's too young to listen. But he seemed amply chastened by you and your lovely sisters."

She snapped the glove open. "Are there any more you need to vouch for?"

"Yes, Jade is a strategist. Pen is a draftsman and a fine engineer. Sophia is a mathematician, and you—"

"I'm overdue for a cup of chocolate." Ivy grabbed her boots and stepped into them. She left with her usual speed.

"And you are brilliant and cunning enough to make this actually work," Collin said to the empty room.

CHAPTER FOURTEEN

Ivy had to agree. Matthew was an excellent cook. "Flavors can be distilled down to simple chemical compounds. A real dairyman should know the chemistry of his product at an anatomical level," he said to his captivated and famished audience.

"Does the lake house have a dairy?" Sophia asked.

They were all crowded around Matthew's kitchen table. Food, her sisters had assured Ivy, was a prerequisite to any discussion of her plan.

"The lake house has a pasture and an ample stable," Matthew said. "I own the cows."

"You really are passionate about your cream," Jade said in her somber tone. Trust Jade to pour cold water on any flame.

Matthew sliced a soft brie and, with a dollop of raspberry jam, added it to toasted slices of a baguette. "I'm passionate about the things I love." He handed the crostini to Jade. "It's not just food. It's a way of life. You could skim your way through it, or you could savor it."

Jade crunched on her toast and then licked her fingers.

Matthew scoffed and returned to his pot of soup on the stove.

"Did you go to the college, then?" Sophia asked.

"I went. Bloody fools. They were determined to shut me up in a laboratory. A kitchen is all the laboratory I need."

"But you learned the fundamentals?" Ivy prodded.

Collin spoke around a mouthful of crostini. "Enough to help me source materials, at any rate."

"There's no subtlety in combustion." Matthew tasted his soup and added a pinch of pepper to the pot. "No mystery that some chemicals just don't get along."

Jade caught Ivy's eye. "Like people."

"Exactly." Matthew tasted the soup one last time, nodded, and banged the wooden spoon against the rim of the pot.

Monty moaned and clutched his head.

Pen patted Monty on the back. "Cheer up, mate. Ives has a story to tell us to make your sobriety worthwhile." She rose and grabbed a stack of bowls from a shelf.

"What are you doing?" Matthew snapped.

Pen stared down at Matthew, easy to do since she was a good six inches taller than him. "I was going to help myself to some soup. Cream of broccoli, yeah?"

Tim looked at Pen and shook his head.

Matthew hefted a pan of large rolls from the oven. "Tim, would you serve Princessa Penelope—"

"I insist on Pen," she said with a scowl.

"—since she clearly does not understand the finer points of soup and fresh bread."

Tim went white but rose and snatched a knife from the sideboard. He cut a lid into the top of one of the hot rolls and ladled soup into it. He placed the plate with the bread bowl and a spoon in front of Pen.

"Are you going to feed me too?" Pen asked.

Tim went pink this time and then twitched his way back to Matthew's side, where he cored the other bread bowls.

They ate themselves into an amenable silence. Ivy couldn't

remember the last time she'd had a hot meal. She'd forgotten how delicious they were.

Jade broke the silence with an appreciative murmur. "Excellent soup, Matthew. Did the cream come from your Guernsey?"

Matthew shook his head, and when Jade pressed him, he looked up, brow furrowed. "Ayrshire."

One of Jade's rare smiles surfaced. "Now, come on, Ivy. It's been a miserable morning." She tore the top of her bread bowl in half and sopped it in the remnants of her soup. "Trot out your plan. I'll poke all the holes in it that I can, and then we can all get to bed."

"It's midday," Matthew said.

Jade licked her spoon. "Yes. It is."

Ivy checked her watch. Twelve minutes past noon. "We have to end the war. Before the snow melts and the roads clear."

"Six weeks if we're lucky," Matthew said, blowing on his soup. He waved his hand. "Farmers know about these things."

Jade leaned forward, resting her chin in her hand. "So you're a farmer now too?"

"Who else can I trust to feed my cows and source ingredients to pair with my cheeses?"

"Next, you're going to tell me you have a vineyard."

"Do they teach princesses nothing when it comes to wine and cheese?" Matthew said. "Incidentally, you're lucky. Not easy to find tenants this far north. Land needs to be worked."

The major sat quietly back in his chair. "Six weeks is not much time."

"Especially since Olcceart has invented a mechanized rifle." Ivy rubbed her forehead and let the moment of shocked surprise pass.

"They have built factories to mass-produce them and a network of railroads to ship them to their soldiers across the front." Ivy felt the persistent pounding start again. "The only thing keeping them from invading is the snow." Always behind her eyes. "We need to end the war before the snow melts." Ivy pushed away from the table. "Cocoa, anyone?" She plucked a pot hanging to dry from the rack and placed it on a burner.

"Ives, what's your plan?" Pen asked, retrieving another bread bowl of hot soup.

"We need to outbuild them."

"We don't have the time." Jade tore another piece of bread from her bowl. "They built their factories long before the war even started. And the railways."

"I said we need to outbuild them. Not match them."

Pen stopped eating. "Ives?"

"We need to build a doomsday machine with more firepower than their mechanized guns. A machine that needs no network of rails to move." Ivy turned back to her compatriots at the table. "We need to build a rail-less engine, a tank that can move across snow. And is indestructible."

Pen blew on her soup. "Is that all?"

Ivy whisked together cream and cocoa on the stove. "We don't need to match the output of their factories. All we need is a prototype and a bluff."

Sophia dropped her spoon, and it clattered to the floor. "We can't risk an entire war on one working prototype and a false promise that we have a factory turning out hundreds of others."

"We can if we couple our bluff with some well-timed subterfuge." Ivy added a pinch of salt to the pot. "Our enemies have factories that we can easily target. We destroy them the same night we unveil our rail-less machine and our boast that we have converted lake houses in the north and schools in the south into factories and are ready to move. My treaty offer will at last get the attention it deserves." Steam rose in fragrant curls from the pot. "We will have a victory we can all live with in the morning."

The major tapped his knuckles on the table. "How many factories do you think I can target in one night?"

"Enough. You're clever, Major. It's why I like you."

Collin might have had a pithy comeback if it wasn't for Sophia's groan.

Jade steepled her fingers. "You'll 'unveil' the prototype the same night a dozen factories are burning in Olcceart?"

"And I'll have a treaty presented by an ambassador to Olcceart's tribunal. We'll call our troops to stand down from the ice fields of Cailin Muire."

Collin pushed back from the table. "A deal."

Ivy dipped a finger into the pot and sampled the cocoa. "Yes. A deal." Always deals. Always and inescapable. "We offer refuge to all their unwanted fey and surrender our ice fields in exchange for peace."

Sophia gawked. "Can we do that? Our ice fields are our national treasure—"

"Our people are our national treasure, and there won't be any of us left if we don't give up the ice," Ivy said.

"What makes you think our enemy will take the deal?" Jade asked.

"Because I would take the deal. And because we will tell them in no uncertain terms that if they don't, our army of armored rail-less tank engines will target their trains first, then their hospitals, their schools—"

"I would never be a part of such an operation," the major said quietly.

"Which is why you are here. We both know it cannot and will not come to this. It's a bluff. But we need to build this machine, and we need to be ready before the snow melts."

"And if your plan fails?" Matthew asked.

Ivy poured herself a cup of cocoa. "The war continues, and we are yet again disastrously behind."

"You'll need more sugar," Matthew said, nodding toward Ivy's cup.

Jade laid a light hand on Matthew's wrist. "No. She won't."

Ivy returned to the table with her cocoa. "Where are the holes, Jade?"

"It's a problem of the factories. You can't target a dozen, or even a half dozen, at the final hour." Jade's eyes narrowed. "Better to start squeezing now, if squeezing is even possible. Olcceart has a soft spot for their industry."

Matthew got up to help himself to a cup of cocoa. "I wouldn't leave off there. I'd target their rails. Mobility might start sooner than you think. Soldiers can be paid to clear snow after all." He tasted the cocoa and spit it out.

Jade said, "He's right."

Ivy pressed her fingers to her forehead. "I don't want innocent lives to suffer."

Jade raised her eyebrows but was careful not to roll her eyes. Ivy had debated with her sister enough to know Jade's perspective.

"When is a life ever innocent?" Matthew grumbled. "I don't know what you've done to this pot of chocolate, but it is ruined."

"The rest of the plan?" Collin asked.

Jade shrugged. "Would depend on what this rail-less engine looks like."

The company turned toward Tim, Pen, and Monty, who was snoring on the table. "Could you take a steam engine off the rails? Build an armored war machine that ran without a track?" Ivy asked.

"And Carved a path of chaos and destruction in its wake," Jade added.

Tim shook his head.

Pen's lips twitched upward. "Yes."

Tim's eyebrows shot up questioningly.

"We have work to do." Pen grabbed Tim's hand and pulled him out of the room.

"As we all do," Ivy said, dismissing the others. "Thank you for the meal, Matthew. I'll wash up."

"By yourself?" he grunted as his eyes wandered to the chair Jade had vacated.

Ivy tied Matthew's apron around her waist. "Monty will help, won't you?"

Monty continued to snore at the table. Just as well. Ivy was too cold and too tired for socializing.

Collin hung back, stacking all the dishes on the table. "Smoke and mirrors."

"Smoke and steel." Ivy set the stack of plates in the sink with a clatter. "Mirrors break too easily."

Collin retrieved the silver from the table. "I'll need to recruit more talent, if you want me bombing factories in Olcceart."

"Fine," Ivy said, running the water. Thank heaven the plumbing had been retrofitted.

Collin rolled up his sleeves. "You might not see much of me. Espionage isn't exactly a desk job."

"Even better." Ivy reached around him for the drying towel. "I have a mountain of briefings to sort through regarding the war *and* the inquiry."

"The assassination attempt. Any news?"

Ivy's hands tightened on the knife she was drying. "Only that Papa is more than willing to blame our enemies. 'Olcceart spies among us'—it's his favorite theory. Not that there is any evidence to support it." Lack of evidence never slowed Papa. "Something is bound to turn up in my review."

Collin paused in his scrubbing. "You think that's what happened?"

"I think my father has always been fond of scapegoats. And jumping to convenient conclusions. There's little to be gained and much to be lost by sowing more ill will for the citizens of Olcceart. I need to uncover the truth before the rumors get out of hand. At least I'll have some quiet while Jade thinks through our strategy to end the war." Collin handed Ivy a handful of spoons to rinse and dry. "She always needs a night's sleep for these sorts of things."

Lines creased Collin's forehead. "Really?"

Ivy waved her soapy hand toward the hall that led to the rest of the manor. "You heard her yourself."

The major hesitated long enough for Ivy to admire how the soap suds clung to his lean forearms. "Quite right," he said.

"Tim and Pen seem to be getting along. Monty will brighten up." Ivy dried her hand on her skirts before she nudged Monty's freckled cheek with her knuckle. He flinched but continued to snore.

"And Sophia?" Collin asked, rinsing the last of the silver before drying his hands.

"I'll tell her you are returning with more dashing young men. Find one or two she can dazzle with her numbers."

"That shouldn't be too hard."

"I was joking."

"I'll find her someone." The major grabbed a coat from the wall of pegs.

"Are you leaving now?" He couldn't leave! She'd only just arrived and...

"No need to worry. I'll write you."

"Stop now, Major, or I will be a puddle of uncontained desire at your feet." The disappointment she felt had everything to do with being left to finish the wash-up alone and nothing to do with Collin's handsome eyes.

"I'll miss you." Collin adjusted the collar of his coat. "Will you miss me?"

"How can I miss you? I barely know you." A sound argument, but not an honest one.

The major leaned against the wall, his hand on the door. "Tim and Monty are harmless. And Matthew is trustworthy." The major hesitated. "I'd keep my eye on Jade, though." He winked and left.

"How do you know?" Collin was older, taller, but still a young sapling that could be snapped in half. It'd be another three years before he filled out. Just in time for the war to begin. "How do you know when to trust someone?"

Gran brayed. "Why trust anyone?"

"But what if you need to?"

Gran stopped short. "What have you done now?"

Collin was quick to step out of reach of her cane. Precaution and all. "I haven't done anything. I've met someone."

"You are too young to meet anyone."

"You're too old to do anything about it."

Gran grumbled and shuffled across the kitchen. "'Fortune-Teller and Matchmaker.' Does it not say matchmaker on my door? I can do anything with the proper motivation. Now tell me why trust has flittered into your naïve little head after having 'met someone.'"

"I like her."

"Because she's pretty?"

Not just because she was pretty. She had a warm voice and a smile always accompanied by a blush when Collin caught her eye. She smelled nice. Like fresh-baked bread.

"Who is she?" Gran demanded.

"Citizen Freud's daughter."

"The baker's girl? It's because I don't feed you enough. Is that it? Always thinking with your stomach." Gran's tremor was particularly violent today. She tried to shuffle toward Collin but just swayed on her cane. Not her good cane either. Today, she used the one made from a solid piece of gnarled elder wood. The one that hurt more when she swung it at him.

"You can't have friends unless you're honest with them," Collin said.

"Preposterous." Gran dropped to her chair with a huff. "Listen to me. One day, when you are much older—"

"How much older?"

Gran jabbed Collin in the stomach with her cane. "Old enough not to interrupt your Gran. You'll meet someone. Someone who makes you feel more alive than you've ever felt. And you won't stop to ask yourself any questions. You'll know."

"What will I know?"

Gran was out of breath. "Risks! The risks fools take when they hand over their trust to another person."

"Mama took that risk," Collin said quietly.

"Yes, and how do you like being raised by your Gran?"

Collin picked at a crumb stuck to the table. "You did it too. You had Mama. You couldn't have done it by yourself."

A brief smile played across Gran's face, cracking the wrinkles in a way Collin wasn't used to seeing. The smile vanished when she saw Collin gaping. Her cane made a quick jab into his stomach. "If you have time to meet someone, you have time to earn a wage. Get your coat. It's about time you started contributing to this household. Let's go."

Risk and rewards. Collin was far too familiar with them these days. Ivy made sure of that, and while Collin was acutely aware that he was the last sort of man a princess would associate with in peacetime, he was determined to make himself indispensable to her now. Regrettable that doing so took him away from the lake house the same day she'd arrived. At least he'd seen her again.

Thankfully, there was no snow in the border town of Grizzle, and the roads were mercifully dry, hopefully dry enough to turn the carriage around and quickly smuggle out an overdrawn fortune-teller. "Let's go, Gran. It's moving day," Collin whispered.

Gran grabbed her elder wood cane and defended herself. "Get your hands off me. 'Sailant!"

"Gran, it's me. It's Collin."

"'Bout damn time." Her words were soft. Collin knew it was not by choice.

"We have to be quiet, Gran. I've not exactly settled your bill."

"Where are we going?"

"I've bought a room in a lovely little farm. South of here. There is a coach outside. Let's go now, and I'll tell you more about it on the way."

"I need my cards."

"I'll buy you new cards, Gran. We need to leave now." Collin didn't want anyone to notice the empty carriage outside.

"Don't be stupid. I'm not leaving without my livelihood. How do you think I've managed so long without you?"

Collin's chest constricted. Heat rose to his cheeks. "Gran, I'm so sorry. I'll explain everything."

"I thought you were dead." Tears welled in Gran's glassy eyes. "I thought—" But her tremor was too much.

"I'll get your cards, Gran. What else do you need?"

"I don't have anything else, stupid."

And to think Collin had missed her. "It's very dark, Gran. I'll carry you down the stairs." She was no longer stout—in fact, she was alarmingly small—so this was an easy task.

"You smell of guncotton and ashes. What have you done, Collin?"

"I started a new job, Gran. Raise in salary and enough money to keep you in the lap of luxury."

"Did you drug the proprietor?"

The man of the establishment was sleeping at his desk and drooling over his ledger.

"Nonsense. I shared a drink with him while the horses needed their harness repaired."

Gran sighed. "I raised you better."

CHAPTER FIFTEEN

Six days later, a scribbled note came attached to a clipping from the *Gazette* about a fire that destroyed an Olcceart train depot. Cleaning rags had burst into flames. No injuries but extensive damage. The note, written in a tight, neat hand, said, *Miss me yet? C.*

That was the last she'd heard from Collin. And when Trina insisted in letter after letter on getting an update...

Slow progress. That was how Ivy described their work at the manor house. Slow progress that could not even keep up with the rate of the ice melt.

I'll pray for another blast of arctic air, Trina wrote. *We've had winters where it has frozen over at the very end. We've had winters where the tulips are buried in six inches of snow.*

Ivy wrote back, *If a hard freeze comes our way, then you must come with it. Bring your ice skates. We wouldn't want anyone in the capital getting the wrong idea.*

Not everyone has their mind in the gutter, Ivy.

"No," Ivy said as she read through Trina's letter, turning over the first page and the next. Trina was going on and on about some new organist. "Some people have their minds entirely stuffed in organ pipes."

A tap came at her door.

"Yes?" Ivy called, not moving from her desk. Why should she? She had letters from the viscount and the bishop, both urging her to persuade Papa to increase the sugar rations. Given the shrill tone of their correspondence, something needed to be done.

"Don't get up on my account." Sophia came in and fell across Ivy's bed.

"Sophia, I need you to run the numbers on the sugar reserves."

"I refuse on the grounds of your impending Treaty of Cailin Muire."

"Come again?" Ivy said, dipping her pen into her pot of ink.

"Your treaty offer. I've seen your draft. It forbids torture against all prisoners of war."

"You are not a prisoner of war."

"Then let me go home."

"Trina has her hands full enough as it is."

"Then send for Gwen, Ang, and Daphne."

"I will. Just as soon as we have sufficient reason."

"Will my untimely death be reason enough for you? I will die of boredom if I have to spend another minute with Monty and Pen and Tim."

"Then find Jade and Matthew."

Sophia snorted.

"What's so funny?"

"If you left your desk for more than two minutes, you'd know."

"Are they still fighting?"

Sophia made a noise of pure disgust. "I want to go home. I'm bored."

"Flirt with Monty."

"I'm not his type."

Thank heavens for that. "Then run the numbers on the sugar. And the wheat supply, too, while you're at it."

Sophia made a whining noise and grabbed the ledger. "Fixed opportunity costs or inflated?"

"Both."

"I hate you!" Sophia reached into her pocket and dropped a small letter on Ivy's desk. "This came for you."

"Thank you." Ivy continued to scribble.

"Read it to me."

Ivy tore open the letter. "Since when did you become a law-abiding citizen?"

"It's not a crime to read someone's mail if you're related."

"Yes, it is."

"I thought about reading it, but the last letter I read was something awful about the declining tenant rate in the country parishes, and the thought of reading something else as boring as that made me want to cry."

"Well, you should have read this one. It's from the major."

"What does he say?" Sophia asked, grabbing the letter. "And why didn't he write his name on the outside?"

"He's coming back. And he's bringing a friend."

Sophia flipped the letter over. "When?"

"Soon." Ivy took the letter back. "Now, go work on your numbers. The major promised to bring a gentleman that would be enamored with them."

Sophia wrinkled her nose and stuck out her tongue but left with the ledger.

Ivy traced the major's signature. He was right. She did miss him.

Ivy hardly left her desk. She'd occasionally take a meal with the others in the kitchen. Matthew continued to create amazing menus from the contents of the larder and cellars.

"But how is the work, Matthew?" Ivy asked.

"How many times must I tell you? Explosives are simple."

"What if I want to detonate one underwater?"

Matthew froze with a spoon of vichyssoise in his mouth.

"Is that something you want to do?" Jade asked icily.

"Some of the factories are converted mills. It may be advantageous..."

"Highly advantageous," Jade said. "But perhaps beyond the skill set of our understudy chemist."

Matthew snorted. "Water solubility is not an undiscovered country of fear and peril."

"Prove it," Jade said, her lips pressing into a tight curve.

Pen sailed into the kitchen, followed by Tim and Monty. "But if we adjust the belt, will it affect the timing?"

"If we don't adjust the belt, it won't matter," Monty said.

"Ives"—Pen grabbed an orange from a crate Matthew had just kicked into the kitchen—"how many blokes do you want running your rail-less engine?"

Ivy considered. "At least three. A driver, a gunman, and a communicator."

"But more is better?" Pen said, tossing an orange to Tim, who fumbled the catch. The orange went skittering across the floor.

Ivy ground her teeth. "This is the type of question that would be better answered by a man with military experience."

"Yes, when is Major Top-Notch headed our way?" Pen began peeling her orange.

"Undetermined. Is there room in your prototype for more than a forward cannon?" Ivy asked.

"We could put cannons on all sides," Monty said.

"The automatics, yes," Pen said, tossing her orange peel into the sink. "Tim reverse-engineered our pilfered model. Improved it, if you ask me."

Tim clanked a set of pots to the floor.

Ivy took off her glasses to consider. "Four gunmen, a driver, and a communicator would be ideal."

Tim scrunched his eyebrows together.

"Communicator—it's Ivy's utilitarian word for commanding officer."

"Six men." Monty pressed his empty hands onto the table.

"It could be done," Pen said, handing half of her peeled orange to Tim.

"It'd be cramped," Monty said.

"Boy, you talk as if challenges are anything but fun. Speaking of which..." Pen sat next to Ivy. She popped an orange section in her mouth. Ivy smelled the citrus in the air. "Haven't seen you in the foundry lately."

Ivy didn't bother to look up from her summary of the court's discussion about the plight of the fey. More refugees were arriving in the capital daily. "I've been buried under an avalanche of paperwork."

"Ah. Sugar. Sophia has been griping about it."

"Now, I've just been informed by Dilbert—"

"Papa's financial secretary?" Pen winked at Tim.

"—that I'm to prepare a budget for next week's cabinet meeting."

"A budget?"

"Papa has put it off, you see."

"Well, come down to the foundry when you have a minute. Tim is very good with a hex wrench."

Ivy kept her glasses on and focused on her latest stack of letters. No need to mark Tim's complexion. He was in a perpetual state of pink whenever Pen spoke or looked in his direction.

CHAPTER SIXTEEN

"Are we there yet?" Eric asked. "My feet are cold."

Collin did up the buttons of his coat. They were close enough to the lake house to be in uniform. And he'd rather be in uniform when he saw Ivy next. "Nearly." A week had passed since he'd bombed the train depot and two since he'd left Ivy—he was most definitely counting the days.

"Isn't it against the law to wear a uniform if you're not enlisted?" Eric asked, tugging at the collar of his sage-green coat.

"What do you care?" Collin answered.

Eric stood taller. "If I'm going to jail, I want it to be because I was declared a public enemy." He jogged a pace to keep up with Collin. "I'm a dangerous man."

"You going to threaten me with paper cuts?"

"Ideas are the most dangerous weapons. Always have been. Always will be."

It was too cold to argue, and Collin hadn't eaten anything reasonable since the night he'd ferried Gran to the farm. Fourteen days of stale crackers and cold spiced wine, the last four with Eric's constant stream of pugnacious insults.

"It's going to snow," Eric said. "Where are we going?"

"To my superior officer," Collin said.

"Shouldn't he have been waiting at the crossroads with transportation orders and, you know, transportation?" Eric clutched his stomach. "I wouldn't say no to a hot meal."

Collin kept going. Not far now. And it was madness to feel so much hinging on his return. And seeing Ivy. Again.

The lake house came into view as the men crested the frozen hill. "A gentry house?" Eric stumbled into a pile of slush. "You didn't mention that. Do they have hot water?"

Collin hadn't mentioned a lot of things. "Yes."

The men wandered up the park to the large estate. "I call the suite closest to the kitchen," Eric said. "Midnight snacking and all."

"I assign the rooms," Collin said evenly. He'd hoped she'd be here. It wasn't as if he expected Ivy to be waiting for him, just he'd hoped she would be. There were, after all, details to be discussed. And knowing Ivy, she'd want to have the final word before anything was said or done.

They pushed through the mud to the back of the house, past the foundry patio to the kitchen garden, all shriveled and iced over.

"No one." Eric peered under a burlap tarp and tossed out a limp stalk of kale. "Shouldn't there be a guard?"

"We're too far north and too far from the front for it to matter." Still, Collin had wondered this himself. Even though the post had been redirected to three different towns before arriving here, he'd wondered. He'd worried. He'd left something too precious here, and it wasn't just hope of securing peace in his lifetime.

Collin heaved open the kitchen door. The kitchen was spotless, save for a bowl covered with a dishcloth near the oven. Only the smell of yeast greeted the weary travelers.

Eric lifted the cloth off the bowl.

"For heaven's sake, don't touch it! It needs to ferment, man," Matthew barked.

"You going to chide us about your sourdough before you sound the alarm for intruders?" Collin asked.

"Out of my way," Matthew growled. "I've got places to be."

Collin noticed the clean shirt. The fresh shave. The wet hair. "Where are you going, Matt?"

Matthew blushed and then blustered through the kitchen. He shoved a half-eaten pie into Eric's hands and a bowl of oranges into Collin's. "I need to borrow a collar."

"You can have all of Collin's collars if it means more food like this," Eric said around a mouthful of shepherd's pie.

Collin set the oranges on the table. "Where are you going, Matt?"

"Well, it's Sunday."

"It's Wednesday." Eric licked his fingers.

"Well, I thought it was Sunday. So I'm heading to church. And after that, I'm heading to the post office to pick up the mail and supplies. Out of vanilla. Can't make croquembouche without vanilla."

"We just came from town," Collin said, "with the mail."

Matt rubbed the back of his neck. "But did you get any vanilla? Or honey, for that matter?"

Collin smiled. "Have a good time. Give Jade my best."

"No need, Major Collin." Jade appeared in her fur coat and hood, along with Ivy's black muff. "You ready?" she said to Matt.

"Just going to grab my collar."

Jade nodded. She leaned against the kitchen doorjamb and turned her attention to the other gentlemen in the kitchen.

Collin came to attention and saluted. Eric fell in line, but not before shoving two oranges into his coat pocket.

"As you were," Jade said.

"Your Highness, may I introduce Captain Eric Bookmonger."

Jade nodded to the gentleman. "They're all in the foundry."

"And we're off to town." Matthew reappeared, proffering his elbow, which Jade accepted with a sly smile.

"Come on." Collin motioned to Eric and headed outside and down the foundry steps.

Pen had goggles on top of her forehead. Grease covered Tim's face. He always stayed messy.

Monty was shouting, "You have to remember the basic laws of physics. If the cannon fires, it will cause an equal and opposite reaction."

Pen rubbed her eyes. "Yes, a recoil."

"It must be considered." Monty grabbed one of Pen's diagrams and threw it on the workbench. "We can't have this engine rocking backward. We have to have some sort of outriggers for the event."

"Planting the outriggers would be too time-consuming," Ivy said.

Collin's heart fluttered. Her back was to him, but just the same, his throat went dry. Her hair was pinned up and under, making her look like she'd cropped her hair clean off.

"Death will be even more time-consuming!" Monty yelled, his face turning a very ruddy color.

Sophia followed Ivy with a book, taking notes and scowling.

"Wouldn't the weight of the engine make this point moot?" Ivy asked. She had a finger resting on her cheek and the others coiled on her chin. "This could be addressed with protocol, could it not?"

Pen pressed her lips together and nodded.

"It should be addressed in the design," Monty continued.

"He has a point. The back blast of a cannon of that size could be considerable," Eric said.

Ivy turned quickly, and her face looked thunderous.

"Orange, anyone?" Eric asked.

Ivy dropped her hand from her chin. "I want a proposal on my desk by sundown. Sophia, come with me." She stood in front of Collin at last, close enough to touch, to hold. And maybe this was worse than being miles apart, because he still couldn't. "This is a classified area, Major. Who is your friend?"

"Your newest recruit, ma'am."

"I'll be the judge of that. Take him to the library. I'll be with you shortly. Sophia, find Jade."

"Jade and Matthew just left," Collin said.

More thunder—and cold, hard steel in her eyes.

"Sophia, finish up the progress report and join me in the library. You'll have to take the minutes of our interview and fill Jade in later."

Collin noted how Ivy gripped the handrail. Her fingers turned clawlike as she brushed past Collin.

Back at the lake house, the stately library desk was in complete disarray. And it was far too cold.

Collin set about lighting a fire. "Where is the kindling?"

Ivy ripped a page from the back of her ledger and handed it to him.

"Excuse me. Ivy, is it?" Eric asked.

Collin winced.

Ivy removed her glasses from her nose and placed them on the desk. "Who are you? And what do you know of Amadanri?"

"I know it's ruddy cold and that Collin is rubbish at making fires."

Ivy gestured to the fire. "Be my guest."

Ivy flipped her watch open. "Major Collin, please give me a reason not to—"

Eric shoved Collin out of the way. "You're doing it wrong."

"These logs are too damp," Collin argued.

"Oh, for heaven's sake." Ivy marched over to a cupboard, reached inside, and procured a bottle of very expensive-looking Scotch, tossed a log into the fireplace, doused it and a few crumpled pages from her ledger with the alcohol, and lit a match. The fire crackled to life.

"Did she seriously just waste an entire bottle of Scotch?" Eric asked.

"Don't make me rethink bringing you along." Collin had rescued him, actually.

"Who is he?" Ivy asked Collin.

He was no one. Nothing. A bone for Sophia and her inevitably arriving sisters to chew up and spit out, marginally useful at best. "He has reliable intel and is handy with a trip-wire explosive. He keeps cool in clouds of smoke." That was key. Smoke made even battle-hardened lads turncoats. "Eric." Collin nodded to his companion.

Eric rose as if seeing Ivy for the first time and bowed suavely. "At your service, ma'am."

"Would you like me to tie him up and throw him in the foundry until you've sat on his lap and questioned him?"

Ivy glared at Collin. That was better. He had her full attention now.

"I volunteer," Eric said eagerly and then, more measured, said, "Ma'am, I volunteer and am at your service. Whatever your service may be."

Ivy stared at Eric until he all but withered up. Maybe Collin should have said something to prepare Eric, but he had wanted to keep all his memories of Ivy for himself.

She rounded on Collin. "You're late. I was expecting you yesterday."

Yes, the detour for Gran had cost him a day. "Apologies."

"We weren't expecting the snow so far south," Eric said.

The library door opened, and Sophia entered with the folio and ledger.

Sophia had obviously spent the last ten minutes in front of a mirror. Her hair was falling becomingly out of her bun. Her glasses were nowhere in sight. Her lips were redder, her lashes darker.

Ivy, on the other hand, looked pale, like she'd not slept in days. She snapped her watch closed and open purposefully. "Sir, you have five minutes to prove yourself loyal to the Crown and indispensable to our efforts to end this war. If I find you have merit, you may stay. If I find you have wasted my time, you will be imprisoned until we can find a competent burgess to argue for your freedom. Our courts are snarled up nicely and have been for the last eighteen months. I would try to be as persuasive as possible."

Eric jutted out his chin. He wasn't as tall as Collin. In fact, he wasn't taller than Ivy, but he never let his height stop him from flirting when the opportunity arose. "Citizen Eric Bookmonger. I ran an independent bookshop in Olcceart and my own small press. That is, until they were seized as property of the people. I published the *Herald*, a circular committed to dialogue concerning the facts of this war—"

"What sort of facts?" Ivy asked.

Eric's attention slipped to Sophia for a moment. "There have been three counts for peace talks that have been ignored just this last year. Half of all enlisted men have been taken to work in factories in the south, and their wages have never materialized. Twice as many fey men are dying than the everyday Olcceart citizen."

Ivy replaced her spectacles and examined a brief on her desk. "What is one to conclude from such facts? Editorialize for us."

Sophia smiled coyly but continued to take notes.

Eric did not hesitate. "The Republic of Olcceart is dragging out the war and using the draft to enslave its citizens and kill the fey."

Ivy's shoulders sagged. "Tell me about your readership."

Eric winked at Sophia but returned to attention. "Ma'am?"

"There must have been some person of interest who subscribed to your paper."

"My subscribers are confidential."

"How do you know the major?"

Eric shook his head. "I will not betray a friend."

Ivy arched an eyebrow. "How loyal."

Collin scratched above his ear. "I wouldn't say 'friend.' I've been a reader since the start of the war. His information has always proven reliable. And entertaining."

"Thanks, mate. I didn't know you cared," Eric said.

Sophia giggled. Eric cracked an enormous grin in her direction.

"We need a list of any sympathetic ears in Olcceart." Ivy folded her arms and turned her full gaze on Eric. "You will supply them, or you will be the Crown's prisoner. Sophia will assist you and brief you on the goals of our operation. Have you any sisters, Eric?"

"Yes."

"Then you know how wicked we can be. Sophia is my sister. Don't give me a reason not to play nice."

"Ivy!" Sophia said.

"I still need the progress report," Ivy called as Sophia hustled Eric out the door and slammed it shut behind them without acknowledgment.

Ivy rose to her feet. "Now then, Major, you said you'd bring someone to keep Sophia out of trouble, but instead you brought trouble with you."

"Eric's all right." Why didn't she call him Collin? He'd have liked to hear her say his name. "Did you know Matthew is getting married today?"

"I thought he was already married. Someone said something about his wife. I'll congratulate him when I have a moment. Now tell me, do we stand a chance? Did you find the location of any of their factories?"

Collin asked for a map, and Ivy rummaged through the papers on her desk until she brought one to the top of the stack.

"They have three factories here, along this river in the northeast. A cluster of factories here in the shire of Westholden." Collin smelled the chocolate on her. "And a final industrialized center here at the foot of the Shale Mountains."

"None in their urban areas?"

"Not yet. Labor is cheaper in the countryside. Also cheaper next to the raw materials."

"So clever. So extremely clever. And so unfeeling. Traditions, livelihoods, and families unbraided in an instant... It's great and terrible all at once," Ivy said, turning over a parchment and scratching out notes. "Is it true what your book peddler said? Enlisted men are working in the factories?"

Collin rubbed a weary hand across his brow. "I fear it's worse."

Ivy stopped writing. "Women and children?"

Collin nodded.

"That makes me feel better about destroying such impressive

innovation. I got your note about the train depot. Were you able to target more?"

"A factory in the south suffered a similar accident when their cleaning rags spontaneously combusted."

"How did you manage it?"

"Guncotton."

"Nitrocellulose. Did you make it on-site?" Ivy sounded excited.

A curl of pride swelled somewhere close to Collin's heart. "I found a way of transporting it wet." Better to leave out the less-than-safe details. "What progress have you made on the prototype?"

"Precious little. The progress reports are filled with squabbles over theory."

"They need more supervision. Monty hasn't taken to the bottle again?"

"No. He's stayed sober, much to our mutual relief. Although, he was much easier to deal with when he was snooted." Ivy took off her glasses. "What?"

"You need to be down in the foundry."

"Impossible. Papa has all but abdicated the throne to me. His secretaries forward all his workload here. It's doubled now that the inquiry is underway." She gestured with her chin to the largest stack of papers on her desk.

"Have they found the assassin?" Collin's fingers brushed against the green hair ribbon lying on the desk. Ivy's ribbon.

She rubbed her eyes, covering her face with her hands. "Not even a lead. Nothing has turned up. Well, nothing of substance." Ivy straightened. "I am to review the testimony of the entire opera production—the stagehands, singers, musicians. All of them. In the hopes that I will find something that our ministers have missed."

"Mars." No wonder the stack of documents was so thick.

"It wouldn't be so bad, but they assigned the scribes with the worst handwriting." Ivy sighed. "I must review, write, revise, and ferry my findings all back to Papa posthaste so that he may apply his seal and signature and suggest next steps." She rummaged in her drawer until she found a fresh pot of ink.

"Next steps that you suggest." Collin would take her silence as a yes. "Will he listen?"

"Sometimes." She was already slashing notes across the margins of the page.

"Meanwhile, there's a war..."

"And the clock is ticking. I'm well aware."

Collin picked up a paper from a smaller stack of documents on her desk and read, "'Commission for a new portrait of King Rupert and Queen Adelaide with subject of hunt for the purpose of legacy and national heritage.' Ivy, you don't have time for this. How is a new portrait more important than winning the war?"

"It's not." Ivy took the document from Collin and started scribbling at the bottom. "Which is why I have asked that only studies of hunts be commissioned by amateur artists currently enlisted in the military. It will boost morale. And create more awareness. We will line a hall with them somewhere."

"Could the population be any more aware of this war?"

"Awareness for Papa." Ivy continued to write. "I know this is trivial, but it's an opportunity nonetheless. And I've not yet fallen behind. I'm still more than capable, and everyone is having fun... Except for Jade. She's been a disaster."

Collin didn't know if prodding would lead to more information, and that bugged him. He should know by now. He should have learned her tics, what led her to open up. But he didn't know. So all he could do was listen. And watch.

Ivy blotted the page. "That's done and will be in the diplomatic pouch under a sack of onions for Papa's courier tomorrow." Ivy smirked. "He hates onions."

CHAPTER SEVENTEEN

It was taking everything Ivy had, but her plan was moving forward. Pen and Tim were a brilliant partnering. Monty was capable, often clever. Sophia was staying on top of her sums. Major Collin was keeping Eric in line. Matthew was a steady hand with Collin's powders—when he could be persuaded to budge from his kitchen, which was not often. Jade had relocated her chessboard to his kitchen table now that she had plotted out a tangled, spider-web strategy of targets.

Collin was gone more often than not, usually taking Eric with him. "He has more connections than you'd think," Collin told her.

Ivy didn't care. "So long as he is kept in hand where Sophia is concerned."

"Oh, don't be stupid!" Sophia screamed. "I'm not the one you should be worried about."

Fair enough. Ivy found herself increasingly concerned with Collin's side of the operation. It would be only natural for a superior to be concerned with the safety of a subordinate when so much of the mission depended on his success. But most superior officers didn't dream about lying in the arms of a subordinate. Such dreams were alarmingly frequent now.

Not that Ivy was sleeping much, or taking anything in besides hot chocolate (Matthew did make a wondrously thick cup), but she had almost caught up on the diplomacy end, which mattered. Ivy was making progress.

Sadly, the same could not be said of the dratted inquiry. They were no closer to finding Papa's dashing assassin now than they had been the night of the opera. After receiving Ivy's review, Papa had ordered a second inventory of the prop rifles and an expanded search of the opera house to include the surrounding neighborhoods. "Something will turn up," he'd said. "We cannot move forward until then." Papa had also expanded the list of key witnesses. Statements from every patron in attendance were being collected now in addition to statements from every Olcceart expatriate. Ivy hated it, and she hated the sluggish pace of the inquiry, but Papa insisted that they proceed carefully, thoroughly. *Excruciating exactness at exorbitant cost* might be a better description of the inquiry. Ivy had tried to explain that time was of the essence.

Can you put a price on my life? Papa had replied in one of his rare letters. *I will not tolerate sloppy work in this matter.*

She'd suggested that perusing new security measures for all members of the royal family and their public appearances might be the only viable solution moving forward. Papa would not stand for the idea. The assassination attempt was not his fault, and limiting his freedoms would punish only him.

There was nothing Ivy could do but await the deluge of reports and briefings that were sure to arrive at the most inopportune time.

Time... Every day, Ivy felt the lack of it pressing against her. The days were lengthening, the snow was too quickly melting. They'd have another two weeks at best before time ran out altogether. The hope that Ivy would find a spare moment to slide down to the foundry alone to pick apart the new firing apparatus was absurd. Spare moments needed to be spent on her family. Trina needed an update. Mina needed a reply about the state of the stables. And then Ivy needed to draft a careful request to Papa for more funds. Steel did not come cheap, particularly when it had to be ferried to the north.

The wind gusted through the study window and blew Ivy's pen across the desk and onto the floor. At least it hadn't blown over her cup of cocoa. Turned out Ivy had been right to pack cocoa in her trunk. They'd already exhausted the lake house supply.

Ivy pulled her shawl tighter around her shoulders. She bent down to retrieve her pen but stopped as the study started to spin around her. She braced both of her hands on the desk and shut her eyes. Darkness could spin all it wanted.

"Working late?" Collin set the pen on Ivy's desk.

She hadn't seen him in five days. When had he returned? And why did he look so relaxed and rested? She wanted to see mud on his boots, snow on his shoulders, shadows under his eyes, new lines across his forehead, a few more flecks of gray at his temples, stubble on his chin at the very least. Instead, he looked as if he'd spent the last three weeks soaking in a hot spring.

But questions were just the sort of thing he enjoyed dodging. Ivy feigned normalcy. "Bracing myself for the next round of communications to review."

Collin took a seat on Ivy's desk. He leaned in close. "News from the front?"

"News from Papa. Adelaide is still not pregnant."

"Must be awkward for you."

Awkward was having Collin leaning over her and smiling. The room began to spin again. "What do you want, Major?"

"Are you dizzy?"

"Of course not." Ivy pushed away from the desk. She moved to the window but needed to place a hand on the ledge to steady herself.

"Then you can do me a favor."

Everyone always needed something from Ivy. "What can I do for you, Major?"

"I need you to raise your hands like this, palms down, and close your eyes."

Ivy eyed her pocket watch on the desk and rolled her eyes. "Major, I have a stack of letters to review."

"This is important."

Ivy complied and stretched out her hands, palms down.

"Eyes closed."

Ivy arched an eyebrow but closed her eyes. The instant she did, she felt herself spinning and moved her hands to steady herself.

"As I thought," Collin said. "Lie down."

"Excuse me?"

"On the chaise will be fine. Although, if you want to find a bed—"

"I know you know you've made yourself indispensable, but if you think for one minute—"

The major placed his hands on either side of Ivy's head and turned it firmly but gently to the right. "Is the room spinning?"

"Of course not."

The major turned Ivy's head to the left, and it was as if the room were being sucked down a drain. Ivy grabbed hold of the major's arm to steady herself.

"Lie down, Ivy."

"Your medic experience?" she asked.

"Gran had vertigo for years."

That's right, he was raised by his grandmother.

"Lie down with your head hanging off the edge of the chaise."

Ivy complied. The major held her head in his hands and tilted it back at a gentle angle. "Your hands are cold." But they did not shake.

"Tell me if you feel dizzy."

"I'm past dizzy. The world is being sucked up a straw."

"Thirty more seconds, then."

"My watch is on the desk if you need to time—"

"No need."

"But it is an excellent watch." Mama had commissioned it

herself. A special present for Papa. *Don't tell him, now. What shall the inlay be, Ivy darling?*

"Look to the right now," Collin said, his voice patient and soft.

Ivy complied. She turned, and her eyes settled on the window. The wind still gusted. "We lost an entire company at the front. Not to Olcceart's guns or their armored trains. To hypothermia. This wretched cold."

"Roll onto your side."

Ivy did, and she stared into Collin's eyes. Eyes with dark lashes. Eyes that caught details the way a spider caught dinner. "This war must end," Ivy said.

Collin gently lifted Ivy until she was on her feet. "How do you feel? Is the room still spinning?"

Ivy reached a hand to the back of her neck. "No."

Collin's mouth twitched into a fleeting smile. "Good."

Ivy grabbed her watch from the table and flipped it open for the comfort alone of seeing the ever-dependable hands.

"How long have you had it?" Collin asked.

"I found it a few years after Mama died. She commissioned the watch as an anniversary present for my father. But he was never fond of the colors and quickly replaced it with a bigger, gold watch. I found it on the floor, kicked under a wardrobe. It's been mine ever since."

Collin's brow was pinched. "Forgive me. I should have been more specific. How long have you had the vertigo?"

Ivy blushed. No one wanted to hear about her mother's watch. She shrugged a single shoulder. Less effort than shrugging the two. "It comes and goes."

"But it's been coming more frequently since the night of the opera."

"That's none of your business."

"I think it is," Collin said. "How many hours do you sleep at night?"

"Too many. People are dying. And if we don't get the prototype working—"

"Ivy, let me put this in terms that will interest you. What happens when a watch is wound too tight?"

"Nothing, because it is impossible to wind a watch or any clock too tight. It only winds insofar as the spring can be tightened."

"The clockwork princess has wound herself too tightly. She sleeps for only four hours a night."

"Three, actually."

"She takes only cocoa. She reads and writes and tinkers and frets. Are you trying to break yourself?"

"Major, your concern is touching but completely unnecessary. I am in perfect health. Even if I were feeling haggard, it wouldn't matter. Those boys are counting on me. I've let too many of them down. I must bring the rest home."

"Ivy, you talk as if this is your war alone."

"It may just as well be. I am the only one determined to do anything about it. Now, do you want to tell me your thoughts on the prototype, or would you like to leave?"

Collin leaned against Ivy's desk. "There's a problem."

"Our greatest natural resource," Ivy muttered.

"The foundry has run out of raw materials. Copper, iron, steel."

Ivy had hoped she would have been able to procure the funds to order them, but she'd underestimated... Or, actually, her father had underfunded her. "Can we use scrap?"

Collin considered. "Are you offering up the manor house?"

Ivy tried to blink back the fatigue. "If we cannot, then we will have to steal it from the other side."

"Steal it?" Collin guffawed. "How would we get away with that?"

"Misdirection."

"It will never work."

"It always works." A shiver ran up Ivy's back. "I'll show you. Take my watch."

Collin did, running his thumb across the tarnished silver and the emerald inlay.

"Put it in your pocket," Ivy ordered.

Collin slid the watch into his vest pocket and patted it in place.

"Now I'm going to take it back without you realizing while diverting your attention elsewhere."

Collin scoffed. "You're welcome to try," he said, smiling and placing his right hand over the pocket. A small draft of wind, from the chimney no doubt, blew his fringe of brown hair gently into his eyes.

Ivy hesitated for a moment. The room was spinning again, but not because of vertigo. Maybe she'd been wrong to try this game. But then Collin had the audacity to smirk and arch an eyebrow. As if he'd already judged the task impossible. She'd show him.

Ivy wrapped her arms around his neck and pulled him close until she kissed his lips. She'd wagered he'd be surprised enough to drop his hand from the pocket that held the watch, but Ivy was not prepared for the enthusiasm of Collin's participation. His hands moved to Ivy's waist, and when her kisses did not stop, he wrapped both of his arms tightly around her.

"You kiss me like you've been holding your breath for the last three weeks," Ivy said against his lips.

Collin did not stop kissing her. And with his hands splayed across her back, Ivy easily fished her watch out of his breast pocket.

She pulled away. "See? Misdirection."

"Explain it to me again." Collin's hands tarried on her neck. They were so warm now, so solid, but they quickly fell to his sides when she shrugged out of his embrace.

"Time's up." Ivy slid her thumb against the watch face. "And I have to send out petitions now for more steel." She took a seat at her desk and prepared to write another request. "In the meantime, dismantle anything of value in the rooms my father remodeled. No need to touch what isn't yet broken. Not just yet, anyway." She glanced up at Collin. His hair was rumpled. His lips slightly swollen. Gracious, he looked as if he'd just lost a fight.

Ivy smiled. That was more like it. "You're dismissed, Major."

CHAPTER EIGHTEEN

Nine days—including two successful, if exhausting, trips targeting converted mills—later, Collin found himself alone with Ivy in the foundry.

Electric light flattered Ivy. The incandescent bulb that hung above the workbench lit her sharp features with an added warmth that suited. Not just suited. Aided. Ivy looked thinner and paler by the day. But in the light of this lone bulb, Collin could nearly forget that stab of worry.

And he could remember. He could remember misdirection. More important, he could remember how right it had felt to hold her. How she'd fit against him in a way that had made him sure that his arms were made for the sole purpose of holding her. Comforting her. Loving her. When she wanted. If she wanted. Mars, he hoped she wanted.

The princess sat hunched over a box of gears at the workbench. Her glasses perched on her nose. Grease covered her fingers. A rough cotton apron protected her tie, blouse, and tweed skirts.

"Good evening, Major."

"Good evening, Princess. Matt said you wanted to talk." Collin shouldn't have felt uneasy. He shouldn't have felt like he was thirteen and Gran was about to lay into him for quitting the hatter's shop. "What are you doing tinkering in the foundry at this hour?"

"This is the only hour I have to try and catch up on everyone's progress."

"Meaning?"

She ran her fingers across the gears in front of her. "This is the only time I get to play."

"Play?"

"Yes, play. I don't get to chase actors or help birth kittens. I don't get to sit all day at the organ and have music spill out of my fingers. I don't get to stand around in the kitchen and play chess. I get to watch my sisters do all these things, while I try to keep a step ahead of disaster." Ivy pulled out a gear and stared at it. "But I can never keep up."

"This is fun for you? All those tiny little gears."

"You mean..." Ivy stooped to peer closely at a cog. "All these marvelous little gears? That fit so"—Ivy jiggled a gear—"precisely and beautifully."

Collin's mouth twitched upward.

"If I didn't have to keep after Sophia with her sums, or stay on top of all those ghastly letters about the inquiry, manage a war effort, or badger Papa..." Ivy adjusted a screw, but her finger slipped, and she swore. "You wouldn't be able to pry me away from these marvelous machines."

"You broke this one."

"Well, you distracted me. So you broke it."

"And it looks like you pierced your hand." He gently grasped her fingers in his own, retying the bandage she'd hastily wrapped around her palm.

"Small hands. Stubby fingers. The kind that can't even manage a single-octave spread. So Trina tells me. She got Mama's long fingers. And she got all the time she needed to play at her piano and then her organ. Papa built her one...after I told him to do it." Ivy looked at him past her spectacles. "I need my hand back now."

Collin nearly kissed it before he withdrew.

Ivy smiled wickedly. "My fingers too dirty for you, Major?"

"I don't want to impede your progress."

Ivy closed the lid of the gearbox. She pushed herself away and moved to examine the crawler track. She smiled as she touched the studded belt. "The prototype seems to be coming along."

"It was a brilliant idea."

"I am a brilliant woman. And one day, when the war is over, when Papa has an heir—"

Collin saw it then. Her dogged devotion to the war, the inquiry, her obtuse buffoon of a father was also ambition. She wanted to be sovereign. She wanted to be her father's heir and was shouldering the work of an entire government to prove herself fit for the task.

"—you'll know it outright. Without having to come guess at it with just a single incandescent bulb casting shadows. Now, then. You have something on your mind, Major. Out with it."

"Misdirection."

Ivy inhaled and removed her glasses before rubbing the bridge of her nose with the knuckle of her thumb. "You're asking for another demonstration?"

"No." Collin blushed but recovered. "Although I wouldn't mind."

Ivy rolled her eyes. "Your plan for your next Olcceart holiday was not on my desk. Jade wants you to bomb three more factories this week. Although, after receiving this letter, I'm not sure if that is wise."

Collin glanced at the letter she held out to him. The incandescent bulb flickered above them. He had to remain calm, even though his muscles tensed, and his mind raced. It was more important to know her response to it than anything else. "What is it?"

"A complaint from a poorhouse in Durbronach. It's the sort of thing that would have stopped with the local burgess, but I asked to be notified of any and all items of interest where the poorhouses of Durbronach and the surrounding parishes are concerned."

Sweat prickled at Collin's collar, but his smile was easy. "Why?"

"For fun."

"You have odd hobbies."

"The letter details the mysterious disappearance of an elderly woman whose bill was disastrously overdrawn."

"Interesting, but what does this have to do with me?"

"She was a fortune-teller. They know this because she kept an old deck of cards with her always. Made a few coins with them." Ivy looked Collin in the eye. It was the kind of stare that made him want to hide under the table. "Do you know what I find most infuriating about my life?"

"The lack of free time?"

"The lies. The constant stream of lies. They make my job harder. They are what rob me of my free time. I did not make this clear from the start of our arrangement, so allow me to do so now. I will not tolerate any more lies from you, Collin. You have one last chance to tell me the truth."

Collin's heart beat faster. His pulse blared a warning in his ears. "The truth is complicated." Made all the more so by how he burned to hold her again.

"And so rarely entrusted into my care." Ivy's voice nearly shook. "Until it is too late, and there is no other choice."

"I found Gran a new home." Collin rubbed the back of his neck. He kicked a scrap of wood with his boot. "No one wants to send their only living family member to a poorhouse. It was all we could afford—"

"Your wages were low, but they weren't a disaster."

"No one else would take a citizen of Olcceart."

The incandescent light flickered again. Ivy was very still. "I'm listening."

"Gran is fey. I mean... She might be. She's a fortune-teller. She has no magic that I've ever seen, but it doesn't matter. She had clients on both sides of the river in Thuaidh Fuar. I was likewise apprenticed to masters in both the Olcceart and Amadanri."

Ivy's brow furrowed. "You are a citizen of Olcceart?"

"I'm nothing!" Collin shouted. "I'm the son of a couple of gypsies who was born in a wagon. I lived in Amadanri and crossed the river to work in Olcceart, then returned back to Amadanri to fall asleep in Gran's shop, before she sent me off to the next mad hatter she found who could teach me something. It didn't matter to her if he was Amadanrian or a citizen of Olcceart. Life is not so neatly demarcated on the margins of countries as you'd like to think."

"You had masters in both Olcceart and Amadanri?"

"Many." Collin ruffled his hair. "Risks are involved with volatile chemicals. People poison and blow themselves up all the time. I couldn't afford to be choosy."

Ivy stared at the gears in front of her. "You speak with no accent. How?"

"Schoolboys are excellent tutors. And a face covered in bruises is excellent incentive to learn."

Ivy picked some sketches up from the table to examine them before slamming them back down. "You could have told me the truth. I would have understood."

"There's more." Collin winced. So much more. "You were right—that morning when we walked to Olivia's—about the rumors. Anyone with even the suspicion of fey blood was..." The ringing started in Collin's ears. The screams of panic. Along with the cold metallic smell of blood. Sticky on his fingers. Dried on his wrists. "You were right. It made our choice easy. We couldn't find refuge for Gran near Thuaidh Fuar. On both sides of the river, everyone knew who she was. Tension was running high. I tried changing our names. It was no use. We exhausted our savings getting Gran a new set of papers. Durbronach was big enough and far enough away to disappear. We looked for rooms, but Gran's papers were not all we were promised. The proprietor of the poorhouse told us he didn't care—for an exorbitant price. Mr. Wesley was only too kind to raise his fees once I was enlisted and sending a portion of my wage. He continued to raise his prices and threatened to take Gran's forged documents to the authorities unless I came up with the money."

Collin's eyes lingered on Ivy's lips. He knew what they felt like. How they tasted. At least he'd always have those memories. "I needed more funds. I was a terrible medic. I couldn't stand the sight of blood. I put in for a transfer. I made it abundantly clear that I was willing to go wherever the pay was best, which correlated to where the risk was greatest. My knowledge of chemical combustion proved useful. I worked my way up, and as soon as I did, Mr. Wesley dug deeper into my wages. It was untenable. So I joined the Olcceart army."

"You did what?"

"I mixed explosives for both sides of the same damn war."

"That's impossible!" Ivy shouted.

"It would have been—without help. Saving a man's life makes him loyal in ways conscripted service cannot."

"Tim." Ivy groaned. "He's not really mute. He never learned the king's tongue?"

"He learned. He just can't shake his Olcceart accent."

"Eric too?"

"Yes."

"And what about Matthew?"

Collin's stomach clenched. "Not Matthew. Although, you should probably have a conversation with his wife to put your fears to rest."

"Dammit, I forgot he married. She'll have to be summoned and questioned with the rest of the men."

Oh no. "You still haven't congratulated the happy couple?" Collin's words were tight in his throat.

Ivy pushed away from the table. "I've been too busy untangling your lies."

All right, he was going to hang for that too. Might as well get it over with.

Ivy didn't give Collin a chance. "You were a captain in the royal army." Her fingers coiled into fists on her hips. "Who were you for Olcceart?"

"Brigadier Colonel Horatio. I advanced faster in Olcceart... Less red tape."

Grease was smeared across Ivy's cheek, and her skin looked sticky with sweat. "Major, I reviewed your file and all your known aliases—"

"My Amadanri aliases. I'm sure my file would be equally fat if Olcceart were as interested in paperwork as you are."

"No one could pull off being a commanding officer on both sides of the war. How would you cross enemy lines? The commanding officers only ever meet if there is a cease-fire."

There it was. The pieces of his past were starting to form a complete picture that was hardly distinguished.

"The cease-fire was negotiated and the armory was destroyed because I was acting as both Captain Collin Dobhareach and Brigadier Colonel Horatio. There were frequent cease-fires called on both sides for various reasons that were never reported. Very little fighting happened on the north countryside. And even then, those trees and trenches made warfare predictable at best."

"You swore allegiance to us."

"And then I swore allegiance to you, Ivy." And he would remain loyal to her for the rest of his miserable life, which could be shortened considerably now that she knew the truth.

Ivy groaned, sinking back down to the bench. "I risked everything on a fraud."

Collin would pretend that didn't hurt. He pulled a piece of paper from his breast pocket. "A fraud with the combined knowledge of every chemist on both sides of the war—well, at least north of the Shale Mountains."

Ivy held her head in her hands. "Shut up."

"You're going to want to see what I made." He held the vellum-like paper up to the light. "Watch the paper." A corner ignited, and the paper disappeared with a single light green flame. "Eric dubbed it flash paper. It combusts into invisible gases, seeming to disappear without a trace."

"How did you do it?"

"I washed paper in acids until I made nitrocellulose."

Ivy slammed a hand on the table, clearly not amused. "How did you play both sides?"

Collin toyed with a stray gear. "We are all of us different people for different audiences. While I am a former prisoner of Amadanri for refusing to execute a pair of farmhands, I am also a courageous commanding officer of Olcceart who is MIA, possibly a prisoner of war."

"But who do you belong to? Who are you loyal to? Who can trust you?"

"You!" Wasn't it obvious? "You want this war to end peacefully. You see the economic and civil necessity of a peaceful treaty. You are willing to do what it takes to garner results. And you have enormous respect for life. Even if you are cavalier with your...charms."

Ivy buried her face in her palms. "It was one kiss, Major. And it most assuredly was the last. What's keeping you from defecting to Olcceart?"

"Have you forgotten about my Gran and what they wanted to do to her?" There had to be more kisses! Their kiss had been too much fun to stop with one. Soft and hard. Reckless and determined. "Not everyone is bloodthirsty. Some people just want to live quiet lives and watch their grandchildren grow up. There are good people on both sides of this conflict." Collin picked up a screw and fit it back into the box that Ivy had disassembled.

"There are bad people too." Ivy let out a noisy sigh before rising. "Major, you've ruined my fun for the evening."

"I'm sorry, Princess."

Ivy rubbed a hand across her eyes. "And my polygraph is at home. Exactly when I could've used a reason to tie you up."

Collin straightened and prepared to retreat from the she-devil. That's what she looked like—fury personified. And who would have guessed that fury could be so strong and so beautiful?

"Have a seat, Major." Ivy grabbed his wrist, and her fingernails bit into his arm. "We have some history to discuss."

"History?"

"What else haven't you been telling me?" Ivy's fingers pushed deeper.

Two other very important facts. Neither of which Collin was prepared to share tonight. He winced. "Are you taking my pulse or torturing me?"

"Both."

"Pain makes the heart beat faster."

"So does lying."

What could Collin say? He *had* lied. "I'm sorry."

"Are you a spy?"

"No! I was upfront about my intentions. I needed money to arrange for a quiet life for Gran in the country. I found opportunities to earn two incomes for the same day's work. I took them."

"How can I trust you?"

"I told you the truth." She pressed her nails deeper into Collin's wrist until he yelped. "I just didn't tell you all of it when we first met."

"Have you been selling our secretes to the enemy?"

"I'm on your side, Ivy. The Olcceart factories I've bombed are proof that I'm on your side."

"You could be responsible for similar feats against Amadanri. You're clever, Major, but I'll find you out."

"I'm loyal to you. I have always said so." And he always would be.

"I don't trust you, Major. But I don't have the luxury of ignoring you. If you are a double agent, I have to uncover whatever it is you're plotting. And if you are who you say you are, then I still need your help winning the war." Her grip slackened as she fished her watch out of her pocket. "Is there anything else you'd like to share about your past?"

Collin swallowed. He couldn't breathe a word. If she found out now, there would be no hope. He had to earn back her trust. He had to win the war for her. And then, if he was lucky, she would understand. Fretting about that would gain him nothing, and what he wanted more than anything right now was to make her smile at him again. "Are you inviting me to lay bare my soul?"

Ivy groaned. She checked his pulse again against her watch. "Your pulse is erratic."

"You are holding my hand and looking very pretty. The grease smeared across your nose is quite becoming."

She gave Collin a look that he knew from his years spent with Gran preceded a good slap. "You're not leaving my side for the next forty-eight hours."

Collin's momentary elation hedged quickly into frustration. "You think I'm going to try to desert you?"

"Or alert your Olcceart contacts, yes. Now, is there something you'd like to tell me before we retire? Do you talk in your sleep? Maybe sleepwalk? You have to leave a window open? Pen's that way, always a window. Trina is the one who forgets to bank the fire. Mina insists on good-night kisses."

He curled his fingers around Ivy's soft wrist. "I'm more particular than Mina in that respect."

"You can wipe that smile right off your face, Major. I don't kiss spies."

"I'm not a spy!"

"We'll see about that." Ivy grabbed his hand from her wrist and pulled him up the stairs. Collin had imagined holding hands in a different context.

"Ivy, this may not be the best plan. How will it look if we are found together tomorrow morning?"

Ivy turned on Collin with an energy that had him pressed against the wall.

"I don't care what it looks like. There is a war, and you have just told me you've played both sides. I am not letting you out of my sight until I know exactly who you are and what you hope to gain." She lifted her chin to stare into Collin's eyes. Mars, she was terrifying—

and so pretty. She had Collin all but shaking. "I know the idea is far from your natural inclination, but would you like to volunteer any information that will make this night more bearable?"

He swallowed. "I have to read myself to sleep."

"Fine."

"And the piano teacher that Trina hired works for me."

"Major Collin!"

"I needed ears in the palace, and Phillip is a stand-up fellow. I'd trust him with any of my sisters." Not that he had any.

"But you trusted him with mine."

"Yes...I do."

Ivy pushed him into the warm, empty kitchen of the manor house. "I will need to see all the letters that he's sent you."

"Burned, I'm afraid. But I can recite them. I have quite a good memory for these things. Where are we going?" He laid a very gentle hand on Ivy's shoulder, but she swatted it off. "Look, Ivy, I'm sorry. But I am the same man that you know me to be. Nothing has changed." Except she was marching out of the kitchen, tugging him behind her. "Where are we going?"

"To your room. I need to search it."

"What?" Collin's heart began beating fast.

"What's the harm if I can trust you?"

Collin's mind lighted on the stolen sketch and the correspondence he had foolishly kept. All screaming signs to an intelligence that was becoming more obvious by the day. Dangerous in its own right, but Collin had told himself the most obvious of facts were just the sort that remained invisible in plain sight.

"Of course. But we will be heard, if not seen. I don't wish to compromise your—"

"My good name will not be impugned by searching the barracks tonight."

"All-all of them?" Oh no.

Ivy marched to the east wing of the lake house. She stomped her boots so sharply down the hall that it wasn't long before doors started to open.

Monty's was the first.

Ivy tore off her grease-smeared apron and tossed it at Collin. "Ah, Montgomery, I'm searching the barracks tonight. Please stand at your doors. Everyone, at the ready. We'll start with the major's room."

Matthew appeared. "What is this, now?"

"Mr. Matthew. You were born in Ionaltradh, yes?"

"Aye."

"Ever travel to Olcceart?" Ivy sounded frantic, giddy.

"Never. My cows wouldn't stand for it."

"Good. Make sure none of these men returns to his room. I'll be listening for their doors. To your room, Major."

Collin spoke quietly, urgently. "Ivy, you should know something."

Onyx eyes framed by thick lashes and framed by the even thicker emotion of frustration fixed on his own. "Did you forget to hide your Olcceart uniform?"

Ivy bustled past Collin and into his bedroom. It had the best view of the east wing. From his bed, he could clearly see through the window to the approach to the house and the windows that belonged to Ivy and her sisters. He'd chosen this room because he needed to keep an eye on Ivy—and wanted to keep an eye on her.

Collin willed his voice not to betray him. "I borrowed some of Pen's sketches."

"Meaning you stole them. I'm surprised by how tidy you keep your room."

"The army, ma'am."

Ivy flinched. She searched through his trunk. The clever woman felt past the seams. "Secret compartments?"

"I've nothing to hide from you." What was the point in trying to hide anything that she'd soon discover?

"Nothing to hide except that stack of papers behind you. Your eyes wandered to it the moment we entered. You have tried to slide them out of sight as I've searched your room."

"You're going about your search all wrong." Her gaze should have been fixed on him this entire time, not on his quarters.

"Hand me the papers, Collin."

The pleasure of hearing his name unattached to his rank, on her lips shocked him into quick obedience. Collin watched as Ivy riffled through the messages, the sketch—the continuous-line portrait—and other doodles Pen had completed of their fearless leader.

"It would appear that you are gathering intelligence on me. Are you trying to forge my penmanship? Or send directives for a body double? Or..." Ivy stopped at the ribbon she'd left on the library desk when he and Eric had just arrived. The ribbon Collin had slipped into his pocket before he'd left on his next mission. He'd taken it for luck, but he'd kept it for an entirely different reason.

"What's the meaning of this?"

Mars, her eyes were nearly swimming with tears.

Collin's flushed. The truth would not be palatable. Especially now.

A door creaked in the hall. Ivy threw the papers and ribbon into the fire and, with clenched fists, entered the hall.

"Sophia!" She nearly screamed her sister's name.

A guilty-looking and flushed Sophia stood in the hall. "Eric was just teaching me how to play poker."

Eric stepped out beside her. "She's quite good at it. Lost my shirt the last night we played."

Ivy's cold stare froze Eric's grin.

Eric stared at the floor and mumbled his apologies. Sophia stepped beside him and laced her fingers around his hand.

"Sophia, go to your room," Ivy said.

Sophia gave an imploring look to her sister, and when that did not work, she stamped her foot, crossed her arms, and stalked down the hall.

Ivy turned on Collin. "Did you know about this, Major?"

"The poker game? Or the lost shirt?"

A stifled snort was quickly followed by Tim burying his face in his hands.

Ivy squared her shoulders. "Pen! Out! Now!" Pen, in one of Tim's shirts, stepped into the hall, shaking with silent laughter.

"What do you two have to say for yourselves?" Ivy demanded.

Pen struggled to keep a straight face. "Well, Tim has nothing—" She broke off and covered her mouth. Tim grinned and folded his arms across his undershirt.

Ivy stormed up to him. "I will cut out your tongue if you do not say something this instant, Timothy. You can blame Collin later. Apologize to my sister."

Tim swallowed. When he spoke, his words were heavy with a thick Olcceart accent. "Pen, I'm so sorry. I'm so very sorry."

Pen stood there, stunned, before she started screaming, "You nitwit! We could have been talking all this time? We'd be light-years ahead by now!"

"I'm sorry. I'm so sorry. Collin told me I couldn't because of my accent."

"And you listened to him!" Pen roared.

"Your room. Now," Ivy said.

Pen thrust her chin out, and before Ivy could stop her, she stripped off Tim's shirt, tossed it at him, and marched down the hall in her knickers.

Ivy grabbed Collin by the sleeve and pushed him back into his bedroom, kicking the door shut. "How could you let this happen? I trusted you! You were supposed to be in charge of your men. And now I come to find two of my three sisters are consorting with them."

Collin winced. "You haven't inspected Matt's room yet."

"What have you to say for yourself?"

"They're all adults. By capital standards, anyone who is seventeen is an adult, yes? They were working. They were team-building. They were letting off steam, having some fun—"

She was pacing, fuming and pacing. "You did this to gain leverage on me. You were going to use this against me."

"Ivy, you are sounding paranoid."

"How am I supposed to sound when the man I hand-picked to win the war turns out to be a spy for the other side?"

"I am not a spy!"

"Then why were you collecting those pictures of me? The evidence—"

"Because you're beautiful!" Collin shouted. "And you're smart and clever. And I never see you for more than two minutes at a time. And as soon as things get interesting, you run away. I was trying to understand why." He'd shared only half the truth. What he was really trying to do was capture the essence of Ivy until the memory of standing before her was as powerful as the reality. Until it was as strong as her gaze. Until it was more than enough to hold on to. Because that might be all he'd ever have.

"All this time, all you had to do was tell the truth. Now you'll not be rid of me. Get your pillow. I'll not have you using one of mine."

Ivy opened the door to a rather guilty-looking group in the hall.

"Did you all just hear that?"

"Everything apart from the pillow, ma'am," Eric said.

"No, we heard that too." Jade poked her head out of Matt's door. "Matthew and I are married, by the way. So it's okay that I stay in his room."

"Impossible." Ivy frantically surveyed the sheepish occupants of the hall.

"They've been married these last two weeks," Collin said quietly.

Ivy stood there, blinking back tears. "Does everyone know?"

"I didn't," Eric said from across the hall. "Congratulations, Matt. Wedded bliss suits you."

"I forbid this union," Ivy said.

Jade flounced. "Too bad. Papa doesn't."

"Papa? You wrote to him. Jade! You of all people! You're not given to flights of fancy. You're the sober, logical sister. And here you've married the first willing man you met without any thought—"

"Good night, Ivy." Jade closed the door in her sister's face.

"It's the quiet ones we have to worry about most," Collin said.

"You are not part of this discussion, Major."

"I do enjoy when you call me Collin. Particularly after hours."

"You are in high water," Ivy hissed.

"I've been in worse." The major followed Ivy across the house and into her room. "Are we sleeping in your room tonight, then?"

"Of course not. You and I will sleep in the library, after you tell me one more time why I should not expose you for the spy you are and send you back to your favorite cell in the palace prison."

"Well, for one thing, your papa will be wondering what I'm doing there when he returns from the Summer Palace tomorrow."

"How do you know that?"

Her room was a disaster, and while Collin would have expected it to smell like her perfume, it smelled remarkably of peppermint and cocoa. "Adelaide's fatigue and lack of a pregnancy will make him extra peevish."

"You assume."

"I don't need to. If Adelaide wasn't barren, she'd have at least two babies by now. You'll need all the help you can get once the rest of your sisters arrive."

"My sisters are safe and sound at home." Ivy kicked off her shoes and felt under her bed, looking for her slippers no doubt.

Collin knelt to assist her. "Yes, and your papa is going to want them all gone in a matter of hours. They are a constant reminder of Adelaide's failure to produce offspring when so many, *many* women have succeeded in that effort." He handed Ivy her slippers. "Your father is not a brilliant statesman, but he is a loving husband. Or so it seems in the case of Adelaide."

"And you know this because of the piano teacher?"

Collin flushed and tried to look away as Ivy unpinned her piles of curls. "Did I mention that the piano teacher is actually an organist?"

Ivy froze, clutching a pin she'd removed from her hair. "My sister loves the organ more than she loves me most days. If I were to lose her, it would be to someone who shares her...passion. You did this on purpose. You're trying to take her from me."

"No, Ivy. I wanted to make sure your sisters are safe, and I needed someone I can trust."

"Describe this organ enthusiast." Ivy struggled with a row of buttons at her neck, obviously agitated. Angry. The correct word was *angry*. "Hopefully arthritic. Grizzled?"

"Young. Early twenties. Dedicated. Trustworthy. Thin. Rather an obnoxious curl. He's a composer."

"Oh, for pity's sake. Must I struggle all night with this damn button, or are you going to help me?"

She'd managed the buttons above and below but couldn't reach one in the middle of her back, and as such, much of her smooth, lovely skin was visible.

Collin obliged, and even though his eyes were fixed on the button and not on the soft skin above and below, his fingers slipped.

Ivy gasped. "I don't know what you do to keep your hands so frigid."

"My apologies, Princess." Collin stood staring at the space where Ivy had just stood. He did not dare look up.

"What has your organist told you?"

"Much of what Trina has told him about your father and the nature of your family."

"I feel exposed."

"Shall I turn around?"

"Oh, don't be stupid. I wasn't talking about undone buttons. I'm talking about how you apparently seem to know all about our nasty little family secrets."

"There is nothing nasty about them."

"A father who is a serial womanizer but has at long last lost his heart to a young opera star? Sisters who are so starved for attention that they throw themselves on the first obliging gentleman they find?"

"Phillip has written at length about his love for the organ and how his passion for the instrument pales compared to your sister's. His interest is not superficial, and it certainly isn't obliging. 'Doting worship of pupil for a master' is the term Phillip used. Do you suppose all musicians are so free with their feelings? I almost blush when he—" Collin looked up to see Ivy belting a dressing gown around striped silk pajamas. "You stole my pajamas!"

"Not on purpose. I was searching your trunk for kieselguhr the other day and forgot to put them back."

"Thief."

"I borrowed them. But truth be told, they are so comfortable I will never give them up."

"At least give me the bottoms."

"So you can then ask for the top? No."

"My Gran... She gave those to me."

"Nice try. Your Gran was a practical woman. She'd have let you sleep in your trousers and coat before splurging on these."

"While you're sleeping in my pajamas, what will I wear? Silk sleepwear is the only thing that sets us apart from the animals."

"I suggest you find another pair. I'm not changing."

Something glowed brighter inside Collin. "You like them because they're mine."

"I enjoy them in spite of their previous owner. Come, Major, there is much to discuss." Ivy grabbed the pillow and blanket from her bed and stormed downstairs to the library, where she kipped on the chaise while Collin answered—but mostly evaded—her questions. When the mantel clock chimed three times, and the major was at last feeling the pull of sleep, he rose, banked the fire, pulled Ivy's blanket to her chin, and tucked it around her. He fell asleep in the armchair, watching the princess who happened to be wearing his striped pajamas.

CHAPTER NINETEEN

Carriage wheels. Not discreet ones. Noisy, ostentatious ones. And so many trunks. Were they all exiled from home until Adelaide had a baby?

But Adelaide would not have a baby. The major was right in this respect. There would be no easy solutions to the succession crisis. Papa had to see this by now.

Ivy's stomach grumbled. It demanded more than just cocoa. She rummaged around in the kitchen until she found the tin of marzipan. She grabbed it and the crock of biscuits. Needs must.

When Ivy returned to the library with her spoils, the major was still sleeping. Ivy padded over to him, the plush wool rug cold even under her slippered feet.

Collin had a nice face. And he was meticulous about it, always so neatly shaven. Ivy felt a twinge of guilt thinking about how he must have suffered in the old abbey's crypt. Since she had entrusted him to Olivia, he'd been the picture of tidiness, everything about his person methodical and fastidious. And gracious, he was obsessed with keeping his feet dry.

But here he was now, rumpled and slightly snoring in a chair.

The whiskers that had poked so marvelously when she'd kissed him could use a trim.

Ivy's fingers pulled and pulsed to touch Collin. He was real. And even though he had fought on both sides of the war and grown up in Olcceart and Amadanri alike, she did not feel that she was wrong about him. She liked his thirst for information. She liked his logical reasoning. She admired his moral compass, although she wished he'd have been more forthright about his past. Still, she understood his reasoning for keeping it quiet.

She admired the lean muscle of his forearms, before edging away to her desk.

It was possible that she was being duped. It was possible that he was a double agent. But then what of his men? Her sisters had placed their trust in them. That counted for something.

Ivy opened the top drawer of her desk and quietly riffled through the papers until she found the folder she'd kept on Collin. She flipped past his correspondence she'd saved to his polygraph tracings from the abbey's crypt. Her fingers ran across the reading until they landed at the end where Collin had sworn his allegiance to her. No twitchy eye movements. No erratic breathing. Steady pulse. Calm. Honest.

Ivy's shoulders relaxed. She could trust him. She could trust her heart when it glowed brighter near him. Ivy knew how to handle men who skirted the facts. Heaven knew she had enough experience. She could handle Collin now. It was not an ideal situation, but she'd keep him close and fortify herself with all the caution and cocoa she could spare.

She shoved the folder back in her desk drawer, and sauntered over to the man who'd kept her letters and her ribbon. Ivy opened the crock and munched a biscuit. And yes, she did gently comb her fingers through his hair.

Collin grunted. "You'll get crumbs on me."

"You would be the man to complain about it."

He opened an eye. "Your sisters are coming."

"They're already here." Ivy continued to muss his hair.

"That feels nice."

"Your hair is"—disheveled, prematurely streaked with gray, over-long—"soft."

Collin opened both eyes. Ivy stared down at her robe and striped pajamas. A blush blossomed on her cheeks. As soft as the pajamas were, she'd kept them because they were Collin's.

"Your godmother liked me."

"What?" Ivy tossed a quizzical, and what she hoped was coy, smile to Collin.

He stretched his back into an arch. "I've tried to think of some-thing to prove to you that I'm not an Olcceart spy." He shrugged. "I couldn't come up with anything more convincing than Olivia liked me. She told you as much."

Ivy sauntered away from the major. Fool hadn't even returned her smile. She nibbled a piece of the marzipan. She needed the sugar to deal with her sisters.

"She must have," Collin insisted.

Olivia had written to Ivy. She'd told her, in terms that Olivia had thought were veiled but had been as transparent as Papa's temper, that she liked Collin. *He's a fine man and a good one. If I were young, I would not let him out of my sight.*

"Auntie fancies herself a matchmaker." Ivy nearly snorted. "She'd like any gentleman I brought round."

"Then I was the first?"

Ivy blushed. The second time this morning. Dammit.

"The first what?" Rachel asked from the doorway.

The wrinkle between Ivy's onyx eyes smoothed away. A worn smile replaced it. With her back turned to the arriving party, only Collin caught the detail. Ivy was exhausted. She needed a good night's sleep in her own bed and a stretch of days where she could nap on the library sofa, dance late into the night, read for pleasure. Ivy needed days that were filled with moments to enjoy herself, think her own thoughts, and do what she wanted. And Collin wanted to be part of those days...and nights.

Ivy hugged her sister.

"Ives, what are you wearing?" Rachel demanded.

Ivy smoothed her hands down the silk. "Pajamas."

Collin's pajamas.

"Do you like them?" Ivy asked.

"But did you sleep in them? And for goodness' sake, why are the hems puddling around your heels? You will wear holes right through that silk."

Collin's thoughts exactly. He'd need those back before Ivy ruined them. She could keep the top. It was more than long enough on her frame to suit. He rose. "Good morning."

"Major Collin!" Daphne and Angelica both said as they burst into the library, quick to preen in front of him. They held out their hands, and Collin bowed over them. He caught Ivy's eye and winked as he did so. "It's been an eternity," Daphne said.

"Four weeks is not an eternity," Ivy said.

"It felt like an eternity," Rachel said, sinking onto the chaise, "what with you ordering Trina to confine us all to the palace grounds."

Harriet rose on tiptoe to whisper in Ivy's ear, "Rachel's been in a mood. And she doesn't travel well."

"Major, have you and Ivy had a slumber party in the library?" Beatrice asked.

Harriet swatted Beatrice on the shoulder.

Ivy grabbed a stack of papers from her desk.

"I fell asleep plotting my latest mission," he said. "I must have nodded off in here."

"No one woke you?" Daphne patted Collin's cheek while Angelica crooked an arm around his elbow.

"The poor dear!" she crooned.

Collin tried to disentangle himself from the sisters, but it was difficult work. There were many of them, and all seemed intent on taking his side over Ivy's. That wouldn't endear him to her, and he was already in trouble as it was. Big, nasty, snarly trouble. "No, no. I nodded off at three ante meridiem. I'm usually the last to fall asleep. Ivy..." Collin fumbled. "Her Royal Highness was just waking me."

All true. But with incriminating information withheld. Except he should not have stumbled on her name.

"The major has proved very troublesome as of late," Ivy said. "Lapsing into informality. Falling asleep in the library. It is a fine thing that you've come to set this house to rights. Where are Mina and Gwen?"

"The stables." Daphne helped herself to a biscuit. "Mina heard there's an expecting mare."

"And Gwen saw a handsome stable hand."

"We have no stable hands." Ivy kissed Daphne in greeting.

"Probably Eric." Collin was about to offer an introduction, but the words dried up in his mouth. Mars, he was an idiot. Ivy needn't look at him like that, her eyes like flint striking steel. Luckily, the igniting spark was smothered when she saw her closest sister.

"Trina!"

So this was what the princess looked like when she was at ease. This was what she looked like stripped of her armor.

Ivy ran to embrace her sister and best friend. She clung to Trina, and any other woman might have started to cry. But not Ivy. Collin moved closer, hoping to capture her whispered words. Trina nodded, before mumbling, "I'm sure."

And just like that, Ivy's armor was back in place.

"Girls, the west wing is ours," Trina said. "There are three unclaimed bedrooms, but I'm afraid most of us will have to share."

"That's not going to be me," Daphne said. The youngest sisters raced out of the room. Ivy arched a single brow in Collin's direction before she left to chaperone. Those dark, lovely eyes had a way of making him forget everything important—rank, station, lies. But as much as Collin wanted to hope and dream about what-ifs, he could not shake the shadows of that unforgiving truth. He'd lied to Ivy. He was still lying to Ivy.

"Major Collin." Trina unfastened her coat. "Phillip sends his regards but regrets that he cannot leave the capital. His papers are apparently amiss."

Collin poked the fire before adding a log. "That's a pretty threadbare cover."

"I should say so. And wouldn't it have been so much better for all of us if you had told us upfront who Phillip was and what he was about?"

Never answer a question if you don't have to. Collin twitched and rubbed his middle. Gran's cane had always punctuated her maxims. "Would you have permitted him to enter the palace otherwise?"

"You underestimate my enthusiasm for the organ. Phillip is a talented player and an even more gifted composer. He is, however, a clumsy and poor spy."

"Yet, his information was accurate, insightful, consistent, and punctual."

Trina unpinned her hat. "Was it his information or mine?"

Collin winced. He could feel Gran's reproach for such an obvious oversight. He should have obtained a sample of Phillip's handwriting at the very least before he'd departed.

"Major, you might be surprised to know this, but you and I are on the same side."

"I wish you could convince your sister of that. This war has her near paranoid—"

"I'm not talking about the war, Major."

Oh. *Oh!*

Trina ran her finger along the spines of the library books. "Phillip is not the sort of spy one would leave behind if one had political goals. And the objectives that I nettled out of him settled the matter entirely."

"Objectives?" Good. More questions. Always questions.

"I believe your words were, 'Learn all you can of them. Not just information but what you feel, Phillip. You are an artist. You feel. You intuit. I need to see the big picture, particularly where Princess Ivy is concerned.' But you missed the mark entirely." Trina leaned a shoulder against the bookshelf.

"I did?"

"Men, even men like Phillip, cannot fill in the pieces about a woman the way her *sister* can." Trina pulled out a tome, thumbing through the pages, before replacing it. "Ivy was determined to keep us in the dark, but I saw the strain she was under. I tried to offer support, but she is stubborn like Papa." Trina rounded on Collin. "Have you seen her smile?"

Mars. He'd seen it. He'd felt it against his own lips on one singular, miraculous occasion. Collin was too embarrassed to speak.

"Not the forced ones, mind you. Not the ones that make you feel as if she is about to swallow you whole. Her real smile."

Sweet peas. Their fragrance and a bit of that milky petal texture. Clean and cool against his fingertips. A few cold bits of dew on the tops of his hands. Yes. He'd seen Ivy's smile. And his poor, war-rotted brain had pulled these cherished textures to accompany the memory. "I've had the honor."

"It resurfaced after she met you." Trina pulled a few slimmer books out by their spines and considered them. "I went to Olivia's, learned what I could. A godmother's assessment and some correspondence are not much." Trina set the books on an end table. "I hardly know you, but I want to help you. I want to see more of my sister's smiles."

Collin fingered the red oak of the bookshelves. The truth. Just not all of it, or he'd lose everything. He'd already lost a ribbon. It was an artifact, yes, but it was gone. And the thought of losing even a chance that there could be more than pilfered ribbons, that there could be smiles and sweet peas... "Ivy thinks I am a spy for Olcceart and will betray her by sabotaging her war effort."

"Will you?" Trina asked.

Never! But there was that pang in his stomach, the one Gran had always told him was far less prescient than the thrust of her cane. "I'm not a spy."

"And still you are relegated to the library sofa and constant surveillance." Trina's eyes were kind, her features benevolent. There was no flint in her gaze or calculation in her smile. She could be wise and understanding, because Ivy was willing to be shrewd. "Ivy asked me to keep an eye on you. She worried she was asking too much after my coach ride." Trina ran a hand across the library books, pulling out a thick book that she'd no doubt find time to enjoy. Thanks to Ivy.

Collin looked at his hands. He couldn't tell Ivy the truth. Not now. Maybe not ever. "What am I to do?"

"The only thing you can at this point. Win the war for her."

CHAPTER TWENTY

Ivy stomped the snow from the bottoms of her boots against the door of the stable. "Mina darling, where has Gwen got off to?"

"Is that all the greeting I get? 'Mina, where is Gwen?'" Mina produced a cube of sugar and offered it to the chestnut mare.

"Of course not." Ivy reached her arms around her youngest sister and hugged her tight. "How are you? How was your coach ride? More importantly, how is Kitty and her kittens?"

"Kitty is cross with me. She would not purr when we parted. And her kittens are vexing. They've clawed through the entire bottom cupboard of linens and your silk cushioned chair." Mina offered another cube of sugar to the greedy horse.

Ivy would have to say something to Mina about the sugar crisis, austerity and all that, but right now there were more pressing concerns. "Mina, there is something I must ask—"

"No, I have not seen Papa's assassin. Trina only asked me every day. It's so…" Mina's face pinched into a fret of anger and fear. "Disgusting."

"And today? Did you see anyone that looked even remotely like him on the journey to the lake house?"

"We left at dark!" The chestnut nickered and snorted. The gelding across the way pawed at the hay.

Ivy gently steered Mina away from the unpredictable beasts. "Let's go inside and talk more."

"No!" Mina pulled away and climbed onto the gate of the chestnut's stall. "I want to go skating on the lake." There was the pout, just like Papa's.

There wasn't enough cocoa to last the morning if this was the new tenor of Ivy's days. "Mina dear, I think the ice has melted too thin."

Mina kicked her feet against the stall and folded her arms across her flat chest in a huff. "Have you measured?"

"Not so loud. You're upsetting the horses."

Mina held out her open palm to the mare. "It's not me. It's you. Horses can tell when people are afraid, distrustful, bossy, snooty..."

Ivy pressed her palms to her eyes and tried to breathe. Stables and barns had never been her place of refuge. If she'd been able to tolerate them at all, she would have found a comfortable perch to wait out Mina's diatribe. As it was, a groan escaped her. The walls began to press too close.

"Is it true Jade got married?" Mina asked.

Ivy squinted, kneading the ache in the side of her neck. "I don't know. She wasn't allowed to if she did."

"Why?" Mina scratched the horse's ridiculously long nose. The beast bared her teeth in a ghastly display of appreciation.

Ivy swatted the straw from her skirts. "Because Papa still has no heir. And marriages tend to produce—"

Mina pretended to retch. "Spare me."

"It could all get very complicated very quickly if any of Papa's children were to get married." It's why Ivy had tried to keep her sisters from chasing after young gentlemen. Too much was at stake with the succession unsettled. "Would his new son-in-law be declared his heir in absence of a baby prince?" Heaven forbid.

"Politics." Mina knotted her fingers in the mare's ratty mane and buried her face in it.

"They are inescapable when your father happens to be the monarch." Yet, Mina found refuge with her animals. Trina with her music. Pen with her engineering. Ivy's lips twitched, and a stab of some old ache gripped her. Maybe she had made a mistake. The lines of duty and her own ambition were beyond blurred. But time was running out, and she wouldn't get a second chance at forging a peace. "Let's get you unpacked. I want to hear about these kittens."

Mina shook her head. "I want to go ice skating."

"Mina, I don't think it's safe."

"What's not safe?" Pen asked, popping into the stable. Tim was following dutifully behind her, still looking chastened and hangdog.

"I want to go ice skating," Mina said.

Pen turned to Tim. "How thick does ice need to be to support people?"

Tim brightened. Ivy would wager her last tin of cocoa that this was the first time Pen had spoken to him since last night. "Four inches," he said, his Olcceart accent curling and swirling his words. "But in this case, I'd say five to seven. To be safe."

Pen didn't smile. She sniffed. "Do we have an auger?"

Mina reached into the mare's stall and thrust the tool toward Pen.

"Right, I think we should measure the thickness of the ice this morning. Don't you, Tim?"

Tim's eyes twinkled, but his presumed relief and joy were contained in a considered frown. "We should sharpen some skates first. For luck."

"Yes!" Mina jumped off the stall door. "I packed mine."

"Excellent," Pen said, taking Mina by the hand and pulling Tim by the wrist. "With any luck, we will be skating before lunch."

"There's no time!" Ivy said. "Every hour, every minute wasted is one we can't get back. We need to work on the prototype. We need—"

"You two run along," Pen interrupted. "I need a word with Madame Warden."

Mina snickered but followed Tim.

"Ives..." Pen began.

"I'm not wrong. We have one shot at this, Pen, and the clock is ticking. There'll be plenty of time to ice skate next year once we've won."

"And what *if* we don't?" Pen folded her arms and leaned against the barn door. "Some of us need memories worth fighting for."

Ivy's shouldered tensed. The horses were making her skittish, pawing at the ground and chuffing like that.

"Look, Ivy, the project is on schedule—"

"Barely."

"But it won't be for much longer. Morale is low. Your tirade through the east wing didn't help matters. You can't run us like inmates in a prison." Pen took in a deep breath before tugging up the collar of her coat. "So we're going to skate. We're going to have a good time today and remember what it is we're fighting for."

The ice was plenty thick, and there was ample skating before lunch. As Ivy surveyed the skating party, a nagging exhaustion filled her. Pen might be right about the others, but Ivy would not grant herself the same latitude. She should be working on the war effort. She should be working her way to the bottoms of her piles of correspondence. She should be delicately uncovering how to annul her sister's marriage. Matt would only complicate the succession crisis. And Papa was already too concerned with that issue at the expense of everything else.

When Ivy stepped into the warm kitchen, Trina was at the stove. "Is there really ice on the lake this late in the season?" Trina asked.

"Don't sound too surprised. We had snow two days ago." Precious sugar and citrus were dancing from the pot on the stove. "What are you making?"

Trina smiled widely. "Honeymoon jam."

"Oh, don't encourage her, Trina!" Ivy rummaged in the larder for the cocoa.

"Jade showed me their license."

Ivy slammed the empty chocolate tin on the kitchen block and groaned. "I didn't think she'd know to get one."

"Do you object to the groom?"

"Not at all. Matthew makes a fine cup of chocolate." She rummaged for another tin.

Trina gave Ivy that look.

"She's too young. The union wasn't blessed by Papa. The decision was completely rushed. She hardly gets along with anyone, and now she's married. Or claims to be."

"She says Papa sent his approval," Trina said.

"Before he thought it through." Had Ivy not just argued the same with Mina? "There are too many implications with her marriage and Papa not declaring an heir."

Trina paused, her knife hovering above an orange. "You object because you see Matt as competition for the throne?"

Ivy again felt the pain pulse inside. "That's what you think I've been doing? I've been competing for Papa's crown?"

"Of course not." Trina continued to slice the oranges in smooth, even strokes. The knife clipped against the worn wood block. "It's just..." The *clip, clip* of the knife persisted in the otherwise silent kitchen. "There needn't be a succession crisis."

No, not again.

"There's nothing wrong with ambition, Ivy." Trina wiped her hands on her apron. "We can't stay princesses locked up like fancy cakes forever, and Papa has no interest in any of it anymore." *It* being the massive work of running a government.

"No need to remind me." Ivy had seen the diplomatic boxes piled in Trina's trunk.

"You have to tell him that you are not just willing to lead but want to lead. Not behind the scenes, slaving and strategizing. But ruling. Reigning."

"That's a choice I can't make for Papa."

"It's a choice he would have already made if you were a son."

Ivy took a deep breath, weary of her wound. It wasn't pleasant knowing she was not enough. Knowing she had failed before she'd even inhaled her first breath. She was not the son and heir everyone had hoped for. None of her sisters were, but none of them were interested in the tedious workings of Papa's government the way she was. Why should they be? Ivy was the eldest; the responsibility was hers to shoulder. She'd realized at sixteen, after a disastrous state dinner where Papa had attempted to seduce a visiting duchess by threatening an invasion of her kingdom, that she needed to start learning the vermilion ropes. Sons did not arrive fully grown and ready to lead a kingdom, and Papa's lack of political acumen was troubling. She learned much in the two years before the war, but not enough to prevent it. She could not politic their way out of the war once it started, as Papa had hoped. Papa hoped for quick and quiet fixes. He'd insisted that if there was a fix for the war, Ivy would find it. *Just look through the boxes,* he'd said. Another set of fresh eyes might find what he'd missed. She'd found nothing for so long. Just misery and a hopeless, senseless conflict. Maybe it was too late. Or maybe if she'd been a son, she would have found a solution sooner.

She'd danced around the topic of succession with her father before, when the threat against their boys at the front had not been so all-consuming. "But what if she can't have a baby?" Ivy had asked him. "What if she does, and it is another daughter? You need to think about these things."

Papa had always waved her off. "They will sort themselves out with time."

The last time she had pressed him, he'd asked, "What do you suggest, Ivy? You care so deeply about this. What should I do?"

She should have had the courage then to say it. *Choose me.*

She loved their kingdom. She spent every moment of her life fighting for it, and she would lead it better than her father ever could. And she wanted to. It pricked her pride that she should have to ask for it. It should be obvious. It should be obvious to Papa of all people. He knew better than anyone how indispensable she was.

"I'm not going to beg to be crowned his heir. If my service has meant anything to him, then he should appoint me heir to the throne of his own volition."

The orange marmalade began to splutter in the pot. Trina adjusted the flame to bring the marmalade to a gentle simmer. "Maybe he will after we win the war."

"None of it matters unless we do," Ivy mumbled.

Trina wiped her hands on her apron. "The jam needs to simmer for forty minutes. Will you keep time for me?"

Nice try. "The clock on the sideboard works just fine. Your jam will be ready at half past."

"Who's going to help me can it?"

"Not the woman who has to review two dozen vermilion boxes stuffed with weeks of neglected work." The thought made Ivy itch with anger. Why hadn't Papa directed them to her in the first place? He'd probably forgotten. *Preoccupied* was the favored term. Yet, diction did nothing to staunch the tide of documents.

Ivy bid her sister farewell and turned just in time to collide with Major Collin. He was solid and quick to catch her, righting her course. Not that Ivy needed much assistance, but she understood the importance of seizing opportunities. Collin's hands lingered for a moment at her shoulders. "Steady," he said.

Ivy shrugged them off. Opportunities be damned. She had work to do. The margins were too thin now for any distractions—even handsome, clever ones. "Major?"

Collin cleared his throat. A sheepish Eric appeared on the stairs behind him. "My proposal for my next...'holiday' is on your desk."

"What's that smell?" Eric asked, brushing past Collin and Ivy.

Was the entire house conspiring to leave her alone with Collin? "I told you not to let him out of your sight," Ivy said to Trina.

Trina added another spoonful of sugar to the pot. "The major is harmless. Besides, he has a war to help you win."

Collin pocketed a peppermint from the tin on the counter. "Matthew tells me more snow is expected. I thought to take Eric and leave now."

"Out of the question," Trina said, tasting the jam. "If you leave, we will not have enough dance partners to have any *fun*."

Ivy clenched her fists. "Trina, now is not the time..."

Ivy trailed off. She could have shouted the words, but they would make no difference. Trina took everything in stride. She stirred the jam and raised a heaping spoonful of it to check the consistency. Runny orange syrup twirled and spun back into the pot. "It doesn't matter. We are going to celebrate. There is a fine piano in the south hall and enough handsome young men for us to dance with."

"Are we really going to have a dance?" Angelica asked, bursting in from outside, skates clattering to the floor. Her coat followed on top of them. She quickly sized up the room. Her back arched and her lips curled when she saw Eric. She sashayed toward her target.

"Do you dance, monsieur?" Angelica asked, linking her arm with Eric's.

"This is ridiculous," Ivy mumbled. She grabbed Angelica's coat and skates and hung them on the back of a wooden chair. She shook out a scant half cup of cocoa and banged the pot onto the stove.

"But it will be fun," Trina said. "And you owe me after leaving me by myself with Daphne and Angelica."

Eric tried and failed to disentangle his arm from Ang's grip. Ivy's headache came snarling back. "Major, you may leave this evening. The snow will have stopped by then. And that will give us enough opportunity to strategize. Perhaps Eric might complete a mission of his own while he accompanies you."

"Enlighten me," Collin said.

"Yes, enlighten us." Ang still gripped Eric's elbow.

"Workers rising up in the factories. Destroying the oppressor. Breaking the chains of indentured servitude. The right rhetoric could incite a riot." Ivy flashed a brilliant smile meant to scare Collin away. He remained at her side.

"A revolution." Ang loosened her grip, setting Eric free in practiced reverence. Always a bit terrifying to see a lioness play with her prey.

"Well, there's an idea." Eric's eyes were like those of a caught deer—dazed, open, and unblinking. Ang was very pretty, and she was very cruel, refusing to admit that hearts could break if handled too roughly. Poor Sophia would be crestfallen.

Ivy whisked her cocoa and cream together. "Unrest and revolt in Olcceart would be useful. Go draft a final issue of your *Herald* and inspire a rebellion, Eric. Ask Bea or Daphne to lend a hand. Gwen too. They have a natural gift for stirring up trouble with their words." Sophia might have a fighting chance if Angelica had to compete with them for Eric's attention. Either way, it would give them all something constructive to do while they batted their eyes at one another.

Daphne appeared at the door of the kitchen and sashayed around Eric and the major so expertly it was embarrassing. "What's shakin'?"

"We're having a dance tonight," Ang said, wrinkling her nose and giggling at Eric. "Right after we put our heads together to plot an uprising."

Now Eric was giggling.

Daphne squealed and shimmied. "Fantastic! Ivy, what are you wearing tonight?"

"Daphne." Ivy felt the color rise to her cheeks. She saw how Collin smiled and raised his eyebrows in interest. "We have company."

"How de do, Major. I'll get to you later, Cap'n." Daphne waved to Eric and leaned against the sideboard. "Are you going to wear your black brocade?"

Ivy whisked her cocoa furiously. "I didn't pack my brocade dress."

"I did, but Trina told me I had to make sure you didn't want to wear it before I settled on it. So... Are you going to wear it, even though you are too skinny now to do the neckline any justice?"

Ivy gritted her teeth. "It's all yours."

Daphne jumped up and down with more squeals. "And what are you wearing to our little dance tonight, Major?"

Ivy pulled her spectacles off and studied the major. No coloring. No smugness. All politeness. "My uniform, ma'am."

Daphne wrinkled her nose and then flounced out of the room. Angelica looked wistfully at Eric before she trailed after her sister. If she'd had an invisible leash tied to his neck and tugged, it would have been superfluous. He followed her instantly.

Trina tasted the marmalade and shook her head. "I need a lemon. Ivy darling, watch my marmalade for me. I'll be right back."

Of course. Because she had nothing better to do than mind a pot of jam.

Ivy poured her cocoa into a sturdy mug and seized the wooden spoon. "Marmalade." It was as good as any curse now.

"May I?" Collin asked, grabbing a tasting spoon.

Ivy shook her head. It was honeymoon jam. And although Angelica and Daphne would have no qualms about explaining it to Major Collin, Ivy was not going to fall into that particular trap. Blushes were dangerous. Plus, she was not about to break a family tradition, even if it was for a ridiculous marriage that she would soon have to spend too many hours proving never took place. "No, but you may rinse out my chocolate pot."

Collin extracted the items from the stove, very careful not to accidentally touch her. Why? They were alone.

"Your sister seemed disappointed in my reply about wearing my uniform."

Ivy took another fortifying sip of cocoa. "Uniforms have spoiled the majority of their youthful frivolity."

"But not yours?" he asked.

Ivy clanged her spoon against the pot. "Reviewing budget reports and summaries from the front is endlessly fun."

Collin swallowed. "Dance with me tonight."

Spoken in the imperative, but with a voice so quiet and halting it was almost—*almost*—swaying.

Ivy hesitated. It was not so improper. Military officers enjoyed a certain distinction from the common man. She and her sisters could indulge in their company, and it was not the same scandal as Jade marrying a cow herder.

But it was all wrong. Ivy knew why Collin was here. And so did he. She'd *bought* him. He'd said as much. She couldn't play pretend with him. Hadn't her demonstration of misdirection proven that point? "No."

"Dance with me right now."

"And risk Trina's wrath over burnt jam?" Ivy lifted the spoon from the pot and blew on it before stealing a taste. Trina was right. It needed lemon. More sugar, too, but gracious, they couldn't exactly spare any more of it.

Collin reached for a taste, but Ivy swatted away his hand. "That's bad luck."

"It is not." Collin tried again with his tasting spoon.

"No, really. Don't."

"Why?"

"Because."

"Are we both twelve? Does 'because I said so' still work?"

Ivy pressed her lips together. "Please don't."

Collin smiled wickedly. He slipped his spoon into the jam.

Ivy's breath caught.

"Tell you what," he said. "Say you'll dance with me tonight, and I will put this jam back without sampling it."

Flirting, keeping Collin off his balance, was about proving there was no attachment. It was a game that kept him close and kept Ivy in control. She wouldn't use her sister's wedding feast—well, the closest she'd get to one—for anything so dishonest. She wouldn't taint the occasion. And she certainly wouldn't dance with the major. That would be tantamount to lying. "No. Now put the jam back. That's an order."

Collin dropped the spoon and raised his hands in surrender. "Who knew jam making was so serious?"

"Not a shop boy from Olcceart."

"Chemist." Collin quickly dipped a finger into the pot, and before Ivy could object, he licked the dollop of jam off his index finger.

And she'd just tasted it moments before! "You idiot! I told you not to do that."

Collin shifted closer to Ivy. His smile wafted between bewildered and amused. "Old habits. Chemists taste everything."

Could they throw out the jam and start over? Of course not. They didn't have enough sugar for that. Oranges were scarce too. Ivy pressed her palm to her forehead. "This is a disaster."

Collin's eyes narrowed. "My finger was clean."

"It's honeymoon jam. It's for the bride and groom."

"You ate some."

"I'm her sister! Sisters make the jam. And I had no intention of feeding it to you!"

Collin shifted so as to be standing closer to Ivy. "Gran must not have understood the finer points of Amadanri marriage customs. I'd be grateful for your insight."

Ivy fumed silently.

Collin leaned closer. His warmth made her dizzy. "Is it supposed to be so tart?"

"Shut up. I'll lose all credibility if they learn I fed you honeymoon jam."

"You didn't feed me."

"The facts don't matter if the results are the same. You ate it. If you breathe a word to anyone—what are you doing?"

Collin had grabbed a spoon and helped himself to a mouthful of marmalade. "Damage is done. Might as well have more."

"Stop it!" Ivy hissed.

"I will. Just tell me why. Tonight even, while we're dancing."

"I'm not coming tonight. I have a mountain of paperwork. I'll have my hands full until midday tomorrow just getting up to speed."

"And Trina will have her hands full chaperoning your sisters. How much of this jam do you want me to eat?"

Ivy seized his spoon and threw it in the sink. She took the pot off the stove, turned off the burner. Trina could sort out the jam. Ivy pulled the major with her into the library and to the assortment of boxes piled on the desk and floor. "Do you think any of this is about what I want?"

"I don't know, Ivy. Why don't you tell me?"

Ivy unlatched a box and dumped it upside down onto her crowded desk.

"You could start with why eating jam with you is such a crime."

Ivy replaced her spectacles. A report on the sugar stores came into focus. "No."

Collin examined a report on the periphery of her stack. "You don't enjoy dances?"

"No. I'd rather not hold tight to Daphne's, Gwen's, and Angelica's reins while arguing with Beatrice, comforting Mina, scolding Sophia, and convincing Jade that her marriage will need to be annulled as soon as we leave for the capital in three weeks. But if I don't do it, who will?"

CHAPTER TWENTY-ONE

"Ives! Come get your face painted." Harriet pulled Ivy away from her desk. "Don't I look just like Adelaide in her last opera?"

"No," said Rachel. "You look nothing like her."

Harriet pouted. "You're just jealous because Pen would not let you borrow her trousers."

The afternoon in the library had encouraged the ache in Ivy's head to spread to her neck. "Where is Trina?" she asked.

"She's practicing," Harriet said, coming dangerously close with a pot of rouge. "Gwen says you need some color at the very least."

Trina was lost to the piano, leaving Ivy completely alone. That was the trouble with dances. Trina was either worshiping at the feet of the musicians, or she was playing music herself. Pen, with her unique understanding of humor, found social faux pas to be particularly delectable and encouraged them where she could. And during the preparations for this dance, Jade was either besotted with Matthew or arguing with him. Very strange dynamic, theirs. That left Ivy to deal with Sophia, Daphne, Angelica, Beatrice, Gwen, Harriet, Rachel, and Mina.

Ivy had to do something to produce an ally among her younger sisters. She gestured to the paint. "Do you think I should?" she asked Harriet, who brightened instantly.

"Ask her to make your eyes smoky. Major Collin will like that. Gwen!" Harriet called, dragging her sister to the adjoining suite. "Ivy wants her face painted."

"Are you sweet on him?" Rachel asked Ivy. She was so charmingly blunt.

"No," Ivy said. But Gwen had Ivy's face in her hands and was twisting and pulling her every which way.

"Then you won't mind if I dance with him?" Daphne said, looking like a very pretty but very tightly stuffed sausage in Ivy's brocade dress.

"Daphne, don't you think a shawl might suit?" Ivy asked.

Gwen grabbed Ivy's jaw firmly once more. "It's a pity your eyes are not green. So much easier to play them up when they are a color."

"My apologies. Where is Mina?" Ivy asked.

"Mina is napping. Poor dear caught a cold skating." Pen helped herself to the array of bobbles on Gwen's vanity.

"Or she's just tired," Harriet said. "Papa did send us off frightfully early."

Ivy's shoulders sagged. "I'd like a nap."

"Out of the question." Harriet held up two different choices of earrings to Ivy's face. "We have to make you irresistible."

"I'm not dancing tonight. There aren't enough young men for all of us."

"Are you going to dance tonight, Pen?" Harriet asked.

"Of course. Can't disappoint Tim."

"Stop twitching," Gwen commanded, grabbing Ivy's chin in a viselike grip.

Harriet giggled. "She's not twitching. She's shaking in passionate desire for Major Top-Notch."

"You've been reading too many novels, Harriet dear."

"She has not," Bea snapped. She was ever protective of her little sister. Ivy tried to apologize, but Harriet wouldn't hear of it.

"Nonsense. This is the first fun we've had since the night of the opera," she said, "and that was six weeks ago. We're not going to waste a moment on boring apologies."

Gwen pulled a stiff brush through Ivy's eyelashes. "Don't rub your eyes, or you'll look like a ferret."

Bea set a circlet of pearls in Harriet's hair. "She looks like a ferret anyway."

"Thanks, Bea," Ivy said.

"Ferrets are adorable. Just ask Mina. I'm borrowing your fan, old girl." Beatrice unfurled it once and closed it just as sharply. "You don't mind, do you?"

Not if Ivy wanted to remain on speaking terms.

"There," Gwen said, admiring her work. "Now you just need a dress. Something sleek and alluring."

"I have nothing sleek or alluring," Ivy said.

"I do!" Angelica called.

It was chaos, all her sisters getting ready at once. All the trading. All the digs and barbs. All the preening. But it was home, and Ivy had missed it. "I am not going to wear anything you brought from home," Ivy informed Angelica.

"But I saved something special just for you, Ivy. I laid it out on my bed."

The girls steered Ivy into the other apartment and laughed and laughed when Ivy found the green monster.

So much tulle. So many petticoats. The absolute worst was the addition of green lace.

"You are wicked, all of you," Ivy said, rolling her eyes.

"It missed you!" Daphne screeched through her hysteria.

"I think you've added even more hideous tulle to the bottom."

"To catch Major Top-Notch's eye. We had to change it a little, since he's seen you in it before."

"That's it. I'm not going."

"Oh, don't be a poor sport," Bea said.

"I can't wear this. I'm the commanding officer here."

Gwen folded her arms defiantly. "Well, you can't wear any of your awful pinstripes or tweeds. It won't go with your face. And I did do a marvelous job painting it up."

"You can borrow my burgundy," Harriet said.

"Trina took that one," Pen said.

"There must be something..." Harriet began to rummage through the wardrobes.

"I'll check on Mina, then." Ivy escaped into the quiet hall. She tapped gently on the south bedroom door. No answer. She pushed through and found little Mina sound asleep in the white linens. Ivy pressed her hand to Mina's forehead and frowned at the heat that greeted her.

The door closed behind her, and Rachel stood by Ivy's side.

"I don't think we should leave Mina alone tonight."

"I'll stay," Rachel said. "I don't feel like pretending to be interested in any of your silly officers."

"It's not about the officers. It's about Jade and her...alleged union."

Rachel scoffed. "Jade is so besotted with Matt, she won't notice me not standing in the shadows. But she will notice if you are not there to keep the girls in hand."

"Rachel, be honest. I will stay if you want to go."

"No, thank you. Social awkwardness is not my brand of fun."

Ivy brushed the hair away from Rachel's face. "You're turning into a hermit."

"Then your work here is done."

"You blame me?"

"Is there someone else determined to keep us isolated from any and all potential suitors at the expense of friendship and happiness because she has ambitions to wear the crown?"

Ivy's shoulders sagged. Perhaps Rachel had a point. "I'm trying to keep us all safe. The assassination attempt is reason enough—"

"There's always a reason, Ivy. Just own up to the real one."

CHAPTER TWENTY-TWO

Collin needed to tell Ivy the truth. How he felt at the very least, more if he could find his courage. The problem was he hardly knew how he felt. He respected her, admired her, but he also could barely stand for want of her touch. He needed to dance with her. Dancing was warranted on this occasion, and it would be as close a chance as he'd ever have of holding her again. What a miserable idea that was.

"Ivy, dance with me. I've danced with all your sisters. How will it look if you alone refuse me?"

She looked so lovely but so sad. "All right."

It was at that moment that Trina stood up from the piano and held a jar aloft. "Honeymoon jam for the bride and groom!" she announced.

"I want some," Eric said, reaching for one of the jars stacked on the piano.

"Oh, no!" Ang said seriously.

"Why not?" Eric teased.

"Honeymoon jam, made by sisters using the oldest magic there is, unites a pair for life," Daphne explained.

The thought of a lifelong commitment must have been a sobering one for Eric. "Come again?"

"Cooking is the first alchemy, fool," Matthew barked before feeding Jade a bite of the marmalade.

"Is it an aphrodisiac?" Tim asked Pen. Now that the two were speaking, they were thicker than the mud Collin would have to trudge through before the night was over.

"No." Pen stretched her long legs across Tim's lap. "It's a pledge, a promise of love unending."

"Bound by the magic of new love and the love of family," Trina said, playing a few chords on the piano.

"Sisters preferably," Harriet added.

Monty picked up a jar and examined it in the candlelight. "So they eat it. And...happily-ever-after happens?"

Daphne giggled. "They eat it and are filled with a burning desire for each other—"

"Daphne," Ivy warned.

"That only grows until they consummate the union and produce an heir," Gwen finished.

Collin cleared his throat. "I'm curious. What would happen to a couple who indulged in honeymoon jam but were not pledged to each other?"

"Nothing," Ivy said quickly. "Because it's a silly tradition based on a sillier belief in magic."

"Not nothing," Beatrice said coldly. "My father unwittingly, so he says, fed my mother an old jar of his honeymoon jam. They went nearly mad for each other until they ran off to his Summer Palace."

"Yes," Ang said, "a couple foolish enough to try honeymoon jam will be tormented by desire that will only grow—"

"That's enough, Ang," Ivy said sharply.

Ang scoffed and flounced her skirts. "I'm not the one who makes the traditions."

"There is no magic in honeymoon jam," Ivy said. "There is no magic left in any of our kingdoms."

"The magic's not gone, Ives," Gwen said, pulling Collin to his feet. "It's just hiding until the war is over."

"You've been reading Mina's fairy tales," Ivy said, her cheeks reddening when Collin caught her staring and winked.

"So what if I have?" Gwen had twisted and twirled until Collin's arms were crossed around her.

Did Ivy look jealous? "Nothing but nonsense and silly traditions."

"Traditions don't have to be serious to be important," Jade said, feeding Matthew a spoonful of jam and kissing his nose.

Ivy flicked open her watch. "But they always have to be a waste of time."

Beatrice nodded toward the door. "You should leave now, old girl. Before you ruin this night more than you already have."

Ivy set her jaw but rose and left.

Collin didn't need Tim to gesture, not at all subtly, that it was his duty to follow. He knew.

He found Ivy outside in the cold. The last of the snow fell lightly on her bare shoulders. At least this time he'd had the sense to stop for their coats. He folded Ivy into hers.

His hands lingered on her shoulders. "I promise I was mad for you long before the jam."

"It's no use, Major. We both know the real reason you are here."

At last, and thank Mars for that. Collin drew closer. Ivy had guessed his devotion, his affection. Telling Ivy he'd fallen for her would be easier now. They could work out the implications of his past together if she felt similarly for him. "Ivy, I—"

"You were the only man desperate enough to sell your soul. Which reminds me." She fished in the pocket of her coat and retrieved a folded piece of paper. "Open it."

"It's a deed to a farm." Collin's voice shook.

"I did some digging and found where you hid your Gran. A lovely place, it would seem, known for its cherry orchard. The tenant informed me that the owner would be more than willing to part with it. Note the date." Ivy indicated a particular line.

Collin's heart hammered. Two weeks from now. "The day after our demonstration."

"As promised."

Collin could scarcely breathe.

Ivy spoke quietly. "I reviewed your holiday. Ten ambitious days in the capital before returning to help us with the final preparations of the engine. I thought the assurance of your reward would be...motivating."

"Ivy—"

"I shouldn't have doubted you."

Collin winced. "Ivy—"

She was determined not to hear him. "A distinguished officer and landowner. What will you do after our victory is assured, I wonder?"

"I'll buy a peerage."

Ivy kicked at the snow. "Whatever for?"

"For you."

Ivy flinched. "The jam is getting to your head."

"You said you didn't believe in it."

"Collin—"

"Dance with me."

"No. Thank you. But I will wish you good luck." She stood before him, rose on tiptoe, and pressed her lips to his cheek. "I need you to bomb as many factories as you can and then hurry back in time to help with our final mission. We can talk of your peerage this spring."

Collin held her close. "Will you knight me with a sword on either shoulder?"

Ivy laughed. "If you want to dig out a tarnished and rusty scabbard from the armory. They were next to the punch bowls when last I checked."

"Ivy, I need to tell you. Something important."

"Later." She buried her face against his chest, and her weight was so pleasant against Collin's beating heart that he forgot his words. "We have no time to spare now."

CHAPTER TWENTY-THREE

A shower of sparks reflected off of Pen's goggles and rained down onto the stable floor. It had been twelve days since Jade's party and six since the rail-less engine had been relocated to the stable, despite Ivy's fear of increased combustibles.

"Hay can be moved. Bessie, not so easily." Pen had had a point, as well as a name for the steel vehicle. Ivy had conceded that the foundry steps and thinning lake ice would be ill-suited to the final stages of assembly. So they'd compromised. They'd moved the hay to the front hall of the lake house, and Pen had allowed Ivy to be present, with Collin's canisters of sodium bicarbonate at the ready, whenever she was welding.

Today, a cohort of sisters had joined them, not that Trina, Ang, or Mina were doing much to help Pen or Ivy.

"Why is Ivy clutching one of Collin's canisters?" Mina asked.

"Because in the absence of the man, she's taken to collecting his possessions. Like a dragon building a horde," Ang called from the empty hayloft.

"The chemical extinguishes flame better than water," Trina explained.

Collin was supposed to have been gone for only ten days, but a full twelve had passed since the night he'd left. There was no word from Collin or Eric. Ivy had had no *Gazette* clippings. No letters. Nothing. And that stretch of uncertainty gnawed at her late at night. It was like the dull ache at the base of her spine—easy enough to forget when she was busy, but in the quiet hours, it became distracting, at times unbearably so.

She should have danced with him the night of Jade's party, possibly the last night she'd ever see him again. She should have danced with him, but instead she'd declined, politely, insisting there was no time. And like the good boy his Gran had raised him to be, Collin had danced with every one of her sisters while Ivy had watched.

She should have made space to examine her own heart. She had feelings for Collin. Admiration and esteem, yes, but something more tender still. Something that made her despair with every new day of his absence.

She should have danced with him. Collin was clever, talented, and by all accounts completely devoted to her. There was that regrettable choice to withhold key aspects of his personal history, but could she blame him for wanting to prove his loyalty before he shared the secret of his past?

Ivy clicked open her watch case and closed it again. Snow had come to the manor house. A late snowstorm should have been a relief, but as the flurries danced and twirled outside the barn window, Ivy felt panic prick her skin. Were the snows to blame for Collin's absence?

Ivy played with the clasp of her watch. She liked the quiet clink it made as it obeyed her. Precise and delicate. She held her watch, and for a brief toggle of the second hand, she was in control. She held time in her hand. It used to be enough. Precision and measurements. Gears that slid beautifully around, adding to the organized whole, did not make up for missed opportunities. They certainly didn't replace lost dances.

Ivy closed the watch and slid her thumb over the facets of the emerald inlay. She, too, had initially withheld key aspects of her person when she'd attempted to persuade Collin to join her cause. But keeping a few cards off the table wasn't lying. You didn't lie to your equal. You confided in them. You lied to inferiors. Children. Dullards.

Ivy's watch continued to clink as she played with its case. Open and shut. Open and shut. She'd kissed him. She'd kiss him again if she ever had the chance. How she hoped there would be another chance!

Open and shut.

Collin must have seen through her veneer before Ivy herself had. She wore his pajamas, for heaven's sake. She was never satisfied unless he was within view. She'd told herself it was because of the war, but the reason was simpler than she'd imagined. She wanted to be close to the young man she admired.

"If you keep doing that with your watch, you'll have to leave," Pen said, twisting off her blowtorch and tugging the goggles from her face.

"Why don't you and I get a cup of cocoa?" Trina said to Ivy.

Ang tossed a horse blanket down from the loft. "Why don't you both stop pacing and acting like idiots?"

"Try to be more sensitive," Trina hissed.

Ang rolled her eyes. "Miss him that much, do you?"

"Who?" Mina asked, clomping down the pigeon-loft stairs.

Ang dusted her hands on her magenta skirts. "Major Top-Notch."

"Who?" Mina asked, turning to Trina.

"Major Collin. You know..." But Trina fumbled and failed to explain further.

"Ivy's beau," Pen said, examining her soldering work.

Ivy pressed her eyes shut and gripped her watch but remembered not to open it. "Not my beau."

"Not her beau," Pen repeated.

Angelica groaned. "When will they come back? It's no fun without Eric." She swung the blanket over the chestnut mare's back. "You won't even let us ice skate."

"True." Ivy had put a stop to further skating expeditions. She didn't trust the ice this late in the season, and there wasn't time. The men had three days at most to practice maneuvers before the final journey to the front began.

Angelica huffed out her exasperation and stormed out of the stables.

"Just as well. She was upsetting the horses." Mina stroked the chestnut's nose while the beast flicked her tail.

Ivy flicked open her watch and garnered Pen's attention immediately. "Have you finished the prototype?" Pen had told her yesterday that it was almost completed. She'd just needed a quiet morning with a blowtorch.

"You do know the definition of a prototype?" Pen asked.

"Show me how to operate it," Ivy demanded.

Pen shook off her gloves and ran her fingers through her short hair. "It's not going to be perfect. There's a leak in the steam compressor. It's causing a whistle I'm not happy about."

Pen always accused Ivy of perfectionism, when really it was she who fussed over details. "Show me now, or I'll send you home with Trina and the others."

"When are we leaving?" Mina whined.

"Soon," Trina said, picking a piece of straw out of Mina's brown curls. Easy for Trina to be calm. She was headed back to her precious Phillip and organ. Not necessarily in that order.

"And when is Major Top-Notch returning?" Mina asked.

Ivy slammed her watch on the workbench. "I don't know!" she roared.

The stable went deathly quiet. Tears welled in Mina's eyes, and she darted out of the stable. Trina gave Ivy a stern look and followed her.

Pen crossed her arms. "You want to try again?"

Ivy exhaled. The musty smell of hay and horses clung to everything. "Trina is taking everyone except you and me back to the palace after luncheon. Collin—" She bit her lip. "The major should have checked in by now, but I've heard nothing since he left." Her heart felt squeezed up against something sharp. "We must marshal our resources and move forward. I will need to take his place, and you will have to take Eric's. At least until we reach the front."

"Ives—"

"Show me how to operate the prototype."

Pen huffed and shook her head. Her eyes drifted like an untethered kite. Bouncing, swimming in a sky that was too wide and too remote. "Not on an empty stomach." She tugged her goggles back into place and lit her torch. "Bring me something edible."

Ivy flipped open her watch again, partially to annoy Pen, but mostly to calm her own temper. She marked the time, closed the watch, and shoved it back into her breast pocket. Apparently, she now delivered lunch. "Fine."

Ivy hoped to satiate Pen with a quick sandwich, maybe a couple of tea cakes, while she brewed a pot of chocolate. Ten minutes, and she'd be back in the stables.

The kitchen, however, was swarming with sisters. She'd be lucky to make it out alive.

"Ivy!"

"Ivy, why are you sending us away? I was just starting to beat Monty at poker," Daphne said with a pout.

"Can I stay behind?" Harriet asked.

"Ivy, can I take your black boots back with me? The ones with the three buckles?" Gwen asked.

The simple act of retrieving the tin of cocoa was like running a gauntlet.

Ivy shuffled and skirted past all of them. "Papa misses you," she told Daphne. "It's too dangerous," she told Harriet. "No to the black boots, Gwen, but you may take my brown ones."

She whisked the cocoa and cream on the stove, adding drops of peppermint oil. Trina's tea had long since run out. "Sophia?"

Her sister was standing in the kitchen corner, sulking.

"Absence makes the heart grow fonder," Ivy said.

Sophia scowled and straightened. "Is that why you keep sending Major Collin away?"

Ivy flinched. Didn't they care at all that she was trying to end a war? She should have taken Collin up on his offer the night of the opera to run away.

The kitchen door burst open. Eric stumbled into the kitchen. He was filthy and frantic, and unmistakable dark red covered the front of his shirt. "Ivy!"

Angelica and Sophia gasped. Ivy's stomach bottomed out. Her fear was nothing compared to Eric's anguished face. "Collin's been injured," he said.

The sunshine was too bright, and the world was too noisy. Everything was wrong.

"Stars and comets," Angelica murmured.

"Harriet." Ivy grabbed her sister by the shoulder. She still had a biscuit in her hand. "Find Tim and the rest of the boys. Send them to me. Hurry now."

Harriet nodded and dashed out of the kitchen.

Ivy turned to Eric. "Show me."

CHAPTER TWENTY-FOUR

The snow that fell from the sky burned as it touched Ivy's skin. And where everything had been far too noisy before, now it was painfully quiet. Collin lay unconscious in the cart. A bloodstained bandage covered half his face. A filthy blanket covered the rest of him.

"Oy." Ivy recoiled at the acidic smell. "Did you bathe him in bourbon?"

"Nearly," Eric said. "It was the only way I could think of traveling with him, so I could say he drank too much the night before and had a nasty fall."

Tim, Monty, and Matthew came running out of the kitchen door. "What happened?" Matthew demanded.

"The blast radius was stronger than we anticipated. We both got thrown, but Collin landed with his head against a wall."

Ivy felt sick. And scared. She wanted to throw her arms around Collin and sob. Instead, she climbed into the cart and peeled back the blanket. Blood had soaked into Collin's shirt and coat, but it wasn't fresh. Ivy felt his neck and spine for injury, and when she was satisfied that he was safe to move, she yelled, "Get him inside."

The men lifted Collin carefully up and out of the cart.

"Easy," Ivy commanded. "How long has he been unconscious?"

"Last two days," Eric grunted as he and the others carried Collin inside.

Collin's bandages had slipped off his face, and a slow trickle of blood had appeared. Ivy swore. Her blood pulsed in her ears. The panicked pace of it reached her eyes as the bile crept up her throat. The snow continued to fall, white and crisp.

They reached the kitchen, and the men laid Collin on the table. Then Mina shrieked, and Jade vomited into the sink.

Ivy should have asked Trina to ferry everyone into the library before she left. She should have thought to spare her sisters the grisly sight, but she'd thought only of Collin and her own battered heart.

"He comes in and out. But..." Eric rubbed the back of his neck. "He's mostly out."

Angelica stood, quiet and pale, in the corner. Ivy wondered if she was about to run headlong into Eric's arms. She instead ran to Daphne and hugged her sister tight.

Ivy took a steadying breath. "Mostly out?"

Collin moaned. "What choice did I have, rattling at the bottom of a cart?"

The sound of Collin's voice, his slurred, weak voice, broke Ivy's heart.

Matthew pushed past Ivy and barked to Tim, "We need to move him. Somewhere we can clean him and sew him up properly."

"I'll die here on the table, thanks," Collin muttered.

Her sisters were sobbing. Collin was hurt. Matt and Tim were trying to drag him away. And Ivy had to rally.

"Leave him there," Ivy said, turning to Tim. "Get a gurney or chaise or something."

Pulse first. Take his pulse first. Ivy leaned over and pressed her fingers against Collin's wrist.

"Ivy?" Collin's voice squeaked out in a rush of surprise and pain and fear.

His breath reeked of bad gin. "Have you been self-medicating?"

"I blew up five factories for you. That's one more than I promised." He was straining to see her, to touch her.

Ivy pushed Collin back down. "Lie still. Can you do that?"

"Maybe, but not probably." Collin sniggered and winced in pain.

Everyone started talking at once.

"Shut up. All of you. Shut up!" Ivy snapped.

But everyone was still just milling about. Half of her sisters had fled the kitchen, but more than enough remained to make matters worse.

Mina continued to sob uncontrollably, but it should be Ivy who was hysterical. She alone knew how important Collin was to the operation and...to her. "You don't get to be hysterical here," Ivy said to Mina. "You can be hysterical in the coach all the way home, but not now!"

Mina cried harder but rose on shaky legs and ran out of the kitchen. The poor dear was scared. It was dreadful to see a healthy young man reduced to a bloody, dead-weight body. Ivy herself had wanted reassurance that Collin wasn't cold, that his skin was still warm, that his chest still rose and fell in a steady, measurable pace. She wanted much more, but Mina had run away, sobbing. Her sisters needed her. And they needed her to be strong.

"Stay with him," Ivy commanded Eric. "See what you can do to stop the bleeding."

He nodded. Sophia appeared at his side and offered a shaky hand, which he readily pressed in his own.

"Trina—" Ivy began, but Trina was already shepherding the younger ones into the library.

Ivy took a last look at Collin's limp body on the table and ran after Mina. She found her on the sixth step of the grand staircase, not that there was much *grand* left about it. Like the other wrought-iron fixtures in the house, it had been cannibalized for the sake of the engine. Ivy slid down onto the stair next to the crying Mina. "I'm sorry, Mina. I should not have snapped. There's no reason to be scared." Ivy put her arm tentatively around Mina, and Mina turned into her shoulder and sobbed harder.

"The major will be all right. He's already talking. He'll be fine."

"No!" Mina cried.

"We'll take care of him."

"No, no, no!" Mina grabbed hold of Ivy tightly. "That's not it! You don't understand."

Ivy's hand paused on Mina's back, and her neck prickled. Ivy had learned that there was always a moment before a fall was sustained, before a horse threw a shoe or a carriage lost a wheel. There was always a moment in which the gears of existence slowed. It was in that moment when she knew everything would fall apart.

"It's him," Mina whispered between sobs, and Ivy squeezed her eyes tight. "He's Papa's assassin."

CHAPTER TWENTY-FIVE

Ivy pulled Mina from her shoulder, where her tears had made the fabric wet and clingy. She had to see Mina's eyes.

"Who?" she asked.

She saw so much fear in Mina's eyes.

Ivy held her sister by the shoulders. "Major Collin? The man on the table with the concussion?"

Mina nodded, and her eyes flooded once again with tears.

The library door opened and closed softly. Trina was on Mina's other side on the stair. "Oh, poor Mina." Trina rested a gentle hand on Mina's back. "What's wrong?" she demanded of Ivy.

The words didn't come easily. They had to be marshaled, berated into doing their duty, into soldiering on when every inch of her wanted to stop, to crumple and despair. "She says Major Collin is Papa's would-be assassin."

"Surely not!" Trina blurted.

Mina wiped her hand across her running nose. "I want to go home!"

Ivy shushed Mina gently. "Just as soon as the trunks are packed,

Mina. You'll be home and asleep in your own bed this night. Every-thing will be right by then. Papa will be so pleased to see you, and he will be just fine. Not a scratch. Not a scratch on any of us." Just Ivy's hemorrhaging heart, which would need to be retrofitted with stronger steel and an artificial pump to keep beating. "I promise. Now..." Ivy took her littlest sister's hands in both of hers. "Can you be brave for me and wait in the library for a few minutes while I take care of a few things?"

"I want to stay with you!" Mina cried.

"I have to put the major under arrest and lock him in his room."

"And hold all of his companions for questioning," Mina said, sniffling.

"Exactly so. Now, why don't you get your coat, and you and Trina can walk outside and see if the sled is ready? Hmm? And then, in the sunshine, you can think of something nice. Like how happy Mistress Kitty will be when you return. I suspect she will not stop purring when she sees you."

Mina nodded and ran up the stairs to the west wing.

"What are you going to do?" Trina asked.

"Pack you and Mina up and send you off as quickly as possible. I can't risk her saying anything to the others. I am afraid I must insist you cease all communications with Phillip. Maybe this is easily explained." Heavens, she hoped it would be easily explained, but three days before their final coup, she could take no chances.

"Maybe Major Collin has a doppelgänger?"

"I doubt it. Dammit. Why didn't I see this before? I should have probed harder when he refused to swear allegiance to Papa."

"But you said he swore allegiance to you," Trina said. "Ivy?"

"Are the sleds ready?" Ivy asked.

"Nearly," Trina said.

Ivy pulled her hair tightly away from her face. "Good. Take everyone."

Pen came bursting in from the kitchen hall. "Yeah, that's not going to happen."

"Pen, the situation has changed." Ivy rose from her perch on the stair. "You have to go home."

"The engine block is cracked." Pen's eyebrows rose ominously. "So unless you want your men in uniform to be pushing Bessie forward during her demonstration, I'm staying."

This wasn't happening. "What's the point of having an engineer and a mechanic if they can't do the work of one princess?" Ivy screamed.

"Ivy?" Pen yelled.

"You're leaving!" Ivy said firmly.

"Stop it, both of you," Trina hissed. "I'm going to find Mina. Ivy, you had better fill Pen in before I get back."

"Bloody hell. What is going on?" Pen demanded. "I asked for one sandwich, and the world falls apart."

Ivy pressed her hands to her temples. "Mina identified Papa's would-be assassin as Major Collin."

"Impossible."

Ivy snorted. "Not in the least." It was all so obvious. He'd left her side before the second act of the opera had started, right before someone had tried to assassinate Papa. Why hadn't she even considered that before now? Infatuation, that's why. Gracious, she was as desperate and needy as the rest of her sisters.

"He couldn't have done it. He was in your box."

"Until intermission. I didn't see him again until the following morning. Why didn't I think to use the polygraph on him after the opera?"

Pen's face twisted into a frown. "Because he's an upstanding bloke who would never do anything of the sort."

Ivy would have laughed, but she was sure her heart wouldn't stand for it. "You don't know him like I do."

"You really think he could have aimed to kill Papa or anyone? The man can't hold a gun to save his life. He refused to use corporal punishment on any of his men. You read his file. I know because you made me read it."

"Mina said she saw him do it."

"So talk to him. Let him explain."

"He's in no state to talk at the moment. And I'm not going to jeopardize his testimony with questions posed under duress."

"Ivy, this is insanity. We've been living with the man for nearly six weeks."

"And he's been away for most of that time."

"We know his friends."

"Do we?" Ivy asked.

"Yes." Pen straightened out of her slouch. "If you work on an engine for six weeks straight, you get to know a bloke."

"And that engine block just cracked. Coincidence?" Ivy asked.

Trina and Mina were on the stairs.

"There we are," Ivy said with a forced smile. "All ready for the journey back home? It will be so much more fun since it snowed, and you'll get to use the sled for part of it. Hmm?"

As they all picked their way through the snow to the sled, Ivy asked, "Where is Mina going to sit? Forward-facing or back?"

"Forward," Mina mumbled. "I don't want to be sick."

"Good plan." Better than any of Ivy's.

Ivy bundled her sister in the sled. "Just until you reach the crossing. I'm told the snow is only reaching us in the mountains here."

Ivy waved goodbye to her sisters, knowing that Pen should have been among them but wasn't because Ivy needed her help to pull this off.

"So what's the plan?" Pen asked.

Ivy marched back to the manor. "Business as usual."

Pen thrust her hands into her pockets. "And are you going to—"

"Confront the major, in time. But not now. There is no margin in our plan for any of this nonsense. We must keep going. I'll advise you not to get more attached to any of them."

"And when this is over?"

The words wouldn't come easily, but Ivy knew she would rally.

She'd soldier on, even though her heart wanted to shrivel and stop from the despair.

"Not all stories have happy endings."

CHAPTER TWENTY-SIX

"Surprised to see me?" Collin said with a half-smile, sitting at the kitchen table. Three days had passed since his arrival and Mina's revelation. Three days that Ivy had spent in coveralls, helping Pen and the rest of the team rebuild Bessie's engine. Three days that she had carefully avoided Collin.

Ivy tried to calm herself. She tried to hastily pack up her avalanche of emotions at seeing Collin upright, with a cup of chocolate in front of him. A curl of fear. A snarl of anger. Relief too. And that dangerous pang of longing. "I was just retrieving the post." Matthew said he'd left the new letters from Trina near the kitchen sink. "Shouldn't you be resting?"

"You haven't come to see me. I thought to update you in person. I survived."

"I see that," Ivy said coldly, before tearing open the first of Trina's letters. She didn't want to look in his eyes. She didn't want to feel betrayed or to wonder. She wanted to avoid all of that. Indefinitely.

Collin fingered the handle of his teacup. "Haven't much of an appetite, though."

"I believe that's common with head trauma." Ivy rubbed her

temple while she read. The news from home was worrisome. Papa was making a fuss over Ivy's insistence that their troops fall back from Cailin Muire. She had written repeatedly that he must call on their men to stand down if they wanted their treaty offer to be taken seriously. She'd explained it all in painstaking detail.

"The house has become devastatingly quiet. Do you miss your sisters?"

"I'm too busy to miss them. We just finished rebuilding the engine." Ivy ripped open the next letter.

"But you miss them all the same." Collin pushed the cup and saucer aside. "How are preparations?"

"The engine is ready. Matt has nearly all the supplies in place. If Bessie leaves tonight, we still have a chance to make Olcceart think we've got them beat with our bluff about an army of tanks. They'll accept our treaty offer, and the war will end." Ivy skimmed Trina's letter. "Will you be ready to leave tonight with the other men?"

"Of course. But what about you?"

Trina had informed her that Papa had stopped reading Ivy's letters and was planning a show of force. "I have to get home as soon as possible. Tonight, at the very latest." Papa couldn't ignore her if she was standing in front of him.

Collin casually rose—too casually not to be suspicious. "Tim is worried about our exit strategy. A rendezvous and letters of transit are not enough." He inspected the sink, which Ivy was resting against.

"Then invent a story," Ivy muttered, not bothering to look up from Trina's letter. She was detailing how Mina had told her she knew Collin was the assassin because he had the same handsome jaw and distinguished nose, even if they had been covered in dried blood when she'd seen him the other day. Mina was certain it was him. Yet Trina insisted that Collin couldn't be an enemy of Amadanri. If he wanted to end the war by assassinating Papa, why hadn't he returned to the capital for another attempt? Why swear loyalty to Ivy? Why indeed. "What would you have me do? Give you all magic tokens, talismans of good luck?"

"It's not a bad idea. Are kisses still considered—"

"No." Ivy looked up from Trina's letter, aware of Collin's closeness. Her body was a traitor. Her arms wanted to wrap around him. Her fingers wanted to close around his wrist. They wanted to examine his jaw, probe the purple and yellow skin at his temple. "Lucky maybe, but not magical."

"I'm sorry, Ivy."

As he said the words, Ivy's heart stopped. She wondered for an instant if he had caught word of Mina's revelation, perhaps read some of Trina's letter.

"I was careless with the blast radius," he said, "and while I do not enjoy you being angry with me, I can't help but hope that maybe..." His hand moved to rest on top of her own.

Her stomach became weightless, while her mind revolted. He'd tried to kill Papa! She should feel only contempt and betrayal. Not butterflies. Ivy brushed one of her curls back into place. "Perhaps if we win the war, we'll have time to discuss why I am so very angry with you."

Collin's thumb drew small circles across her hand. "I'd like that very much."

"I need you to be ready to leave tonight." She winced. She needed more. She needed to know if he'd betrayed her by telling Olcceart of their plan. She needed to know if he was plotting to return to the capital to finish what he started the night of the opera, and she needed to know how she fit into his scheme. Maybe then she'd be able to sort out the web of feelings she'd spun around the man. But she didn't have time for that nonsense now.

As Ivy huffed out of the kitchen, she heard Collin say, "Anything for you."

CHAPTER TWENTY-SEVEN

The steel tank hissed steam. Monty and Matthew were loading supplies into the hold. Eric and Tim were scurrying about, too, performing one last systems check.

Pen pulled Ivy aside. "I'm not saying you should elope like Jade, but if you don't thaw out, he's going to suspect something's up, and it will affect our chances here." Pen nodded to the steel tank.

"What do you want me to do?" Ivy hissed. They had a half hour at best to finish up if they wanted to meet the coach, and they needed to meet that coach.

"Can you just pretend that he is innocent for the next half hour?" Pen pleaded. "Please, Ives."

"They could all be his accomplices. They could be planning a coup. How do we know they won't all run off with Bessie for their own traitorous purposes?" Ivy felt for her watch, but it wasn't there. She'd either left it on the bureau or slipped it into her trunk. One more reason not to stay in the stables for a moment longer.

"Ives, we've talked about this." Pen had argued tirelessly for Collin and his men whenever she and Ivy had been alone these past three days. *Why would Collin return to enemy lines injured? Why would he go above and beyond to destroy Olcceart's factories? It doesn't make sense.*

"These men put their entire lives on the line for you. Please, see what they've done." Pen gestured to the rail-less engine. "Forget the rest."

"I don't have the luxury." Ivy had to trace every path and shepherd the details as well as champion the big picture. Because she couldn't trust another to do it. She couldn't trust anyone. Not her father. Not his sycophantic court. Not the major. Not even her sisters; they were too close to Collin's men now to be objective.

Pen snapped her fingers in front of Ivy's face. "Collin is beside himself. Do something about it. For king and country, if not for him." Pen folded her arms.

"That reminds me." Ivy extracted a letter from her pocket.

Pen set her jaw but accepted the letter. Her eyes scanned the words before she snorted. "This is the thanks I get?"

"Professor August is most intrigued by your portfolio. I secured a fellowship for you in the Engineering Department and one for Sophia with the mathematicians. Jade will read poetry with the other fellows."

Pen folded the letter and shoved it into her back trouser pocket. "What about Tim? And Eric? And—"

She didn't have time for this. "Don't start."

"Talk to him," Pen said. "Give him a reason to succeed one last time."

Collin lay on a horse blanket in the empty hayloft. He looked awful. Thin. Pale. His characteristic meticulousness had given way to a scruffy stubble, untucked shirt, and unkempt hair.

"How is your head?" Ivy asked.

He looked up. Shifting to sit on the blanket. "The ringing in my ears has stopped."

"A good sign." Ivy sat next to him. She wanted to take him by the shirt and scream in his face, but Pen had a point. They needed this— for king and country.

"I was trying to impress you. I thought I'd make it an even half-dozen bombings."

Horrifying. He was attempting to flirt. He'd shot at Papa, and now he flirted with her as if it meant nothing. "Why would I be impressed with more explosions?"

"It's a complete mystery. Gran, when she had a mind to tell me about these things, told me women like flowers. But here I find the girl of my dreams is more impressed by pyrotechnics." He smiled, a sly, tentative half of a smile that carried just as much pain as it did enjoyment.

Smiles were carefully honed tools of deceit. Ivy knew—Papa smiled all the time. "And steel machinery. Let's not forget that."

"Eric said I had to do better than mere explosions. You remember the project you gave him and the triplets?"

Ivy laughed a single tired note. Not because she wanted to, but because she had to. Pen's pep talk had been thoughtful, but completely unnecessary. Ivy knew her duty. "Inspire a rebellion, was it?"

Collin slid a little nearer. The floor boards beneath them creaked as he moved. "We found a press, leafed out hundreds of issues of his *Herald*. Printed some of them on my flash paper. They're supposed to rise up at midnight tonight. Loot factories. Burn storehouses. Angry mobs in the streets will riot." He rubbed the back of his neck, blushing. "You're going to just gloss over 'the girl of my dreams' bit?"

Ivy shrugged. "It's a little trite, but I understand. Every man fancies a princess."

Collin laughed and then winced, clutching his side.

"Did you break a rib?" Ivy asked.

"I don't know. I was promised a castle full of competent nurses to tend my wounds once I woke up. But I wanted only one—and she refused to even visit me."

"Lie down," Ivy said. Collin complied. She rolled up his shirt, exposing skin marbled with purple, blue, and yellow splayed across his left side. Ivy counted his ribs with her fingers.

He sighed with pleasure, and her stomach twisted. This was the man who'd shot at Papa. She'd been sitting right next to him. She'd kissed him and pined away with hopes to kiss him again.

And all this time, he'd been lying to her.

Ivy pressed too hard, and Collin yelped in pain. "You did that on purpose!"

"Perhaps it was better that I was too preoccupied to nurse you back to health." Ivy rose. "Get some rest. Godspeed."

She climbed down the stable ladder. The steel engine hissed to life. A hatch opened, and Monty climbed out.

"If I had known I would have to ride in this tin can, I wouldn't have been such a miser on interior space in the design." Monty rolled his neck and stretched. "I'd dearly love to stand up straight again in my lifetime."

"If I had known how ripe you chaps smell, I would have designed better ventilation," Pen said.

Matthew placed two more parcels onto the deck of the tank. "You were out of your daft mind, all of you. It's against the nature of the universe. Men—"

"And women," Pen quipped.

"—are not supposed to spend their lives canned like pickled beets in steel monstrosities." Matthew had been short of temper since Jade's departure. Ivy had insisted, for safety, that Jade relocate to the capital with the rest of the sisters. She'd left out that the separation would be indefinite.

"Her name is Bessie," Pen yelled, "and if you don't say something nice about her, she might take offense and quit on us."

"Please, Pen." Ivy reached for her watch and stamped her foot in frustration. Of all the days to misplace Mama's watch. "Are the supplies in place?"

"All accounted for," Eric said.

"Systems check?" Ivy asked.

Pen dusted her hands on her coveralls. "Done."

"What are we waiting for?" Tim asked.

"Goodbyes, you ninny." Pen shoved her goggles into Tim's chest and stormed out of the stable. He stood motionless for a moment, staring down at Pen's goggles, before he ran after her.

Matthew shuffled forward. "The cart's been loaded with your trunks, and the horses are ready and waiting."

Ivy could not bring herself to look him in the eye. "Thank you, Matthew. Thank you for your service."

Matthew fumed. "Looking after an old house is hardly the work of a hero."

"Just the same." Ivy took a deep breath and faced the remaining men. "Good luck, gentlemen." She was too overwhelmed to say anything else. She slid the barn door open and trudged toward the cart and horses.

This night should have been electric, sharp and crackling with the hope that their hard work would end with peace, but this night, the wind blew its own sermon of disapproval. What else was Ivy to do? Matthew had to remain behind at the lake house. It was his official appointment. And although Ivy knew that Jade's marriage had to be annulled, she also knew that she could not put Matthew in harm's way.

The wind gusted. Risk and rewards. Why should it matter if the others were willing to take the risk? She'd done what she could. They all had. And even though it ate her up to admit it, her sisters had aided tremendously. They'd created rewards and motives for the men that Ivy never could have duplicated on her own. She'd come dangerously close with Collin. It made her stomach curl to pretend these last three days that nothing had changed. She'd done her best to avoid him, but tonight she'd had no choice.

Collin was waiting for her near the cart and horses. The snow had melted into icy, muddy piles. They'd be lucky to make it to the coach crossing alive.

Ivy squared her shoulders and approached the horses rather than look Collin in the eye. "I thought I left you in the hayloft. How did you manage to escape?"

Collin arched an eyebrow and shrugged.

"You're slipping, Major. Where is your thirst for facts and details?" She placed a tentative, gloved hand on the chestnut mare. It chuffed and bucked at her touch.

"I'm distracted," he said, stepping nearer.

Ivy's stomach curdled. Risk and reward. If Pen and Trina were right, and there was no betrayal to Olcceart, no further plot against their family, then she had to pretend for ten minutes more or risk jeopardizing their last chance for peace. The wind blew a reproach. Ivy swatted her tresses out of her eyes.

"What will you do after the war?" Collin asked, and in the pale starlight, Ivy had the satisfaction of seeing him color.

Flirtation was a weapon, and she'd arm herself one last time. Her voice purred as the wind again blew bitter. "I'll catch up on my correspondence and hopefully balance this year's budget. That is, if Papa will let me." She drew her lips into the ripest of smiles. "Provided, of course, your last mission is a success."

"You should be his heir." His hands were not gloved. A painful lattice of cuts covered his knuckles.

She wanted to scream. She wanted to run back to Mama's lake house and hide. "Perhaps our success this week will convince him of that as well." She knew he wanted to touch her. There could be no other reason to forgo gloves in freezing temperatures. It was an open invitation.

Ivy stepped closer. Maybe now, in the honest moonlight, she could find it, the lie in his concern. If she was indeed being used, it'd be nice to know for sure. But he looked at her so sincerely. And when he touched her...

Ivy tilted her chin up to him. He slowly reached a hand out, giving her every opportunity to turn away, but she didn't. He ran his fingers from just below her ear across the length of her jaw. His touch was warm, pulsing with need. It was easy to remember why she'd entertained ideas of infatuation. Ivy forced herself to remember that one of the fingers touching her now had curled around a trigger.

Ivy froze, trying so hard not to cry or scream. "I wish you good luck."

"And a safe return?" Collin was so still. Ivy felt his warm breath on her face. All she had to say was yes. All she had to do was stand there for an instant longer. Perhaps plant a goodbye kiss on his slightly parted lips. Tell him he'd be successful, and she'd be awaiting his return to the capital after the armistice. Then she'd arrest him on charges of attempted assassination. At best, he'd spend the rest of his life in prison. At worst...

She shuddered. "You're not coming back, Major."

Collin froze. His hand retreated from Ivy's face. His features knotted in concern.

She couldn't lie. Not like Papa. Not like Collin. She was better than that. "The night of Papa's opera..." Ivy's heart beat fast. "I know you were holding that gun."

A cascade of anguish as precarious as new snow on a winter's worth of accumulation fell in Collin's eyes. From there, it caught and tumbled to his expression, his posture. He appeared barely able to face her standing.

"Do you care to deny it?" Ivy asked.

"No," Collin said. He drew in a breath. The earnest young man had been transformed in a moment. His youth had been stripped away. The moonlight caught the lines in his face. It highlighted his recent injuries. He was an old, wounded soldier. It would be helpful to her to remember him this way, if her heart insisted on remembering.

"Care to explain?" she asked.

"I don't have enough..." Collin fumbled. His eyes glinted in the moonlight. The horses chuffed and flicked their tails.

Not enough what? Time, nerve, honor?

Collin pressed a hand to his neck. "Information. You see, I've been trying to help you win this war. But I didn't plan—" He was breathing hard. "There are things you don't know about. Conversations you've been intentionally left out of—"

"What are you saying? If you know something I don't, then tell me!"

"I can't, Ivy. Not now."

"Why not?" Had Papa been using her as a pawn all this time? Had she been sacrificing all her days and nights for a political game that had already been decided? Rage burned inside her. "Is it because I'm a woman?"

"No. Ivy, please."

Or was this all just more oily Olcceart tactics? "You've lied to me for the last time. I took a calculated risk that I could persuade you to help our cause." That was her mistake.

"And haven't I?"

"I don't know. You and your men could all be traitors to Amadanri. The moment I turn you loose, there's no telling what you might do. But it's a risk I must take now." The only one that could lead to peace. Or the deaths of the entire royal family at the hands of Olcceart assassins.

"We'll complete our mission. Trust me—"

"Trust you? After you intentionally left me in the dark about so many important details."

"It's for your own good."

Ivy's words were as sharp and as hard as steel, "Says the Olcceart spy—"

"I was an officer, *not* a spy!" He drew nearer, as if proximity would lend credence to his words.

"—who tried to kill Papa. No." Ivy laid her head against his shoulder. She wanted him to feel what he'd thrown away. Collin's heart beat fast. She felt it. She felt him breathe in. She remembered how, days ago, she'd have pledged her heart to him. She dreamed about embracing him. They could have had so much together. "You see, I can't trust you. Not now. Not ever." She ran her hand up his neck to his hairline.

"This is easier." Collin pulled her away and looked in her eyes. Instead of anger, all Ivy saw glinting in the moonlight was pain. "This way, you needn't worry about sending an honest man on a suicide mission."

A red, hot magma bubbled out of Ivy's heart. "Are you calling me a coward?"

"Pragmatic, madame."

Ivy knotted up her fingers. She wanted to sink them into Collin.

"You've found an easier way of saying goodbye and a noble reason for detaching your heart," he said.

"Yet, neither one of us is forthcoming with any declarations." It cut deep to realize that he did not love her. It hurt that she had fallen in love, or imagined herself in love, with a man who did not reciprocate such feeling. But Ivy would heal. Hers at least was a superficial wound, created from shared spaces and convenience. She'd temper her heart until it could withstand mere infatuation. "I'd ask where your courage fled, but one cannot declare feelings they do not possess."

The major winced. She'd hit her mark. And although it was a relief to not witness a man tightrope-walk across the rope bridge of doomed love, it was also...disappointing. And lonely.

Ivy climbed into the cart and busied herself among the furs and blankets. "This is goodbye, Major. I wish I could say I have no doubt of your success, but the truth is I have many. If we should succeed, I hope you are able to enjoy your freedom and our hard-earned peace, but if I find you in the capital or hear any word of you at all in my kingdom, you will be back in prison, waiting the rest of your life for a trial that will most assuredly result in your death."

"Am I really so dangerous? Or would you say the same to any man you grew fond of?"

In the distance, Ivy saw the stable door swing open. Pen and Matthew approached.

"Be a good boy. Drive the tank into Olcceart. Blow up one last factory to get their attention and then deliver our terms for armistice." Ivy grabbed the reins and flicked them. The horses stumbled to attention. The cart wheels rattled and lurched in the mud.

"And then what?" Collin yelled above the noise.

"Disappear."

PART TWO

Years later, people claimed they could see the distant light of the explosion from the capital. They told stories of how the shock blast ricocheted off mountains until it collided with their own hearts. They told of the wind carrying the smell of smoke over forests, across farms, through city streets. And then after the smoke had passed, they smelled the magic.

Their stories were true.

CHAPTER TWENTY-EIGHT

Two weeks after sending her special unit off on their last mission, Ivy stood outside the palace in the fickle, spring sunshine. Vermilion and emerald pennants flapped everywhere: streetlamps, turrets, rooftops, gutters, the bandstand. They crisscrossed the square in a motley spider web of patriotism. It was as if Papa had been planning this celebration since the first invasion. Papa did excel when it came to making a spectacle, but if ever there was a suitable occasion for it, it was armistice. Peace.

Ivy's plan had been a success. Bessie made quick work of Olcceart's impenetrable front, destroying their biggest armory and capturing their attention. They had quickly agreed to a cease-fire, peace talks, and then armistice. Through it all, Ivy had tried not to think about Collin and his men. She didn't know if they'd survived. She preferred to think they had but refused to make inquiries despite her sisters' frequent pleas. If she were to find out they were alive and well in her kingdom, then her duty demanded she make good on her threat. She'd have to arrest Collin and his suspected accomplices. Nothing good would come of it.

But now, outfitted in their finest spring dresses, they were celebrating their hard-earned peace with a public assembly in the palace courtyard.

Papa gripped his gold-leafed podium. He wore his dress uniform, not the hat with the dyed-red ostrich plume. Papa worried about squashing his wigs, and today he had on his very best blond curls with a pompadour. He smiled, lips pressed together, and squinted into the sunshine. "Let us bask in our glorious peace. Let us remember our fallen. Let us forgive our neighbors. Let us build anew with the foundation of hope and the brightness of victory."

It was exactly the sort of speech Papa enjoyed. Simple. Repetitive. And it would have brought genuine comfort to Ivy's own heart had she been able to assuage her conscience. She'd let an attempted murderer, a talented, shrewd, calculating young man, escape. Collin had completed his mission. He'd helped win the war, but he was no friend of Amadanri.

"But let us now turn to urgent matters at home…"

It would have been nice if the end of the war had solved all their problems—the overcrowded cities, the lack of funding, the food scarcity, and the refugee problem. Papa had to inspire and rally the people now, or else a revolution would be brewing. And while Olcceart's revolution was due some credit for their peace, it was far from welcome at home. Interestingly, the start of the revolution had been attributed to the final issue of a small, private paper called the *Herald*, but that could not be proven, as all copies had vanished without a trace.

Trina smoothed a lock back into her coiffeur. "Convenient that an editorial from an anonymous author incited factory workers to riot, break their own machinery, and burn down their warehouses on the same night that Bessie and our steampunks arrived."

"Steampunks?" Ivy asked.

Trina shrugged. "They needed a nickname. And you tear up anytime we so much as say 'major.'"

A small smile cracked Ivy's composure. She was relieved that Trina was speaking to her again. "Not merely convenient." Ivy would have to find a way to thank Jade for her brilliance. She'd insisted Eric write that editorial with the help of the triplets' flare for dramatics. "Damn lucky."

Papa stared at his notes at the podium before placing his hand on top of them and crumpling them. "I know. I know you didn't believe me. But what did I say?" The king wagged a finger toward the crowd.

"Ivy?" Trina hissed urgently. Papa was going off script.

Ivy silenced her sister with a glare.

Papa continued. "Look at this crowd. Look at the soldiers. They fought for me. And I brought them home."

Ivy stared at the cobbles of the square. Looking at Papa when he was posturing was almost unbearable. She smoothed a wrinkle out of her skirts and eyed her sisters, lined up oldest to youngest behind their father. Ivy clenched her fists. Of course Daphne would forget her coat on a day like today. Especially when all the young men were assembled before them.

"I said I would win the war. And I was right."

"If only he'd let you give his speeches," Trina whispered as she expertly brushed a curl back, carefully shielding her words from the paper boys who were too clever when it came to reading lips.

King Rupert sighed dramatically. "But I'm afraid I have some bad news."

Ivy's gaze fixed on the alley. Her heart panged with the memory of the last time she'd headed down it with a young man in filthy clothes, his face covered in bruises. She flinched, realizing the last image she had of Collin was painfully similar.

Pen leaned out past Trina and mouthed, "What is Pops talking about?" She didn't even try to disguise her words for the boys at the *Gazette*.

King Rupert spread his arms wide and let them fall. "I still have no heir."

The crowd erupted in shouts, but King Rupert silenced them when he spoke. "I've done all I could for you, but I have no son. And Adelaide can't do it. Not that she hasn't tried. She can't. You under-

stand. So... I've come up with a plan." Papa swept his hand toward
Ivy. "I have the most beautiful daughters. They're gorgeous. They
take after their Papa, don't they? I propose..." The king held up his
right hand, curling his forefinger to his thumb.

Ivy's fingers twitched, and her pulse quickened. He was going to
do it! He had to. All those years of her hard work and devotion. He
was going to modify the law of primogeniture to include daughters.
And with Ivy's role in the open, it would be that much easier to
manage the statesmen and balance the budget. With her father's
open show of support for her capabilities, she'd be able to enact real
and lasting change. And she'd be able to do it faster. She might even
be able to find some free time of her own to sew a cushion or learn the
northern dialect or—

"I propose a contest. And the victor will win not only our kingdom, but one of my daughters as well!"

Ivy watched the crowd erupt into cheers. She watched hats soar
into the air and fall to be stepped on and ignored and left behind. She
felt as if she were falling, rolling off a table and clattering to the floor
like a stripped screw or worn-out gear. She felt cold and hard, and she
felt a fresh stab in her aching heart. She'd done all that she had done
—won a war, protected her people, worked herself almost sick—for
what? For a father who did not value her, her efforts, or her sacrifices.
For people who were willing to accept her or a sister—mercy, they
were all interchangeable—as a trophy. For people who cheered and
lost their hats at the very idea of it.

A smug smile stretched across King Rupert's face. His eyes
nearly disappeared into the satisfied grin, and with the cheers from
the crowd, his smile only grew. This was victory on his terms, a
victory he could dictate and understand. Not a peace, hard-earned
with personal sacrifice and even greater cost. But a spectacle, a cheap
trick to garner sloppy, drunken toasts to the king by even sloppier,
drunken men who then would march up to enter this contest in the
hopes of undressing Ivy or one of her sisters with more than just their
eyes.

A cold, bitter wind rippled the spider web of pennants and had ideas about Ivy's skirts. She swatted them back into place and hazarded a glance at her sisters. Fear. Disgust. Anger. And, in the case of Jade, nausea.

Trina had gone pale. She blew into her hands to shield her lips. "Did you know about this?"

Ivy cocked an eyebrow and smiled broadly. It was almost impossible to read lips when they were stretched so wide. "No." She felt like screaming, ripping her dress, and challenging every last man in the square to a duel. They looked at her now. They looked at all her sisters as if they were pieces of marbled meat hanging in the butcher's window.

Pen was less discreet and swore a storm before she asked Ivy, "What are we going to do?"

"We're going to play along. For now. We play along. Smile, girls. Wave to your people."

Rain tapped against the windows of King Rupert's personal study. Ivy tapped louder at her father's door. It had taken her all afternoon to find a moment alone with her father. And while she'd very much like to open a downpour of criticism on the man, she, like the rain, remained light. Restrained. "Papa? Papa, may I have a word?"

The king sat at his red-felted card table. A frown graced his jowls as he studied his hand. "Did you like my speech today?"

"Yes, Papa. But why didn't you tell me about your plans for the succession?" And for turning all twelve of your offspring into trophies?

"My game, you mean? I'm tremendously fond of games." The king returned his hand to the deck and shuffled the cards clumsily.

"Papa, our government is not a game."

"What do you want me to do about it? Statesman... Oh, what's his name? You know, the short one with the snaggled tooth. He tells me we need to discuss my heir now that the war is over. But I have no son, Ivy. I have daughters. Twelve of them." The king dealt his cards, as well as a couple extra.

"Yes, but it's a very complicated and delicate situation." If Ivy could only explain why the proposed solution was dangerous, if she could just make Papa understand her position—

"It's not. You always bring me problems to solve. Everyone tells me about problems, problems, problems. And what do I say? What do I always say?"

Ivy pressed her lips together. She twisted her fingers around one another. Gracious, it'd be lovely to twist them around Mama's watch right now, but she still hadn't found it, even after unpacking her trunk and scouring the sisters' apartment twice. She pressed her heels into Papa's lavish Easterlie carpets. "'Bring me solutions.'"

"That's right." The king pulled a card but returned it to the middle of the deck and pulled another.

"But, Papa, it could be very dangerous to award just anyone your crown, not to mention one of your children."

"If you're so worried about it, then bring me a solution, Ivy." The king inspected his cards and retrieved yet another from his discard pile.

"Will you consider an alternative plan for the kingdom?"

He didn't even bother to look up. "I promised the people a game. I promised them a game that any man can enter."

"But, Papa—"

His chest puffed out before he huffed out a blast of frustration. He dog-eared his ace of hearts and sent it back into the deck. "Now what kind of king would I be if I went back on my promise?"

It was no use. The rain continued its measured tap, and she would continue to patiently sift through her father's plan. "What sort of game do you have in mind?"

"Oh, I don't care. So long as the people like it. We can fill in the details as needed."

The wind gusted, and a heavy downpour rattled the leaded windowpanes.

Or Ivy could create the details to suit her own ambition.

"The other girls have gone out shopping, except Jade, who is in bed with a megrim." Trina was waiting in the hall outside the sisters' apartment. An extra wing especially for the princesses had been added to the palace when Mina was born. It was the first edifice in Amadanri with electric lights. Papa had declared they'd always be left on.

Ivy toggled the switch. The hall was a dim affair in the thunderstorm, but the lights were unresponsive. "Maybe the fuse," she mumbled.

"They said if they were going to be a door prize, they might as well look the part." Trina closed the door behind her sister. "So, what's the plan?" she demanded.

"There is no plan." Ivy unbuttoned her jacket and threw it on the floor of their private salon. The room was spacious, well-appointed with furniture that showed hardly any signs of frequent use, but it was also a complete disaster. Twelve sisters in a common living space meant books were lying haphazardly on chesterfields, end tables, and the floor. Pen's sketches took up the remaining available tables. Discarded shoes were piled against the wall. The *Gazette* was dissected and strewn about the room. Gwen's pastels smudged into Harriet's unrolled meditation rug. Ivy's jacket joined the collection of discarded garments that littered the floor.

Trina's pretty face scrunched into a frown. "What?"

Ivy untied her cravat, balled it up, and tossed it at the wall. "I work so hard, and this is the thanks I get? I'm told, along with the rest of the country, that a stranger, a know-nothing man, can come in, compete in some silly game, and become king?" Ivy raked her fingers through her hair. "I should be sovereign." She stormed into her bedroom and slammed the door.

Trina entered and quietly closed the door behind her. She stared at her sister with wide eyes. "Should I have gone shopping too?"

"It should be me!" Ivy screamed. The injustice had weighed so heavily and for so long that the scale had broken. Ivy crumpled next to her bed, sobbing. "I already do all the work. Papa shirks all the tough decisions and leaves them for me to handle at the eleventh hour." Snot ran from her nose, and she wiped at it with the back of her hand. "And then when he finally makes one, it's not just stupid but dangerous!"

Trina sat on the edge of Ivy's bed. She laid a gentle hand on her sister's neck. Ivy sobbed harder.

"I was the one who finally forced peace! I worked hard. I sacrificed everything!" And everyone. She wouldn't be nursing a broken heart if it weren't for the stupid war. And the only reason why it had been bearable was because she knew—she'd thought she knew—that monarchs had to make personal sacrifices for the common good. Now, none of it mattered. Now, everything was lost. "I tried to be good. I tried to prove to Papa that I could do the job."

Trina stroked her sister's neck.

Ivy groaned and shook her sister off. Collin had been right when he'd said, *The man is a selfish, incompetent disaster.* She'd not say as much out loud, but he'd been right. Papa wasn't fit to be king. No man was. Selfish and stupid brutes, the lot of them. It made her skin crawl to think how they'd gawked at her, at her sisters, after Papa had announced his blond-curled-and-pompadour-brained scheme.

Ivy rose and shouldered open the window. The rain was still falling at a roar. "I should be king," Ivy said to the rain.

Trina was beside her sister but made no attempt to touch her. Instead, she snatched up her music books from the chaise below the window.

Ivy inhaled the sharp notes of wet earth and sky. "I know my country better than any of those men. I know the duties. I know the hard decisions..." Ivy stared beyond the rain to the spring garden. Tender green sprouts were beginning to blanket the muddy furrows. Papa hated that more of the grounds had to be sacrificed. He'd finally agreed to the proposed farmland so long as it wouldn't interfere with his views. They'd settled on tucking the new fields back here, near the sisters' apartment. Rain bit Ivy's face as she stared down at row after row of cotyledons. "And I can make those decisions." Ivy slammed the window shut and drew the curtain. No need to further torture herself. She'd proved her point. "I should be king... And I will be."

"What?"

"I'm not letting some oaf steal my birthright or marry any of us. I'm going to rig the game."

Trina dropped her music books. "Ivy?"

"I'll make it impossible. The idiots will spend years trying to win the contest. Meanwhile, I'll have an amenable statesman quietly change the law, allowing for female succession, and if they all refuse, then I'll just have to outlive Papa."

"Ivy?" Trina said again, with a note of genuine alarm in her tone. "What are you talking about?"

"Glass mountains. I'll build one for all of us." Ivy forced a laugh. "Let them try and climb it!"

CHAPTER TWENTY-NINE

The squeaking carriage wheels woke Collin from his nap against the cherry tree. He'd not intended to fall asleep. He'd not intended to fall in love with Ivy either.

"Young man!" An elderly gentlewoman with feathers in her hair poked her head out of the carriage door. "Is this Oswald's farm?"

"Madame?"

"The Oswald farm? They make the most extraordinary rhubarb pie."

Collin rose and dusted his trousers. What would Gran think of him if he were to make this poor woman go on shouting like that? Collin quickly crossed over to the carriage. He tipped his nonexistent hat and bowed. "Fran makes a delicious rhubarb pie. But she's married to an Elis now, and the farm has changed hands quite a bit recently. I'm not sure on the name." Fran had insisted that Collin and Gran could pick a new name, but they'd yet to land on one they all could agree on.

"Fran remarried? Good heavens. At her age. It's a scandal."

Collin smiled. "The lady continues to make an excellent pie."

A low chuckle sounded within the carriage. "Excuse me, Sylvia dear."

The carriage door swung open, and an old woman dressed in a smart fedora and heather cloak swept out of the carriage.

"Florence, where are you going?"

"Fresh air, Sylvia. Go on and enjoy your pie. I'll have a stroll with this young man."

Sylvia blinked her large eyes at Collin. "No objections?"

"None." Collin winged an elbow toward Florence, who grasped it firmly. "I'm Collin, madame."

Florence nodded. "You're a long way from the fight, Major. And please call me Florence."

"The war is over."

"Then why are you not at the capital celebrating? I'm sure a smart young officer like you had much to do with the peace."

Collin and Florence strolled under the avenue of cherry trees. The buds on the trees had swollen nicely, yet still were closed tight. "My invitation was rescinded."

"Oh?" Florence unbuttoned her gray cloak and spread it underneath a cherry tree. The shadows of the branches danced across it in the bright sunshine.

Collin assisted Florence as she sat on her cloak. "Thank you, Major. My joints are all the stiffer from that infernal carriage ride. Peppermint?" Florence produced a candy from a pocket of her dress.

"Thank you." Collin unwrapped the red-and-white-striped sweet.

"You're the first young man I've met in ages who didn't snub an old woman's offering. Your Gran taught you well."

Curious, he'd not mentioned being raised by Gran. He'd not mentioned his former rank either. "Gran taught me that sharing a drink, a sweet, a meal is the fastest way to make a friend."

"Or acquire information?" Florence produced a second sweet for herself. The paper crinkled as she unwrapped the peppermint.

"Gran would put it in those terms, yes."

"You're a good boy, Major. Now tell me what you are doing camping alone under cherry trees."

Collin bit the peppermint in half and choked on one of the pieces.

"What's her name?" Florence said. She produced another peppermint for Collin.

He nodded his thanks but turned the sweet over in his hands. "Ivy. Princess Ivy. If you can believe that."

Florence hmphed. "Princesses are such a nuisance. As soon as you've rescued one, two more crop up that need saving."

"Not this one." Collin carefully unwrapped the sweet. "This one's different."

"Then why are you here?"

"She thinks I tried to assassinate her father, King Rupert."

Florence snorted. "And she was mad that you didn't succeed?"

Armed with a sharp wit, this woman. Gran would like her. Collin leaned back on Florence's cloak and covered his eyes with his arm. "She told me if she ever saw me back in the capital or anywhere near her father or family, I'd be tried and hanged."

"And she didn't drag you back to stand trial because..."

Collin scratched at the hair above his left ear and blushed.

"I see." Florence squinted up at the branches. "Look at those buds. No one does cherry blossoms so well as your little Kingdom of Amadanri. You know, Sylvia and I came here many years ago, before the war, of course, hoping to see the cherry trees in bloom. We were too early. Trees thick with swollen buds were all we saw. And I was so mad." She looked Collin in the eye. "I was furious with disappointment. What on earth were those trees thinking? Didn't they know we had traveled for weeks just to see them bloom?"

"Our cherry trees are known for their rudeness. I must apologize for them."

Florence smiled and patted Collin's hand. "They just made me more determined. That year, we could not stay to see them open. But I told Sylvia that next year would be different. And it was. King

Rupert invaded our friends in the east. The cherry trees had to wait. But now. With armistice and your hard-earned peace, we are back. And we will see the cherry blossoms."

"They're beautiful. My favorite time is the end of the season."

"When the petals rain down as a gentle, fragrant snow." Florence's smile spread wide, and she rubbed her hands together. "I shall stand in this spring snow. The trees cannot exclude me this time. My victory will be all the sweeter for the waiting."

Collin offered his flask to Florence. She unscrewed the top and sniffed the contents, took a sip, and nodded. "Don't stop fighting, Collin. Ivy needs you. She's put herself in a dangerous position."

"You fear another assassination attempt?"

Florence looked down her nose at him. "Do you?"

Collin blushed. "No."

"No, Ivy has placed her trust in people who care only about themselves. No one is looking out for her best interests. She, like Cinderella, believes that if she will only work hard enough, she will earn their love, merit the same careful consideration that she has for them. But the poor dear is as good as invisible."

"Her needs certainly are."

"Exactly so. She needs someone to look after her. She needs a handsome, young man who will pull her away from her squabbles with statesmen while turning her head on the dance floor."

"I never could get her to dance."

"I never saw the cherries bloom. It only made me more determined."

Collin took a sip before he screwed the cap back on his flask. "You know an awful lot about Ivy—"

"I know an awful lot about princesses."

The carriage wheels squeaked across the hill. "Will Madame Sylvia be joining us?" Collin asked.

"Heavens no! Sylvia is determined to arrive by teatime. At least one of the five pies she is buying is a gift for our hostess and mutual friend. I believe you know Olivia of Whiting Street."

Collin rose to his feet and assisted Florence to her own. He shook the dust from the cloak and handed it to Florence.

"Keep it. You may find it useful."

She was a fey matchmaker if ever there was one! A fairy godmother to the lucky families who could afford it, and she was giving him a gift. Collin would be a simpleton to refuse it. "Thank you, Florence."

"Hullo!" The carriage stopped, and Sylvia, her smile enormous, swung open the door. "Fran is ever a delight, and her young husband...ooch! Such a charmer."

Collin assisted Florence into the carriage.

"Did you have a nice respite with the major?"

"An absolute delight. I do love the boys who were raised by their Grans."

"Thank you, Major!" Sylvia sang out. "I am much obliged. It is so much easier to travel with Florence when she is in a good humor."

"If you let me plan the destinations instead of just dragging me hither and yon, you might be surprised—"

"If there is anything I can do to repay the favor?" Sylvia asked.

A warm breeze blew through the cherry branches, and sunshine dazzled off the polished steel of the carriage. "Might I join you ladies? Florence has convinced me to enjoy the capital's cherry blossoms for the season."

Sylvia turned to her companion with raised brows. "A working holiday, then." Sylvia cleared her throat. "Major, it would be our pleasure."

CHAPTER THIRTY

Ivy hadn't wanted to go shopping. But after three days, the rain had at last turned into a drizzle, and it was time for a respite. So Trina had argued. She'd caught Ivy more than once swatting tears from her eyes as she scribbled away at a proposal for Papa's inane game. Now Trina insisted on playing chaperone. A change of scene would do Ivy good.

In other words, Trina wanted to go shopping.

Ivy could have begged off, and Trina would have sighed deeply and returned to scratching away at her sheet music, but Trina was growing restless, her music morose.

A-shopping they would go.

The polished pine floors of Olivia's shop glinted ocher in the afternoon light. The bell on the door rang. The crystal chandeliers winked as they swayed gently, while bolts of buttery fabrics stood at attention along the walls. Olivia was both tailor and milliner. And her shop was something else. It was absolutely magical. Something about it made Ivy want to believe that change was as easy as donning a new costume. She had only to find the right dress, and she'd be recognized as Papa's true heir. If the dress were combined with the right set of heels, the men in her life might even regale her with the truth for once.

"Shall we start with gloves? I'll need a new lace pair as soon as the rains stop." Trina stopped at the glass counter. "I do hope this cold snap ends soon. I feel as if winter has lasted for years."

Or it felt like spring had never come. Ivy fingered a bolt of silk with green, burgundy, and cream stripes.

Trina joined her. "Oh, that's lovely. Excuse me?" The attendant behind the counter came to attention. "Has anything been made in this yet? We want to see it." The attendant nodded and slipped into the back room.

The shop was wonderfully quiet. Had Trina sent word that they were coming and asked for an empty store? Ivy hoped not. Olivia had to make a living after all. Ivy wandered over to the pinstripes and tweeds.

"No, none of that. You need color, dear. You need something fun. Maybe this beautiful floral?"

"Trina, please. I'm not Daphne."

"She would scratch it off your back. It is so much her taste. But you need something. You can't wear tweed for the rest of your life."

"I'm certain I can."

"Mademoiselles, we have a waistcoat in the silk stripe." The attendant, a slim gentleman in an expertly tailored coat, laid the waistcoat on the glass counter.

The bell on the door jingled, and the door burst open, but no one entered.

"Must be the wind." Trina fingered the silk waistcoat. "Perhaps with brass buttons?"

The attendant nodded and returned to the back room. Trina twirled through the bolts of velvet. At least Trina was having a good time.

"Remind me to tell Auntie she has a problem with her door," Ivy said, making sure it had clicked shut. She leaned against the glass display case and startled as her arm encountered a soft cashmere. She looked down but saw only Trina's lace gloves.

"Ivy," Trina called from an aisle in the back. "Come look at this charmeuse. It's just your color."

The bell jingled again, but this time a chic gentlewoman, dressed in white with plumes in her hair, strode into the store. "I need woolen socks."

"Yes, madame. At the counter, if you please," the attendant said.

The woman waved her bejeweled hand. "I'm in no rush."

Ivy stopped the attendant before he could flitter into the back room once again. "Excuse me, do you have any cashmere?"

"Apologies, mademoiselle. We have only our spring collection on the shop floor. I could look in the back—"

Ivy dismissed the notion.

Trina came to Ivy at the counter, carrying a bolt of dark green fabric. She held it up to her sister and squealed. "It's your color, darling."

"Papa has already made me the joke of his stupid game. I'm not going to make an even greater fool of myself by wearing *ivy* green."

"It's perhaps not the color but the cut that matters here, my dear." The woman in white had wandered over to the girls. She fingered the green material. "How do you do? I'm Sylvia."

Ivy bit her tongue. She hated forced introductions. But what else could she do? "It's a pleasure to meet you, Sylvia."

"Oh, I'm sure it's not. Here you are, wanting two minutes to yourself, and some stranger imposes on you. But your sister is right." She tapped the shimmering fabric with a finger, and the andalusite of her ring glinted on the shop walls. It was a ring remarkably like Auntie's. "This color suits you."

"Forgive me, but I will not be ridiculed for wearing a dress that matches my name."

Trina munched a chocolate from the dish on the counter. "It has happened before, which is such a shame, because it is a lovely hue."

"It brings out the fire in your eyes," Sylvia said. "Your other dresses before were..."

Ivy picked at the raw edges of the charmeuse. "Green monsters."

"Full-skirted?" Sylvia asked.

"Embarrassingly so." Was the attendant laughing in the back room? Someone had just snickered.

"Strapless?"

"Naturally."

Sylvia tsked. "Little-girl dresses. No. If you had a floor-length sheath made out of this—tight clinging sleeves, draped bust, scooped-out back, slight train." The woman tapped a finger to her lips. "Perhaps a bit of embroidered beading for some sparkle." She nodded brightly. "No one would ever make fun of you for wearing green again."

Trina jumped in before Ivy could derail her. "And what if Ivy wanted a red dress?" She set a bolt of crimson taffeta on the counter with a thud.

"A modified mermaid fit. So she could dance in it. Are you girls fond of dancing?"

Trina spoke before Ivy had a chance. "We are indeed!"

Sylvia clasped her hands together. "You must come to the soirée my dear friend and I are hosting. She doesn't know it yet, but I will convince her. Some dancing is what we all could use on chilly spring nights like these. Some of us more than others."

"My sister and I would be delighted." Trina caught Ivy's withering look. "However, we will not be able to attend. You see, our younger sisters are even more fond of dancing than we are, and if they were to learn we had gone without them, they would never forgive us."

"Yes, they'd probably cut off your hair when you were sleeping. Pretty hair too. I can see why he likes it."

"Excuse me?" Ivy asked. Her skin prickled once again, as if she'd brushed up against cashmere.

"No matter. They are invited too. Young people need ample opportunity to enjoy their youth."

Trina was absolutely no help. "We should be delighted to come to your party."

Sylvia squealed. "How marvelous!"

Delightful. Another impossible situation. Invitations from unvetted, opinionated old bats.

"I shall send your invitation with Monsieur Wind. Just give me some time to work out the details. And none of that fretting, Ivy. We are long-standing friends of Olivia's, and she's an excellent judge of character."

"You're friends with Auntie?" Trina's enthusiasm was almost embarrassing.

"Lifelong friends."

"Then you're family!" Trina and Sylvia embraced and screamed, and the poor attendant, who had a collection of wool socks draped over his arm, turned pink and tried to discreetly back away, but Trina stopped him. She pointed to the bolts of green and red fabric.

"I'll see to ordering your dresses," the attendant said, and they swept away, chattering about *buttons* and *modified mermaid* and what all.

"There now," Sylvia said to Ivy. "Some pretty new dresses and a reason to wear them, but still no smile. What is wrong, Ivy darling? Is it your critics? Pay them no mind. Your new green dress will silence them for good."

"Do you really think any solution is as simple as a new dress and an invitation?" The bite in her words was regrettable, but so was the instant familiarity this woman had assumed.

"Trina's spirits have certainly improved."

Trina did look remarkably happy as she chatted with the attendant.

"Simple pleasures should be indulged." Sylvia tried on a ring from the display. "Now and then."

Splendid. Ivy must now endure life lessons from a complete stranger.

The attendant at last commanded Sylvia's attention and showed her the selection of wool socks. "You know, I think I'd prefer silk. I am fond of this one, though. Would you be so kind to send me the bill?" The gentlewoman rounded on Ivy. "Now you listen to Auntie Sylvia. Dancing, my dear. It's the only remedy. Now I must be off. Look for my invitation. Hmm?"

"We should be going too," Ivy said, feeling once more the sensation of cashmere brushing against her arm.

"Ivy darling? The waistcoat?"

"No, thank you, Trina." Ivy wandered over to her sister. A dark emerald tie lay on top of the counter. "But perhaps this new tie."

CHAPTER THIRTY-ONE

"Tim!" How could a bloke sleep through the racket below? Collin shook his friend's shoulder once more. "Tim!"

Tim pulled the pillow over his face and continued sleeping.

Collin reached for the alarm clock on the box beside Tim's bed and twisted it until it exploded into a riot of dings.

"I'm up. I'm up!" Tim rubbed his eyes. "Collin?"

"Surprised to see me?"

Tim was on his feet and hitting Collin with his pillow and then his fists. "What are you doing here?"

"I could ask you the same question." Collin grabbed his cloak and pulled it over his shoulders. Tim stumbled backward onto the bed with a yelp, then extended a tentative hand. Collin sidestepped out of reach.

"Where did he go?" Tim muttered, blinking and rubbing his eyes.

Remarkable. Florence's cloak was remarkable. It obscured the wearer completely as soon as it hung from his shoulders, though Florence had warned Collin that the cloak's magic did not extend to fey eyes.

"Collin?" Tim hissed.

Collin shrugged out of the borrowed cloak and folded it over the only chair in the cramped little room. He would have to see if Tim could afford a room in a nicer part of town. Preferably far away from Sutherbee's. "Are you done with fisticuffs? Or do I need to put the cloak back on?"

"What do you want?"

"I need your help. I need a roommate, too, but that can wait until tomorrow night."

Tim groaned and picked up his alarm clock and a screwdriver. "I thought a certain princess told you to never come back to the capital."

"And I thought I'd change her mind. I need a favor."

"Knowing you, you probably need more than just one. How's your Gran?"

"She can't recognize me anymore."

"I couldn't even see you with that awful cloak. Where'd you get it?"

"I made a new friend."

"Fantastic. Now I won't feel bad when I tell you to bugger off."

"Look, I'm sorry I left you and the others sleeping at the border, but it was for your own good."

"We could have both ridden back in the tank. There was a hero's welcome big enough for the two of us."

There was not. And Collin had worried that an arrest would follow his return of the tank. He hadn't wanted to risk—or involve—Tim unnecessarily. But things had changed dramatically thanks to the king's game. "I preserved your anonymity! Without it, you couldn't be here working in the capital." Ivy had meant what she'd said. "Do you know where Eric is?"

Tim put down his clock and tool and lay back on the bed. "No."

Collin sat down on top of his cloak and tipped his chair back against the wall. "How 'bout Monty?"

"Nope."

"Phillip?"

Tim threw an elbow across his eyes and pointed a finger at the floor. "He plays downstairs every night. Helped me get my room. Nice bloke."

Collin squinted in the dark light. The electric streetlamp outside the small window cast a yellow haze on the small washbasin and the sorry table that had assumed the role of desk in the narrow room. The notes of the pipe organ rose above the raucous laughter and shouting for a few notes. "You sure about that?"

Tim had dozed off. Collin let all four legs of his chair clatter back to the floor. Tim woke with a start.

"What about Matthew?"

"He never left his dairy cows."

It was worse than he'd feared. "I need them all back. All of them."

Tim rolled onto his back. "What for?"

"We're going to win the king's game. Together."

"Yeah? And which one of us will be king after we do that?"

"Does it matter? You'll get another chance with Pen."

Tim climbed out of bed and slid his suspenders over his shoulders. "Phillip will know where Monty is. Eric won't be far."

CHAPTER THIRTY-TWO

Ivy stood while her father sat at his breakfast table. Never mind that she had been the one up all night for the past week engineering a game to satisfy Papa's need for spectacle, the people's need for sport, the country's need for pragmatism, and her need to pursue her own ambition. She'd be bald and wearing one of Papa's blond wigs before she'd allow another man to rule the kingdom.

King Rupert's eyes narrowed. "This is a clever start."

Start? A complete outline, cost analysis, and summary of cultural significance were nothing more than a start? "Thank you, Papa."

Rupert flipped through her neat stack of papers. Her meticulous cursive spiraled in regimented lines across every page. "Your sisters helped you make it?"

Ivy massaged her aching hand behind her back. "No. I thought to spare them the trouble." Working against a deadline was not exactly pleasant. Particularly when the deadlines were a perpetual surprise.

King Rupert grunted. "Three tasks... It's a good start but not enough. Your sisters need to add something."

"For instance?"

"Oh, I don't know. But..." Papa flipped through the papers. "I must have final say in the applications. It is my game after all."

A tight smile spread across Ivy's firmly pressed lips. "Of course, Papa. Now, if we could talk about the timeline—"

"No time." The king shoved an entire strawberry scone into his mouth. Crumbs splayed across his cravat as he spoke. "I invited a crowd of hopefuls to the palace. They're outside now." The king licked his fingers. "Go explain the game to them."

"Papa, you said yourself the game isn't ready."

"Tell them what you just told me."

Ivy's heart hammered. "Don't you wish to speak with them directly? They are your guests."

The king snorted. "A crowd of rowdy men my guests?" He shook the crumbs from his cravat. "I'll stop by once you've explained the process." He rose from the table and inspected his blond wig in the mirror, tugging it back into place. "Is that a new tie, Ivy?"

Ivy fingered the knotted green bow at her throat. "The war is over. I thought I'd celebrate with a new tie."

"You should get a dress to match. We named you Ivy for a reason, you know." The king grew uncharacteristically somber. It was the most he'd spoken of Mama in...forever.

"Yes, Papa."

Ivy braced herself, finished her cocoa, and proceeded to the west salon. It was crowded with men and boys of every age.

"Gentlemen, it's a pleasure to welcome you to the palace this morning. Thank you for your dedication and your service. On behalf of your country and monarch, I thank you."

A man called out from the middle of the crowd. "The rules, sweetheart."

Ivy's toothsome smile did not falter even though her skin prickled and her fists clenched tight. "You must each complete three separate tasks, all designed to find the natural leader and future king among you. The first task is also the application to the rest of the contest. As you can imagine, my sisters and I are busy people."

A roar of laughter filled the salon. Charming. A princess obviously had nothing better to do than powder her nose and look pretty.

Ivy chuckled, a sound that would have set a person with a discerning ear on edge. "Only those who succeed at the first task may proceed with the competition. Are we clear so far?"

There was a murmur of agreement.

"A monarch must be a statesman. He must be able to draft important documents. The first task will be to write twelve official state letters in a single night."

Silence indicated their lack of amusement. They'd love this next bit.

"All as perfect and clearly legible as the first."

There was a roar of indignation.

"You may bring your own pen if you like, but we will supply the parchment. You may also bring your own ink, as my sisters tell me this can make or break an effort. You will have from sundown to sunup to draft your documents. You will present them to me when the sun rises. Those whose documents are in order will advance to the next task." And no one would. Ivy would make sure of it. "Are we clear, gentlemen?"

Grunts and nods to the affirmative. Such primitive beasts. Ivy suppressed a shudder. "Excellent. You may return to the palace entrance and sign up for the night of your choosing. Should you require assistance preparing for the application process, classes will be available to you at the college free of charge." That they were disguised literacy and vocational classes need not be mentioned. "Captain Hector and the other guards will assist you if you have further questions. Good day, gentlemen."

Ivy exited the salon and, with a shaking hand, donned her glasses to scratch a note about future crowd-control measures. She jumped when she spied a familiar figure, dark, dashing, and draped in a gray cloak, slouching against the hall wall. She blinked and removed her spectacles, but the hall was empty.

CHAPTER THIRTY-THREE

Collin didn't know how, but Tim had found their friends. Monty, Eric, and Phillip, along with Tim, were waiting for him at Sutherbee's.

Monty cradled his head in his hands. "Do you have to play so loud?"

Phillip removed the pencil from his teeth long enough to scribble a note on his sheet music. "Shut up. I'm composing." He shook out his right hand before playing a thunderous round of chords.

"So, what did they say?" Eric asked.

Tim was even more direct. "Did you see Pen? Did she look like she missed me?"

Collin's brow furrowed. "I did not see her, but I'm sure she's pining for you."

Tim almost believed him. "Shut up."

Collin shook out Florence's cloak and hung it on the pegs just under the sign that said Sutherbee's: Established Who the Bloody Cares. Have a Whiskey.

"How did you find employment in such a charming establishment?" Eric hollered to Phillip.

Phillip muttered something with his pencil between his teeth that sounded like, "They let me compose all morning."

"Couldn't you do that later, less early?" Monty winced.

Eric clapped Monty on the back. "Drink too much again?"

Monty groaned. "Absolutely bottled. Thanks, mate."

Collin beamed at his friends. His found family was almost reunited. They'd just have to play Ivy's game. And win. "Where is Matthew?"

"Who?" Phillip asked.

"Jade's husband," Tim explained. "He'll be round soon. He has deliveries all over the capital on Wednesdays now."

"And you're sure Sutherbee is out for the morning?" Collin asked Phillip.

"He's probably out of his bloody mind, letting Phil play that ruddy machine," Monty muttered.

Phillip straightened and pulled the pencil from his mouth just long enough to declare, "I'm creating art. It matters!" Then he went back to it.

"Right, well..." Collin toggled a switch on the organ before Phillip swatted him. "We need to get crackin' on Ivy's first challenge."

"First challenge?" Monty poured himself a drink, which Eric quickly snatched away.

Collin fetched a chair that had been stacked on the bar and sat. "She said there would be three tasks."

"Is that all?" Eric asked.

"No. The king says the game must be expanded." Collin colored slightly. It was one thing to overhear information that was carelessly discarded. Quite another to collect it without permission. "He wants more input from all the sisters."

"Such as?" Tim asked.

"I dunno." Collin considered. "Additional tasks. Riddles, maybe."

"Riddles would definitely be the easier option," Monty offered.

Phillip played a murderous chord on the organ.

"Something wrong, Phil?" Collin said, drumming his fingers on the pipe organ.

"Don't touch my organ," he snapped. "Think you could answer a riddle Sophia wrote?" He scowled at Tim. "Or maybe one both she and Pen collaborated on?"

Tim turned deathly pale.

"That's what I thought," Phillip said. "This is a disaster. No bloke has a prayer of ever understanding a woman, let alone a collective effort. Egads!" He closed the keys of his organ. "It's a trap if ever there was one."

Eric shifted awkwardly at the bar. "How about the tasks, Collin?"

"Ivy only mentioned the first. Draft twelve state letters in a single night, all equally legible."

"Well, that's not so bad," Tim said.

If that was all there was to it, but Collin knew Ivy. "Ten to one, there's a soporific involved."

Monty woke up. "I like those odds!"

"She'll lace some edible with a powerful soporific or hypnotic, and half the men will fall asleep before they've even written their names at the top of the submission form." Collin folded his arms. "Whoever competes will need to fast while at the palace. What do I say, boys? What do I always say?"

"Trust me," the men chorused.

Mars! "Never taste an unknown substance."

"You never say that," said Tim.

Phillip brushed a speck of dust off the top of the organ. "So we know not to eat anything. That doesn't help us at all with penning these letters."

"Can we write them beforehand?" Eric asked.

Collin arched an eyebrow. "No. Ivy said the paper will be provided. I'm sure it will carry an official watermark, and then there's the question of the unknown prompts."

Tim tapped his finger to his teeth. Odd habit. But one Ivy had confided that Pen found endearing. "And the ink? Is she supplying the ink?"

"It sounds as if Pen convinced Ivy to let the applicants bring their own."

Tim's wry frame froze before his mouth cracked into an enormous smile. "She would too. Gads, I love that girl." Tim blushed. "I mean—"

"It's all right, Tim." Phillip raked his fingers through his wavy blond hair. "None of us would be here with Major Dunderhead if we didn't feel the same way about one of the sisters."

"But which one..." Eric mumbled to himself.

"I love them all equally," Monty said with a hiccup. "Like a brother. Except Ivy. She scares me."

Collin could not disagree.

"And applicants can bring their own pens," Tim mumbled, clearly turning that over in his head. Then he grabbed Phillip's composition and flipped it over.

"Hey!" Phillip protested.

"For true love, mate." He began sketching. "The problem, gentlemen, is legibility"—he continued to hastily sketch—"and speed. Ivy's banking that either or both will be enough to cog up most of the applicants."

"And if all else fails—the soporific." If they'd only seen her. She'd become a live wire— stripped, exposed, and extremely dangerous. "She'll add it to warm milk, maybe the coffee." Or, knowing Ivy, the chocolate.

Tim scratched out a portion of his sketch but continued drawing. "We need to create a pen-and-ink system that will ensure both accuracy and speed."

Eric slid off his stool and squinted at Tim's rough sketches before shaking his head. "It's times like this when I miss those girls the most."

"Something like that." Tim leaned back so the others could scan the drawing. He tucked the pencil behind his ear before he realized it was Phillip's and returned it.

Collin squinted at the design. "With keys like Phillip's organ?"

"More like a piano," Tim explained. "But instead of hitting a tuned string, they'll hit a ribbon of ink that will then stamp onto the paper, which will be rolled through like a tiny printing press."

"The configuration of the keys would correlate to the speed, would they not?" Collin asked.

Tim's eyes darted after ideas in his unique brain as he considered.

"Yes," Phillip said. "Leave it to a man who sits at a keyboard all day. Configuration matters."

Collin searched behind the bar for something to eat. "Monty, could you calculate the most frequently used letters in the alphabet?"

Monty lifted his head from the table. "Using what as a sample?"

Something minty perhaps. "Eric?" Collin asked.

"State documents, of course. The recent armistice would be good. The Declaration of Sovereignty. The Charta. Anything that conveys the typical language of state."

"Can you find the documents?" Collin asked, grabbing a peppermint from a dish shoved behind a row of bottles. Was there chocolate anywhere?

Eric shrugged. "As long as you are content with copies."

"Copies are fine. You can assist Monty with the calculations?"

"You mean babysit him until he sobers up?" Eric slapped Monty on the back.

"Hang on," Phillip said, grabbing the sketch. "If keys are involved, someone will have to learn how to play."

"Well, that can be you, Phil, can't it?" Collin smiled—he'd found a tin of cocoa.

"I'm not staying up all night writing letters of state. I have a paying gig here."

"He's right," Tim said. "We can make this contraption, but we still need someone familiar with writing state memos for this to work."

"Who's had ample experience corresponding with various government officials?" The company turned expectant eyes on Collin, who at this moment had his nose in a tin of cocoa and a peppermint in his mouth.

"What are you doing?" Eric asked.

Mars. What was he doing? Inhaling chocolate and mint because they reminded him of Ivy? "I can't just walk into the capital and apply for the king's game."

"Why not?" Tim asked. "You were there this afternoon."

"Yes, but Ivy didn't see me." No one saw Collin.

Monty looked confused. "I thought you two were..." He brought his pinched hands together.

Tim grabbed another sheet of Phillip's music and continued his clumsy sketching. "Did you have a row?" The bell at the door jingled, and Phillip rose to answer it.

"She still upset that you almost blew us up?" Eric asked.

Mars, if it were only that simple.

"More likely she was upset that he didn't blow himself up." Matthew stood in the doorway. He heaved a crate of clanking glass bottles onto the bar counter, and rather than take in the greetings from his friends, he went straight to Collin and punched him square in the jaw.

Collin staggered backward. The blow cascaded pain through his joints.

Tim pulled Collin upright. "What was that for?"

"Don't ask," Collin mumbled.

"This is your fault." Matthew's stocky frame was out of focus, but Collin felt a finger jab him in the ribs.

"What did he do now?" Tim asked, sounding every bit as long-suffering as Collin's Gran.

"I can't see my wife, and it's because *he* did something unspeakable."

Collin squinted around the throbbing pain. Phillip, Monty, Eric, even Tim, were all expecting answers now, while Matthew's fists were ready to force them.

Collin pilfered a bottle of milk from Matthew's crate. "I can explain everything." He applied the cold bottle to his tender jaw. "Trust me."

There was a chorus of groans. Mars, he did always say that.

Matthew retrieved the bottle and wiped it clean. "You'd better."

CHAPTER THIRTY-FOUR

Mina cradled the invitation in her gawky hands. "Are we really all going to go?" Goodness, she was growing. In another two months, she'd be taller than Ivy.

"What does the invitation say?" Ivy scratched out the last line of her manuscript. She needed to be careful when it came to drafting more-lenient tariffs. Not that the sanction on coastal grains could be lifted without Papa's approval.

"'To the Princesses Twelve of His Majesty King Rupert's Court in the Kingdom of Amadanri. We invite you to be our guests.'" Mina looked up from the invitation. "Who is 'we'?"

"Auntie Olivia's friends, Madames Florence and Sylvia," Trina said, playing a major scale up and down her spinet. She'd moved it back to the sisters' suite now that the library was being used for billiards.

Harriet looked up from her atlas. "Who?"

"They're fey matchmakers." Rachel did not bother to look up from her novel. She'd grown so sullen since Papa's announcement.

Angelica snorted. "Auntie must have sent for them when she

learned how badly Ivy botched things with Major Top-Notch." The triplets erupted into unbridled laughter.

"Girls!" Trina scolded.

Ivy looked quickly to Mina, who'd gone pale and quiet. She'd asked Mina not to say anything about Collin to their sisters. She'd instructed Trina and Pen to do the same. As far as the rest of the sisters were concerned, Ivy had failed abominably to capture Collin's attention in peacetime, or she had, unforgivably, failed to reciprocate his interest. The details didn't matter since her sisters were more than happy to fabricate them. Accounting for the absence of the rest of Collin's compatriots was more difficult. Spite seemed to be the prevailing theory.

"Aren't you lucky, Ivy," Jade snarled, "to have not only an entire kingdom clamoring to win some stupid game for you, but also to have hired matchmakers doing their part behind the scenes."

Jade had been most sour about Ivy's insistence that she remain separated from Matthew. He could be part of Collin's network. His relationship with Jade might have been completely nefarious... Or it could have been genuine. In any case, it would not do for Papa to have a son-in-law before he had an heir. It would be all too easy for some halfwit courtier to propose that Matthew be named successor over an upsetting game of billiards and for Papa, in a fit of frustration over a missed ball, to agree to the proposal.

Mina came quietly to Ivy's defense. Sweet thing. "The invitation says the ball is to celebrate the cherry blossoms."

Daphne grabbed the invitation from Mina and read, "'A series of three private midnight balls hosted by Madames Sylvia and Florence and Monsieur Wind to celebrate the fleeting beauty of the spring cherries and newfound peace.'"

"I told you!" Mina crossed her arms and huffed into the chair beside Ivy's desk.

"Who is Monsieur Wind?" Gwen read over Daphne's shoulder. Did sisters have nothing better to do than haunt the salon while Ivy was trying to work? If only the college had reconsidered Ivy's appeal.

But no, Professor August had insisted that the college was overrun by veterans and that accommodating young women, including Ivy's sisters, was impossible at this time. It was a game for additional funding, but one Ivy had no time to play.

"It doesn't matter." Jade lay down on the chaise and clutched a pillow to her stomach. "Ivy will tell you you can't have him or ever see him again." She burst into sobs.

"Politics is one thing, but Ivy can't deprive us from a few nights of fun," Daphne said, rubbing Jade's back.

"Oh yes, she can." Sophia slammed a stack of papers on top of Ivy's desk. "Here's your precious analysis. I hate algorithms, and I hate you!"

Fantastic. A mob of unhappy sisters. Ivy reached for her cocoa cup, but it was empty.

"Ivy, why can't we go?" whined Gwen. "Have you no heart?"

"She has none," Jade wailed. "You don't have to ask."

"Or are you afraid your allure will disintegrate once everyone sees what a terrible dancer you are?" Bea smiled as affably as she could manage while hurling insults.

Why had Ivy insisted on fiscal responsibility when Papa had wanted to build a new billiard room? Then she could have camped in the library indefinitely. Ivy scratched out another line of her manuscript. Her hand ached as she thought of the hours she'd lose rewriting the proposal. "I've never been alluring," she said.

"You've tried to be," Rachel mumbled.

"You're worried the rest of us will outshine you," Ang said.

"You're jealous of our beaus," Sophia added.

"Husband," Jade amended.

Not this again. "I've only *ever* had your safety and happiness in mind. Trina, help me persuade them."

Trina ceased her playing. "Ivy loves us all very much, which is why she has already accepted the invitation and shuffled funds for new dresses."

Delighted squeals punctuated the chaos of the sisters' salon.

"Better yet, new shoes," Harriet said. "We'll wear holes in them every night with our dancing." She twirled and spun around the salon.

Ivy locked eyes with Trina, who merely shrugged and returned to her playing.

"Can I paint your face?" Gwen asked. "You'll never doubt your allure after I'm finished."

"Oh, I can help!" Mina beamed. "Just think, my first ball!"

This was a disaster. This rivaled Papa's game in level of disaster. Unknown and unvetted hosts. No details about the location or other guests. Sky-high expectations on the part of her sisters. Not to mention the fortune they'd want to spend on their dresses. And shoes.

CHAPTER THIRTY-FIVE

A week later, Collin stood in front of the doors to the palace. Pink and orange already highlighted the sky, though the sun had not yet set.

Tim handed Collin the attaché case. "Oof. Heavy."

"There wasn't time to build it with a lighter alloy," Tim countered. "We're lucky we found the parts for it as is."

"It's magnificent."

"You remember how to change the ribbon? There's nothing I can do about having to press the carriage-return lever at the end of every line. Maybe if I had more time to tinker—"

"Tim, you are a genius."

"You will give me credit. I know Ivy loves gadgets, but Pen appreciates workmanship."

"Pen will know your work immediately."

"She's so... I'd build a bridge to the moon for her." Tim grabbed Collin's sleeve. "Don't mess this up."

The weight of his trust was heavier than the attaché case. By far. "I won't let you down. Trust me."

Collin followed the applicants into the palace, the front portions of which had become a public museum. He walked through galleries of paintings that alone were twice the size of Tim's flat. Painted on the ceiling above were likenesses of amused courtiers, fat cherubs, and spun-sugar clouds.

A captain of the guard motioned them into a smaller gallery that contained marble sculptures. "This way, sirs. Any of the desks will do."

Ocher rays of sun slid into the room. Collin selected a desk in the back left corner of the room, behind a bust of some ancient hero, and set down his attaché case. He heard both of the double doors swing open and donned his cloak as a precaution.

"Good evening, gentlemen." Ivy sailed between the sculptures, walking among the applicants. "Thank you for coming. We thought we'd have you in with the antiquities, as it is already set up for our students at the college. Young minds must be educated now that they are no longer patrolling trenches."

She wore the green tie, the one he'd picked out for her in the shop, the one that brightened her eyes and made Collin's knees buckle. He pulled his cloak closer and pressed himself against the wall.

Egads, she was preening, flirting even. "Paper is at the front. As are ink and pens if you did not bring your own. There will be no talking amongst you. Hector and his men will chair this application. Libation and victuals will be available throughout the night. Please enjoy yourselves."

She smiled one last time, a dazzling grin. She'd eat them all alive, but Collin would be careful. Once she'd left, he removed the cloak and folded it on the back of his desk.

The sun slid down out of the sky. The electric lights of the gallery already hummed contentedly. Collin paced up to the front of the room and commandeered a stack of papers. He examined the first prompt. An embargo on barley and flax seed. Very well, he'd read enough of those when he'd been a captain. The second prompt was a sanction on the export of dairy cows. Mars, it was going to be a dull evening. The third prompt was a rededication of some hall at the college, and so it went. All tedious. All similar to the requests and responses Collin had read daily during the war.

Collin returned to his seat. He carefully withdrew the type machine from its leather case and threaded the first piece of paper into it. He began punching the keys, enjoying the action and clacks. A few chaps took notice, but when the margin bell rang, and it was time to hit the carriage return, the entire room stopped.

Collin pressed on. It was dull work, but no challenge since he'd practiced all week. The quick action of the keys matched the rhythm of his thoughts.

A disgruntled, middle-aged man with pug eyes and jowls to match huffed and stormed to the captain at the front of the room. Collin raised an eyebrow but continued working the type keys.

"I tell you he's cheating. He brought a machine!" the portly fellow bellowed. The captain of the guard held up his hands and spoke in whispers. Collin was focusing on his memo, so caught only a few words. "Calm down... Cookie? ... Cocoa? ... I'll have a look."

The portly fellow grabbed a biscuit and a punch glass. Hector came weaving between the marble sculptures toward Collin.

"Major! Fancy seeing you here."

So Ivy had not shared her plan with the captain of the royal guard to arrest Collin the moment he returned to the capital. Collin rose and shook Hector's hand. "Captain! How's the family?"

"Noisy. Some peace and quiet tonight is a real treat. What's this you got here?"

Collin stood tall with pride. "It's my pen and ink."

Hector whistled through his teeth. "Is it, now?"

"Would you like a go?"

"I would!" He took a seat at Collin's desk.

Collin unwound his paper and inserted a new sheet. "You just press the keys, and when it's time to start a new word, you press this bar to make a space."

Hector retrieved spectacles from his breast pocket. Even so, he squinted as he pecked out, *Hello. My name is Hector.*

"Let's have a look." Collin unwound the paper and handed it to Hector.

"Blimey. It does look smart."

"He's cheating!" the man said, still grasping his punch glass.

"And where's the ink?" Hector asked.

"Soaked into this ribbon here."

Hector whistled low.

"He should be disqualified!"

Something about how Hector's shoulders stiffened put Collin in mind of his long-suffering Gran. "Have you had some of the coffee?" the captain said to the pug man. "They do make excellent coffee here at the palace."

"If you're going to let him continue with his cheating contraption—"

"Now, hang on. This is just the application process. Nothing anyone else does is going to affect your standing in the game. You do your work, same as anybody else here, and you'll push on through to the next round. But look"—Hector handed the man a tea cake—"if you're so upset about his pen and ink, I'll write it up special and have the princesses review it. Sound fair?"

"Yes, but the noise," the man grumbled.

"Ah. We could move the major to a separate room. You don't mind, do you?"

Collin did not, and the pug man snorted and squeezed behind his desk once more.

Collin rose, hefted his type machine, flung his cloak over one shoulder, and followed Hector to a closet door at the front of the room.

Hector unlocked the door, pulled a chain on a lightbulb, and shoved a desk inside the cloakroom. "After you."

Collin set down his type machine.

"I do apologize, Major."

"Quite all right."

"Can I get you a coffee? Maybe a biscuit?"

"I'll come out after I finish this prompt. Don't want to lose my train of thought."

It was a quarter to eleven when Collin opened the door and noticed that a full half of the fifty-two men in the room were sleeping.

Hector, too, was yawning.

When Collin opened his door again at half past, the entire room was snoring. The chap closest to him was drooling over his letter and had an ink stain across his face. Three empty cups of coffee littered the floor around him.

Collin heard the door of the gallery jiggle. He toed his own door shut, placed the type machine under his desk, and threw his cloak over his shoulders.

"Good evening, gentlemen." Ivy's voice.

"Boys." Pen had come too.

Their heels clacked across the parquet floor. Collin strained his ears, eager to catch any information.

The girls wandered near Collin's side of the room. "But what's this about a boat ride?" Pen asked.

"You saw the invitation same as me." Mars, Ivy sounded peevish.

"Yes, but why boats?"

"Why any of it?"

Pen sighed. "How far did that one get?" Collin heard the rustle of parchments being shuffled.

"He appears to be working out of order. He's drafted prompts twelve, seven, and eight."

"Maybe taxes are his comfort zone. I don't know why you had to keep the topics all so dull."

"Only the strong will survive." Sad, too, Ivy's voice tonight.

"Tim's back in town," Pen said.

"I forbade communications with any of them—"

"I didn't have 'communications' with him, Madame Warden. I saw his work in a shop window on Grove."

Ivy groaned. "You don't know—"

"Oh, I do. I could spot his work anywhere."

Collin was grateful he and Tim's type machine were hiding in a closet.

"What that boy can do with a box of gears and springs—"

"I didn't think you still cared for Tim," Ivy said.

Pen muttered something Collin couldn't hear. "I didn't think you'd be so hung up on Collin that you'd banish him from our little country."

"You're impossible."

"And we're going to be late for our dance party. Can't keep the others waiting."

"Particularly when this ill-conceived evening is the only reason any of them are speaking to me." But Ivy hesitated. "A desk is missing. I told Hector that applicants could be moved to one of the closets if there were an issue."

She opened the door and looked straight through Collin.

"Ives?" Pen called.

She stood there, her hand on the door, looking as still and beautiful as one of the statues in the hall. Ivy swiped a tear from her cheek. "Coming."

Collin heard the door creak shut. He quickly counted his memos. Ten so far. That wasn't bad. That was quite good. That sort of work warranted a break. He replaced the type machine on the desk, pulled his cloak close, and followed the girls out of the room.

CHAPTER THIRTY-SIX

Beatrice pounced the moment Ivy and Pen returned. "How are our future husbands doing?"

Ivy grabbed the necklace Mina offered her. "They're all sound asleep."

"Dreaming of their victory, no doubt," Trina said, handing Ivy a pair of earrings.

"More like drooling." Ivy tugged at the shoulders of her dress. Maybe this was the right thing to do. She couldn't go on seeing Collin's ghost every time she opened a door. Still, the entire business of these balls was too slapdash for her taste.

Pen linked her arm around Ivy's. Her tight curls and her beaded headband bobbed with the movement. "Who feels like dancing?" Her strappy blush-pink dress covered in scalloped fringe shimmied with her every movement.

They climbed down the back spiral staircase of their apartment.

"Where are we going?" Jade whined. She was looking pale, poor dear. At least she'd escaped Gwen's creams and powders. Ivy had not been so lucky. Mina assured her she looked just the thing, but the fact remained that she looked nothing like herself.

Trina put an arm around Jade's shoulders. "Sylvia said she'd meet us outside our apartment door."

"That's an odd place to meet us," Jade grumbled. "We'll have to walk half a mile just to get to the carriages."

"Well, we have to meet somewhere. The garden, I suppose, suited." Trina adjusted Ivy's necklace. "When did you find time last fall to plant the sweet peas?"

What was Trina talking about? "I didn't."

"But I was sure I saw sweet peas in the garden."

Ivy's brow wrinkled. "Weeds, then." She heaved against their arched wooden door. It stuck tight against a forceful gust of wind. Ivy tried again, this time with her shoulder against the door.

"Ives, open the door! Jade's going to be sick." Her sisters erupted into a chaotic chorus of shouts and whines.

"I'm trying. It's stuck. The wind—"

But the wind stopped blowing, and Ivy swore she heard a soft chuckle outside.

She pushed open the door and stumbled, not into their familiar paved garden of tidy box elder and vine-covered walls, but an alpine forest of birch and pine.

The wind prodded the birch trees until they rustled their leaves into a soft clamor of applause. Ivy shifted closer to the door. Her eleven sisters screamed with delight and raced past her into the forest.

Magic hung thick and sweet in the chilled night air. Ivy should have known. Midnight balls were always the work of magic, their invitations the tools of fey matchmakers.

"I don't believe it," Ivy murmured, taking a tentative step into the forest.

"I told you magic was real!" Mina skipped ahead into a clearing where their hostesses stood waiting in the moonlight.

"There they are!" Sylvia sang. "Come quickly, girls. Come, come, come. We have just a little stroll toward the lake."

"Lake?" Jade sounded like she'd faint. The other sisters ran on ahead, squealing with joy and excitement. Trina hung back to assist. Jade was prone to dramatics, but tonight she was taking it a bit too far.

"Is this a dream?" Trina asked.

Jade pinched Ivy hard on the arm, who yelped at her sharp nails. "No."

"Good heavens, where are we?" Trina should have spoken with alarm, not wonder and enchantment.

"The Shale Mountains, it would seem." Ivy reached out to help steady Jade, but of course she would have none of it. Instead, Jade quickened her pace, pulling Trina along with her and leaving Ivy to bring up the rear.

Ivy shuddered, watching her sisters thread their way through the birch trees to the lakeshore. How were they ever to get home? She turned and saw their garden door standing alone in the middle of the forest, like some strange sculpture. A soft glow, no doubt the electric lamps from their hall, seeped through the cracks in the doorjamb. If she shepherded her sisters back to the door, could they simply open it and return home? Or would the door connect with their home only at the behest of their hostesses?

"You needn't worry, Ivy."

Ivy jumped, feeling the soft brush of fabric on her arm. Yet, Florence was a good distance behind her. The woman moved slowly and deliberately through the tangled tree roots.

"I should have brought my cane," she grumbled.

Ivy offered the woman her hand, which she grasped tightly with weathered fingers. "The wind won't blow away your door. It'll remain standing in the forest until you're all safely home. You may all come and go as you please until then."

"We shouldn't be here," Ivy said.

"A warm fire and a book would make for a far pleasanter evening," Florence agreed, "but we make sacrifices for those we love."

That hadn't been what Ivy had meant.

Sylvia clapped her hands in obvious delight. "Oh, I do hope you don't mind. Florence and I, we took the liberty of inviting some strapping young muscles to help us row. Come quickly, girls. The boat ride is the best part."

Florence laughed, an alarming noise that sounded like a donkey braying. "Sylvia can't get enough of boats. Not since we went to wherever it was with all those canals and bridges."

"It was so romantic. Come, girls. Come!" Sylvia beckoned.

A beautifully still alpine lake reflected the brilliant gibbous moon. There was no mistaking that they were miles and miles from their home and in some concealed valley of the Shale Mountains Ivy did not recognize.

Twelve little boats rested on the pebbled shore, each with a handsome attendant. Sylvia beamed. "We told everyone you were coming, and some of our strapping friends rowed out to meet you. Isn't it wonderful to have so many friends? It makes the dancing such a treat. Come, come. Into the boats, girls. Florence, you ride with Trina. Yes. And I'll ride with whatever my new friend in the pink's name is over there. And then what to do about our dear friend in cashmere?" She gestured toward Mina, who was standing alone at the edge of the lake.

"Mina isn't wearing cashmere," Florence supplied hastily.

Sylvia swatted a feather from her headdress out of her eyes. "Who said I was talking about Mina?"

The fey women stared at each other in impatient silence for a moment. The wind blew afresh, and once again, the sharp sweet notes of magic swirled around the party on the beach.

"Oh... *oh!* Yes, indeed." Sylvia giggled. "On second thought, perhaps Florence should ride with Ivy. Yes, that young gentleman over there doesn't look quite strong enough to row all of you. And I'll go help Mina, who is standing all alone just now at the edge of the lake, and make sure her boat isn't too heavy for... Yes, for all of us."

Trina whispered to Ivy, "If I didn't know any better, I'd say they were up to something. It's like they're shuffling the place cards."

Ivy tugged at her bodice. "Does it matter?"

Trina's brow furrowed. "Don't snap at me!"

"They're using magic! We're hundreds of miles from home. We may as well be their prisoners," Ivy hissed.

Florence brushed past them. Again, Ivy felt the press of cashmere, but the woman was draped in violet silks. "That's an interesting way of looking at social invitations."

"We never should have come." But there was nothing to be done now. Half a dozen boats were already in the middle of the lake.

"You object to magic?" Florence asked, seating herself staunchly in the middle of Ivy's boat.

"Into the boats, into the boats," Sylvia sang. "That's it, dears. Nothing so fun as a boat ride across a smooth lake."

"Shall I have a row, then?" Pen asked the gentleman in her boat. He blushed and handed her the oars.

The young man in Ivy's boat, who quite decidedly looked as if he'd just rolled out of bed, proffered his hand. Ivy took a deep breath. In for a penny, in for a pound. "I am wary of magic," she said to Florence. "I stepped out my back door and find myself inexplicably hundreds of miles from my home by artifice that I do not understand and frankly believed lost to time."

"Not lost. Biding its time," Florence said.

The boat lurched forward, and the youth at the oars jumped aboard with a nimbleness that was bewitching.

"I don't understand it," Ivy said.

"That's part of the fun," the young man at the oars said.

"Is he fey too?" Ivy asked.

"Don't answer," Florence commanded the youth before he could reply.

The boats cut through the still lake water, rippling the full moon's reflection. The giggles from the younger girls and the sloshing of the oars sluicing the water bounced off of the Shale Mountains.

Jade moaned from her boat ahead, which prompted Harriet to ask why they'd not held their soiree in Amadanri.

"Neutral territory, dear," Sylvia called from her boat. "No one ever claims the mountains. Not the impassable ones, anyway."

Ice-cold lake water splashed onto Ivy's slippers.

Rachel pressed Sylvia for more details.

"This was the palace of an old friend of ours," Sylvia said, "and it, along with her memory, has been abandoned for many years. But on a night like tonight, and with so many dear friends eager to celebrate, you will perhaps catch a glimpse of its former glory."

The crumbling palace loomed closer with every tug of the oars through the water. The palace leaned tight against a mountain wall. It glowed golden in the dark night and hummed with music.

The boats scraped onto the opposite shore. The princesses, gentlemen, Sylvia, and Florence disembarked.

"You know, I think we should have a few peacocks about," Sylvia announced. "When the music fades, it's far too quiet."

"I love peacocks!" Mina cried.

"Tasty birds, aren't they?" Florence chuckled. No one joined her.

"Inside, girls. Inside," Sylvia urged. "The night is as young and fair as yourselves. Enter. Enjoy. You are our guests. Isn't that right, Mr. Wind?"

"Indeed." An ageless gentleman appeared at Sylvia's side, and although he looked well-dressed and elegant, there was a disheveled air about him. "How did I do with the invitations?"

Sylvia clasped her hands together with a delighted smile. "Mr. Wind, you excelled."

The party walked up the crumbling and cracked palace stairs, thick with slippery moss at this time of year. A solitary birch tree had the tenderest of green leaflets on its branches. The gentleman held it out of the way as the last of Ivy and her sisters stepped through the open archway.

Candlelight illuminated a glorious throng of bodies, most moving in time to the spirited music coming from a cluster of musicians at the center of the hall. Vines grew through the cracks of the leaded-glass windows and tangled and twisted across the walls of the great palace in a web of breathtaking and chilling beauty.

"I see you added to the guest list," Florence said.

Mr. Wind folded his arms, and a gust of mountain air rustled the leaves on the vines closest to them. "No one should have to celebrate without their friends."

"Or pet projects?" Florence squinted a single eye.

The wind smiled his dazzling smile. "You've lost your cloak, Florence. Shall I retrieve it from your pet project?"

What had he meant by that? Ivy wondered.

Florence gulped down her champagne. "I won't be needing my cloak. It's stifling in here."

A cooler breeze swirled gently around them. "Better?" the gentleman asked. "Introduce me to your friend."

Sylvia bustled forward and pulled Ivy with her. "This is Princess Ivy, eldest of Rupert's brood." Ivy curtsied. She nearly choked on the smell of perfume, sweat, and, above all, magic. "Ivy, this is our old friend, the wind."

"We've met before." The gentleman bounced one of Ivy's loose curls. "But it is a pleasure to stand before you." He took her hand and pressed it to his lips. His touch was warm summer breezes, harsh winter winds, crisp autumn mornings, and cool spring nights.

"Say something, Ivy," Sylvia prodded. "Don't just gape at our gracious host."

"Forgive me. I didn't know a force of nature had a corporeal form."

"There's a lot you don't know," Florence mumbled.

"Excuse me?" Ivy said.

Sylvia's lilted laugh surfaced, yet she turned bright peach with embarrassment.

"Some champagne?" the wind asked.

Florence shook her weathered finger at him. "And a promise that you will not blow away the cherry blossoms before I've had a chance to enjoy them. Then maybe we will talk about your sad young man from the boat."

"He's Doris' great-grandson."

Sylvia gasped. "I see the resemblance!"

"And his name?" Florence asked.

"Henry." The wind gulped down his entire glass of champagne. "Ivy should dance with him."

CHAPTER THIRTY-SEVEN

It was good of Sylvia and Florence to arrange a place for Collin in Mina's boat. It was even better to see Ivy in her green dress. Collin had nearly fallen out of his chair when she'd opened the closet. Sylvia had been right: No one would ever have a laugh at her expense for wearing green after that dress.

She looked so alive now, and so beautiful, even if she was pressed against a wall, scowling and straining to keep an eye on all her sisters.

Sophia and some bloke swirled past Ivy but then stopped. "Ivy, Ivy! This is Fredrick. He's promised me that he will win Papa's game and marry me. Isn't that splendid?"

"The young lady is so pretty, I would promise her anything."

Ivy's eyes lost more of their twinkle. "What about Eric, Sophia?"

"Eric who?" Sophia twirled away with her new partner.

Poor Eric.

The musicians continued to play a waltz. Ivy paled and skirted toward the edge of the room. Collin shadowed her, desperately wishing to throw off his cloak, take her hand, and—

"Something wrong, Ivy?" Trina asked. She was seated next to Mina, trying to pin Mina's strap.

Mina shrugged. "It ripped."

"Hold still," Trina said, and then huffed. "I can't do it. Ivy, you give it a try, please?"

Ivy cocked an eyebrow and took the place next to her youngest sister on the settee. "Mina, how did you manage to tear the strap off your dress in the first waltz?"

Mina giggled. "Peter did it."

"Who is Peter?"

Collin's thoughts exactly. Ivy needed help, a partner, if she hoped to keep her sisters safe and out of mischief. Collin would have volunteered for the job, but then who would look after Ivy?

"He stumbled, and his hand slipped and caught my strap and..." More giggling.

"There. I've laced it into your stays and tied it tight."

Mina was on her feet and back into the crowd of dancers without so much as a thank-you.

Trina returned to the settee. "Will you be keeping an eye on Peter?"

"Of course." Ivy trailed her fingers across the smooth green silk of her dress. "Go on. I know you want to inspect the musicians."

"They're so talented. Do you think if I asked nicely, they'd let me play?"

The smile was merely a shadow on Ivy's lips now. "Well, that depends. What favors are you willing to trade?" Trina did not hear her. She was already halfway to the chamber orchestra.

Ivy folded an arm across her waist and rubbed her shoulder. Her chin trembled, and a sheen came to her eyes. Collin was standing close enough to wrap Ivy in his cloak, to pull her close and hold her, but she stared right through him.

"Ivy? Ivy!" Rachel was at Ivy's side, hanging on to the arm of a beautiful young woman whose hands were covered in filigree. "This is Naomi."

Ivy patted her eyes briskly with the back of her hand. "Hello, Naomi."

"Naomi wants to know if women can also compete in Papa's game." Rachel and Naomi fell against each other, laughing.

Ivy toed her slipper into the cracked and crumbling stone floor. "I wish it were possible, Naomi. We could all benefit from more female leadership."

Rachel and Naomi turned to each other, blushed, and again exploded into laughter.

Ivy sank onto the settee. Collin took a seat beside her. He should say something to comfort her.

"Spectators this night, are we?" Mr. Wind looked first at Ivy and then at Collin. He gave Collin a quick wink before turning his attention completely on Ivy.

"I don't feel much like dancing," Ivy said.

"And why is that?" the wind asked, gesturing for Collin to move so he might sit next to the princess.

"I never got a chance to be like them. I was never young."

"The lady is young now."

"Not like them. They are carefree. I never was allowed to be."

"Why?" The wind asked a decent question.

"Why else? War, politics, work. And then they needed tending."

He handed Ivy champagne. "And governesses were scarce?"

"Papa had a habit of stealing them." To put it mildly.

"Ah, yes."

"I don't get to be the debutante. I get to chaperone and mend ribbons. I'm an old maid before I had the chance to be a young one." Ivy set down her champagne, which Collin tossed onto the nearest vines. He didn't trust their host, however gracious he appeared. "At least they are having a good time."

The wind agreed. "Your sisters are instructing all of us in their revelry."

"The poor dears haven't had fun in ages." The wind was comforting, and Ivy must have felt a safety not normally afforded her to be so unguarded.

Collin swatted and shifted at the cloak around his shoulders. The heat was making the cashmere itchy. Which was annoying. That Ivy was always guarded with Collin, that he was incapable of offering her comfort now was immaterial.

"At least I can enjoy the ball through their eyes."

"Mademoiselle, you speak as if infected with heartache."

Ivy's lips twitched for a moment into a halfhearted smile. "Promise you won't tell?"

Collin forgot to breathe. He needed some air, a moment to catch his breath. He stood and stumbled into Bea, who snapped at her partner something fierce. He returned in time to see the wind wipe a tear of mirth from his face.

"Fortunately, I have the proper prescription for such an ailment." The wind waited until Ivy was staring into his quick, ageless eyes. "Dancing." He pulled her to her feet and pointed to the boy who'd rowed her boat.

Collin stood next to Ivy. All he'd have to do was pull off Florence's cloak and explain. If she'd give him the chance. He still didn't know if she would.

Ivy marched over to the wallflower, who had to be at least a half-dozen years younger than she. "Got a name?"

The young man fidgeted with his cuffs and cleared his throat. Please heaven, let his voice crack. "Henry."

"You up for some dancing, Henry?"

The boy went pale but nodded.

The curious thing about dancers was that they didn't have any tell. Particularly when they were standing by the wall, blanching and twitching. Collin had all but written off Henry as inconsequential, but the second the youth straightened and offered Ivy his arm, Collin's throat tightened. The young man had a natural grace.

Mr. Wind chuckled. "I've always been fond of that boy." He swilled his champagne and bumped Collin's shoulder, spilling the rest of the champagne on his head, before rejoining the fey women.

He'd done that on purpose, Collin thought, shaking the moisture out of his hair.

"Where did you say you found Henry?" Collin overheard Florence ask Mr. Wind. A crescendo in the musicians' melody drowned out his response. Collin crept closer.

Sylvia fluttered her fan. "While I'll admit he is not as physically impressive as Florence's specimen in the still life, all changes when he moves."

"It's always about movement with you," Florence said.

"Naturally," the wind replied, popping an olive into his mouth.

A syncopated beat started from the musicians. Henry and Ivy danced and soon cleared the floor. "Henry is an excellent dancer." The wind adjusted the lace at his throat. "Almost as good as me."

Collin felt a visceral shock seeing Ivy in the arms of another, beaming, blushing, and having by all accounts a marvelous time. Fun. She was having fun. Fun that Collin would snatch instantly from her if he appeared before her now. He'd already broken her heart, the least he could do was ensure she enjoyed herself, even if it did fill him with seething envy for his rival.

Collin's feet felt like bricks as he moved forward to take an inventory of Ivy's sisters. He'd keep an eye on them this night. He'd make sure no harm came to them. The same, however, could not be said of his jealous heart.

CHAPTER THIRTY-EIGHT

"Good morning, gents." Pen was at the front of the small gallery, biting into a doughnut she'd pinched from the fresh trays. "Sleep well, did we?"

Bright sunshine streamed unfiltered into the room through the many lunette windows above the state paintings. It danced off the smooth limbs and flowing robes of the marble sculptures until it collided with the polished wood desks and sleepy eyes of the applicants. The men in the room winced and grumbled. One poor fellow wilted when he saw the ink of one of his documents completely smeared by a puddle of drool.

Collin, who had returned his desk to the back corner hours ago after finishing his prompts in the closet, quietly stretched then returned the extremely heavy type machine to its case—careful, of course, to keep it shielded from Pen's view. He wondered if Florence's cloak, folded neatly over the back of his chair, would disguise objects as well as people, but Collin thought better than to experiment with magic tricks in a room full of witnesses, albeit groggy ones.

"Papers to the front now." Pen caught Collin's eye, and an enormous smile spread across her face. Fifty-two men all stood up, shuffled their manuscripts, and stumbled forward to form a line. Collin slung the cloak over his elbow and took his case and papers to the back of the queue.

"Your Highness, will you be reading every document, or only those from applicants who completed all twelve of the assigned topics?" a hopeful contestant shouted from somewhere in the middle of the line.

Collin strained and spotted Ivy sitting at a desk near the exit, looking fresh and poised and not at all like she'd spent most of the night dancing. He knew she had—and with just the one young man. His fingers clenched around the handle of the carrying case as he ground his teeth with the memory.

Collin had pulled not one but three scoundrels off of Ivy's sisters last night, had tripped up another handful of young men who'd been too enthusiastic where Pen, Trina, and Jade were concerned, had switched Bea's champagne for seltzer water repeatedly, and had kept Harriet from falling into the timpani. He could attest that clumsy Peter ripping Mina's strap had been the least of Ivy's problems.

Ivy cleared her throat. "We will consider all applications, sir. Thank you."

She wore a crisp gray-and-green-striped blouse with ruched sleeves and a smart line of silk buttons down the back with high-waisted herringbone skirts. Modest heels today. No doubt because of the dancing.

Collin felt his eye begin to twitch. He'd love to blame it on lack of sleep, but fatigue did not make his chest burn or stomach harden. Nor did it quicken his pulse. Yet, this was how Collin felt when he remembered watching Ivy dance with another man. And try as he might, he could not stop picturing the two dancing. So the youthful Henry could dance. Collin could too. Definitely not as well, but did it matter when all he wanted was an excuse to hold Ivy close?

The portly man passed Collin with a doughnut in hand. He sneered before snatching Collin's stack of papers and waddling to the front of the line, where he presented them to Ivy. "Your Highness, this was the applicant I was telling you about with the illicit machine." He pointed wildly toward the back of the line.

Ivy winced but didn't look up. She kneaded the back of her neck and momentarily closed her eyes. Ah, the late-night dancing had left her with a headache. Collin knew those signs. Ivy carefully donned her spectacles and calmly took the papers the man thrust at her chest. Hector appeared at the portly man's side and suggested he take a step back.

"I told your captain it was unseemly!" the man said.

Ivy studied the papers, dragging her fingers across her soft, kissable lips as her eyes moved quickly across the pages. A soft flush came to her cheeks as she bit down on a smile that threatened to escape. Watching her excitement was more satisfying than drinking ice-cold water to quench an extreme thirst. Collin would never stop inventing machines for her if that was the way to her heart.

"He should be disqualified," the portly man bellowed. "The machine wrote his entries for him!"

"Perhaps if we had a demonstration of the machine in question from Mr....?" Ivy scanned the printed sheet, looking for a name.

Now or never. Collin cleared his throat. "Major."

Ivy froze. Her smile fell, and her hand tightened on the pages, crumpling them somewhat.

Collin stepped forward. Thrill and dread mixed inside him until he was sure he'd be blinded by the effects. "Major Collin Dobhareach. I fought in the war, Your Highness."

A man, easily old enough to be Collin's granddad, slapped him on the back. "And a fine job you boys did in the end."

Ivy's eyes narrowed. Collin would wager his borrowed cloak that her pulse was hammering while her mind chased down every available avenue. Would she arrest him? Would she try to avoid a scene now? Was she happy to see him?

Collin scratched above his right ear. Gran had said the habit was to blame for his bits of gray. "My handwriting hasn't been the same since I served on the north front last winter. I improvised."

Granddad slapped Collin's back again. "And a fine job you did!" Was the coffee laced with spirits this morning?

Collin removed the type machine from its case. New technology could stall Ivy, and from the hard steel sheen in her eyes, stalling was an excellent idea. "The paper is threaded like so. The keys stamp through this ribbon of ink onto the page. Would Her Highness like to try?" Collin smiled at Ivy, a poor, shaky attempt at a smile. His insides were twisting into knots, and he had to count his breaths to keep his head. In the morning sunshine, she was even more beautiful. And formidable. Ivy was the kind of woman who would take an entire lifetime to understand.

Ivy rose. She smelled strongly of chocolate and mint this morning. She regarded the machine with narrowed eyes before punching out I-V-Y.

Pen perched on the desk. "Nifty sound, those keys clacking and punching."

The portly gentleman guffawed. "Bloody distracting. A bell kept chiming all night long."

"Surely not all night. Even at four a.m.?" Pen asked. That was when the girls had returned and found most of the men, Mr. Portly included, passed out on the desks.

"Can the machine be preprogrammed?" Ivy asked.

Collin opened his mouth to speak, but the question had been addressed to Pen.

Pen nodded toward the machine. "May I?"

Collin gestured to the type machine. "Please."

Pen pressed a few keys. "How do I make a space? Oh! It's this bar down here. Clever." She pressed a few more. She examined the top, felt underneath. "It's entirely manual." Pen turned to Mr. Portly. "It's spring-loaded and runs on manpower. Without fingers to push the keys, nothing happens." Pen handed the paper to Ivy. She looked at it and then crumpled it in her hand.

"I prefer to think of it as brain-powered." Collin shouldn't have said that. He shouldn't have said anything. He should've just fallen to the ground and begged Ivy to forgive him.

"The major will leave his typing machine here for further inspection. Hector!" Ivy called. The captain appeared at the princess' side. "Please detain Major Collin. The king will have to decide if his peculiar interpretation of pen and ink is admissible."

Hector hesitated, and when he cast a look of bewilderment toward Ivy, she mouthed, "Arrest him."

What? No! Ivy couldn't detain him over a type machine and then conveniently lock him away for the rest of his life. But she was sitting with her chin high and her back so stiff that Collin knew he was wrong. She could do anything.

"Your documents, Major?" Hector asked, placing a firm hold on Collin's arm.

Collin felt the uncomfortable pricks of sweat. "The princess is holding them." Ivy continued to study Collin's papers. Sunlight reflected off her spectacles, but behind the glint, he saw her eyes were red. She was angry, most certainly, but maybe flustered too? Would that work in his favor? He took a deep breath and betted that he could exploit her fluster. "Delightful morning, is it not? Puts one in mind to hike up to the mountains. Visit an alpine lake."

Ivy stopped riffling through the papers and examined Collin. "Major, there are thirteen letters here. Do you have a duplicate?"

"I wrote an additional public service announcement warning younger boys against the wiles of older women. I thought it would be appropriate now that the war is over. Young men are so impressionable. You agree, sir?"

The granddad behind him did and spluttered on a little too enthusiastically about desperate widows.

Collin wrinkled his brow. Hector was still tightly gripping his arm. He'd not go quietly. "Some of these boys in here look too young even to have fought in the war." He leaned in close enough to whisper to Ivy, "Or dance with the woman responsible for ending it."

Ivy slammed her palms on the desk. "Take him away, Hector."

The men, who were already on edge from the unique coffee and uncomfortable sleeping accommodations, grew rowdy at the sight of one of their own—a veteran, no less—being taken away by the captain of the royal guard. A man needn't be an explosives expert to understand the potential kinetic energy building in the gallery, but Collin of course was. He tried to turn back around and show that he was cooperating peaceably, but the action was misinterpreted. Collin was slammed forcibly to the ground, Hector's boot pinning him down. The men erupted into angry shouts, which ended almost as soon as they'd begun.

A pair of red velvet slippers with massive gold buckles stopped just short of Collin's nose.

"What's the meaning of this?" King Rupert demanded.

CHAPTER THIRTY-NINE

Collin forced to the ground with a mob of tired and angry men as witnesses was exactly the sort of spectacle Ivy had hoped to avoid. She perhaps should have been more afraid, but all she could feel was a numb ache. Why did Collin have to turn up now? Why couldn't he have just listened to her, trusted her for once, and stayed away?

But now Papa was here, preening in his favorite pink and gold coat with the heeled red and gold slippers that he insisted matched. Olivia had begged Ivy to do something about the ensemble—something about courtiers demanding equally tacky garments for themselves and the fall of good taste as they knew it—but Ivy could not work miracles, unless one counted that whole business of ending the war. No one ever did.

"It's well in hand, Papa."

The king dismissed his daughter with a wave of his hand. "I'll be the judge of that." He motioned for Hector to bring Collin to his feet. Papa peered at the major, squinting until his burnt-peanut eyes nearly disappeared.

Ivy took in a slow, shaking breath. "Papa, you remember Major Collin? You met at the opera." She left out that this was the same man who'd helped her win the war but had been missing in action ever since. Papa had never asked her about the particulars of her task force, and now, much to Ivy's shock and dismay, she was inclined never to tell.

"Ah...yes. The opera. Entered our little game, have you?"

Collin was visibly seething. "Sir."

Ivy stared resolutely at her new watch, the replacement for her mother's. The contempt in Collin's voice made her blush. Or maybe it was the knowledge that she was up for grabs just as much as the throne in this foolish game.

"Hope to take my place, do you?" the king asked.

"Hardly," Collin said.

Papa sneered. "Then what do you want?"

"I want to make sure that the people I fought for stay safe, that their interests are protected."

Unbelievable! Surely a man as practiced as Papa would see through the lies and faux sincerity.

Papa sniffed. "A patriot. Your application, Sergeant."

"Major," Ivy muttered, handing Papa the documents.

The king perused the file. "He pushes through."

"Papa—"

The king rounded on his daughter and raised an eyebrow. "What now, *Ivy*? Is there something *you* know that you'd like to share? Silence, please," Papa said, addressing the crowd. "My eldest daughter is clamoring for more attention. Take note, men. This one may not be worth your trouble."

The chuckles that accompanied Papa's words stung more than Ivy cared to admit. Had she been twelve, she would have run away sobbing, but she was twenty-two and had work to do. "There is a concern with the major's contraption."

The king grunted. "What did you bring, Major?"

Collin said nothing.

Hector roughly prodded Collin, "Answer His Majesty!"

Ivy reconsidered running away sobbing.

"My machine is a set of mechanical pens, sir."

Papa scowled. "Applicants were allowed to bring more than one pen?"

It wasn't that simple! "Well, yes. But—"

Papa waved his hand dismissively. "He pushes through. In fact, all enlisted men push through to the next round. Did you hear me?" Papa said to the crowd. "All enlisted men push through."

Cheering and applause erupted in the hall. Neither Ivy nor Collin clapped. Ivy was furious. Collin was, too, judging by the fire in his eyes.

"What? No thanks for your king?" Papa said, turning to Collin.

Hector prodded Collin again.

"Thank you." Collin clenched his jaw, his fists too. "Sir."

Papa tugged his wig back in place. "Carry on."

CHAPTER FORTY

Ivy left with her father. She didn't even cast a backward glance. Just slammed her ledger shut and followed the king. There were a few things Collin would like to slam, too, but Gran wouldn't stand for such disrespect.

Pen took over the paper shuffling. "Thank you, gentlemen. Good luck today."

"The test is over?" Collin asked.

Pen pressed her lips together for a moment. "Ah, no. You see, a king must be able to rule and govern in the most physically and mentally strenuous of situations. The next half of the application awaits you in the royal portrait gallery."

Of course it did.

Collin followed the line of exhausted men out the door. Several of them shrugged and headed for the exit.

"After all, I've got as near a wife as I'd ever want at home," one told another.

"How long do you think these questions will take?" Collin's grandfatherly friend asked.

Collin considered. "I suspect until they've thinned out at least two standard deviations?"

"What?"

"The questions will no doubt continue until the rate of attrition has stabilized."

"What?"

Go home. Sleep it off, Granddad. "They'll keep going until men stop leaving."

The remaining men entered the domed portrait gallery. Dozens of small tables filled the area, while the many likenesses of King Rupert on the walls looked on. Behind each table sat a woman—young, old, middle-aged, lots of women. All with pen and paper in hand.

"Gents." Pen's voice bounced across the gallery. "Please take a questionnaire. Do not lose it. Your questionnaire is very important. Note the number on your questionnaire. This is how you will be identified on the next portion of the entrance exam." Pen hopped onto the desk Trina was seated behind and continued. "These lovely volunteers have all submitted questions they think are important to ask future kings. They are going to ask you their questions and record your answers on your questionnaire. They have the right to ask additional questions. Please understand that you will have two minutes with each of our volunteers. After two minutes, Princess Katrina will ring her bell, and each gentleman will collect his questionnaire and rotate to the next volunteer." Pen paused as Trina whispered something in her ear. "Right, we thank our volunteers for their service to the kingdom and will not tolerate any disrespect. Any questions?"

"Yeah. How is our response scored?" a bloke asked.

Ivy stormed into the gallery. "Confidential, gentlemen. But please understand that our volunteers are taking this matter as seriously as we are."

Pen folded her arms, and her smile beamed bright. "All right, then? Ready, set, go."

Collin walked over to a slightly graying woman seated at one of the small tables. He bowed, presented his questionnaire, and waited with his hands clasped behind his back. A quick survey of the room confirmed his suspicions that all of the women at the tables were single. About a third of them wore wedding bands moved on other fingers, indicating widowhood. All were well coiffed. All were smiling. All had their own set of papers, and Collin strained to see that they were ticking boxes that seemed to have three answers. *Yes. No. Unsure.*

"Good morning. Thank you for your service, ma'am," Collin said with a warm smile.

She patted her hair. "A pleasure, to be sure."

"You have some questions for me?" Collin asked.

"If you were an *eau de toilette*, what would you smell like?"

Collin couldn't suppress a laugh. "I think I'd smell like woodsmoke and roasted apples and rain before dinner. I'd probably wear into cut grass and cherries as the night went on. You?"

"Oh…" The woman patted her hair again. "Peach blossoms and gardenia, I suppose."

"Lovely. My Gran was fond of gardenia. Do you have more questions for me?"

"Oh… No." Her giggle made her sound young.

"May I ask you a question?"

More giggling.

"How did you learn of the princesses' need for volunteers?"

"Oh… Well, my vicar told us all at our prayer meeting. Said it was our duty to help the kingdom in this effort."

The bell rang, and it was time to move to the next volunteer.

He easily answered a question about his favorite meal—soup and fresh bread, followed by a cup of chocolate. And while Collin listened to the volunteer's recitation about meaty pies, he overheard the question from two tables down: "Which princess is the most beautiful?"

"You are," the man said in reply.

"I'm not a princess," the volunteer said quietly.

When it was Collin's turn for the same question, he considered. "If I tell you the truth, do you promise to keep it a secret?"

The damsel blushed and nodded.

Collin rose and leaned over to whisper his answer in her ear.

She made a quick ticking on the paper—a checkmark next to *Yes*.

"Tell me about the longest relationship you've had with a woman," a widow of midyears said.

"Her name was Gertrude. She made the most delicious fry bread. Her hands were so beautiful, even though they shook at times." Collin felt an ache in his stomach from the years of being poked with a cane. "She made me a better man."

"An older woman?"

"Well, of course older. She was my Gran."

"Your Gran?"

"The longest relationship I've had with a woman. Gran raised me."

"Sir, I meant romantic relationship."

Ivy was pacing close to his table. Collin cleared his throat. "Oh, I see. I've had a rough time of that with the war."

"Did you have a sweetheart before the war?" This woman was persistent.

"No. Not before."

Ivy was staring resolutely at a gold pocket watch. Collin felt the lump at his breast pocket.

The questions continued, and Collin moved from table to table like an item on a conveyor belt every time Trina's bell rang.

Did he like animals? "Yes, of course. Although, am I allowed to say I'm shy of horses?"

How did he spend his spare time? "I have an affinity for the opera."

Did he want children? "Only daughters."

"Thank you, gentlemen." Ivy stood at the front of the room after ninety minutes of questioning. "Our volunteers have recorded your responses, as well as their opinions of you and who they recommend should continue in the king's game."

"That's not fair," a sour-looking gentleman shouted.

Ivy held up a hand. "It is your turn now to tell us which of our volunteers' opinions we should consider in your evaluation. There is no limit. You may choose all, none, or any variation thereof, but please consider carefully. Your future is in your hands. Our volunteers will stay seated at their numbered desks for a moment so that you may have a minute to walk around and remember."

The watch ticked against Collin's chest so loudly in the now-quiet gallery, he was certain everyone could hear it. He crossed the room and stood behind Ivy, who was scratching notes into her dossier.

"That was clever," he said softly, bracing a shoulder against the pillar at Ivy's back. "Giving the ladies ample time to interrogate perspective mates. I take it their questions have nothing to do with finding a future king and everything to do with how well they like the applicants?"

"I was serious when I told you about the decline in birth rate. We need babies, and we can't all be king. There are forty-five attractive and eligible women here."

Forty-six, by Collin's count. "Some well past breeding years."

"Oh, don't be stupid. It's not just about population growth."

Collin traced the row of buttons on the back of Ivy's blouse with a single knuckle. "What is it about?"

Ivy ignored his touch. "Productivity. Quality of life. Social harmony. Some of these men are far too old for our soon-to-be mamas. Alone, they pose a risk of discontent and revolution—"

"Is it really all risk management with you?"

She snapped her dossier shut and rounded on Collin. "What would you have me do, Major? I asked the men their opinion. I will not and cannot force anyone to socialize outside of this contrived setting." Ivy's lips curled into that same mischievous smile he'd noted early this morning. She had a plan. Somehow the data from the applicants and volunteers who ticked the same boxes would be correlated, and invitations to the same luncheons, committee meetings, or prayer groups would materialize for those who matched.

Pen trotted up. "Major Top-Notch needs to complete his exit exam."

Ivy rolled her eyes but stayed to listen.

Pen cleared her throat. "Major, of the volunteers you spoke with today, whose opinion would you like us to consider as we contemplate your continuation in the competition?" Pen handed the paper to Collin. "There are also questions about who you felt understood you best and who you would trust."

The gallery had emptied of the other contestants and volunteers, and their conversation echoed off the many likenesses of Rupert. "A little on the nose, don't you think?"

Ivy tilted her chin upward. "Communication and trust are the key indicators of a successful relationship."

"Says who?" Collin asked.

"Me! Now answer Pen's question!"

"All of them." He folded his arms and noted with satisfaction how Ivy colored. "I'm curious. Did Her Royal Highness author any of the questions the applicants asked today?"

Ivy did not look up but busied herself reviewing Collin's application. "I did."

Pen's smirk appeared. "She did."

"Which one?" Collin demanded.

Before Ivy could stop her, Pen grabbed Collin's application and flipped to a particular page. "Number twelve: What quality do you most admire in a woman?" Pen skimmed the page. "And Collin's response was, 'Pragmatism, but resolve is a close second.'"

Did Ivy recognize her own words from so many weeks ago after his comment in the library about her lips?

Ivy glared at Collin. "Liar!"

"Tastes change, Your Highness. But you can read my response to the question about which princess is the most beautiful, if you're worried that I've soured on your very pretty lips."

Ivy looked as if she was about to slap him.

Meanwhile, Pen squealed as she skimmed through Collin's application. "Oh, that's good. Ives, you should read this."

"Burn it," Ivy said, grabbing Collin's application and tearing it in two.

"Ivy." Trina appeared at Ivy's side, grabbing her sister gently by the arm and taking the pieces of Collin's application from her. "Darling, I think it best if you retire. It is so early, and you've had barely any sleep."

Ivy huffed and tugged her vest straight. "I'm fine. At least I'm well enough to dismiss the major's application."

"On what grounds?" Collin asked. "You'll find all forty-five women highly recommend me." Gran had raised no ill-mannered fool.

"He's very popular," Pen agreed.

"His machine," Ivy said.

"Tim's machine," Pen corrected. "And Papa approved it." She kicked at the parquet floor. "Not that it matters. You'll never let me see it again."

Collin dug his hands into his pockets and leaned against a hideous portrait of Rupert in a toga. "He'd be more than happy to build you another."

"Ivy." Trina took her sister by the shoulders. "Pen found no fault with the major's machine. Papa told everyone, including a half-dozen boys from the *Gazette*, that all soldiers stay in the competition for this round."

Ivy took out the gold watch, only to force it back into her pocket without looking at it. With a huff, she opened her dossier. "Your address, Major?"

"You plan on visiting me?" Collin lived for the way her voice purred when she teased him back, but Ivy was all seriousness.

"I plan on mailing you the next set of instructions for the game."

"You're collecting information." It was smart too. Know thy enemy and all that.

"Do you wish to continue?" Ivy demanded.

Collin fluttered his lashes. "Sutherbee's on Grand Avenue."

"A saloon. Of course. Congratulations, Major Collin. You've just won entry into the king's game."

CHAPTER FORTY-ONE

"So how did she run, mate?" Tim looked hopeful. Expectant. "Did she jam up? Did the q-strike stick? Sometimes it does that."

"It was perfect, Tim," Collin said.

"Brilliant. Let's have her back. I'll get her oiled and into the shop window on Grove. I might even find a sponsor with this one. At the very least, I'll be able to..." His shoulders sagged. "You don't have it, do you?"

"She took it," Collin said.

Tim sank onto a barstool. "Cripes. I was going to sell it."

"What for?" Collin asked.

"For money, stupid."

Collin rubbed his eyes. "I thought you were applying to university."

"With my illegible handwriting and lack of funds?"

"Have some faith." Collin slid a hand to the watch in his pocket. It was wrong to borrow something without asking, but he'd done it only because the memory of Ivy taking it back the first time was so compelling.

Phillip looked up from his sheets of music. "What are you grinning at?"

Collin had almost forgotten the good news. "I got in. My application was approved. The game is on." A warm spring breeze brought Collin's attention back to his scrappy, ragtag friends. "But I think we may be a little preoccupied tonight."

Phillip snorted. "Are you planning on manning the bar with Sutherbee?"

"No."

"Then our fearless leader has made plans for us to celebrate," Eric said.

"Closer." Collin grabbed his cloak. "I think it might be prudent for all of us to find some formal attire for tonight."

"For what occasion?" Phillip asked, scribbling away at his music.

"Dancing. You'd be surprised how fond the princesses are of it."

"Where are you off to?" Tim asked.

"To procure us all invitations. Official ones."

Olivia beamed when she answered the door. "Major Collin, what a lovely surprise. Come in, come in. I've made the most extraordinary strawberry sandwiches." Olivia ushered Collin into her apartment and closed her door against the wind. "Did you have a good time at the ball? Sylvia and Florence mentioned you came. We'll have to keep it down this morning. The poor dears are still sleeping."

"Why didn't you come last night?" Collin asked.

Olivia settled in an armchair. "Oh goodness. Take your pick. Too loud. Too hot. Too late. And...I'm a homebody. I don't like venturing too far from what I know."

"Where was the ball exactly? I must admit I felt a little lost when we arrived."

Olivia took a slow sip of her tea. "Was there sand?"

"No. No, there were mountains. A little lake."

"And a cracked and crumbling old villa?"

"Yes. Very ornate columns and flying buttresses that were an engineering masterpiece…if they'd still been standing."

Olivia shuddered. "The North Mountains. Not that they had much of a say. Those two go wherever the wind will take them. And Mr. Wind does love dancing around in those mountains."

"Forgive me, but how did we get to the North Mountains? We're at least a good two days' journey from the eastern border—"

"Not as the wind blows." Olivia winked. "Did you meet him?"

"Him?" Collin accepted the cup of warm tea Olivia offered him.

"*Monsieur* Wind."

Collin blew on his tea. "You talk of the wind as if he were a fellow one could shake hands with."

Olivia pried off the lid of a hand-painted tin. "Turkish delight? Sylvia brought them. We discovered that none of us is a fan, but there must be someone in this world who just adores them. Otherwise, why make them?"

"No, thank you."

"Have you tried one?"

"You don't build a convincing enough argument to justify the attempt."

"But won't you forever wonder what you are missing?"

Collin took a powdered sugar square and bit off a nibble. "Hmm."

"Would you care for another piece?"

Collin placed his half-eaten square on the saucer of his teacup. "No, thank you."

"It is a puzzle, isn't it?"

"Am I to understand that the wind carried us to an old palace in the North Mountains last night?"

"With Sylvia and Florence's help. What's a party without hostesses?"

"And the other guests?" Collin asked.

"Sylvia and Florence have many friends, particularly in the

North Mountains. And the wind is handy at bringing people together. He has his favorites, you know."

"And tonight will be more of the same?"

"Oh, of course. I don't think you could stop the party now that it's started. Once these paths are made, they are easy to follow."

"Is that so?" Collin asked, his head spinning.

"Of course it is," Florence said.

Startled, Collin turned to see Florence and Sylvia descending the stairs.

"You're fey godmothers, the pair of you?" he said.

"We are retired," Florence said.

"Truly?" Olivia asked.

"Yes," Florence said.

But Sylvia shook her head behind her companion. "The world needs matchmakers. It needs meddling. It needs to be peopled. Young people are the only ones to do it, but goodness, you could not find a sillier group if you tried."

"Ill-suited for the task." Florence clanged about, fixing her tea.

"It sounds like Florence woke up too early," Olivia whispered to Collin. In bolder tones, she said, "You'll need a nap before this evening's adventure, Florence."

"I don't need to return tonight. I'll send Collin." She found a seat next to him on the settee. "You'll keep an eye on Olivia's goddaughter, won't you?"

Sylvia snorted. "Well, of course he is going to keep his eyes on Ivy. He wants to people with her after all."

Collin reddened, but there was no denying any of it. He was completely besotted, which was something of a problem, because Ivy was less than cordial. No matter. She'd change her mind once all the pieces were in place. Clever minds could not ignore information, and he'd bring her more than anyone ever dared. He cleared his throat. "Might I bring a few of my chaps with me this evening?"

Sylvia smiled until her plum lips were as flat as butter knives. "Yes, do! The more, the merrier!"

"How is the contest going, Major?" Florence asked.

"Excellent," he said, remembering how Ivy had lit up over the type machine.

"Solved their riddles, have you?" Sylvia asked.

Collin's skin pricked. "Riddles?"

"And what will you be building for her next?" Olivia asked.

"Whatever Ivy wants."

There was a knock at the door, followed by the jiggling of the handle. "Auntie. *Auntie!*"

Olivia jumped. "Speak of the devil. Does that cloak conjure as well as obscure? Put it on, Collin. She'd never speak to me again if she knew I am on your side."

Ivy pounded on the door. "Auntie, let me in. It's too windy this morning to stand in the shadows."

Clearly, Olivia was in no mood to be scolded. Collin grabbed his coat and dashed behind the Easterlie screen in the corner.

Olivia opened the door.

"Auntie!" Ivy swept into the room.

"So sorry, Ivy darling." Olivia paused to yawn. "We had something of a late night."

"We?" Ivy tossed her black hat onto the chesterfield. Her wrap and gloves quickly followed.

"You know my friends Sylvia and Florence?"

"Yes. How are you?" Ivy did not wait for a response. "Auntie, it's a disaster. All of it."

The major, safely tucked behind the Easterlie screen pulled the cashmere cloak silently around his shoulders. Even so the ferns on the wall tickled his face. This was as close as he'd ever come to seeing Ivy act her age. He'd seen her swathed in her pinstripes and tweeds, outfitted to do battle with politicians and rascals thrice her age. He'd seen her protective and motherly toward her sisters. He'd seen her worrying over the problems of people she would never know or meet. But now she was a twenty-two-year-old, come to her matriarch for soothing and reassurance.

"Would you care for some tea, dear?" Olivia busied herself with the tea service.

"It wasn't supposed to happen like this! This stupid game wasn't supposed to happen at all. Papa was supposed to propose an addendum to the charter, primogeniture, et cetera, et cetera. Now he's created a stupid game because *he* thinks it makes him look magnanimous. Fine. That's fine." She clawed her hair tightly back from her face. "He told me to write the rules."

"Did you?" Florence asked.

Olivia handed Ivy a gold and black teacup.

Ivy met the question with a pout on her lips. "I schemed a door so tight that no camel could possibly push through."

"How is that fair?" Sylvia asked.

"If we were playing fair, we wouldn't live in a monarchy! There'd be a populous government. There'd be opportunities for every citizen to voice her opinion." Ivy drained her cup of tea completely and set it on the table with a clatter. "And princesses would certainly be allowed admittance into the college!"

"Oh my dear!" Olivia soothed. Ivy crumpled into her lap and submitted to some shushing.

"Now I have to tell Pen, Trina, and Jade the bad news. Whose cup is this?" She was, of course, pointing to Collin's cup with the nibbled square of Turkish delight.

"It's mine," Florence said.

"You're holding a cup."

"I didn't care for my first. Too strong."

"Ivy," Olivia soothed, "I realize this game has been trying for you, but maybe—"

Ivy sat up. "Don't you see? All I had to do was outlast the villains. They could answer riddles for years. They could be sent off on impossible quests. They could be trifled with until their interest waned. I could pick off the truly terrible, power-hungry, and dangerous and let the rest idle." She beat her fists into the chester-field. "I can't do that now!"

"Why not?"

"Because of *him*! Papa told me, 'All enlisted men push through.'" Ivy let out a strangled moan. "Foolish, selfish—"

"Particularly with the assassination attempt still unsolved," Florence said.

Ivy blanched. Collin reddened under the safety of his cloak.

"What is the latest word on the inquiry's progress?" Sylvia asked, taking an innocent sip of her tea.

Ivy's shoulders bunched before she forced them back. "As none of our leads has turned up any suspects, the official theory is a prop malfunctioned. Not that we've found any bullets..." Ivy dropped her head to her hands, rubbing her tired eyes for a moment.

"The unofficial theory being spies from the Olcceart are responsible." Olivia rose abruptly and called for her terrier. "As if there weren't already enough hard feelings for our neighbors." The sound of claws clacking preceded the little dog. Olivia scooped him up and handed him to Ivy, much to the dog's obvious delight.

Ivy absently stroked the dog's ears as she held him close. "Papa's latest plan is to re-create the night of the opera and the events as they unfolded, down to the very last crystal punch bowl. He wants us to re-create this 'Night to Remember' quarterly until the assassin is found." Ivy set Ottis down, and the dog promptly began sniffing his way toward Collin. "I hoped to distract him from this preposterous idea with his succession game or any number of our pressing matters of state, but he is adamant 'the people must remember the night they nearly lost their sovereign.'"

Ottis had found Collin and was tugging on the hem of his pant leg.

Olivia gently rubbed Ivy's hand. "Ivy darling, I realize this is a very stressful time for you. That's why my friends have organized these weekly balls to look forward to. Hmm? Dancing. Revelry. You of all people have earned a chance to let your hair down."

Ottis was now growling as well as tugging.

"Yes, tell us about the ball. We were so delighted by the turnout."

Sylvia rapped her teaspoon loudly against her saucer. "And the talent. The young man you were with was such a marvelous dancer."

Collin felt like growling, too, but was most gratified to see Ivy's puzzled frown. "Who? You mean the boy from the boat?"

"You should have seen them, Olivia," Sylvia said. "Such an elegant pairing. Some individuals are natural dancers. This young man—"

"Child really," Florence said, rolling her eyes.

Collin stooped to pick up the little dog, who proceeded to lick his face all over.

"He was dance itself personified," Sylvia said.

"I really didn't notice." Ivy poured herself another cup of tea.

"What did you notice?" Trust Florence to ask the right questions.

"I noticed Rachel fell in with a young lady I've never seen before. I noticed Sophia was already too interested in a young man who hardly looked trustworthy. I noticed Trina danced only twice, and spent most of her time looking upset near the musicians. And we were all damn lucky to return home in one piece given the amount of champagne Bea guzzled and the looks the triplets and their new beaus were garnering."

And Collin had thought she hadn't paid any attention. He set the dog down, but not before scratching his belly.

"Well, I think we may have a solution at least where Trina is concerned." Sylvia nibbled a piece of Turkish delight but shook her head and put it down.

"Ivy darling, you cannot always be your sisters' chaperone and guardian," Olivia said. "The ball was for you just as much as it was for them. You must try to enjoy—"

"How can I, when there are dangerous, clever men determined to win Papa's game?" Ivy groaned and plunged her fists into the chesterfield once more. "Papa is too stubborn to listen to reason. My sisters have not the least bit of sensibility when it comes to...revelry." She looked as if she struggled to blink back tears. "And at least two of them are beside themselves with grief."

"Three of them," Florence mumbled.

Ivy had keen ears. "What do you mean *three*?"

"Was Major Collin at the ball last night?" Florence was not one to mince words.

Ivy twisted a tassel tightly on the cushion beside her. "What do you know of the major?"

Collin stepped out from behind the screen. He shook his head, desperate to indicate to the fey women that they should not defend him or implicate themselves in any way.

Florence propped her legs on Olivia's table. "I know he's a decent man."

Ivy laughed. It was a strangled sound. "You sound just like my family. Why in heaven's name is he so damn likable? It seems everyone is willing to overlook not just facts but common sense for the man."

"What facts need to be overlooked?" Florence asked.

Ivy froze. Lips pursed. Eyes tight and flashing. Back painfully straight. She was visibly bristling. "Yes. I, too, misjudged Major Collin during the war. It was a mistake."

"One you'd make again?"

"In war, sacrifices must be made. In peace, we don't have to stomach the same choices. Major Collin betrayed my trust one too many times. I will not make the mistake again."

"No. You'll just make worse ones that will lead you to attend a ball and not enjoy a single moment of it." Florence sipped her tea. "Ones that will make your pride hiss at outstretched arms."

Ivy placed her cup and saucer on the table. "It would seem the major is more popular here than I am."

"No one is picking sides, Ivy," Olivia said quietly.

"Well, they should. The major is dangerous and not to be trusted."

Florence grasped the arms of her chair and rose stiffly to her feet. "You alone are of this opinion because you alone feel your independence threatened by his affection."

Ivy was as still as saltpeter before it ignited. "Old crone. You may be a friend of Olivia's, but you are no friend of mine. The major is cunning. He's obviously charmed you. He charmed me, too, for a time. But I'm telling you he is—"

"Dangerous?" Florence brayed a single note of amusement. "He is not dangerous. He has not made designs on the monarchy."

Sylvia put a hand on her companion's arm. She squinted a single eye. "That's not entirely true. Peopling... Remember?"

"I meant he has no interest in replacing the king," the old woman explained.

Sylvia pulled a frown. "That's accurate."

Florence shuffled forward. "Why should his interest in you be so threatening?"

"I do not owe you any answers!" Ivy hissed.

"And the major deserves no explanation either?" Florence asked.

Ivy opened her mouth to speak but froze. "He's here, isn't he?"

"See for yourself." Florence spoke the words, and Collin, who felt his insides curdle with embarrassment, straightened and removed the cloak.

It was some sort of ploy. They'd been baiting her, trying to get her to reveal something advantageous about the contest. Obviously, *he* was in league with the two newcomers. But how had Auntie been persuaded? Maybe by his oily smile or his too-interested, beady eyes. Ivy told herself they were beady, not bright and attractive. She would recategorize them, and her mind would adjust. Her heart, however, was another story.

The major, with his cuffs rolled up and cloak slung across his shoulder, looked like more of a common laborer than an enlisted officer. Ivy should have had him stripped of rank, but then that would lead to questions and a court-martial, imprisonment, or death. Or all three. Her heart demanded the avoidance. Even now. The traitor.

"Good morning, Ivy," Collin said quickly. "Forgive me. I should have greeted you sooner."

"You skunk. Hiding behind Auntie's screen!" Ivy snatched up her hat and wrap. Her gloves toppled to the ground, but she left them there. She'd not be stalled a moment longer.

"Yes, I impugned on Olivia's excellent manners this morning by arriving unannounced. It was wrong. I am sorry. I only thought to spare her..." The major looked to be wrestling inwardly. Perhaps his anemic conscience finally was manifesting. He looked red-faced, guilty.

Good. But not good enough.

"Auntie, you appear to have your hands full this morning. I'll call another day, perhaps once your other guests have pushed on." Too rude, but it didn't matter. There was nothing to salvage. She shrugged into her coat. This was a disaster. Another one in the long line of disasters this morning.

Ivy donned her hat and stormed out the door. She was still on the stairs when Collin came after her.

"Ivy." He'd stopped just shy of grabbing her arm.

She wished he had. She would have retaliated instantly with a solid slap across the face. "So familiar, Major. Although I suppose when you attempt to assassinate a girl's father and then plot a coup, you feel entitled to such familiarities."

"Ivy!" He exhaled her name as an exasperated whisper.

"What do you want?" Because he was always after something. She used to like that about him. She liked the feel of the gears whirring constantly inside a man, a ticktock that made her feel reassured. Used to, anyway.

"To apologize. I didn't know you'd be visiting your aunt this morning. I wouldn't have come." He acted genuinely sorry. And that was the trouble. His sincerity was so achingly realistic.

"If you want to apologize, you've started in the wrong place." Good. Very good. He could start with the failed assassination, ebb into his sorry instinct to lie about it and everything else, and finish with being stupid enough to almost kill himself over a miscalculated blast radius. Ivy shuddered. "What gives you the right to even consider calling on my aunt?"

"She's my friend."

"No, Collin. She's *my* family! She's off-limits to you."

"Ivy, please." His voice was urgent and aching with something. Annoyance. Longing. It was too much. The weight of it all. The cruel loneliness. Once upon a time, Collin was to be the one man who understood. She'd thought him intelligent, charming, and handsome. It was maddening that her heart still maintained the attraction. She'd thought him the one man she could trust. But he was a farce. And while her heart was more than ready to dismiss his past transgressions, she would be smarter.

"If you so much as walk this corner again, I will bring charges against you."

He looked stunned, wounded. "Ivy, you can't believe that I'd do anything to hurt you."

Did she think this man standing in the empty morning street was capable of harming her? Or anyone in her family? She'd avoided asking herself that question. Partly because she knew how willing her heart was to answer, but mostly because it was too dangerous. What if she was wrong?

Her country had survived the war by operating with an abundance of caution. Risks had been carefully managed. The probability had been examined with integrals and sums, and only the most sanguine chances had been taken. She'd adopted the same protocol when Mina's intel had come to light. Had she made a mistake?

The street was empty, and just for a minute, just because it was delicious to remember the rising swell of sunrise, Ivy moved closer to Collin. Close enough to smell the cut-grass and woodsmoke scent he inexplicably carried. Close enough to measure the stubble on his chin. Close enough to feel his warmth.

It was a mistake. She'd made too many mistakes around the major. But this one would be costly.

"I was there," Collin said. "I saw you last night. And you were so completely and breathtakingly..." He swallowed. He seemed to struggle to remain calm, to breathe evenly. He bent down, and his forehead almost touched her own.

Ivy's stomach bottomed out, and she'd berate herself for it later, but right now, she'd hear what Collin had to say. His eyes weren't beady. They were lovely eyes.

Collin took her hand and pressed it, and gracious, she was enjoying the pressure of his fingers and thumb against her skin.

"...sad. You could have danced with me."

The idiot! A man didn't call a woman *breathtakingly sad*. He called her breathtakingly beautiful. Breathtakingly emboldened. Breathtakingly intelligent.

Ivy, for the one hundred and forty-fourth time that hour, wished for her watch. Not Papa's gaudy, gold timepiece that she'd borrowed for the morning and returned before coming to Auntie's. It kept atrocious time. She longed for the tarnished silver and emerald watch. If she'd had it at that moment, she would have flipped it open and inspected its face. Mama's watch had never lied to her. Nor had it disappointed her with stupid observations, however true they might be. Ivy pulled away her hand. "Says the invisible man?"

Collin grabbed Ivy's arm. "Am I invisible now?"

She stood there in the wind. Not caring. Enjoying his frustration. Hoping his heart was demanding action against his better conscience. "Yes."

CHAPTER FORTY-TWO

They were seen by one of the boys from the *Gazette*. Rumors of favoritism started. The eldest princess favored a contestant. A certain war hero. A clever spy. A major who'd probably won the war and, rather than seeking fame and fortune in the capital, had retired to a quiet farm well outside the city borders where only the promise of the princess' hand could persuade him to return.

"How did this get into the morning *Gazette*?" Ivy threw the paper down and poured herself a generous cup of chocolate with steeped mint.

Trina eyed the paper. "When did you have a clandestine rendezvous with Major Top-Notch?"

Ivy groaned. "Did Papa see this?"

Pen patted Ivy on the shoulder. "He was quite proud of the story. He says intrigue is good for national morale."

"Since when has Papa cared about national morale?" Ivy asked.

Pen grabbed her sketch pad and flopped on the chesterfield. "He asked when you would meet your fella again."

"I can't believe Auntie. Her friends are atrocious. I blame them, and not her, for this." A gust of spring air billowed the curtains near

Ivy's desk. It pulled at the curls at Ivy's temples, but she swatted them back behind her ears. When the wind did it again, she jangled open her desk drawer until she found pins to keep the curls in place.

"Can you tell me one more time why it's more important to stay up here when it is such a lovely day outside?" Rachel asked.

"We have to work on Papa's game." Ivy threaded a paper into the type machine and punched at the keys.

"If it's Papa's game, why is Ivy spending so much time on it?" Mina bounced a shuttlecock against her badminton racket.

"Because, Mina, Ivy doesn't want to get married," Jade said with a pout.

"No one said the winner had to pick her." Daphne stabbed at her embroidery with renewed vigor.

"Good thing too." Angelica snickered.

"Girls!" Trina gave them a sharp glare.

"Oh, come on. We were just teasing. Ivy knows we love her." Beatrice sauntered over to her sister. "I just feel like there is more than one way to approach this problem. One that doesn't involve calculus and pages and pages of postulating." Bea's shawl fell over the type machine. "Ivy darling, what is really going on? Don't write me a treaty when I merely want to shake hands."

Ivy looked at Bea's beautiful demure face that was so completely at odds with her mischievous eyes. Her half sister had a demonic sense of irony.

"Papa places too much trust in chance. He says that Lady Luck is more an expert on succession than any of us." Ivy swept aside Bea's shawl and punched out the last of her thoughts. "He'd assign us all to husbands based on the roll of dice. I will not do the same. I've read each application." Not entirely true. She'd avoided Collin's. "I would not trust Amadanri to any of these men, to say nothing of the happiness of my sisters."

Trina put down her sheet music. "Did the volunteers do nothing to help the effort?"

"The volunteers did a great deal to help in a separate effort.

Bishop Cardew tells me that he has been asked to officiate many marriages this coming fortnight. Olivia writes that midwives have taken on twice as many new clients since last spring."

"Capital." Pen, who had been leaning her chair against the back wall, brought all four legs clattering back to the floor. "How does that help us?"

"Yes." Rachel looked up from her book. "What stands in the way of us marrying some depraved, power-hungry beast?"

"Ivy." Trina slammed the lid shut on her instrument. "Ivy stands in the way."

The sisters became sheepishly quiet. Ivy's shoulders sagged under the weight of their trust. "I won't let you down. I won't let your fate be decided by some half-baked idea." She rubbed her eyes and muttered curses about the stupid contest.

"Is that why you insisted the application process be so ridiculous?" Mina asked.

Pen shook her head. "Ives was trying to weed out as many undesirables as she could from the start."

"Which explains why she drugged them all," Jade said.

"I drugged only the applicants who were foolish enough to trust our coffee and sweets," Ivy said, punching out another line on the type machine.

"Did it work?" Harriet asked.

"A little. Papa insisted that veterans be admitted to the contest anyway."

"And what is the contest exactly?" Beatrice asked. "Now that the application process is over."

The silence in the salon sizzled now. Ivy took a deep breath. "I can't trust any man who would compete for Papa's enjoyment to rule this country or marry one of my sisters..."

"So?" Mina asked.

"So... I've invented some impossible tasks. The first was sent out today to the most"—Ivy winced, thinking of a certain gentleman—

"promising of applicants." Ivy handed a copy of her missive to Pen, who was tearing Ivy's desk apart, looking for it.

Pen let out a low whistle. "A horse that needs no food, water, or pasture?"

Mina wrinkled her nose. "I don't want to see starved, skinny horses in our city."

Trina laughed. "It's a metaphor, darling. Ivy wants the applicants to invent a machine that could take the place of a horse."

"Oh." Mina rummaged behind the couch for her straw hat. "Is that possible?"

"Reaching for the impossible might inspire innovation." Ivy drained her cup of chocolate.

Pen snorted. "And there's going to be a race on these mounts against Papa's favored gelding?"

Ivy smiled. "I might have included that one just for giggles."

"What else have you been cooking up?" Angelica asked.

Ivy almost felt a wave a relief surge through her, but it was a swell that rose and left her still adrift. "Find a branch silver with frost in the full summer sunlight."

Gwen helped Mina pin her straw hat in place. "Fiddlesticks! An ice merchant could manage that."

"If he could, I'd propose to him." The girls didn't hear Ivy's comment, and she wasn't about to explain the capital's food-storage problem that would only worsen in the summer heat. The numbers she'd projected were distressing, to say the least.

Trina thought for a moment. "The first task tackles a problem of transportation? The second one of food supply?"

"And if an applicant has elegant solutions for any of these problems, plus proves himself reasonably handy with a pen—"

"Or a type machine?" Pen smirked.

"—then maybe he deserves to be king." Ivy stood up from her desk. Mina and Harriet were volleying the shuttlecock back and forth across the apartment. Ivy caught it. "I believe Frankfurt has set up the net in the garden. Shall we adjourn?"

"At last!" Mina ran out of the room.

"Hats, girls. Gloves too," Ivy called.

The sisters, properly attired, made their way into the exquisite spring sunshine. The cherry trees were full of white and pink clouds of blossoms. The spring breeze carried their fragrance to Ivy as an offering of amends for the bit about the curls. The lawn yawned before them, sweet and fragrant. It was a lovely day.

"It would be nice if the roses would bloom." Trina admired the glossy, dark green leaves of the hybrid teas and floribundas.

"It's too soon," Ivy said.

"But not for the sweet peas."

Ivy and Trina stood in front of the wrought-iron trellis. Tangles of light green vines grew up them, and the delicate clusters of lilac, pink, indigo, white, and vermilion blooms sprang from them. "Someone must have planted them."

"I think they reseeded themselves." Trina called to the party on the lawn, "Mina! Harriet! Fetch us some shears! And baskets too!"

"What's in it for us?" Mina asked, running to a standstill in front of her sisters.

Trina arched a brow. "I'll let you borrow my best dresses for next week's ball."

"Deal!" Harriet said and ran with Mina into the kitchen, where they assaulted Frankfurt with their needs. They returned posthaste.

Mina thrust a basket and pair of shears into Trina's hands. "I get your red dress with the bows."

"Not if I take it first," Harriet shouted, dropping her basket and shears at Ivy's feet.

The wicker felt dry and brittle in Ivy's hands. She slid the handle to her elbow. "We could have just pulled the flowers off."

"The right tool lends itself to the right amount of attention." Trina cut a gorgeous white sweet pea.

Ivy snipped off a deep burgundy bloom and inhaled a scent that was uncomplicated and delicious and made her feel happy and carefree for a moment. She fingered the soft petals of the flower.

"Did you mean it?" Trina asked.

"Mean what?" A smile was on Ivy's lips. The smell of the flower, the happy *plunch* of the shuttlecock being served and returned, the warmth of the sun—it was all almost enough.

"That you'd happily marry a man who invents solutions to your political problems."

So Trina had heard her. "They're not my problems. They're our country's problems. Our people's problems. We can't afford to lose any of our harvest, particularly with everyone descending on the capital now that the war is over. And the population concentration means we don't have the space to keep horses the way we did before." Ivy tossed a blush-pink sweet pea into her basket. She grabbed a handful of the closest blossoms and cut them all off the vines. "I never said I'd *happily* marry anyone."

"But you'd do it just the same?" Trina smelled a lilac bloom.

"It isn't fair to ask any of you to make the same sacrifice."

"But why is it okay for you?"

"Because I'm the eldest. Such sacrifices are incumbent on me to bear with grace and—"

Snip, snip. "I won't allow it," Trina said firmly.

Ivy stopped. Oh really?

Trina continued to make a careful selection of the sweet peas. "There is more to leading than innovation and sacrifice."

"Innovation and sacrifice are what won the war," Ivy said quietly. Also what broke her heart.

"The war is over, and we are talking about your future, Ivy darling. You may have devised acceptable terms for your surrender, but I will not allow it. If you are willing to marry this champion who can freeze branches and build mechanical mounts, then I insist he and the other hopefuls answer a series of riddles."

Ivy froze. The *thwack* of the rackets and swoop of the shuttlecock mixed with the laughter of her sisters. "You want me to add riddles to Papa's game?"

"I do. How a man thinks through a problem and the solutions he invents speak volumes about his character."

Ivy snorted.

"Have you considered that one of these men may have designs on a different sister?" Trina asked. "Papa said the winner would get to choose. I agree that the eldest daughter is only fitting, but I know you would not agree to additional screenings for your sake alone." Trina inspected a white bloom but chose a pink sweet pea instead. "Do it for them."

"Riddles? As in, the more there is, the less you see?"

Trina paused with her shears open. "Pride?"

Ivy huffed. "I believe the textbook answer is darkness."

"Well"—Trina bent low to retrieve a red sweet pea—"the girls and I have been thinking up riddles of our own. More complex than your example. A few are quite clever."

"Tell me."

"And have you accused again of favoritism?"

"Oh, Trina." Ivy closed her eyes and winced. "I had no idea *he* would apply. And you must know he cannot win."

"I think he might."

"I can't allow it. He's a security threat."

"A handsome one. With an even handsomer machine."

Ivy's spine went warm as she thought of the type machine on her desk. "Have you tried it?"

"I have not, but Pen explained it to me."

"Oh, you have to. It's brilliant. No one will be able to blame anything on illegible scripts as soon as these are implemented. I swear I can type faster than I can write now."

"Is that so?" Trina inspected the blooms in her basket. Hers was nearly full.

"It's just the sort of thing we need moving forward."

Trina began cutting and adding sweet peas to Ivy's nearly empty basket. "Major Collin is a clever man."

"Pen says she all but saw Tim's signature on it."

"I stand by what I said. The major is clever. He knows who to turn to when he needs help." Trina pruned off another blossom. "Why else would he call on Auntie?"

Ivy huffed and snipped at the blossoms, not caring that she cut mostly leaves. "You need to put your hat back on, Trina. You're getting a little too much sun."

"You are forever mothering all of us. Give me your word that I will be able to shoulder some of this responsibility for you. I'll see Captain Hector and will arrange all the particulars for our riddles. I'll get the girls to help me. We'll have such fun."

"How could I refuse?" Ivy sheared off another handful of leaves.

CHAPTER FORTY-THREE

A week later, Collin sat in the long hall outside the palace library at noon as directed by the missive he'd received. The drapes were open, and the expanse of the shared abbey lawn was glowing green in the sunlight.

All around him, blokes were doing what blokes did when they waited. Some dozed. Some read. Some paced.

"I'm so nervous," the chap to his left said.

"Why?" Collin asked.

He fidgeted with the seam of his pant leg. "I got a callback. It means something."

Collin shrugged. "What good does being nervous do about it?"

The bloke opened his mouth and then closed it. There was something different about this group of men. Collin began to drum his fingers, taking inventory.

"Hah. You're nervous too. I see the way you beat your fingers against your knee. That's a tic."

"Perhaps. But not of nerves. I'm thinking."

The bloke with sandy hair and a well-trimmed mustache scoffed. "So am I."

"Is that so?" Collin asked absently. All the other men were under thirty years, with one or two possible exceptions. All healthy. Not a lame man among them.

"I was thinking that there should have been a class at university for this," the blond chap said.

"All educated, then. I wasn't sure about you."

The man patted his mustache. "What's that?"

"The class rings and officer insignias. Of course you'd want those on your person today." Any and all proof that they were men of substance. "You'd be a fool not to do all you could to plead your case."

The library door opened, and the room tensed like a tightly wound clock. "Sir Reginald Blake."

"Wish me luck," the bloke said, uncrossing his legs and rising.

Collin watched as more and more of the gentlemen were called away. They did not return, he noted. Not ten minutes later, he saw Sir Reginald picking his way back to the college, head down, hands in his pockets, toeing at the clover.

The complement of guards opened the library door. "Major Collin," one called. The hall was empty. Of course it was empty. Collin strolled over, his cloak resting over his arm.

"Their Royal Highnesses have retired to the dining room for refreshment. They ask that you wait on them in the library, if you are willing. Help yourself to a game of billiards."

"Shall I take your cloak, sir?"

Collin wandered over to Ivy's old desk. "Thank you, but that won't be necessary." After the guardsmen had left, he slipped the cloak around his shoulders, effectively obscuring himself, and headed for the dining room.

He found Angelica and Rachel standing at the sideboard.

"Pass me the cream," Angelica said.

Rachel obeyed, and once Angelica had hold of the pitcher, she dumped inordinate amounts of cream into her cocoa.

"You'll need the sugar too," Rachel said, sliding the pot over to her sister. "I swear the coffee isn't even as bitter as Ivy's cocoa."

Angelica took a slow sip of her chocolate. "How much longer?"

"Not having any fun?" Rachel stirred her chocolate carefully.

"Who knew all these men could be so dull?" Angelica bit into a crumpet.

"And so stupid?"

Angelica added more sugar to her cup. "It's almost enough to put you off them entirely."

Rachel tapped her spoon against her cup twice. "Maybe it is."

Angelica brushed the crumbs from her fingers. "Maybe if you weren't so busy daydreaming. A little preoccupied thinking about tomorrow's ball and a certain young lady, are we?" Angelica waggled her eyebrows. "Don't think I didn't notice the two of you dancing last week."

Rachel could not contain her smile. "She has the most cunning pair of green eyes and a gorgeous, unapologetic laugh."

"I'm sure she's equally excited to see you tomorrow too." Angelica looped her arm through Rachel's. "You can tell me everything after we finish up in the library. I saved the best for last."

Collin dashed back to the library just in time to take a seat at Ivy's old marble-topped desk.

"Major Collin!" Rachel beamed.

He rose from behind the desk. "Lady Rachel, Lady Angelica. Good to see you both! How have you been?"

He spoke in an affable way, as if the princesses were his treasured sisters and also his best mates. In truth, they were a little of both to him.

"Bored silly," Angelica said with a pout. "We had to revive our spirits with a cup of cocoa, but that did very little for us."

"I think I ended up drinking more cream than chocolate." Rachel shuddered dramatically. "Ivy does like it so very bitter."

"How do you like your cocoa, Major Collin?" Angelica smiled and batted her eyelashes with great exaggeration.

The pocket watch ticked loudly against Collin's chest. "Stolen from Ivy's cup when she's not looking. Is that the sort of question you've been putting to all these young, eligible men?"

"Oh no," Angelica said with mock solemnity. "We don't get to have any fun with the young gentlemen."

"Why's that?" Collin leaned against Ivy's desk and braced his arms on either side of him.

"Always so amiable, this man," Angelica said, flopping down onto a settee. "Why did Ives send you away so quickly after the war, anyway?"

"Why indeed?" Collin stammered.

"Pen knows. Trina too. But the old girls don't see fit to share their secrets with us. Did you and Ivy have a falling out, Major?" Rachel asked.

Collin slipped and knocked a couple of books to the floor. "Did Ivy say something?"

"It's just that we saw so much of you during the war and see so little of you now."

"The war is won"—Collin retrieved the books—"and I lack the pedigree or education that garners invitations to the palace."

"And yet, here you are with an invitation." Rachel led him by the arm to the settee.

"Your father is at heart a democrat," Collin said.

Rachel slouched into the opposite armchair. "Or he's just a dumb fool who is lucky enough to have a dozen very clever daughters."

Collin's eyes twinkled. "That too."

Angelica cleared her throat. "We have a riddle for the major, don't we, Rachel?"

"Are you ready, sir?" she asked.

"I am."

"Are you ready, Angelica, with your scorecard?"

Angelica tapped her temple and winked at Collin. "Ready."

"Excellent." Rachel interlaced her fingers. "Now then, a decorated general's son returns home from the war a hero. The father is congratulated for their mutual service. Confused, the man says, 'But I was never in the army.'"

Angelica smiled. "Explain."

Collin hesitated.

Rachel shrugged. "You may ask us any questions you like."

Collin's smile resurfaced at a collected, mischievous angle. "That won't be necessary," he said. "Although... I am curious what sort of questions the other hopefuls have been asking."

Rachel opened her mouth, and a squeak of a giggle escaped.

Angelica laughed, throaty and loud. "Most are too precious to bear repeating."

"Of course." Collin's gaze wandered over to Ivy's old desk. "The decorated general was the boy's mother." He straightened. "In any effort, you will usually find an unsung woman doing the heavy lifting."

"Well, now." Rachel sipped her cocoa. "That's refreshing."

Angelica's eyes narrowed for a moment, taking on a stately seriousness. "Thank you, Major. Your answer has been recorded, and should it meet favor with His Majesty, you will advance to the next round of the competition."

"Thank you, Lady Angelica, Lady Rachel." Collin bowed. "Oh..." He fished into his pocket and pulled out Ivy's old, battered watch. "I found this." He colored for a moment. "I noticed the drawer of Ivy's desk wasn't closing flush and investigated. It had slipped down behind."

"Did it now?" Rachel accepted the watch. "She'll be beside herself with joy at its safe return."

Ang showed Collin to the door. "Maybe she'll even give us all a day off."

Collin was called back to the palace at teatime the next day, but he was escorted to a private gallery on the second floor. He found Jade sitting on the purple upholstered chesterfield. She was stone-faced and looked a good deal paler than last he'd seen her. Thinner too. She sat against the cushions of the sofa as if they alone were supporting the weight of her spine.

The butler, Frankfurt, introduced Collin, and Jade waved him away and then clutched her stomach.

"Good heavens, Jade, are you all right?" Collin asked.

"No, Major. My marriage, although perfectly legal and lawful in the eyes of the church, has not yet been recognized by my papa, though he said he didn't care when I wrote to him to ask permission." Jade sniffed. "But Ivy got her claws into him, and now he pretends he didn't understand. He says it would not do to have a son-in-law until after he has recognized an heir in this silly game." Jade clutched her side. "It is most distressing." She took a shallow breath and reached for her ginger tea.

"Allow me." Collin poured her a cup. "Sugar?"

Jade moaned. "Heavens no."

Collin handed her the cup and saucer.

"I'm supposed to ask you a riddle, Collin. But I'm too upset to remember it." Jade started to cry but quickly patted her cheeks dry. "What do you do as a rule when a woman is upset?"

"I listen." Collin sat on the sofa and produced a handkerchief that he laid between them.

"I miss Matthew!" Jade wailed. "We've been apart for six weeks. We were only supposed to be separated until Papa made his big announcement. Ivy promised that he'd name a successor, but instead, he turned us all into prize pumpkins. I told Papa I've already married and don't want to be a pumpkin, and he said that I married without his *official* permission, so it doesn't count. But somehow it counted when he didn't marry my mama, only to do it as soon as she was close to giving birth?"

Collin nodded and eyed the white square handkerchief.

Jade grabbed it, blew her nose, and sobbed. "What if this actually happens? What if some moron does win Papa's game, and he picks *me*? I love Matthew. I married Matthew. We were going to move to the country and raise dairy cows and grow raspberries and have cream and raspberries with our luncheon every day." Jade sobbed harder on Collin's shoulder. "But Papa doesn't care!" Jade blew her nose again and sniffled into Collin's sleeve.

"Matt cares," Collin said quietly. "I promise he won't let that happen."

"But he hasn't even completed an application!" Jade wailed. "Why?"

"Matt nearly beat me bloody when he found out I applied."

Jade sniffled. "He did?"

"He told me that I am a disgrace, and I'm mocking the humanity of not only the crowned princesses but his wife."

Jade's sobs subsided. "But you did it anyway."

"I did," Collin agreed.

"Why?" Jade demanded. Her eyes were red with tears but also with rage.

"Well... What do I have to lose?"

"You never answer questions, Collin."

"Life awards more points for asking them."

"Not when you are playing some stupid game and I decide if you move on to the next round. Answer my question, or I will vomit all over you this instant and tell everyone you failed to answer my riddle."

Collin had to work hard not to wretch himself. "That's not very sporting."

"Then persuade me to reconsider. Why did you enter this horrid game?"

Jade demanded the truth, but Collin's instincts were to protect the truth at all costs. It was all he had left, but he had to share at least a part of it with Jade. "I am worried about Ivy. I am worried about what sacrifices she'll make to protect all of you."

Jade sniffed. "Ivy doesn't need a martyr."

"No, but she needs someone who will put her needs before his own. She needs someone who loves her and cares about her and won't let her become a pawn in a political ploy. She deserves someone who will fight for her."

"Someone who will lie to her too?" Jade asked.

Collin stared at his hands. "I made a mistake."

"You made more than one."

Collin sighed and scratched above his ear. Before he said anything more, Jade shook her head and held up a hand, which she promptly returned to her stomach with a moan. "No, don't say anything. You're a better listener, and listening is more important than telling the truth." Jade, with a great grimace, sat upright and scribbled across a paper on the table. "Take this to Bea. She's in the music room. Go now. The sooner we push you through, the sooner this will be over, and Matthew and I can leave for the countryside. I've never liked the capital. Your handkerchief, Major."

"It's yours. Matt sent it with me."

Jade ran her finger across the monogrammed MF on the white linen and started to cry.

Collin hesitated. "Is there anything I can do, Mrs. Ferbent?"

The lady seemed soothed by hearing her married name. "Hurry."

Collin did, straight down to the music room, where a flautist was playing behind the closed door.

Collin knocked.

"What now?" Beatrice opened the door slightly. "Oh, it's you. I truly wasn't expecting to see any contestants today. I wasn't expecting to see any contestants ever, after Jade finished with them."

"Jade sent me. I do apologize, Lady Bea, for disturbing you. Jade insisted I come and inquire after your riddle. I can, of course, return at your convenience." Collin set the note scribbled in Jade's hand on Beatrice's music stand.

"Dear Jade, always willing to hand off the tedious." Beatrice silently fingered a few notes on her flute. "Might as well get this over with. My riddle is more of a role-play."

"I'm at your disposal."

"Let's pretend for a moment that you are king, and you've given a speech to your public, as kings so often do. You've given a good speech. A very good speech. However, a faction in your kingdom has taken offense where none was intended. They are angry and hurt." She played a few notes and nodded. "How do you handle the situation?"

Collin gestured to the chair next to Beatrice. "May I?"

The young woman eyed the chair with a slight nod.

Collin murmured his thanks and took a seat. "I'd apologize. I hurt someone else's feelings. I wasn't as careful with my words as I should have been. I ought to be sorry first and explain second."

"So you would try to explain?"

"I'd ask for forgiveness, and then I'd ask for their help in understanding where I went wrong. I'd listen until I'd gathered enough information never to repeat my mistake. Those would be my priorities."

"Interesting." Bea tuned her flute once more. "Most everyone is preoccupied with explaining why they meant no offense and why the other party is wrong to feel offended."

"I passed, then?"

Beatrice snorted. "Does Ives still wear a striped, silk pajama top to bed?"

Collin reddened.

"Go home, sir. Build Ivy a love letter out of a machine. The more cogs and gears, the better. It is the only way to her heart." Beatrice rose, as did Collin.

"Surely not," he said.

"Perhaps I am being too cruel. I shall amend. It is the only way to her fancy."

Collin hesitated. He ran a hand through his hair, combing it at the sides, right where it was flecked with gray. "This game is terrible. It isn't fair to any of you, and it is particularly unfair to Ivy. She should be your father's heir."

"She's certainly worked hard enough for it, hasn't she?" Beatrice rubbed a smudge off her flute with her thumb.

"You disagree?" Collin asked.

"I'm not a fan of absolutes in any system. Ives and I are not especially close, but she deserves her happiness. I doubt all of it is wrapped in the trimmings of 'heir to the throne.' I have much more faith that it is wrapped up in a former soldier who will not admit defeat and has a knack for getting anything done to make her smile. You should see her with that type machine." Beatrice jabbed a finger into Collin's chest. "And gads, if you do not make a quieter prototype, I swear I will come and find you and play scales out of tune outside your window at night so that you, too, can know the joy of trying to fall asleep amid a relentless racket. Now go on. Back to your hovel. Await the next missive. Remember, I have a piccolo should you consider making anything so noisome in the future."

Collin turned down the corridor toward the kitchen. What good was a cloak of invisibility if it didn't let him roam around the palace unescorted? Not that he'd roam anywhere too exciting. He wanted to see the kitchen gardens in spring and remember standing in them last winter with Ivy. He rounded the corner and passed the butler's pantry but stopped when he saw Ivy inside. With her hair down, a basket of sweet peas in her hands, the sunlight streaming across her shoulders, she looked young. She looked her age—and not at all like a woman with the weight of a monarchy on her shoulders.

Collin pulled off his cloak and waited.

Ivy considered a sweet pea but dropped it when she saw Collin in the doorway.

"Major."

He bowed.

"I didn't know you were here today," she said, blushing.

"I just answered my last riddle...with Bea."

Ivy reached for a silver creamer on a high shelf but struggled. Collin entered the small room and slid it closer to her.

"I take it it's going well. You expect good results."

"I don't expect anything," Collin said.

Ivy snorted. "Why would you? Everything you want is so easily within your reach." She added the sweet peas to the silver creamer as if they were darts flung at a target. "My sisters tell me that you've achieved high marks on your answers. In fact, Jade told me that if Matthew were not so entirely fulfilling, she'd want you as a second."

Collin's ears felt remarkably hot. "I'm sure I've no idea what that means."

"Everyone I love seems hell-bent on helping you win this stupid contest."

"Very generous of them." Collin handed Ivy a deep indigo sweet pea.

Ivy glared at him but took it. "It's so easy for you. My family adores you. You have a natural rapport with the people. Even my father is on your side, which is remarkable, given you tried to kill him."

Collin grabbed Ivy by the shoulders. He kicked the door closed to the pantry. "Will you at last let me explain?"

Ivy appeared too angry to hear explanations. "I dare you to try!" Her gaze moved sideways to one of the major's hands on her shoulder, and then her onyx eyes moved to his own. "I dare you to uncover all the secrets to my sisters' riddles. I dare you to become king of this bloody country."

She had a smudge of dirt on her forehead. Her shoulders were supple and strong under his hands. She was impossible. So real. And impossible. "Maybe I will," Collin said.

Her eyes flashed fury. "You'd like that, wouldn't you? A kingdom complete with a bride."

"I don't give a damn about the kingdom!" Collin might have shouted those words. He might have said them in an angry whisper. But his arms went around Ivy, and her hands were on the base of his neck, in his hair. And her lips...

Her exquisite lips were pressed against his own.

CHAPTER FORTY-FOUR

Collin went rigid. His jaw went slack, and Ivy felt him gasp then sigh against her lips. That was perhaps the most satisfying bit, but certainly not the highlight. No. That was when he reclaimed his wits and kissed her back. Ah, the tortured young man. The desperation. The want. Ivy had seen glimpses of such passion. It had on occasion surfaced like steam escaping from an open valve. Now it was pouring out of him. He pinned her against the cabinets. Silver and china clanked behind her.

She kissed him to prove she was in control...and because she wanted to.

His arms were wrapped around her, and his hands against her back urged her closer to him.

Until they didn't.

A gasp at the slightly open door, followed by a giggle, and Collin let her go. Not just let her go, but pushed her off of him as if she'd done something wrong. He turned bright crimson, his eyes retreating from her own to the floor. It had happened almost instantly. More important, Collin had pushed her away before Ivy had had the chance to do the same.

It was insulting, embarrassing, and all Ivy could manage was to roll her eyes. Really, she'd expected more from Collin. He was not some schoolboy who kissed her in secret and was too ashamed to even look at her afterward.

Anger chased embarrassment. Ivy brushed past the major and left.

CHAPTER FORTY-FIVE

"Ivy?" Collin called after her. Who kissed a man like that and then left without a word?

But she'd disappeared. Collin rubbed the back of his neck. He'd been startled. Someone had walked in and then quickly closed the door when she'd discovered the pair of them. It shouldn't have mattered. He shouldn't have pushed Ivy away. What had he been thinking? What did it matter if anyone saw them? If he'd not pushed her away, would they still be together in the butler's pantry?

Collin righted the creamer that had clattered to the ground.

There was only one explanation. He was a complete idiot, and should he ever be in such a position again, where the most beautiful woman in the world locked her lips with his own, he'd never let her go. Never.

Collin returned the fallen sweet peas to their silver vase, telling himself the situation was far from hopeless. Far from it.

Upon his return to Sutherbee's later, Collin asked, "Has it come?"

Phillip sat at the organ, pencil in hand. "Has what come?"

"The second task from the princess."

Phillip nodded toward a stack of papers at the bar.

Collin riffled through the papers until he found what he was looking for. He ripped open the official seal. Vermilion and emerald. And gold. Always gold when King Rupert was involved.

"What has Ivy asked for now?" Tim said.

Collin read quickly. His fingers trailed across her words as if he were brushing them across the smooth skin of her cheek. "Very clever."

"Well, what does it say, man?" Matthew demanded.

"She's tackling the problem of transportation." Collin read from the letter. "'Gentleman, congratulations on your successful admission.' Et cetera, et cetera. 'Your responses were inventive and promising.' Et cetera, et cetera. Here." Collin pointed to the third paragraph. "'I've never been fond of horses, but I require a mount. One that does not eat, needs no water, no pasture—'"

"Impossible." Monty set one of Matt's crates on the counter.

"Not impossible. She's inspiring innovation while tackling the problems of urban living. There's not enough room in the capital for all the horses. Nor enough money in the coffers of the average man to afford the upkeep. The space alone to keep a horse in the city is almost impossible to come by." Collin's heart pounded. "It takes insight to even recognize the problem. But it is one." He moved his arms to his chest. He twitched his hands to the nape of his neck. The skin there still held the memory of her touch. He giggled.

"You all right there, mate?" Tim asked.

"Brilliant." Collin remembered how her fingers had tangled in his hair. "She's brilliant, and she needs a brilliant solution." He grabbed a pencil from the bar and flipped the letter over.

"What are you thinking?" Eric asked.

"We could use a steam engine," Tim offered.

"No. We can't." Collin scratched notes on the back of the letter. "She said no water. And the noise of the engine would be a problem... More than you can imagine." Collin smiled. "That reminds me. Tim, is there any way of making the action on our type machine quieter?"

Tim's eyes rose upward as his mouth closed in consideration.

"Forget the type machine." Monty hoisted jugs of milk onto the counter. "How are we going to make the princess a vehicle without an engine?"

"We need something quiet. Elegant." Collin drummed his knuckles on the table. "It will have to be self-propelled."

Monty snorted. "Are you sure we can't just find some horse that runs on rainbows and sunshine?"

"Lightweight. Simple." Collin made more notes. "The type of job that could be manufactured on a large scale. Affordable."

"Nothing with four moving pistons could be affordable," Phillip said.

"Who said anything about four?" Tim was tapping his fingers to his teeth.

Collin beamed. "You have an idea."

"Of course he has an idea. He only ever makes that ridiculous noise when he has an idea." Phillip flipped through his sheet music haughtily.

"She wants a mount. We could make something like this scooter..." Tim sketched quickly.

Eric peered over Tim's shoulder. "Yeah, I've seen those scooters around town. Told Matt he should find one for his deliveries."

Collin rose to stand behind Tim. No sense in staring at his progress upside down.

"Only, it would be with two wheels of equal size," Tim continued.

Collin grabbed the drawing. He wasn't as patient as he'd thought. "With a saddle in the middle."

"A very small, lightweight saddle."

"Maybe something closer to Phillip's organ stool," Collin said.

"What about propulsion?" Matt asked as he set the last crate on the bar.

"Well..." Tim grabbed back the drawing.

"We could strap a motor to some gears," Monty said.

"No. She was very clear." And so very pretty. "No water. No food. In other words, no fuel."

"You could pedal," Phillip said, rising from his organ. "I push my pedals, and the music plays."

"Pedals with a gear and ratchet system," Tim said thoughtfully.

"Three wheels for stability?" Eric asked.

"We want this to be affordable," Collin said. "Make it with two."

Tim's pencil broke. "It's not going to be very stable with two."

"But it'll be fun. Do it. Make it pretty. Make it simple. I need the drawings by tonight. And, gentlemen," Collin said to the room, "we have a date with the tailor."

"Whatever for?" Matthew demanded.

"We are headed to a midnight ball," Collin said.

"Dancing?" Phillip sneered.

"Music. Revelry," Collin clarified.

Matthew groaned. "We have music and revelry right here, and we don't need to shell out from our coffers for fancy suits. Or stay up all night for it."

"Did I mention that the princesses will be in attendance?"

Matthew straightened. "All of them?"

"Jade will be devastated if you are not there. Now off we go to Madame Olivia's. She promised to take care of us. And you boys might need naps if you hope to keep up with your better halves tonight."

CHAPTER FORTY-SIX

The moon had shrunk to a third quarter in the sky above the alpine palace. Matthew hooked a finger into his frilly cravat. "Why on earth do they have peacocks? I'm gonna go bloody mad if I have to listen to those stupid birds shriek all evening."

"Don't worry." Collin clapped his friend on the back. They'd spent the afternoon at Olivia's, where the good woman had fetched this and that for all six of the men. She'd been in heaven. They had not, but Collin and his friends had endured the smartening with all the social grace they could muster. The sun had set ages ago, and the moon was high in the sky before Olivia shooed the men out her back door. And just like with the sisters' garden door, the men had stumbled out into the mountain forest and not into the back alley behind Olivia's townhome.

Now they were threading their way through the trees while the smell of magic blew heavy on the night breeze. "The music will start soon, and you won't be able to hear anything else," Collin said.

Matthew swore as he tripped over a tree root. "Why did I come?"

Collin held a low branch out of the path of his friend. "To see your wife. Now come on. If you don't put a good face on, she's going to think the romance is completely gone."

"You've been married less than three months. Hardly seems fair," Eric called from ahead of them.

"Give me strength," Matthew mumbled.

"Gentlemen!" Sylvia cried from the shore. "You made it! Don't you look smart?"

Collin greeted Sylvia and Florence, who stood in the moonlight at the lakeshore, dressed in their finest and armed with a fan and a cane, respectively. "Madame Sylvia, Madame Florence, allow me to introduce—"

"Oh, no, no! No time for that. To the boats, to the boats." Sylvia waved them onward. "Your ladies await."

"Boats?" Matthew rounded on Collin. "Boats!"

Apparently, Matthew was not a fan of open water.

"Oh, don't be silly, Monsieur Matthew," Sylvia crooned. "Nothing could be easier. No tricks there."

"Jade will be sick," Matthew mumbled.

Florence brayed. "Jade would be sick in a boat or out, monsieur."

Matthew glowered.

Sylvia continued to urge the gentlemen into the boats. Collin was determined to captain a vessel, but a hand on his shoulder stopped him. "Major Collin?"

The grizzled gentleman, who had spilled his champagne on Collin at the previous ball, stood before him. "Sir?"

"How do you do? I don't think I introduced myself before. I'm the wind."

Collin froze. Never having met a force of nature personified, he wasn't quite sure what to do. He settled on a bow.

The wind nodded in acknowledgment. "I am sorry to do this to you, but you see, I am Henry's sponsor here." He gestured to the young man at his side. "He will be the gentleman to escort Ivy to the party this evening. Nothing against you, of course."

"Even the wind plays favorites?" Collin squinted in the moonlight. The wind was not so handsome, but he was quick and had an energy about him. An intelligence. A confidence. It all made a man stop and obey. Not willingly.

"We all do, or else what's the point?"

"Why him?" The young man, Henry, was embarrassingly thin, not exactly tall, decidedly self-absorbed, and completely uninformed when it came to Ivy's character, history, talents, and predilections.

The wind gestured to the cloak slung across Collin's arm. "You chose invisibility last time, and Henry was there to partner with Ivy. He'll partner with her again tonight." The wind's eyes crinkled with a cunning smile. "Henry needs my help. You do, too, just of a different sort." He winked and bumped against Collin's arm. "Enjoy yourself."

For people who approach life with purpose and a great deal of forethought, emotions such as annoyance often get bottled up and set on a shelf so as to deal with pressing matters at hand. For people like Collin, the danger is that all emotions, good ones, too, are bottled up and shelved. The world becomes colder and grayer, and the carefully stocked shelves start to get overcrowded. A single break could set off a chain reaction of small explosions that could lead to quite the impressive combustion.

Sylvia whispered to Florence, "Exciting, isn't it?"

She tried to, anyway. The woman had a voice that carried.

Florence wandered over to Collin. "Why the pout, Major?"

"I've been uninvited to the boats."

"Who needs an invitation with that cloak?"

"Maybe I'm tired of being invisible."

Florence rapped her cane gently against Collin's stomach. "Maybe that's the point."

Collin clenched his knuckles tightly but threw the cloak over his shoulders and disappeared into the night.

"Now, old friend," Florence said to the wind, "what are you up to?"

But the wind was too satisfied to answer.

Twelve boats rested on the pebbled lakeshore. They were admirable little crafts, if a bit small.

"Matthew, might I ride with you?" Collin asked.

"Cows above, Collin! You nearly killed me."

Collin apologized and persuaded Matt with an offer to row the first leg. Henry was too small not to notice the extra weight.

"Get in," Matthew grumbled. "And not a word to Jade. This is supposed to be a romantic evening."

Romantic, it was not. Jade vomited her supper into the lake water. She cried when she saw Matthew and was hysterical for nearly a half hour after. All of this meant that Collin was very tardy when at last they arrived at the crumbling palace.

Collin had wanted to see Ivy's face when she discovered the twerp in the boat. Was she disappointed? No. But she looked annoyed. In fact, Ivy looked very annoyed with everyone and everything this night. Collin wandered closer beneath his cloak.

"It's stifling in here," Bea complained, tugging at the high neckline of her black gown.

"I told you, Bea, that dress would prove too hot," Ivy said.

"So do something about it!" Beatrice snapped.

Ivy's eyes narrowed, and rather too adeptly, she tore the long sleeves off of Beatrice's dress. "Happy?"

Beatrice fingered the frayed, raw seams at her bare shoulders. "If you had just lent me your red gown, I wouldn't look like an intoxicated peddler!"

Ivy handed Beatrice the torn sleeves. "My red dress is lovely, but even it can't work miracles."

Beatrice threw the sleeves on the floor. "Hilarious, Ives. Pace yourself tonight, old girl. Wouldn't want you looking haggard when you're trying so hard to catch the eye of Papa's contestants."

Ivy went white with rage as Beatrice flounced away.

"Who was that?" Henry asked.

"My sister."

"You have quite a lot of them, don't you?" The lad was all smug smiles and fluttery movements.

"Yes, Papa had to build an additional palace wing for all of us and another besides for Bea's ego."

Henry chuckled lightly. Good heavens, it sounded almost like a giggle. "You say the cleverest things."

Ivy scoffed, but a smile lingered on her lips. "But I'm being unkind. She is my sister."

"That's hard to believe."

Ivy's stare grew cold. The fool had opened a fresh wound. "I know. I look and act like her mother."

"No, I meant you are so different. Intelligent. Sophisticated."

"Seasoned?" Ivy asked.

"Beautiful." He took her hand in his own.

Ivy arched an eyebrow. Collin had to chew the inside of his cheek to keep from throttling the idiot. "You hardly seem old enough to be paying such compliments."

"Am I old enough to dance with again?" The rascal pressed her hand to his lips. And, damn the young fool, but he made her blush.

They walked arm in arm to the dance floor, and Collin bottled a fresh vintage of emotion, and Mars, if he didn't feel like pinching the silver, stealing the crystal goblets, and breaking the china.

The familiar jig tumbled from the musicians' enclave. "This was my favorite," Ivy said. Henry had sweat on his upper lip, sticking to the bit of peach fuzz. "You need a shave, darling boy."

Henry's eyes flashed, and a frown cracked his grin for an instant. He shrugged. "If the mountain jig is the matron's favorite song, then I shall ask the musicians to play it again."

"No, don't." *And don't call a young woman* matron. *Ever.* But, of course, Ivy did not say this. And, of course, Henry did not listen. Nor did he ask Ivy why the jig was her favorite. He dashed off, leaving her alone. The boy was quick to adore but not to understand. And adoration without understanding was...empty.

Ivy wandered through the couples who were thick in conversation to the balcony and cold spring air. Air that demanded all the blossoms shudder and close up shop until morning. Air that forced the birds and crickets into silence.

Why, Ivy? Why is it your favorite?

Those were the right words, the only words, she'd wanted in reply. And they wrapped around her now like a soft, cashmere cloak. They were proof positive that someone had heard her and understood.

"Because I used to stand on Papa's feet, and we'd dance to it together. And Mama held Trina in her lap and clapped her hands together. And we were a happy family. None of us were missing any pieces and trying to stop up holes with silly wars and sillier operas. And we danced because I wanted to and because everyone knew it would make me happy. No one stopped to ask me if I had earned my happiness. No one weighed the frivolity against other sacrifices. No one asked me to fight wars or negotiate trade deals or satisfy both the society of arts and the hospital with the same small pot of gold. No one expected me to live my life only for king and country. No one wondered if it was right for me to take moments to enjoy myself, to think my own thoughts, or do what I wanted."

It was too cold a night for Ivy to be out in nothing but her red dress. As Collin wrapped his cloak around her shoulders, the question tumbled out.

"Why, Ivy? Why is it your favorite?" He spoke softly, almost too afraid of her response to ask the question at all. What if it was because she enjoyed dancing it with Henry? He'd overheard that Henry was the heir of some little mountain kingdom. Damn royalty. The boy was unbelievably talented. The women he danced with... It was like they transformed into visual embodiments of joy and passion. But Collin had needed to know why.

Ivy had answered, and it was as if her words had reached inside him and grasped his heart until it beat in the palm of her hand. Raw, tender, as vulnerable as a cherry blossom on a frost-ridden night. He loved her. He'd never stop loving her. He was an idiot. Mars, he was such an idiot, but if she gave him a second chance, if she would just hear him out...

A strong gust blew the cloak off Ivy's shoulders.

It was about this time that Henry found Ivy and pulled her back into the ball with his puppy eyes and insistence they dance the jig one more time. And although Collin knew that there must be something to the lad for Ivy to have taken an interest in him, he personally hated him.

As Collin stood alone (and invisible) in spring's cruel night air, he also knew that his mind was made up. He would confront King Rupert and put the attempted assassination behind him once and for all.

CHAPTER FORTY-SEVEN

Collin spent the entire week arranging the details of his rendezvous with the king. He'd hoped to find an opportunity the morning after the ball, but rain had postponed all the king's public appearances. Then Adelaide had caught a cold, and His Majesty had refused to leave her side. Now it had been a full week since he'd last seen Ivy, and on the morning of the third and final ball, Collin seized his opportunity.

The day was pristine, calm, and clear and the hour early. Procuring a livery uniform had been all too easy with the use of Florence's cloak. Collin had no trouble persuading the king's regular coachman that he should enjoy the morning in bed, followed by a leisurely breakfast. "Sit this one out. I can ferry His Majesty to the barley fields and back."

"Thanks, mate." The coachman handed off the reins to Collin before trotting off to the kitchens. He disappeared just as Rupert and his valet rounded the garden wall.

"Where is Adelaide?" King Rupert asked his valet as he stopped beside the royal carriage, not bothering to acknowledge his new coachman.

The valet bowed. "Resting in bed, sire. As per doctor's orders."

"Can't we postpone this...this..." King Rupert waved his hand in the air.

"Traditional inspection of the barley field?" the valet supplied.

"Yes, that. Can't it wait? Adelaide needs me. No one knows how she likes her sausages cut except me."

"If you hurry, Your Majesty, you will be back before Her Majesty wakes."

The king nodded and hoisted his portly figure into the carriage.

Twenty minutes later, the royal coach stopped outside a row of cherry trees on the edge of a freshly plowed field. Collin hopped down and opened the carriage door.

"It stinks," the king whined, poking out his head. "What did they put on that field?"

"Horse manure," Collin said. "Which is exactly what His Majesty is full of."

The king's face turned red with rage. "Excuse me?"

Collin grabbed the king by the lapels. "Back into the coach, Your Majesty. It's time we have a chat."

His wig was up in a high pompadour today and already sliding forward. "Touch me again, and I'll have you hanged!"

"If I don't return within the hour, my letter will be delivered to Adelaide," Collin said evenly.

"What do I care of letters?" King Rupert snapped.

"She'll know that it was you, Your Majesty, who arranged your failed assassination."

The king's burnt-peanut eyes grew wide as his mouth grew tight in a firm line. "The coward has at last found some courage?"

Nearly two months earlier, before Collin had met Ivy, joined her task force, and fallen hard for her, he'd been awaiting a grim fate in one of the monastery's dark cells.

Colonel Cervantes—the same colonel who had witnessed Collin's insubordination and who all the men called Colonel Raisin (for obvious reasons)—was with Collin in his cell..."interrogating" him.

The purple-faced colonel shoved Collin onto a chair. "Keep your hands behind your back."

"They're shackled." Collin shook his fettered hands in front of him. "I can't do anything about them."

The colonel slapped Collin in the face. "Do not speak!" Little bits of spittle sparked in the light of the incandescent bulb as he spoke.

Collin took a few quick breaths to balance out the pain. When he lifted his head once more, the colonel was quick to slap him again.

A door opened, and a too-old dandy impersonating a younger version of himself strutted into the cell. He wore a blond wig. The buckles on his red leather shoes were gold. His gut, which was of some notable size, was cleverly disguised by vests and coats. The lace of his enormous frilly cravat would have been worth twice the number of stolen rations that had started this stupid affair.

In hindsight, Collin should have realized this was the king, but his focus had been off from the pain.

The king stood before Collin and brought an exquisite incarnadine square of silk to his face, covering his mouth and nose. "Leave us," he commanded Colonel Raisin, his voice the easy whine of a man who'd never known the absence of power and luxury.

"Sir, I don't think that would be wise," the colonel said. "This man is not to be trusted."

Collin drew his eyebrows together. "Bit unfair."

"Shut up!" the colonel screamed.

The king outstretched his hand. "Your coat, Colonel." The raisin wiggled out of his coat and, with a bow, handed it to the king, who tossed it across the filthy chair arranged opposite of Collin. "When have I cared about being wise? Leave us."

"I shall be outside the door, Your Majesty."

"You're the king?" Collin scoffed. That might have been the reason the colonel slapped him one last time before he left.

The king lowered himself with a grunt to the chair. "You like that?"

No, Collin did not enjoy being slapped, but saying as much would only encourage them.

The king primly crossed his legs. "It stinks in here."

"One grows accustomed to all kinds of atrocities."

The king drew his eyes into a dull squint. "I need you to fire at me."

"I beg your pardon?" Collin said.

"Tomorrow, at the opera. This gun"—the king pulled a pistol from a pocket inside his vestment—"will be backstage right."

Collin swallowed and shrank in his chair. "Put the gun away."

"Squeamish. I would have thought more of a captain."

"Put the damn gun away!" Collin shouted.

"Watch your mouth."

"I can't fire at you. I'm a lousy shot." More accurately, he was too haunted by his memories to even grip the gun.

"I didn't say to kill me. I said to fire at me. Make it look believable." The king considered. "It might be suspicious if you use my gun. We'll have a rifle or something for you backstage."

"Why me?" Collin could barely breathe.

"Why not? I need someone to do it. It may as well be a discredited coward. Probable cause." The king rose. "Your record precedes you." He snorted. "You can't even kill a pair of know-nothing Olcceart farmhands." He found his snuffbox and applied a liberal portion to the back of his hand before inhaling into each nostril. "After intermission, before the second act. One shot, maybe two. Try to get them in the box. But if you have to aim for the sky, I'll understand."

"No. Absolutely not."

The king picked a medal off the colonel's coat and tossed it on the filthy floor. "You know my eldest. She's tenderhearted." He sat.

"Helps out at the palace. Loves to read through the appeals." He crossed his legs at the ankles. "I know the officials have yet to assist you in that effort."

More to the point, they had been ordered to delay—at least that was Collin's guess. He'd asked for paper repeatedly, but it never came. He'd had to be creative and penned his appeal on the back of a receipt of sale. Had the king confiscated it?

"You do this," the king said. "And I'll make sure your appeal finds its way to her."

"And if I don't?"

"I'll find someone else, and you'll rot away in this prison."

Collin swallowed.

"I'm not asking you to do anything wrong. You've fired guns into the air before. Do it tomorrow at my opera, and you could be a free man."

"How do you know I won't aim to kill?" Collin asked.

"Because you're a coward." The king inspected his nails.

"This can't be right."

"What do you care? Do it, and your appeal will be heard. Refuse, and you'll die in this cell."

Collin's heart hammered. The ringing in his ears grew to a terrible racket. Sweat trickled down his back.

"Now"—the king brought his lace handkerchief to his nose and inhaled—"do we have a bargain?"

Being close to this perfumed dandy buffoon again made Collin nearly ill. Pretty green leaves rustling a gentle percussion in the morning sunshine were easily seen and heard from the windows of the carriage and did little to quell his disgust. Their delicate harmony was quite at odds with the smell of the manure.

The king covered his nose with a handkerchief. "You have no proof it was me. No one does."

"The gun was loaded with blanks. That's why no bullet was found," Collin said.

"Still no proof."

"Colonel Raisin never liked the idea, did he? He even voiced his dismay to your captain of the royal guard."

"Hector is my captain of the royal guard."

"Hector was promoted hours before the assassination attempt. And your former captain was paid off and sent away. Don't you think he'd more than happily return at Ivy's behest?"

The king scowled and sat with his shoulders high and hunched forward in the royal carriage. Outside, the sunlight was warm, and birds tittered their gossip.

"Why did you do it?" Collin asked.

"I did it for Adelaide. You... You don't understand. I may be king, but I'm... I'm thirty-two years older. Adelaide is the love of my life. I did it for her."

King Rupert was more senile than Collin had thought. "The assassination attempt was directed at Adelaide?"

"No. It was to make her value me. Appreciate me. People hold on tighter to the things that are nearly snatched away."

Anger curled through Collin. "And what of your daughters? What of the nights Mina cried herself silly because of all of this? They were all of them terrified—"

King Rupert waved his hand. "They have each other. Ivy has assured me that it is under control."

"And you believed her?" Collin demanded.

The king grunted. "Ivy is a better statesman than you'd think."

"She's your daughter. She's had to mother her sisters and calm their fears, win your war, and manage the succession crisis—all thanks to you."

King Rupert's nose wrinkled, and his blond wig slid forward a fraction of an inch. "I did what I had to do."

"You staged your assassination attempt, allowed the blame to fall squarely on the citizens of Olcceart, let your daughters live in fear, and then trusted your eldest to handle the situation just so you could be assured of your wife's devotion?"

"You have your answers. Now what do you want?" the king snapped.

Collin ground his teeth, trying to stay calm. "Tell Ivy the truth."

"You have answers and proof. You tell her."

"Oh, no. You're going to do it. I'm going to trust you to do the right thing," Collin said.

"Why?"

"Because Ivy loves you, and she deserves a father who loves her back. And in the absence of that love, she deserves the truth at least. You are going to tell her the truth. Because"—Collin's emotions choked him—"she still remembers standing on your feet and dancing with you."

The king snorted. "Of course she does. I'm an excellent father."

Collin clenched his fingers into a fist. "You will tell her. If you don't, you will answer to me."

"And just who are you?"

"God willing, your future son-in-law."

"No, no." King Rupert shook his head and chuckled. "Ivy willing."

"She should be your heir," Collin said.

"She would be if she were a son and not a daughter." He tapped his cane on the roof of the carriage. When nothing happened, he rolled his eyes. "Are you also my driver?"

Collin folded his arms across his chest, grinning. "This carriage doesn't move until you swear you will tell Ivy the truth."

Rupert tugged at his wrinkled lapels. "You've ruined my coat."

"I could ruin more. I learned some tricks from my stay in your prison."

"Indeed." The king chuckled. "Fine. I'll tell her. On my honor. Now can we depart, or do we need to stay here and smell more manure?"

Collin left the carriage and climbed to the box to urge the horses forward.

After the interlude with the king, Collin made a mad dash to Sutherbee's. His friends had taken over the saloon as a sort of base of operations during daylight hours. They needed someplace to build all of Ivy's machines. Phillip had begrudgingly assured them that Sutherbee didn't care so long as the booze behind the bar remained untouched.

"Is the prototype ready?" Collin asked on arrival.

Tim did not look up from the gears he was tinkering with at the counter. "A 'hello, how are you?' would go a long way, Collin."

"Yes, where have you been?" Eric demanded before dumping a crate of scrap metal on the counter.

"Hello," Collin said deliberately, conveniently avoiding the question. Wouldn't suit to tell the chaps that he had borrowed the king's coach—with the king inside. "How are you? Did you enjoy yourselves this morning? Looking forward to more dancing tonight? It's the last of the midnight balls."

Matthew groaned from his table near Phillip's organ. A pile of receipts and a long list of sums lay in front of him. "Thank merciful heavens for that. You'd have to be a numpty to enjoy that ear-splitting, hot, crowded—"

"We are all in excellent spirits today, apart from Matthew," Tim said.

"Jade still sick?" Collin asked.

"She threw up all over his trousers on the boat ride back," Eric whispered before cracking up with laughter.

"Ah, so married life suits her," Collin said.

"Do I need to crack your ignorant skulls open?" Matthew said. "The farce is eating her up. She's terrified she's going to have to marry some crackpot contestant."

Collin rubbed his forehead. "Well, if you'd show me the proto-type, we wouldn't have to worry about that, would we?"

Matthew nodded toward the back door. "Phillip and Monty have it out back. Don't hold your breath. They can't get it to balance."

Collin found the pair in a heated argument.

"I'm telling you, thicker tires," Phillip said.

Monty shook his head. "Thinner tires are more elegant."

"But they aren't going to survive these cobbles."

"Gentlemen, hello." Collin jogged up the steps. "How are you? What have you here?"

"Your pedal cycle, just as you wanted," Monty said, pushing the contraption toward Collin.

"Except no one can ride it because no one can balance it on those two tiny wheels," Phillip said.

"Since when have you become a mechanic?" Monty shouted at Phillip.

"Who needs to be an engineer to know that the streets of the capital are uneven?" Phillip retorted. "Those tires aren't going to work."

"Gentlemen, please. Not now." Collin rubbed his eyes. A nap would suit right now. It would suit very well. "Can you make hybrid tires?"

"Not in time for the demonstration this afternoon," Monty said sullenly.

"The demon—what?" Collin asked.

"The princesses want a demonstration of ideas this afternoon. They want to see our progress, officially 'so they can show their enthusiastic support for the king's game and encourage their favorite suitors.'"

"And the unofficial reason?" Collin asked.

"Beats me." Monty was screwing a tire to the front of the frame. "Just be grateful the race against the king's gelding was called off."

"Why the change of plans?" Collin asked Phillip.

"I don't know! I don't understand women any better than you do. I wish I did."

Collin considered. "Something happen between you and Trina the other night?"

"Why does something have to happen?" Phillip roared. "Can't a man just feel like shouting?"

Monty spun the tire, checking its fit. "Trina was crying when she left the ball last week, and she wouldn't talk to Phillip about it. Hasn't spoken to him since."

"Oh," Collin said.

Phillip snorted and scoffed and looked so agitated it was painful.

Collin sat next to Phillip, careful to look straight ahead. "You two going through a rough patch?"

"How the hell should I know? She won't talk to me! I was only sitting at the clavichord for one song."

"Three," Monty said, spinning the fixed wheel in place.

"And I look up, and I see Ivy stomping away with her dance partner, and Trina is fighting back tears."

Collin's brow furrowed. "They quarreled?"

Phillip threw up his hands.

Collin tried to fit the pieces together. "The prototype evaluation wasn't supposed to be until next week. Why speed up the timeline?"

"Maybe they're bored," Monty said, checking the chain between the pedals.

"Ivy doesn't have time to be bored," Collin said.

"She could be outnumbered," Tim mumbled, joining them.

"How was Pen the night of the last ball?" Collin asked.

"Bored," Tim said.

Collin lifted his brows. He'd stepped in it, then. "Dancing's not really her thing?"

"Ivy's forcing your hand." Matthew set a load of crates at the back door. "She's forcing everyone's hand."

"Why?" Collin asked.

"Because she can," Matthew offered.

Collin kicked at the cobbles under his feet. "The inspection is this afternoon?"

"Teatime," Tim clarified.

Collin nodded. "Then we'll have time."

"Time to what?" Phillip asked.

Collin stood, brushing the dust from his trousers. "To paint it green."

CHAPTER FORTY-EIGHT

To say that the beautiful spring sunshine was at odds with the current mood in the sisters' apartment was an understatement.

"I don't know how you can drink hot chocolate on an afternoon like this," Beatrice said.

"It warms my hands," Ivy said.

"Good. Maybe it will warm your cold, black heart!" Jade yelled before bursting into tears and running out of the room.

"Steady on?" Pen said as she strode into the room. "What's that about?"

Ivy sipped her mint cocoa. The bitter taste wrapped around her like desperately needed armor. "Jade is upset with me."

"It's somewhat understandable, given the exchange I witnessed," Trina said without any emotion. She was, of course, right.

Beatrice rose. "You missed it, Pen. Ivy here was explaining why the game had to be moved up. She told Jade that it was her fault."

Ivy was forever and always at fault. "Yes," she said. "I'm worried that Jade's swollen belly is beginning to show, and this game needs to end as quickly as possible so that she can get back to her husband,

and Papa can bless the marriage before there is explicit proof that a union preceded his game."

"Jade's pregnant?" Pen asked.

Ivy gritted her teeth. "Yes."

Pen tossed her sketchbook on the chesterfield. "What does it matter? Jade's of age. She went ahead and married the man. More importantly, they love each other."

Ivy snapped the case of her watch closed. "How would it look if even the king's own daughter circumvented him? Can you imagine his tirade?"

Trina continued to play at her spinet. "Last time he lost his temper, we went to war."

"I don't want to spend another four years fighting Papa's next war," Sophia whined. "There'd be nothing left to save."

Eye-rolling from a half-dozen young women had a palpable taste, like stale garlic and onions. Ivy drank more of her cocoa to fortify herself. "I did what I thought was expedient. I don't see why it is so upsetting."

Beatrice snorted. "You don't see how talking about your sister's 'swollen belly that will only grow more and more indiscreet' could be unfeeling and rude? Trust Ivy to offend and be oblivious."

Ivy set her cup in her saucer and winced at the clacking it made. Her migraine, which was something of a constant fixture these days, always made sounds so painful. She turned her full attention to Beatrice. "Educate me, Bea. The pupil is ready for more lessons."

Beatrice snapped her book shut. "It's her baby, Ivy. Her child. She's going to be a mother now, and she doesn't even get the chance to tell everyone how proud or excited she is to be one. Instead, she gets you telling her that, at best, people will think she's just eaten too many pastries, but never mind, we need to hurry up and auction off one of us to the highest bidder quickly so that dear Papa can save face!"

Pen chuckled. "You unfeeling monster."

"It's not funny, Pen!" Angelica said, crossing her arms.

Pen crossed her eyes.

The resulting scuffle of sisterly regard ended only when Frankfurt announced that the competitors had arrived and awaited them in
the courtyard.

The princesses smoothed their habits and frocks. Ivy tugged on
her gloves. The cold leather felt too tight on her hands. "I didn't mean
to be insensitive," Ivy said, mostly to her gloves, but she hoped Trina,
who lingered, might be listening. "I'm trying to fix this."

Trina again got that mistiness in her eyes.

"Don't cry," Ivy said. "I promise I can do better."

"It's not that. I don't want to do this anymore. The other night...at
our last ball, I thought—" Trina shook out her skirts. "I was so tired I
thought, 'I need to go home. I need to go to bed.' But I remembered
I'd have to wake up, and it would all start again. And it's too much. I
don't want to stand in a row and smile as a bunch of strangers
posture, trying to become heir and husband. And you... You looked so
beautiful but so unhappy that night. I want more for you than to just
be twirled around on the dance floor."

"Who's to say I couldn't find happiness twirling there every fortnight?" Ivy asked quietly. "People work every day at a job they hate
their whole life, and then they go home and enjoy life for a few hours
before it starts all over again. That could be me."

"No, Ivy. Being the center of attention at some magical midnight
ball is not the same as having a home."

Ivy swallowed. "But if it is all I could have..."

"Why couldn't you have more?" Trina was crying.

Ivy did her best to smile, but the corners of her lips would not
turn upward. "Silly Trina. I don't need more."

The truth was that the happiest Ivy could remember feeling was
dancing with Henry at the enchanted palace at the lake. She didn't
love Henry. He was too young for her, and he was far too amused by
all the squabbles she'd had with her sisters. But love wasn't a prerequisite for dancing. And dancing with Henry, who she'd heard Sylvia
whisper had fey blood, was such fun. He had a knack for making Ivy

feel seen in the most flattering way. And to feel people's eyes on her in an appreciative way, to know they admired her for a moment, that was enough. It wasn't complicated. It wasn't deep, but it was something.

And so, Ivy could pick the least dangerous of contestants, the least likely to have a spine, the least likely to attempt an assassination on her father and then lie about it to the detriment of all. She could pick a boob. She could marry an imbecile and quietly run the country behind his back. As long as there were dances to fortify her—something at least to look forward to—she could sacrifice her days.

If she had to.

Papa was a reasonable man. He had explained that he hoped the winner would choose Ivy, because as he'd put it, *You have so much experience. You'd be able to train him so easily. I wouldn't have to worry about a thing for the rest of my life.*

She had thought about conscripting Matthew into service and ensuring he won Papa's game. Then Matthew would become heir, Jade his bride (officially), and the two of them would rule and reign after Rupert's demise. And Ivy... Ivy would remain working away in the shadows. Invisible. Like she'd always been. And Jade and Matthew would be miserable. They both hated the capital. In fact, Jade had screamed that she didn't care what anyone said, she was leaving for the lake house today, and then the poor dear had vomited her tea cakes into a bucket and cried herself to sleep.

At the last ball, Trina had insisted that Ivy deserved love. She deserved to know what it was to love a man and be loved in return.

Ivy had laughed and said, "Who on earth would love any of us? We are trophies, Trina. That's all we are to any of them." And poor Trina had seemed to take that a little hard.

"Then why did you kiss Major Collin in the pantry?" she'd asked.

Ivy had stood there, stunned and angry. The memory of Collin pushing her away was still too raw.

"Mina told me," Trina had confided, looking so very serious, waiting for an explanation.

"Mina. Of course. No doubt checking for Miss Kitty." Ivy had shrugged. "I did it for fun."

Trina had raised both eyebrows. "I thought you said Collin was dangerous."

Infatuation could be very dangerous. A red-hot curl of indignation had slithered through Ivy when she'd remembered again how Collin had pushed her away. "And I thought your penniless organist was only going to play one song."

Trina had looked completely wounded. "Phillip is not penniless."

Ivy had grabbed a flute of champagne and drained it. "He's also too engrossed in the instrument to care that you are standing here all alone."

Ivy continued to say things she regretted, but what she regretted most was leaving her sister upset while she had laughed and headed off to the dance floor in search of Henry. That was what young women did. They looked out for their own interest. They had fun at the expense of others. Except for Trina. She'd insisted they talk about Collin and about love and about Ivy deserving both. All that had done was anger Ivy. Did trying to kill a king and father mean nothing to anyone anymore?

Ivy was in the wrong, and she knew it. In the honest morning sunshine, she had apologized to her sister for everything. And Trina, although still clearly upset, had accepted her apology and gone on again about Ivy deserving love.

Some things were just impossible. Like loving a liar.

The proceedings were held in the inner courtyard of the grand palace at noon. It was an enormous space. The salons and the formidable facades towered above them. The formal fountain in the middle gurgled and splashed. The sweeping staircases, freshly scrubbed of coal dust, glistened in the spring sunshine. It was all decidedly different from that crumbling villa in the North Mountains.

King Rupert sat under a canopy of gold silk, Adelaide seated at his side. His daughters stood in a fan around them. Poor Jade did not look comfortable standing. As soon as Papa had his fanfare and said his piece to all the contestants in attendance, they could sit or amble with their parasols and ask questions of the gentlemen. Maybe Papa would be compelled to brevity this afternoon.

"Gentlemen, suitors, potential sons-in-law," Rupert began.

"Papa should have opened the contest to potential daughters-in-law," Rachel muttered.

Mina and Harriet giggled. Ivy was too tired to reprimand them.

Papa scowled, and his wig began its descent. "Welcome! As you know, my daughters have asked for an invention, a horse that needs no food, no water, no pasture. And..." As Papa beamed, his eyes nearly disappeared behind the swoop of his blond wig. "You learn what a husband knows firsthand: Ladies are impatient for their gifts."

Polite chuckles. Trina leaned over to Ivy and, under the shield of her hand, whispered, "I don't see Major Collin."

Ivy smiled. "Good." Except her disappointment was sharper than a new quill.

"We commend you for your courage, for your ingenuity, for—for your valor—"

The pleasant ring of a bell sounded, and through the arched entrance to the courtyard, a man on an in-line, double-wheeled cycle pedaled into view. He held on to two handlebars and sat on a small seat that was attached to a frame. The man, tipping his head to the guards, pedaled, and gears on a ratchet system spun the two large, slim wheels.

Ivy was so enamored of the contraption that she didn't mark the rider.

"What's the meaning of this?" Papa demanded.

"My apologies, Your Majesty," Collin said. "It's my first time riding this, erm, horse. I grossly underestimated the amount of time" —he was panting—"and energy it would take to get to the palace. His Majesty's palace is set atop quite an impressive hill."

Papa's chest nearly burst with puffing. "The steepest hill in the capital."

"I believe it." Collin skidded to a stop, hopped off the cycle, and shook out his legs and rubbed his knees.

Ivy watched, eager to witness what her father would do to Collin. Reprimand him? Arrest him? Behead him? But no, Papa turned to Adelaide, who was smiling at the major. She coughed delicately into her handkerchief before leaning over and whispering something in her husband's ear.

Papa's eyes narrowed, and his wig slid another centimeter. "We invite you all now to present your horses, starting with our late-comer..." Papa hesitated.

"Major Collin," Ivy supplied without amusement.

"Major Collin, come forward," Papa demanded.

The major somewhat awkwardly stepped over the frame of his cycle until he straddled it. He then stood on the pedals and attempted to move the cycle forward. He listed and hopped off.

Gwen squealed. "Isn't the major adorable on his contraption? Look at him. He's like a little baby learning to walk."

"Starting is the hardest part," Collin explained. "But I've almost..." He mounted the cycle again and moved it slowly and evenly forward, picking up speed. "There! I didn't have much time to practice, and it takes a bit of balancing to, um"—the cycle wobbled—"to keep upright."

"Ingenious," Pen said.

"Another love letter from Tim?" Trina asked.

"Oh, no. It's too quaint for him." Pen shielded the sun from her eyes and squinted. "Although the ratchet system looks like his work."

Ang snapped her parasol open. "Look at him go! Gol, that looks like fun. I want a go."

"No," Ivy said. Truly, this cycle was the most delightful machine she had ever seen. It was whimsical yet practical. It was impossible but completely real. It was delightful, and it was green.

The major pedaled to the front of the tent. "Would anyone like a go?"

"Yes!" Pen leaped down the stairs, followed closely by Ang.

Adelaide spoke, and the shuffle toward the major immediately ceased. "The major would please explain how this satisfies the rules of the contest."

"Yes, of course, Your Majesty." Collin bowed to Adelaide. "My pedal cycle is a one-man transportation equivalent of riding horse-back. It requires no fuel and can stand against a building for days on end. All it needs is a rider."

"Ingenious," Papa said. "Can anyone ride it?"

"With practice," Collin said.

"Prove it." Papa brushed his thumb across Adelaide's hand before kissing it.

Collin wheeled the cycle forward. "Perhaps one of the princesses would like to volunteer?"

"Ivy," Papa said without hesitation.

No. Never. Ivy refused to aid Collin in any future success. "My skirts would get tangled in the gears."

"We fitted the gear and chains low so as to avoid..." Collin almost looked like he was blushing.

"If you won't get on the cycle, then I will," Pen whispered to Ivy, "and I'll spend the rest of this silly game lying and cheating to help Collin win."

Ivy shoved her parasol against Pen's chest and strode to the pedal cycle.

Collin's smile was guarded. "Balance is something of a trick, but if you go slow, I can hold your seat."

Ivy glared at Collin.

"Or not," Collin said.

"Is the seat adjustable?" Ivy asked.

Collin twirled the seat down. "It could be better. We borrowed parts from an organist we know."

"The handlebars are fixed?" Ivy asked.

"They are." Collin held the bike as Ivy stepped across the frame and straddled it.

"Explain the trick about the balance," Ivy demanded, carefully avoiding eye contact.

"Momentum. You have to be moving forward to stay upright." Collin's face was so close to Ivy's own, the missed whiskers of his hasty shave were glaring. "I was a coward to push you away."

Ivy's stomach bottomed out. Her pulse quickened. "Who designed this pedal cycle? Pen said Tim's stamp is on the pedals."

"I sketched it out, with Tim and the others' help, of course."

"Phillip's work, then?" Ivy slowly, shakily began to pedal forward.

"Did you not hear me?" The major sounded exasperated. "I designed this. I built this."

"Let go of my cycle, Major."

"Who says it's yours?"

"You painted it green. You might as well have painted my name on it." Ivy pedaled some distance away from the gold canopy and moved in wide, steady circles around Collin. "Estimated cost of production?"

Collin jogged next to her. "Couple of crowns. Particularly if some of the parts can be scrapped from military materials."

"Excellent." Ivy gripped the handlebars.

"Do you like it?" Collin righted the handlebars whenever Ivy listed.

"If you'd stop doing that, I'd tell you."

"If I don't, you might fall."

"I'd rather fall than be pushed away again."

Ivy pedaled faster and sailed away from him. But not before she rang the bell twice.

≈

Collin grabbed the reins from the lad standing near the horse and mounted the beast.

"Stop! That's my invention," shouted a young nobleman who had been chatting with the triplets.

"It's a horse," Collin said.

"A horse that needs only love and attention to survive."

"I'll bring it back." Collin kicked the horse's sides and rode after Ivy. Phillip had been right about the tires, thank heavens. Ivy wouldn't get far on the palace's gravel paths. But goodness, she was speedy. "If you crash that cycle, I will kill you," Collin shouted as he approached her.

Ivy picked up the pace. "Get your fat, smelly horse away from me!"

"I have it on good authority this horse is neither smelly nor fat, just brimming with the fruits of tender-loving care."

Ivy veered onto a path through the palace orchard, but a tire skidded on the pebbles, and she went down with a crash.

"Ivy!" Collin pulled the horse to a halt and jumped off the beast, who promptly went to sniffing the blossoms and nibbling the crab-grass around the trees. "Are you hurt?"

Her sleeve was torn from the elbow to the shoulder of her left arm. A nasty rash blistered on her skin. Ivy struggled to pull herself upright. Collin reached down to assist her.

"Don't touch me. This is your fault!" she spat. "If you hadn't chased me on that stupid horse, none of this would have happened."

"You ran off with my pedal cycle!"

Ivy staggered to her feet. She hissed in pain at the raw skin on her arm. She felt like crying. She'd slept for only two hours the night before. Her head pounded behind her eyes. And she had just fallen off her new pedal cycle, with Collin as witness.

His jaw clenched in that unfathomable way men's jaws did. "You need to go to bed, Princess."

Ivy counted her breaths to make sure she did not start screaming in anger. Still, her pulse beat mercilessly in her ears. She folded her arms across the black and emerald stripes of her dress. "No."

"Let me take you home, before you do something else you'll regret."

Ivy's mouth turned into a wicked smile. "What do you know of regret, Major Collin?" His name came out as a sneer that would have startled Ivy had she not been so angry. The man stood there, too tall for her to stare down at and too proud for her to ignore. "You, who are content to only observe life and collect your little stores of information. Why? What good will it do you now?"

Collin's eyes softened. His brows puzzled upward and together. The show of concern would have been heartening if it hadn't been so patronizing. "Ivy, this isn't you. You've been rude, if not mean, to your sisters. Last week at the ball, you bullied some of them to tears—"

"They deserved it!" Ivy's fingers contracted and clawed into her palms. She felt so stupid, so foolish. She wanted to seize Collin and dig her nails into him until he felt as she did. "I've had enough of mothering them, coddling them, babying them. I've tried to protect them, but all they do is take." Ivy paced. The movement brought a fresh stab of pain to her battered extremities. "All they want is more. I'm done. Don't you understand? I'm done!" She rounded on Collin, her fists positioned to pound on his chest. "You of all people should have seen. You, who are so interested in watching and carefully considering the outcomes. I've sacrificed everything for them. Now there is nothing left."

Collin nodded and rubbed his forehead. Repeatedly. "You're talking about more than just your sisters now."

Of course she was! She was talking about everything—family, king, country.

"Ivy, please. Just listen—"

"No, you listen! I've spent all my life taking care of everyone else. Not a day has gone by that I haven't done what other people needed me to do. I always put their needs before my own. I don't even know who I am or what I like. I'm done with that!"

Collin's cool veneer seemed to crack. His eyes flashed, and for a moment, his lips turned up in a contemptuous sneer. "Because you've at last found someone to dance with?"

She would have laughed at his schoolboy jealousy, but her shoulder felt like it had been burned open. Little bits of gravel bristled in the slick red rash. If anyone learned she'd been injured on the pedal cycle, it would never be mass-produced. "Why couldn't you have worn a cravat? Or a vest?"

"I was somewhat rushed in my preparations this afternoon. News of the schedule change barely reached me in time." Collin feigned sincerity. "Did you not want to see me?"

"Give me your jacket."

He obliged, even though he was decidedly underdressed, and with only the white linen of his shirt and no waistcoat or cravat in place, Ivy found it necessary to remind herself of important facts. "I like dancing. I like dancing with Henry, and nothing you say is going to make me stop."

Ivy carefully shrugged into Collin's jacket and buttoned it over her dress.

"You have a habit of stealing my clothes."

And why is that, dunderhead? "If anyone asks, I was cold. Did I damage the cycle?"

Collin righted the pedal cycle and made an inspection. "Only the paint job."

"Excellent. I need this to work. How fast before you can get it into production?"

"I have the schematics, the prints, and a report prepared of projected costs and necessary labor. It will be on your desk before morning. I would have brought it with me, had I been given more notice."

"Oh, don't you start too." Ivy took the cycle from Collin.

"Are you riding the pedal cycle back?"

"I'm not riding that creature. I hate horses." She really did.

"Fair enough."

Collin's shirt billowed in the wind. Ivy shivered. "You should have made two pedal cycles."

"I'll get right on it, Princess."

"But this"—Ivy tapped the center frame—"needs to be lower. And although I love the exposed gears, it might be easier to ride with the gears covered. My skirts, you see."

"Wouldn't it be easier to change your skirts than the bike?"

He had a point. "Do it anyway."

"Fine, but tell me what else I should be working on. I take it I will be advancing to the next round?"

He would. The cycle was magnificent. "I haven't thought that far ahead."

"No? No, you've been too busy thinking of dashing little dancers with puppy-dog eyes. But, Ivy, it's not going to be enough." Collin grabbed the reins, and the horse reluctantly left off the crab-grass and stood at attention. "Your puppy is an excellent dancer, and people are quite amused by the pair of you, but it won't be enough." Collin dropped the reins. "It's not what you need. You don't need a boy to worship you and fawn over you for your clever insults or biting wit."

He stood so close. The pedal cycle was all that separated them. "What do I need?" She felt a fevered haze shiver up her spine. His jacket smelled like him—cut grass and woodsmoke. She'd keep it. His scent had worn off his pajama top, but she'd keep that, too, because it was so cozy.

Collin's eyes sharpened. He leaned forward. His lips parted, and for a moment, Ivy didn't care that he'd lied...or brandished a gun at Papa's opera. But he didn't kiss her. "A man who will build you a pedal cycle and write up a business proposal for efficiently and sustainably mass-producing it."

Her spine went cold. "Charming." Ivy stood on the pedals and lurched forward.

They returned to the courtyard and to the canopy that had been abandoned by everyone save Trina and Pen.

"Did you have fun, then? Is it my turn for a ride?" Pen asked.

"Do not leave the courtyard." Ivy handed off the bike to Pen. "Where is everyone?"

Trina took in a deep breath. "Jade was unwell."

"Properly sick, in point of fact," Pen said, wobbling slightly forward on the cycle.

"Papa and Adelaide left immediately. Sent for a doctor." Trina put a hand to her brow, rubbing small circles at her temple, a tic that only ever surfaced when she had her hands full. "Drank preventive doses of spirits."

"And the other contestants?" Ivy asked.

"We had a camel ride. Yeah. We did." Pen beamed as she lurched in circles around them. "Can you imagine if we all rode around on camels?"

Trina suppressed a smile. "Nothing even came close to Major Collin's cycle. But you knew it wouldn't."

"I'm flattered." Collin bowed low. It wasn't a sweeping, elegant bow like Henry's, but it was something. The major wasn't lithe; he was athletic. And healthy. And handsome. And a liar. A committed liar.

"Thank you for your entry, Major Collin," Ivy said. "We shall carefully consider it and return it when we have finished our examination." Would she? Ivy pulled Collin's coat closer. "Instructions for your third and final task will arrive via post—"

Pen skidded the cycle to a stop in front of Collin. "For pity's sake, Ives, just tell him. He's the only one who deserves to push on."

Ivy was annoyed that the other contestants had left. How would she find the most flaccid of them all now?

Collin wheeled the cycle to Ivy. "I would appreciate any and all additional time to complete the task," he said, handing over the cycle.

Ivy shivered as the wind gusted. "I want a branch—"

"A branch?" Collin pulled the collar of his coat up around Ivy's neck.

She swatted his hands away. "Would you let me finish?"

"Apologies," Collin murmured, not that he looked sorry.

"A branch thick with frost and sparkling like diamonds in the noonday sunlight." Ivy delighted in Collin's look of dismay, dare she say horror? "A branch covered in ice."

CHAPTER FORTY-NINE

Collin retreated to Sutherbee's, where he slumped, exhausted, onto the nearest stool and rested his head on the bar.

Phillip left his organ. "Went well, did it?"

"She wants a frozen branch now."

Phillip reached around the bar for a couple of glasses and a bottle. "What?"

"Ice crystals frozen all over a branch. It's impossible."

Phillip poured them each a drink. "I don't think so."

Collin accepted the drink, but hesitated. "Sutherbee won't mind?"

"I won't tell him, if you won't." Phillip touched his glass to Collin's. "Matt and Tim have been working on some sort of cooling technology over on Grove for weeks now." Phillip reached again behind the bar and procured a paper and pencil. He scribbled an address on it and handed it to Collin. "Better hurry if you want to catch them before we're all expected at Madame Olivia's."

Not twenty minutes later, Collin found himself panting in front of a dusty, old storefront on Grove Street. A bell rang as he pushed open the door. He tripped on a cloth splattered with sawdust and paint that covered the floor. He toed up the corner, revealing black and white marble tiles underneath. "Matt?"

"Yeahup?" Matthew yelled from behind the large glass counter at the back of the shop.

"What's going on here?" Collin asked.

"Did you think you were the only bloke playing strategy all this time?" His voice sounded muffled, like he had a wrench in his teeth.

"Is this place yours?" Collin asked.

Matthew rose and set a handful of tools on the counter. "It is for the next three weeks. After that, I'll default on the payment."

Collin sniffed and then sneezed. "Charming."

Matthew swore. "It was available for the right price and has the wire working I needed. Thanks to Sutherbee."

That's right, Phillip had mentioned Sutherbee's was expanding. "A new saloon?"

"The other proprietors on Grove didn't take kindly to the idea." Made sense. Grove catered to a decidedly more posh clientele than Sutherbee's. "I pitched Sutherbee my idea for the place. He liked it so much he became my chief investor."

Collin inspected the paint cans in the corner but stopped short of prying open the lids. "I didn't know you were interested in staying in the capital."

"I didn't either," Matthew grumbled. "What is a man to do when his wife is being held hostage, and his entire future and happiness are put on hold?"

"This is...a lot of construction for... What is this? A deli? A bakery?"

Matthew rummaged in the toolbox behind him for a screw. "You may call it a confectionary for the time being. But let's get on with it, man. I can smell it on you."

"Smell what?" Collin asked innocently.

"The favor you are about to ask."

Collin chuckled. "Dairyman's nose can smell all that?"

Matthew disappeared behind the counter. "What do you want?"

"I want to freeze ice crystals onto a birch branch."

Matthew snorted. "Why?"

"Because I love Ivy."

Matthew straightened, leveling Collin with a serious stare.

Collin fiddled with the closest of Matthew's tools. "Although I do find increasing merit to your plan—"

"Jade's plan," Matthew corrected.

"Jade's plan of settling out in the country and letting the capital rot, Ivy will not allow it. She cares so deeply." Collin loved that about her.

"Careful, now." Matthew crouched low and tinkered with a coupler and glass coil. "Can't have you melting into some sordid puddle in my parlor."

"Help me?" Collin asked.

"It's proprietary knowledge," Matthew said.

"I don't need to know how it works. I just need to give her an ice-covered branch. Phillip said you and Tim have been working on this for weeks. Help me do this, and we've won the game."

Matthew wiped his hands on a linen towel. "How do you know this will end the game? Hmm? How do you know she won't just keep stringing you on, asking you riddles, inventing more tasks?"

"She said it was the last."

"Let me be plainer." Matthew tossed the towel on the floor. "How do you know this—you and Ivy—will work? Have you told her the truth?"

Collin fingered the trimming on the glass cabinet. "Almost."

Matthew rested both hands on the shop counter. "The refrigeration technology, including the submitted patent information, is the sole property of Tim. Even I don't know how it works."

"It's not for the lack of me trying to explain." Tim crossed the room, grabbing a screwdriver from Matt's collection. "But Matt's right. I'm not going to disclose the information and lose my best work. Again."

Collin's shoulders sagged.

Tim considered a pair of pliers before shoving them into his back pocket. "But when I get the freezing rooms working, I will toss in a branch for you."

Relief and gratitude washed over Collin. "How long?"

"Another hour or two. Longer if you stay here pestering me with questions."

"I'm happy to assist in any way," Collin offered.

"Yeah." Matt handed Collin a brush. "You can start painting. Then you can start cleaning this place up."

"Cleaning?"

"I won't pass the state inspection with the place looking like this. And my investors are counting on me." Matthew stood taller. "Not to mention the missus."

CHAPTER FIFTY

It was to be the last night of the spring balls, but they'd proven so popular that the hosts had decided to extend them indefinitely. The musicians did a quick job of tuning before they slid into the next set.

Ivy watched Henry tug at his lace. For all the attention he gave his cuffs, he should have spent more time on his cravat. "Shall we dance, Ivy?"

"Again?" She willed herself not to pant. Nothing was more infuriating than being out of breath while one's partner showed no signs of being winded. "Your cravat is an absolute mess. Let me help you." Ivy twisted the knot apart before she began the new knot. It was just the sort of job she was accustomed to, fussing over the younger and more cavalier. Henry's hands moved gently to her own, and she realized that the action was more flirtatious than she'd intended.

The youth took her fingers in his and brought them down until he was holding both her hands and staring at the tangle of their fingers.

The beadwork on Ivy's shoulders was starting to itch. This was not going to be easy, but better to end it now. "I really like you," she said.

Henry's crooked, mischievous smile broke across his face in a brilliance that matched his talent on the dance floor. "I like you too."

Ivy pressed her lips together but could not summon the energy to tug them into a smile. "But I need more than just dances. I need to start thinking of the future."

"The future." He said it with such gravitas. He spread Ivy's hands wide and stared at the shale floor between them. His smile disappeared, replaced with a slight frown that looked altogether too at home on his features. Maybe Henry deserved more credit.

"You know my father has no successor..."

Henry swallowed. "I do."

"I have responsibilities to my family and kingdom that I cannot ignore." Ivy's eyes darted to her sisters, to the beautiful fractured glass of the old palace windows, to the vines that had wound their way between the cracks. "I thought that this, dancing with you, could be enough." Her voice broke. "But I was wrong, and it's not fair. I'm sorry."

"No. Don't be sorry." Henry gently brought a finger to Ivy's chin, tilting her gaze back to his. "I understand."

Ivy heard how his voice had drifted into somber tones, tones that reflected all-too-familiar territory of duty and responsibility...sacrifice. She could not breathe against the amber-and-gold-beaded stomacher of her dress. "I need some air."

"Of course." Henry bent over her hand one last time before Ivy withdrew from the heat and press of the dance floor.

Collin watched the pair of them from a distance. He wore his borrowed cloak, which, although made of lofty cashmere, felt tonight like chain mail and nettles. Stupid cloak. It was supposed to be such a boon, but being invisible was the worst. The woman he loved was being fawned over by a self-entitled young dandy, and all Collin could do was watch.

Collin clenched his cracked and sore hands, the artifact of hours of painting and scrubbing. He'd not cleaned like that since Gran was in her prime. What made it worse was that Matthew was tight-lipped about the project. He would not even let him into the back of his shop, just the infernal "parlor," as he called it.

Collin was exhausted, out of sorts, and incredibly tired of being dismissed by the woman he loved and, he was sure, loved him too. Why else would Ivy wear his pajamas? Why else would she kiss him not once, but twice? Why else would she create task after task that he alone—well, no, that he with the help of their friends could manage? And he'd managed them well. The type machine was genius, particularly with the quieter action and return. The pedal cycle was the most heartfelt poem he could manage to relay his feelings for Ivy. Because that's what loving her felt like. It felt like riding a pedal cycle at sunset as the petals rained down from the cherry trees. It also felt like stumbling, lurching, and sometimes crashing forward. But it was worth it.

He'd even confronted the king about the regrettable assassination business. He'd given him the chance to make it right. That was the right thing to do. Give the man a chance to explain himself to his daughter, let Ivy learn about it from the source, and give her some privacy to process. Had the king done that, and had it made no difference to Ivy? Because she was still dancing with that idiot boy.

"Your jaw will get sore if you insist on clenching your teeth like that," Florence said.

"Ah, Major Collin." Sylvia flitted to her companion's side. "How did your demonstration go this afternoon?"

"I don't know," Collin muttered.

"Well, you were there. What did you invent for Her Royal Haughtiness?"

Collin clenched his fists as he watched Henry titter over Ivy's hand. "A pedal cycle."

"About time someone invented a bicycle," Florence said.

Sylvia rapped her fan on Florence's shoulder. "None of that," she said under her breath before turning back to Collin. "I'm sure Ivy adored it!"

"She rode off on it before I had a chance to ask her, and when I finally caught up to her..." Breathless, wild-eyed, her beautiful hair blown loose in the wind. Collin reddened. "She was quite preoccupied with other matters."

Florence chuckled. "Capricious."

The music swelled. Sylvia launched into a tirade of how it was the duty of youth to be both impulsive and cavalier. Collin tried to be a good boy. He tried to be attentive to his hostesses, but when he stole a glance in Ivy's direction, she was gone. "What happened to Ivy?"

"Oh? Well, let's ask Henry. Henry?" Sylvia waved toward the scoundrel. "Henry, my boy. How are you this evening?"

Henry bowed low and with great flourish. Collin should have expected as much. Henry bumped into Collin when he straightened.

"Steady on!" Collin said.

Henry swore a pretty oath before he straightened and apologized. "I didn't see you there in the shadows."

So he was fey. Major Collin inclined his head and tried to be civil. He did not try hard. "How do you do?"

"Excellent. Excellent!" Henry beamed. "The woman I love, the most beautiful woman here, and the quickest wit in this room..." Henry pressed his lips together and shook his head. "She and I have reached an understanding."

Collin's mouth went dry. He struggled for words. "You're joking."

"I can scarcely believe it myself." Henry ran his fingers through his wind-tossed hair. "She spoke of the future. Of *our* future."

"Oh, Florence. I did not see that coming," Sylvia said through tight lips.

Florence's eyes looked so strained and tired that Collin thought the woman would pass out. "Excuse me," Collin said to Henry. "My friend is unwell."

"Of course. Please attend to your date."

"She's not my date!" Collin shouted, but Henry had already disappeared into the crowd. "Florence, are you all right?"

Florence swatted Collin away. "I'm not the one you should be worried about."

"Go to her, Major," Sylvia said. "You don't need magic to know those two won't suit."

Collin ripped off the cashmere cloak. "My sincere thanks for the use of your cloak, Florence; I no longer need it." And with that, he ran after Ivy.

The crickets chirped amiably in the night air, but it was still too early for cicadas. The winter had been too hard for the frogs to begin their serenade. Pity. Frogs were Ivy's favorite, as they were a sure sign of warmer nights. Ivy ran her hand along the side of one of the boats at the shore. The wood was smooth and cold under her fingers. Tight buds of new green leaves studded the birch trees like jewels.

"What do you think you're doing, dancing with that child?"

Ivy turned and squinted in the dim moonlight until she found Collin storming through the clump of birch trees. "What are you doing here?"

"What on earth does he have that I lack?"

"You're still jealous?" Wonderful. He could sit with it awhile.

Collin closed the distance between them. He was seething. "And you're insane. Why would you propose to him? He's a sniveling little dachshund. Is dancing really that important to you? I swear I will take lessons and hire tutors—or whatever the hell you call dedicated dancing teachers—if it matters that much to you."

"What are you talking about?"

"Henry, who I had the pleasure of meeting in there just now. He tells me that he and 'the woman he loves' have reached an understanding. He was going on and on about your future."

Ivy scoffed. "It's a joke. He was teasing you."

"How simple do you think I am that I could mistake pure, unadulterated joy for a joke?"

Ivy pressed her fingers to her temples and groaned. "Well, then, it was a pure, unadulterated misunderstanding. I was trying to gently tell him the truth."

"The truth?"

"Yes, the truth. I know it's a foreign concept to you."

It was Collin's turn to groan.

"But that's what adults do. They tell each other the truth. They have hard conversations."

"What did you say to dear Henry?"

Ivy folded her arms across her chest. "I told him that I liked him very much."

"And then he turned his puppy eyes on you and stopped listening." Collin kicked at the pebbles.

Ivy thought about it. "Well, now that you mention it, that's possible. I told him I liked him very much—"

"Yes, you said that. No need to repeat it."

"—but that I had to think of the future. Dancing isn't enough. And... Oh my stars, he thought I was talking about marriage, didn't he?"

"Yes. He did," Collin snapped. "He's dancing on air at the very prospect."

"He's four years younger than me! He's like a little—"

"Pet dachshund? Adoring, devoted, small, but not someone you want to have and to hold from this day forward for as long as you both shall live?"

"You're insufferable." But also right.

"How was your cycle ride today? The one you took after I left. Did you enjoy it? Did Henry build you a pedal cycle? Did he build you a type machine? Did he spend the last fourteen hours scrubbing a tacky shop so that he could get you that branch covered in frost?"

Ivy's eyes stung. "He's not complicated. What he and I have is not complicated. *Everything* between me and you is complicated!"

"I understand your obligations. I am prepared to support you in them and do anything in my power to help you succeed. How is that complicated?"

Ivy felt like bursting into tears, screaming, or pushing Collin backward into the cold lake. "I don't know, Collin. Why don't you try to kill my father and then lie about everything, and then we can reassess?"

"Ivy, please. There is more going on here than you know."

Not this again. "Then tell me! You want me to think you had a good reason for trying to kill my father, when there can't possibly be a good reason. Stop trying to save face and just tell me the truth."

"I can't tell you." Collin scrubbed a hand across his face.

Ivy pulled off her heavy emerald earrings, turning them over in her hands. "I've only ever cared about two men in my life. Both insist on lying to me. Repeatedly." She dropped the earrings into the pocket of her gown. "Now the moon is full, the night is fine, and I have to go inside and break my little dachshund's heart and set him free before I stare down the loneliness of the rest of my life."

"If you let me play your father's game to completion, it doesn't have to be lonely."

"Do you really believe that? Do you really think it is that simple?"

"Forgiveness is a yes-or-no choice."

"And one that would have to be made hourly if I were married to you."

"The way Gran explained it, I'm fairly certain that's how all marriages work."

"Collin, you trying to kill my father for some unknown reason that you seem to think is legitimate and forgivable but refuse to explain is a problem bigger than forgetting to turn down the bed or bank the fire. It's unforgivable." Ivy lowered her voice and tried to regain her composure. "I've never pursued bringing charges against you regarding the attempted assassination, because I felt I owed you for your service in the war, but I swear if you don't tell me the truth, I will expose you."

"You're right," Collin said. "I should have explained better—"

"You didn't explain at all. You never do. Why are you even here?"

"I love you."

Ivy felt her heart shrinking and stretching. Her eyes burned as hot tears spilled out. "You can't just say that!"

"Why not? I love you."

"Stop it." Ivy sank onto the edge of one of the beached boats. "It's not true." If it were true, then... Then everything changed.

Collin was quiet. He drew closer and sat next to her on the edge of the boat. "It's very true."

Ivy could feel his warmth. She inhaled, hoping to smell the characteristic cut grass and woodsmoke but coughed. "You smell like bleach."

"I was cleaning Matthew's—and Jade's—new shop. Inspector comes tomorrow morning."

"Shop? Jade has a shop?"

"All I know is that it's now a very clean one, thanks to me."

Ivy brushed a bit of dust off the front of Collin's shirt. "Why were you cleaning Jade's shop?"

"For you. Asking Matthew for a favor was the only way I knew of getting your diamond-studded branch." Collin rested his hand on top of Ivy's.

"Frost-studded," Ivy corrected.

His fingers wrapped gently around her wrist. "Diamonds, I'm sure, would be easier to procure."

"Jade has barely spoken to me since... since I made her return with us to the capital. She's the reason..." *Be fair now.* "Well, there are many reasons why this game must end, and soon. I thought if I could come here night after night, I might be able to stomach marrying some harmless, self-absorbed nitwit. I'd continue to quietly run the kingdom while my father and his understudy unknowingly try their best to erase all my efforts, but at least I'd have some dancing to look forward to." Ivy should have untangled Collin's fingers from her own, but his hands were so warm in the cool night air. "I had hoped to stretch this game out indefinitely, but that isn't fair to my sisters."

"It's not fair to you. You deserve more, Ivy. You deserve love. Not because you've earned it, but because you do. We all do. And you deserve to lead this country and to have your efforts out in the open, recognized—"

"And yet, that only happens if I am lucky enough to be picked by Papa's champion." It wasn't fair. "But we come back again and again to the potential champion also being Papa's attempted assassin."

Collin's hand trailed softly down Ivy's arm. "I'll tell you the truth now. He should have been the one to tell you, but I did warn him."

"Who?"

"Your father. In the abbey crypt, he approached me hours before you did."

"No, no. That's ridiculous. Only a monster would put his family—"

Collin looked so pained, his face showed the strain. "The assassination attempt was staged. The gun held blanks."

Ivy's shoulders sagged, crushed by the weight of trading one massive betrayal for another. "Why?"

"For Adelaide. He wanted her to... He said she is the love of his life. He wanted proof that she cares for him. And if she doesn't, he thought to inspire her regard."

Collin recited every last sorry, pathetic detail.

Ivy snorted and blinked back tears. "I should have known."

"I thought you did. I was sure you knew right up until I came to you the morning after the opera, and it was abundantly clear you didn't... And then I was a coward. I didn't want your ill opinion of me. I was embarrassed and ashamed. I was going to tell you everything, but you caught me lying once about my involvement with Olcceart. I was determined to prove myself to you before I told you all of it. It was a coward's excuse, followed by another that it was not my place to explain your father's actions." Collin tilted Ivy's chin up and brushed away an errant tear. "I was a fool. I made too many mistakes. I worried that the truth and my abominable behavior would color me a villain forever in your eyes. I should have told you everything from the start. But then...my sorry mind reasoned I'd have no chance, none, of winning your affection."

"Winning." Ivy batted his hand away. "Must it always be a game?"

"No. I'm sorry. I'm an idiot. I love you, and I'm an idiot."

"You're an idiot for loving me?"

"No. I'm certain loving you is the smartest choice I've ever made."

"It's a choice, is it?"

"Forgive me. Forgive me for everything."

Could she? She didn't know. A white-hot rage boiled inside. "I should have known this was all Papa's work."

"He's not worth your tears, Ivy."

Ivy brushed more tears away with the heels of her hands. "You don't understand. Everything would fall apart without me."

"Let it fall apart. It's too much for one woman to shoulder."

Ivy bristled. "But it's enough for a man to handle? A man like you?"

"That's not what I meant."

"It doesn't matter." And it didn't. Ivy was too mad. And too embarrassed. And too bewildered and upset. Hot tears stung her eyes. She should have tackled him to the ground, pummeled him with her fists for everything. Instead, she wrapped her arms around him. "You should have told me. You should have told me everything." She loved him. She'd wanted him always, and with a sort of relief, she at last understood the frenzy of her heart to be something greater than attraction alone.

"Ivy?"

As she buried her face against the chest of the man she loved, Ivy asked her heart, *Will it be all right now?* It was simple. Collin would win Papa's game. He'd choose her. He'd be king one day, and she'd be his queen.

"No!" Ivy pushed him away. She loved him, but she couldn't do that. She wouldn't do that! She'd not be queen consort to any man. Something lay deeper in a corner of her heart, deeper than her love for Collin. And it wasn't power-hungry or sinister. It wasn't raw, unsettling ambition. It was a belief, as hot and as real as a lightning flash, that she could lead her people. That she'd do it better than anyone else. That she was meant to do it. That she had to and wanted to. She was done living in the shadows, begging for attention, never for a moment in control of her future. "I love you." Ivy said. "But I can't—" She couldn't untangle the words from the sob lodged in her throat.

Collin's eyes looked wet and strained. He was too clever at collecting pieces of information not to understand. He shuddered. A weaker man would have collapsed. "What are you going to do?" His voice was hoarse with grief.

She did not know. She needed more time. "I'm going to dance, and then I'm going to go home. Good night, Major Collin. I'll expect your final answer to the king's game in the morning."

Collin nodded and bowed low. "Good night, Princess."

Ivy returned to the dance, and it wasn't long before she found him. "Let's dance, Henry."

"But I thought—"

"Forget what I said. We'll dance one last time as friends before you row me back to the opposite shore. Do you understand?"

Henry nodded solemnly. "One last time."

"As friends," Ivy repeated.

Henry's smile was pained. As if he were cherishing the last rays of carefree summer sunshine. "As friends."

CHAPTER FIFTY-ONE

"Good morning, Papa." Ivy closed the double doors of the breakfast room behind her. The king and his courtier appeared somewhat startled by Ivy's unannounced visit. "Senior Rudolpho, my father and I have delicate and urgent matters of state to discuss. You are dismissed."

There was no mistaking Ivy's tone this morning. The senior bowed and left the table.

The king gulped his glass of wine. "Ivy. I don't remember inviting you to breakfast. But since you are here, you may as well try the sausages. They are excellent this morning."

"Papa, we need to talk," Ivy said.

"The cantaloupe is superb. Really top-notch."

"We need to talk now."

The king wiped his mouth on the tablecloth. "Oh, not now. You know talking at the table gives me gas. And I have Adelaide's dressage display to attend before the Cherry Blossom Festival begins. Adelaide has planned a picnic under my favorite tree for luncheon. Why don't we talk then?"

Ivy stared at her father.

"Or perhaps you would join us at the croquet game this afternoon before the parade? You know what Rudolpho was just saying? He said he's never seen my game as good as it is now. He told me my best days are ahead of me. What say you to that?" The king belched. "The croquet pitch will do just fine. We will talk then. Now have a liqueur."

"No. We are going to talk here," Ivy insisted.

"I don't want to talk—"

"I know you staged your own assassination attempt."

The king pressed his lips together and puffed out his jaw. He looked so much older then. Frail too.

Ivy was furious as she calmy poured herself a glass of water. "Did you even consider what that would do to your family?"

"Of course—"

"To your daughters?" Ivy took a seat at the table.

Papa waved his hand. "You're strong girls."

"Did you consider the economic consequences of such an attempt?"

"Well." He gestured with his hands. "Economies are volatile and...and—"

"Did you consider how such a plot could fail? What if Colonel Cervantes in a drunken stupor, had spilled the entire plan?"

The king pouted out his lower lip, but an eyebrow struggled upward as if he had a furtive thought.

Ivy continued. "How easily do you think that information could have been used against you, or Adelaide, if it had gotten into the wrong hands? What if there had been Olcceart spies? You and our entire family could have been killed."

"But we're all fine. Not a scratch on any of us."

"It doesn't change the fact that what you did was wrong. It was very wrong, Papa!"

Papa's wig slid forward, until he grabbed the blond thing and pulled it off, revealing a head full of white, wispy hair. "You don't understand, Ivy. I planned the assassination attempt on my own life to boost support for the war effort. I was never so popular as I was the day after my opera. People value what you threaten to take away. And demonizing the enemy is a useful tool—"

"A king should never use a war to inflate his popularity."

Papa shrugged. "Wars have been fought over less."

Ivy gripped the stem of her water glass. "You don't deserve to be king. A king must think of others first and always. A king must consider the best interests of his enemies as well as his friends. A king should be the first to sacrifice everything for his country. I love you, Papa, but you are a terrible king!"

Papa glared at her with his burnt-peanut eyes and tight lips.

"And that is why you are going to form an official Parliament, and Parliament's first act will be to make the monarchy pass to the primogeniture of the king regardless of sex. Parliament's second act will be to limit the power of the monarchy, starting with mandatory retirement at age sixty."

"That's less than two years from now!"

Ivy drummed her fingernails on the table. "Yes."

"You'd put the fate of our country into the hands of a bureaucracy?"

"You put it in the hands of your twenty-two-year-old daughter and the band of steampunks she could persuade to join her."

"But you succeeded."

"At what cost? I've been cleaning up your ill-conceived messes for the last six years. I have a life to live. I have books I want to read and studies I want to make. I want to sleep for more than four hours a night. And I want to travel, and I want to have children of my own. And I want them to stand on my feet as I teach them the jig." Ivy splayed her hand across the lace of the breakfast table before rising. The mantel clock ticked softly, and outside, a songbird lilted the first tentative notes of a cherished reprise.

The king's jowls sagged deeply. "I did a good job raising you, Ivy."

"What?"

"I did. I've taught you the most important thing a parent can teach a child. Life is filled with problems. Big problems. And what have I always said?"

"'Don't bring me problems. Bring me solutions.'"

"And here you've brought me solutions at last. Parliament. Primogeniture. Retirement. They're good, Ivy." The king smirked, and a soft twinkle came to his dark eyes. "Why didn't you think of them sooner?"

Ivy rolled her eyes, but a small smile fixed to her features.

The king bit into an enormous cherry pastry. "Now, what about my future sons-in-law? You going to let me save face and name your major the winner and future king? Or will there be a scuffle over Jade's fella?"

Ivy stammered, "I...I don't know." She pressed her hands to her forehead. Truthfully, all her fight had been focused on confronting her father. She wasn't prepared to tackle the question of Collin.

"I like the major. A little hot-tempered. But resourceful. Scrappy. Honest to a fault. I like that in a man. Does he win? It's up to you." The king shoved the rest of the cherry pastry into his mouth. Crumbs fell all over his lace cravat. "You'll know where to find me, if you make a decision."

"Thank you, Papa."

The king wiped his mouth on the table linen. "Finally, some gratitude. Now may I finish my breakfast in peace? Or are you going to drag me with you to talk to Rosecrans about convening this Parliament before I've finished my sausage?"

"No." The songbird's reprise became merry and confident. A warm breeze brought in the smell of the fresh grass and sweet peas. "I think I must see your game to its conclusion."

The king grunted. "A word of advice. Consult with your sisters—all of them—before you make your move."

∽

Ivy's sisters agreed to meet her in the salon off the courtyard terrace not twenty minutes later. Ivy had started with what she intended to be a lengthy apology, followed by an explanation of Collin's innocence, the mistakes she would not repeat in the future, and the news that she was to be Papa's heir with the understanding that a new Parliament would from this day forward share in the power of the monarchy. "Thank you all for coming. First, let me say that I owe you all an apology—

"Save it, old girl." Beatrice handed Ivy a folded note. "We know everything."

"I was listening at the door when you met Papa for breakfast," Mina said, stroking Mistress Kitty, who purred loudly and smugly.

"And we've known of Collin's innocence for some time," Trina said.

"Matthew beat the truth out of him when he arrived in the capital," Jade said bluntly.

"Why didn't you tell me?" Ivy asked.

"Would you have listened?" Rachel asked.

They had her there. "And Papa's game?" Ivy asked.

Jade snorted. "We all knew how it was going to end."

Trina smoothed one of Ivy's stray curls back into place. "We got Matt and Tim started on the most complicated of your impossible tasks weeks ago."

"Helped out a bit too." Pen kicked her feet up onto the arm of the chesterfield. "You didn't think we'd let our boys have all the fun?"

Ivy beamed with pride at her talented, clever, incredible sisters. "Thank you." She slid her finger under the seal of the note.

"Don't open it yet!" Harriet shrieked. "You can't read it until Collin comes."

"It's his last riddle," Sophia explained.

"If he can answer that one, he deserves to win." Gwen winked at Ivy.

Ivy held the last riddle in her hand. "Are you sure this is all you want me to ask him?"

"Well, actually"—Daphne considered—"it would be nice to know if he has any younger brothers."

"Or sisters," Rachel added.

"Just ask him," Trina said.

Ivy opened her mother's watch. "He's supposed to be here by now."

A bike bell rang from outside in the courtyard, and Trina gave Ivy a quick hug before swatting her out the terrace doors. From the top of the courtyard stairs, Ivy could see Collin approach on the green pedal cycle. Her heart fluttered as he rode toward her with a messenger bag over his shoulder. He dropped the bike and ran up the steps, stopping a few below Ivy.

"I have it," he said.

"Major Collin—"

"It's in here." He rummaged through the bag.

Ivy tried again. "Major Collin—"

"There." Collin placed a birch branch in Ivy's hand. It was thick with ice crystals and sparkled in the noonday sun. "Just like diamonds. The frost makes it look silver, yes?"

Ivy held the frozen branch. "Collin." Saying his name without his rank made her blush. "I have one last riddle."

Collin nodded. He looked tired, and crestfallen. "One last riddle," he repeated.

Ivy unfolded the note from her sisters. "Why does a beautiful princess who dances holes in her shoes many a night in the arms of handsome young men seldom smile?" She arched an eyebrow, pleading silently that he'd have an answer. Any answer.

Collin dropped his bag and climbed the rest of the palace steps. "My answer is twofold." He drew nearer, and Ivy found her eyes settling on the stonework at her feet. "First, she's tired of dancing in the dark. Her brilliance is going unnoticed. I'm sure she'd prefer dancing in the daylight, where her efforts—namely grace under pressure, intelligence, industriousness, and altruism—can be seen and appreciated for what they are: outstanding service to king and country at the price of enormous personal sacrifice. Second..." Collin swallowed and tilted Ivy's chin up to meet his gaze. "She is not dancing with the right man."

Ivy dropped the branch, grabbed Collin, and kissed him.

He kissed her back, naturally. He wrapped his hands around her waist and pulled her closer to him. From behind them, Ivy heard a chorus of happy shouts.

"The game has changed," Ivy said against his lips.

He kissed her, and only when they were both struggling for air, he said, "Has it?"

Ivy pressed her forehead against his neck. "You've won, but you will not inherit the crown or be allowed to marry the princess of your choice."

Collin pulled away while keeping his hands firmly on Ivy's waist. She enjoyed them there. His eyes came back into focus. He was about to speak, but she stopped him with a kiss. "As Papa's heir, that choice is now mine."

Collin smiled widely. He hesitated for the briefest moment before kissing her again. Ivy gasped when his attention turned to her neck, her shoulder. "Would you like to see how I froze the branch?" His words pulsed and pulled across her skin.

Ivy laced her fingers through Collin's. "In a minute."

"You're sure?" the king asked, adjusting the pink lace at his throat in front of the stately mirror of his personal salon. Collin, Ivy, and all of her sisters had just managed to catch their father before he set off for Adelaide's dressage exhibition.

Ivy beamed at Collin. "Ardently."

He returned her smile. "Passionately."

Her sisters stood all around them, vibrating with excitement and shared joy.

"Fine." King Rupert waved a hand. "You're married. Wife and husband, the pair of you."

The second raucous cheer of the morning erupted from Ivy's sisters.

"Well done, Pops," Pen said, squeezing their father's shoulder and shaking his hand vigorously.

Rupert looked smug. He did love an adoring crowd.

"Don't...don't we need to exchange vows or say something?" Collin asked.

"You'll have to say an awful lot in the state ceremony that will happen..." The king looked to his daughter.

"In a month or two," Ivy finished for him.

The king nodded. "A late-summer wedding. We'll announce it after the Cherry Blossom Festival. Adelaide will have fun planning the details."

Ivy blushed as Collin brought their intertwined fingers to his lips and kissed her hand. "Exactly so."

"Off you go. Enjoy some time to yourselves. Have a proper honeymoon." The king left to admire his wife atop surely the prettiest horse in the kingdom and share with her the happy news.

Collin pulled Ivy into his embrace, holding her against his heart while his lips grazed her temple. Ivy closed her eyes, savoring how delicious her husband's arms felt around her, how his lips trailed slowly, gently down her cheek, her jaw, her neck.

A sniffle interrupted Collin's progress and then a sob. But not from Ivy or Collin. Ivy opened her eyes.

The triplets and Sophia were holding one another and crying.

Daphne bit her trembling lip. "It's just...everything!"

Trina cleared her throat. "We have a Cherry Blossom Festival to attend. Come on, girls. Lots to do this morning." She shepherded her sisters out the door. "Chin up, Gwen. Yes, it's wonderfully happy, Ang. Your happy ending will be next, Sophia, I'm sure. Let's find your spring dresses, hmm? Aunt Olivia sent over new shoes, too, when she heard about the pile we've danced holes through." Trina blew the happy couple a kiss before snicking the door shut.

Ivy ran her hands across Collin's strong shoulders and down to his chest, where she kept them, enjoying the pulse of his heart under her fingers. "Now, husband, about that branch... It will have to wait until this afternoon. I want to show you the palace. Particularly the north wing."

Collin's hands traced a long, slow line down Ivy's back. "Why the north wing?"

"It houses the suites where Papa hides the foreign dignitaries when they come to visit. Private, gorgeous suites with big, luxurious beds. They were designed with the hope that they'd be so comfortable the guests would never want to leave and bother anyone about their state business."

"Very quiet and out of the way?" Collin pressed a kiss to the hinge of Ivy's jaw.

"Empty of everyone, since there have been no state visitors for years. Yet, one suite is always kept ready. Just in case."

Collin kissed her lips. "Show me."

Ivy kissed him back before leading the way.

CHAPTER FIFTY-TWO

The sun was low in the sky by the time Ivy and Collin found their sisters and friends in the avenues of blossoming cherry trees. Clouds of pink and white blossoms formed a low billowy canopy over their heads, and when a gentle breeze shook the trees, a soft flurry of petals fell. Jade and Matthew were sprawled out on a picnic blanket. Pen and Tim were on a blanket of their own, contemplating a chessboard. Monty lay in the grass, dozing with a straw hat over his eyes. Eric, the triplets, and Sophia were in the process of climbing the largest cherry tree.

"Where have you two been?" Eric called. "You've missed all the fun."

"Where are the others?" Ivy asked after she'd greeted her sisters.

Pen rested her chin in her hands. "Mina convinced Harriet and Rachel to go with her to hear the festival storytellers. Although I suspect she was more interested in visiting the fey fortune-tellers. Beatrice volunteered to chaperone."

"And Trina?" Ivy nudged Pen's queen a square closer to Tim's knight.

Pen swatted Ivy's hand away and moved the queen back. "She went with Phillip to church to prepare for this evening's concert."

"Is Phillip playing the organ?" Collin asked.

"No." Pen took Tim's rook. "Trina is."

Ivy radiated happiness. "Trina's playing?"

"One of Phillip's compositions," Tim said, taking Pen's queen with a pawn.

"You're going to pay for that," Pen said to her beau. Tim leaned over the chessboard and kissed Pen's cheek. She rebuffed him playfully.

"We're all going to the concert after we wave to Bessie and Papa in the parade," Gwen said, dangling from a branch above them.

Sophia giggled. "Papa was so impressed when he finally saw our rail-less engine, he said he'd write her into his next opera."

Nice to see Sophia content for a change. "As long as Collin and I don't have to sit in his box on opening night. What's this?" Ivy asked, admiring a pedal cycle that had a large, interesting steel box attached to the front.

Jade, who was sprawled comfortably on a blanket next to Matthew, propped herself up on an elbow. "Open it."

Ivy raised the lid and gasped. Tin cylinders brimming with pastel shades of feathered cream were inside the ice-cold box. "Ice cream."

"Secret family recipe." Matthew kissed Jade's nose before hopping to his feet. "Ordinarily made by freezing cream from my best cows with Easterlie sea salt and ice harvested from the manor's lake in the dead of winter."

"Tim worked out something infinitely cleverer," Pen said as she fit a fallen cherry blossom behind Tim's ear before putting him into check.

"With your help," Tim said.

Jade stretched and yawned. "Matthew built me a confectionary, but I think calling it an ice cream parlor might be more fitting." She sighed happily. "There's enough room in the refrigerated display cabinet to name a flavor of ice cream after everyone in our family."

"What's my flavor?" Ivy's voice grew serious. "Is it chocolate?"

"We call it Ivy's Victory." Matthew handed Ivy a wooden spoon with a sample of the concoction.

"It's green," Ivy said, accepting the sample.

"I told him it had to be," Jade said. "Taste it."

The smooth, rich cream melted on Ivy's tongue. "Mint. With chocolate shavings?" Ivy offered the spoon to Collin, who readily took it and even more readily wrapped his arms around her.

Jade and Matthew exchanged a knowing look.

Ivy cleared her throat.

"Hey, we got married," Collin said, smiling hazily at Matthew.

Matthew struggled not to grin. "I heard. Well done." He served up a waffle bowl of Ivy's Victory and handed it, along with two spoons, to Ivy and Collin.

Ivy broke off a piece of the crunchy waffle and dipped it in the ice cream. "Another edible bowl. What's Collin's flavor?"

"Collin didn't get a flavor," Matthew said with a scowl.

Monty moved the hat from off his face. "Ruddy fool would have ruined everything if we hadn't stepped in."

A young man in an army dress uniform stopped in the avenue in front of the group, mouth open and eyes wide. "Montgomery?"

Monty gasped and was on his feet and embracing the young man in a moment. "Ramon. I didn't think I'd ever see you again."

"My regiment came back for the parade. What's left of us, anyway. How you been—"

Ramon didn't get another word in because Monty kissed him. Ramon dropped his helmet and kissed him back.

The triplets, Sophia, and Eric cheered and whistled from their perches in the cherry trees.

"Who are they?" Ivy overheard Ramon whisper to Monty. "Are you going to introduce me?"

"Yes, Monty! Introduce us!" Ivy shouted.

"Have some ice cream at the very least," Collin suggested.

Monty considered. "Later?" he asked Ramon.

Ramon slipped his hand in Monty's. "Later sounds good." They walked off into the avenue of cherry blossoms.

"Why didn't he want to introduce us?" Ivy asked Collin.

Collin pulled Ivy closer. "I think they were in a hurry to catch up. There are a lot of us."

"Enough to inspire an entire cabinet of ice cream." Ivy took another bite of her flavor and turned to Matthew. "What's your flavor, brother?"

"Raspberries and cream, naturally."

"Mine is fresh ginger." Jade rose and slipped an arm around her husband. "I'll have another scoop, love."

"Collin has to have a flavor," Ivy insisted. "He's family now."

Matthew gazed fondly at his wife. "What do you think, my dear?"

Jade took a taste of her ginger ice cream. "If we added a ribbon of chocolate and a hint of smoked almonds to the cherry ice cream you made for the festival... We could call it Major Top-Notch."

Ivy took another bite of her ice cream and couldn't believe she'd lasted this long on cocoa alone. "Matthew, this is extraordinary."

Jade leaned into her husband's broad chest. "It is all I've wanted to eat since I learned I was going to be a peopler."

Matthew glowed with pride.

"Are you coming to the ball tonight?" Sophia asked, scrambling down from the tree.

Eric hopped down after her. "You going to finally dance with Ivy, Collin?"

Ivy said, "No," at the same time Collin said, "Yes."

"No," Ivy said. "We're heading to Trina's concert, and then we are leaving on our honeymoon. We have a coach headed for a particular cherry orchard and an even more particular Gran, before we make our way to the North Mountains. In fact, we should probably head to Sutherbee's now to get you packed before the concert."

Ivy blew kisses to her sisters and headed off, arm in arm with her husband through the blossoming cherries.

"Wait!" Mina ran down the avenue toward them. "Wait!" She skidded to a stop and handed Collin a bright red jar.

"What's this?" Ivy asked.

"It's your honeymoon jam. Rachel, Bea, and Harriet helped me make it. I wanted to use cherries, but they aren't in season yet. The strawberries are good, though, and Frankfurt helped us find the fresh cherry blossom honey." She handed a second, still-warm jar of jam to Ivy. "We didn't have time to make more than two."

"Thank you, darling." Ivy kissed Mina.

Mina beamed but then became very serious. "Don't eat it with anyone else. You will eat them, won't you?"

"Of course." Ivy wrapped her arms around her husband, delighting in his warmth and scent. He really did smell like roasted apples, cut grass, and woodsmoke.

Collin opened his jar and offered it to Ivy. "The magic won't work unless we do."

Ivy dipped her pinkie into the hot jam and licked her finger. It tasted like the sweet notes of spring and all her hopes for happily-ever-after. She dipped her ring finger, now adorned with her mother's elegant wedding band, into the jam and offered Collin a taste.

Collin's lips closed around the tip of Ivy's finger. When he kissed her next, he tasted of strawberries, honey, and happily-ever-after. And something else too. Something that carried the smell of cherry blossoms, the laughter of her sisters and their friends, the wind rippling over an alpine lake, and the enchantment of first dances. Magic.

A NOTE TO MY READERS

Once upon a time, I took a folklore class. I learned among other things that fairy tales are folklore, and by design they are supposed to be told, tweaked, and retold. It was all the invitation I needed to retell my childhood favorite, *The Twelve Dancing Princesses*. I had so. much. fun. playing with this story, tagging along with Ivy and Collin, and weaving in a few Gaslamp/Steampunk artifacts that make my heart happy. I hope you had fun too! If so, please consider leaving a review.

In that same folklore class, I discovered another tale of nightly balls, mischievous fey, plucky princesses, and dashing princes. I'm happy to share that I'm working this story into another fairy tale retelling, *The Forgotten Storyteller*, which I hope will be published in early 2023. Before I put my fantasy hat (crown) back on, I hope to see a sequel to my debut, *My Cosplay Escape*, published by the end of this year (ambitious, I know, but an author can dream). *Turnabout Is Fair Cosplay* spins another sweet, sassy yarn in the world of costumes, superhero fandom, and happily-ever-afters. You can read more about that story here, and I'll have the pre-order links up just as soon as I can.

Sharing stories makes us human. Readers are often writers, and independent publishing makes it easy for anyone to share a story. Don't be silly (like me) and wait for an invitation. There are plenty of seats at the author table for everyone. Retell your favorite fairy tale. Write that epic fantasy novel. Put down on (digital) paper the characters you've created. Pen your memoir. Whatever form your story takes, know that readers are out there, and they're hungry for more. Fudge, I'm hungry for more.

Speaking of more... Pop over to my website, amytrent.com, for extras or to say hi. I love to hear from my readers! Sign up for my newsletter if you want to be in the know about my new releases and writerly life. I'm sometimes on Instagram @authoramytrent and occasionally on TikTok @authoramytrent, so if socials are your thing come find me.

However you like to keep in touch, know that I will always be wishing you,

Happy Reading!
Amy Trent

P.S. Coming attraction excerpt below!

ACKNOWLEDGMENTS

I would not be a writer without the support, love, and mentorship of my aunt, the amazingly talented Grace Burrowes (graceburrowes.com). Love you always, Aunt Grace. Thanks for helping me get this story, like the other one, off the ground. Thanks for talking me through imposter syndrome and the finer points of indie publishing. I'm forever grateful!

I've been so lucky to work with talented editors on this journey. A big, heartfelt thank you to Deborah Halverson (deborahhalverson.com). Thank you, Deborah, for being a champion of New Adult, and thank you for being a champion of this story. I can't believe I got to work with you again! Thank you to Joyce Lamb (joycelambediting.com). You are a copy-editing legend, and I am so grateful for your help!

Everlasting thanks to my talented cover artist, Bianca Bordianu of Moonpress Design (moonpress.co). Thank you for your patience, your understanding, and for figuring out how to work in the perfect crown into my cover. You are amazing! It was so much fun to work with you!

Sincere thanks to my talented and wonderful proofreaders: Sarah Rosenbarker and Arianne Costner. Y'all are geniuses!

Special thanks to my big sister, who told me that this was her favorite book that I've written. I wouldn't have survived the thornier days of editing without you! Browned-butter chocolate cookies to my brother, who's been a fan of The Horse Opera for decades. Hugs to my little sister, who's friendship and grace shows up in all of Ivy's eleven sisters. I'd be nothing without you all, and I am so lucky to be your sister.

Big thanks to my loving and supportive parents. Thanks to my father, who blazed the author trail with his debut novel. Thanks to my mom, who has always been my cheerleader and hero.

Eternal gratitude to my kiddos—I am so proud to be your mommy. Lucky too. You both are thoughtful, compassionate, and delightful humans, and I love you always. This book would not exist without you. Thank you! And you are one-hundred percent right; *Rain, Goats, & Ivy* would have made for a flashier series title.

Biggest and brightest thanks to my husband. I love you, Mr. Trent. Let's get married and runaway together. I'll have your babies, and we can live happily ever after. Oh, right. That already happened. Wink. Thanks for being one of my proofreaders. You're getting really good at it. I love you forever, and I promise to try my utmost to never have revision season line up with perf season again. Two Trents stressed out about writing is too many for one kitty to manage.

It would be incredibly weird to thank our family pet, Aspen the cat, but this furry purr-motor has brought all the Trents so much love, well-being, and delight that she deserves to be at least mentioned. People and animals go together, and I'm forever grateful that RezDawgs Rescue gave her a home until that fateful day when the lack of cat became incredibly and irrevocably clear in the Trent home. Aspen, you filled the whiskered, four-legged, twitchy-tail hole in our hearts, and we're all the better for it. Thanks, Miss Kitty.

Hey, dear reader! I wanted to thank you too for taking a chance on me or for sticking with me as I bolted into a different genre. It's an honor to share these stories with you. Thanks for making my dream of an HEA with horse operas and honeymoon jam come true.

COMING ATTRACTIONS

Please enjoy this snippet of my next fairy tale retelling, The Forgotten Storyteller. *To stay updated on my progress, check out this page on my website.*

The smell of thyme and onion pressed against Kate as she stood shaking in the dim kitchen. The waves at the shore crashed, while on the stove the bubbling chowder whispered its own despair. "How?"

"A spell from the North by the look of it." Cook's rough hands shook as she gathered a few tarts, some cheeses, and a loaf of bread. She took the dish cloth draped reliably over her shoulder and laid it in the center of the table.

Kate's voice was tight between her sobs. "Can it be undone?" She watched Cook wrap the lunch in the soft linen.

"Dark magic can always be undone, Katy." Cook's fingers fumbled as they tied up the parcel. She pushed it in Kate's hands, until Kate held the knotted meal against her own knotted stomach.

"How?" Kate begged.

"I don't know," Cook said, shaking her head. "You'll find a way, though. I'm sure of it. But now you need to run." Cook grasped Kate by the shoulders. Tears pooled in her eyes, and the wrinkles on her face were drawn tighter and deeper than Kate had ever seen before. "You're not safe here. You need to run now. Far away. Understand?"

The hot summer air swelled inside the kitchen and smothered Kate until she could not breathe.

Annie bleated miserably at Kate's side. The salt of the surf lingered in the air and the pound of the waves hummed in her ears.

Away. Far away from ocean breezes and white sand. Far away from her mother and stepfather. Far away from the warmth of Cook's kitchen and the comfort of the court. And farther away still from her stepfather's influence and friends. Away. Until the memories of home—and the stories—were all that remained. Kate nodded.

Cook's hands left wrinkles in the silk of Kate's sleeves that could not be smoothed away. "I'll find another lamb to serve for dinner. That should buy you a little time—"

Annie bleated impatiently.

"A very little time."

Memories unraveled with use. And in the weeks that followed their flight from home, poor Kate had recalled those last moments with Cook until it was a threadbare story that haunted more than it consoled.

"I am sorry, Annie." The white lamb stood in the mountain road, chewing on the hem of Kate's cloak. "Our story is so thick sometimes..." Annie stared up at Kate with her obstinate, big brown eyes. "I get lost in it."

The lamb bucked at her rope and bleated angrily.

Kate ran a hand through her tangled tresses. "Yes, but normal lambs can't be trusted to follow their people the way big sheep can."

Annie snorted and headed straight across the lawn toward the manor. Her hooves carefully picked out the driest tufts of grass.

"Now don't be like that." Kate told her. "We both have to be at our most persuasive for this to work."

Annie looked back at Kate, and bleated. The rope was taut.

"Yes, I'm coming," Kate said. She stood up and shook the dust off her trousers and cloak.

The manor house, planted stoutly at the end of the lawn, would have been considered a castle if it had taken a little more architectural risk. A palace perhaps, if it had more finesse and subtlety. But the lines of the manor paralleled the plateau and hugged the safety this rare bit of flat land offered.

"Slow down, Annie." Kate tugged on the lamb's rope. "I need to catch my breath."

Annie bleated haughtily.

"Well, I'm sorry, but I only have two legs. And I'm the one who has to do the talking."

Kate stood in front of the manor for a moment. The morning light crested the mountains. Still, it would be sometime before any sunshine fell on the house. In the cold, unwelcoming shadows, Kate's skin pebbled.

"Bit of a missed opportunity. Don't you think?" Kate and Annie had reached the gravel walk before the stone steps of the front door. Annie said nothing. "It's just... If I were a big manor house in the middle of the North Mountains, I'd be tall and grand like the mountains." Kate scraped her feet through the gravel smiling at the crackle they made. "Soaring towers, steep roofs, natural stone. Not this crumbling old plaster. Still," Kate shrugged. "It is out of the way."

Kate lifted her hand to knock on the large oak doors, but hesitated. She turned to her lamb. "Do you suppose I should use the back door?" She stared down at Annie's woolly face and soft pink nose, half forgetting there would be no reply. "Mama said that noble guests arriving at the back door demonstrate great humility and respect for their host."

Annie folded her front legs and laid down.

Kate continued. "She also said that messengers arriving at any

entrance besides the main door belittle the importance of their work."
Kate pulled her hair tightly away from her face. "I'm not sure where
that would leave a wandering teller."

Kate stood in the morning shadows. The air was so different here-
-dry and tasteless. Not to mention thin. The air at home was salty and
heavy with the responsibilities, trades, and errands of a busy port.
Heavy with sounds too—the surf, the ringing of ships' bells in the
harbor, the cry of the gulls. But all was distractingly silent here. Kate
was used to noise. This manor house was set high above the sleepy
village below. It rested at the foot of the mountains, like it was ready
to climb them at a moment's notice. Quiet with a quick getaway.
Excellent.

Annie bleated impatiently.

"Right. It's just a door." Kate took a few steps forward, but hesitated again. She could not afford any mistakes, particularly with cold
weather approaching. "Oh, for heaven's sake." She took a deep
breath, squared her shoulders, and knocked.

Nothing.

Kate knocked again. Footsteps. A latch moved. A lock turned.
The door opened. A girl dressed in grey, curtsied and stepped aside.
She kept her eyes down, but they widened as Kate tugged Annie
inside behind her. The girl closed the door heavily.

"Hello." Kate bowed with practiced flourish. "I am Kate, the
storyteller, apprenticed to Hammond the great storyteller—"

The girl gave a small gasp and ran off.

"Of the Midlands who learned stories under the master teller,
Ashmund, of King William's summer court." Kate sighed and bent
down to stroke Annie's soft head. "At least you heard my speech."
Annie bleated. Kate looked around the empty hall before she whispered. "Was I that bad?"

"Hello?"

Kate started. With as much poise as she could feign she straightened and turned around. The girl returned with a severe woman
dressed all in black.

"Hello," the woman in black repeated. "Miss Kate, is it?"

"Yes." Kate smiled and nodded. She hoped very much that this woman had not heard her speak to Annie.

The woman's eyes narrowed. "Forgive me; Sarah says you are a *storyteller*."

Kate could feel her knees shake. She swallowed and hoped that her voice would not falter when she spoke. "That's right. Apprenticed to Hammond, the great storyteller—"

"Yes, yes. Wait here." And the woman in black and Sarah disappeared.

Once more Annie and Kate were alone in the great hall. It was an immense room, but quite dim. Its few windows were covered in stiff, dusty curtains. Not open. Not flaunting views to even the lowliest of guests. Kate shivered. The coolness of the night before was still trapped inside the hall. "Never to escape," Kate murmured. It seemed to be the type of place that was perpetually cold and still.

"You?"

Kate jumped. An impressive woman was standing in the center of the hall. She wore an elegant sapphire dress, much in the same style that Kate's own mother wore. But there was an added air of restraint about this woman. Her features were delicate and her olive skin was exquisite, marred only by fine lines around her eyes and finer lines still around her lips.

"You are the storyteller?" the woman asked.

"I am—Kate, the storyteller." Kate bowed low, but hesitated mid bow wondering if a curtsy would have been more appropriate for this lady.

"You can't possibly be done with your apprenticeship," the lady said, her eyes narrowing.

Kate tried to smile. "Only just finished--To Hammond the great storyteller of the Mid-lands...ma'am." Kate bowed again, but the lady continued to stare. Kate cleared her throat. "Hammond learned stories himself under Master Ashmund, who was the greatest jewel of William the Wise's summer court." Kate fished out the apprenticeship contract from inside her doublet and handed it to the lady.

"And now you are seeking your fortune?" the lady said as she examined the document.

"We both are, my lamb and I, yes."

Annie bleated and made delicate clacking noises with her hooves as she paced across the hard granite floor.

The lady pursed her lips. Her narrowed eyes widened as a smile spread across her face. She handed Kate back her contract. "I think there might be a place for you here, Kate."

"Really? I mean--" Kate squared her shoulders. "Wonderful."

The lady held up a slim hand. "Provided of course we approve. You have a fortnight to show your merit. After which time, if we agree that you are well suited to our court, we shall discuss your terms. Now, come with me." The lady started down the long hall.

"I just have one question—"

"Sarah, take the sheep to the stable," the lady called.

"Lamb," Kate said. Sarah, the girl who had answered the door, curtsied and took Annie's rope. "Her name is Annie," Kate whispered. "She hasn't yet had breakfast. She's very fond of strawberry tarts."

"Kate," the lady called from the foot of the stairs.

"Good bye, Annie. Be brave!" Kate kissed her lamb.

"Kate!" the lady called again. She had nearly reached the middle landing of a large, twisting staircase. "Kate, while you are here, you are to wait on this family. Do you understand?"

"I was saying goodbye to—"

"Do you understand?" the lady repeated.

Kate swallowed her frustration. "Yes, ma'am. I understand."

"M'lady."

Kate froze. She hadn't been called 'M'lady' in weeks.

"M'lady. You may address me as Lady Teresa or M'lady. Ma'am is entirely inappropriate."

"Yes, M'lady." Relief finally steadied Kate's shaking knees.

Kate followed Lady Teresa up the stairs to another grand hall-way. After walking past several closed doors and large portraits of grumpy looking men, the lady stopped at a heavy wooden door. She gently knocked twice and entered.

"Henry..." she cooed before Kate even entered the room. "I found you a storyteller."

Made in the USA
Thornton, CO
04/30/22 14:26:55

397fe5b4-ba23-4784-b066-c4b4c45b8e03R01